# Summer of the Plague

## GORDON JOHN THOMSON

# DEDICATION

For my friend and fellow Sunderland supporter Brian Charlton.

# Summer of the Plague

**In the spring of 1665,** England is recovering from a terrible winter, yet the country has other severe problems to face as the sun finally returns. The King, Charles II, had been welcomed back as a saviour on his restoration five years before, but is now resented by increasing numbers of his own people. And in March, the King declares war on the Dutch, England's great seagoing trade rivals...

Worse news comes to Restoration London, though, when there is an outbreak of the plague in April. This is terrible news in particular for the wealthy young physician and merchant Henry Raven, who believes that the outbreak is not natural but has been caused by an old enemy plotting his revenge against the city of London. Henry Raven, together with his friends from the Royal Society, Dr William Croone and Robert Hooke, organizes the city's fight against the spread of the disease.

Raven's delectable young mistress, Molly Titchen, is a precocious seventeen-year-old actress at the new King's theatre in Drury Lane who is torn between her devotion to Henry Raven, and her love of strutting the stage in breeches parts. When Molly gives a bed for the night to one sick young actor, her kind action is misunderstood by Raven who believes that she has been unfaithful to him...

Henry Raven has other problems to tax his mind too, apart from his fight against the plague and his wish to save his relationship with Molly. Firstly, a close childhood friend, Esther Linney, has disappeared from her cottage on the estate of Raven's family home in Dorset, Salwayash Manor, and gone to London. Raven's sister Catherine asks her brother to find Esther in London, and discover why she left Dorset in such mysterious circumstances...

As the plague rages through London, Raven finds himself having to defend Esther Linney against a charge of witchcraft, while also trying to save Molly from an implacable enemy. But his greatest challenge is to discover the secrets of an old family curse, and to unmask a cruel murderer...

# CONTENTS

# PROLOGUE

Brothers are often blind to the virtues of their sisters, and Henry Raven was little different in this regard from most men. He had always considered his younger sister Catherine to be a pretty and vibrant girl, of course, yet today – on this fine April morning, walking with her beneath the emerging green canopy of the twelve-acre beech wood at the western borders of their Dorset estate, and with the dappled sunlight emphasizing her fine features and fresh pink complexion – he realized for the first time that she truly was an unequalled English beauty.

Catherine was a little bemused by his long look. 'What is the matter, brother? You stare at me suddenly in a most provoking way. Have I a smudge of soot on my nose? Or something even worse…?' She laughed gaily at the thought, a delightful girlish sound that put Raven in mind of the impish girl she had once been.

'Nay, thou art far too much the grand country lady now ever to be caught out with a snotty nose…' As a girl, Catherine had been a child of boisterous and playful disposition, and up to the age of ten or so had enjoyed sharing the vigorous rough and tumble of games with her brother rather than the more genteel pastimes usually preferred for girls. Henry was six years older than his boisterous sister so it had taken much patience on his part to indulge her in this way, yet he was glad in retrospect that he had. At that time she had never given any thought to her appearance, he remembered fondly, leaving her chestnut hair to grow wild, her frequently runny nose to go unchecked by the attentions of a clean handkerchief, and only washing her face when she was forced to by her weary nurse. Yet that boyish upbringing seemed to have done no irreparable harm, and now, at one-and-twenty, she was grown into a feminine and enchanting young woman, if one still of very determined character.

They walked on, their boots crunching on the leaf litter and the remains of last year's beech mast, which still decorated the forest floor in a thick coat of red and gold. Catherine had preferred to walk today rather than ride, as it gave her so much more opportunity to study the spring flowers at close quarters. 'If you must know, I was but musing on the fortunate chance that you took after our mother in your looks, rather than after our worthy father, like me,' Raven continued, after another long pause to enjoy the glowing beauty in his sister's face.

'Oh! And why is that?' Catherine came to a sudden halt, not sure of his meaning.

'Because, otherwise, it might cost me a great deal more in the matter of a dowry when the time comes, in order to tempt some young man to make you an offer,' Raven reflected dryly. 'If you had been cursed with such a plain face as mine —' he tapped his own prominent nose with a regretful smile — 'and were endowed with this same rough complexion, and this large misshapen nose - then I believe it would have been a monstrous struggle to find a suitor for you at all. I might even have had to resign myself to you remaining a lifelong spinster of this parish.'

Catherine relaxed her face into a smile again. 'Then, O skinflint brother, I am heartily glad that you consider me comely enough to be saving you the cost of a huge dowry, even though I think you overstate my charms. You will still need to dig mightily deep to rid yourself of me, I fear, because my shrewish tongue and less than servile manner will still deter many suitable young men.' Her eyes gleamed for a moment with humour. 'And do you have anyone particular in mind for me yet, Henry?' she asked with a deliberately straight face, although Raven knew full well that it was not a serious question and that Catherine would eventually do her own choosing in this regard, with little or no recourse to his opinions.

'I have just rid myself of your sister Mary this very week,' Raven said lightly, 'so I will need a little time to find another equally wealthy pigeon for you.' Raven had come to Dorset from London two weeks ago to give away his other sister Mary — a girl as equally determined as Catherine if not blessed with the same natural beauty — to a long-time acquaintance of the family, Sir Francis Middleton of Kent. 'It will not be easy to ensnare someone for you as wealthy and serious as Sir Francis.'

Catherine pulled a most unladylike face at the thought. 'I am sure that stern gentleman will make Mary an excellent husband because she is a very serious and sober girl herself. Yet he would not suit me. I need some lightness and humour in the man that I will share my life with, and Francis is sadly lacking in those qualities. If the only suitors I could "ensnare", as you put it, were such eternally serious young men as Sir Francis Middleton, then I might perhaps even prefer to remain a lifelong spinster of this parish.' She glanced beyond the edge of the wood and down the hillside into the emerald vale of the River Simene where the distant water gleamed under overhanging willows, and kingfishers flashed their brilliant jewel-like colours, while, on the chalky slopes above, lambs gambolled in contentment under the watchful and protective eyes of their patient ewe mothers. 'And why should I not stay here for all eternity if I wish? There is no more beautiful parish in all of England than Salwayash, after all.' She touched his arm as they began to walk along the woodland path again, then leaned up to kiss him on the cheek. 'Your face may lack conventional beauty, Henry. Yet, for myself, I would not change one whit of it. I never saw my father's face so if yours truly carries a good likeness of his features, then I am fortunate indeed to be able to see the traces of him, living still in you. Anyway I prefer a man who looks like a man, not a powdered and bewigged fop. And you do bear more than a passing resemblance to the King in your features too, Henry – at least if I judge from his likeness on the coins in my purse - so you should not disparage them too much, otherwise it might sound treasonous. And our lusty monarch certainly has no problem attracting the attentions of ladies, from all that I hear, even if he does have a swarthy complexion, and a large Roman nose like yours to boot...'

Raven interrupted with a wry comment. 'Yet I doubt that the successes of his amorous adventures have much to do with his swarthy skin or the ill shape of his nose...'

'No, indeed,' Catherine conceded. 'After all, a lady cannot judge the virtues of a King's face with quite the same detachment that she would judge a normal gentleman's features. Nor can she reject his advances with the same detachment – Kings are born to command their subjects' actions after all. ' Catherine eyed him mischievously. 'But, despite your resemblance to our monarch, promise me that you will never ape the King in his more foolish fashions and take to wearing a periwig. I will never speak to you again if you even contemplate such an unconscionable thing. Those crisped snaky locks are often known to be the dowry of a second head,' she quoted, 'while the skull that bred them lies already in the sepulchre...'

'You are the second lady to demand such a thing from me, and I have already promised her never to yield to the temptation,' Raven stated breezily, '...even though it must be exceeding convenient to have your own hair shorn like a sheep, and then to simply clap a wig on your shaven head like a hat whenever you cross the doors. Especially with summer coming, and the City of London so full of fleas and ticks.'

Catherine's face darkened and took on a more serious aspect as she realized instantly that the "lady" her brother must be talking of had to be his young actress mistress, Molly Titchen. This young woman was presently a sore subject between brother and sister because, although Henry would never truly have dared to interfere and find a suitor for his sister, she was certainly not similarly constrained by her personality from interfering in the search for a suitable wife for him. Particularly when his current paramour, Molly Titchen, was so far from Catherine Raven's ideal of a perfect future wife for her only brother that yesterday at dinner she had expressed the wish to come to London Town and to throw this importuning young actress off London Bridge.

Catherine held her temper with obvious difficulty as she said, 'I am still surprised and disappointed that you would bed a common sixteen-year-old actress, Henry, but I do hope that this unsuitable liaison will go no further than her sharing your bed from time to time. I also trust that you will soon tire of her...'

'We shall see,' Raven responded evasively. 'But for the sake of accuracy, I must correct you. Molly is now *seventeen* years old, and nothing about her is "common", sister.'

With a shrug of resignation, Catherine apparently decided not to spoil the rest of their walk with talk of this upstart girl and made no further comment. For his part too, Raven decided to say nothing more on the subject, even though annoyed by Catherine's dislike of Molly since it was based not on any personal acquaintance, but merely on her own prejudices about actresses, laced with a little hearsay from a third party, namely his own forthright housekeeper Dora Bagwell. Dora had been back at the manor last Christmas to visit her sick sister, and had no doubt been the source of most of Catherine's misinformation about Molly. Henry Raven held the sanguine hope however that Catherine, unlike Mistress Bagwell, would warm to Molly if she ever did meet her in the flesh - though even if he was wrong in this supposition and his sister's dislike of Molly proved to be a more permanent and vexatious thing, he had no intention of breaking with Molly over it. When it came to his own inclinations in love, this was one area of his life where he had no intention of ever yielding to Catherine's judgement.

He decided, though, that now was not the most opportune time to inform his sister that he had recently rented pleasant rooms for Molly in a house in Bow Street. This was mainly for Molly's sake since she had grown uncomfortable visiting his home in St Martin's Lane under the inquisitive eyes of his servants, and particularly because of the clear hostility of his housekeeper Dora Bagwell. Raven could have dismissed Dora from his service of course, yet he was reluctant to take such a drastic step with a loyal and long serving family retainer, and in any event Molly had insisted he should not. Yet Dora was becoming increasingly crotchety of late so Raven had decided that he would soon have to send her back to Dorset for good anyway, which might perhaps cure the real reasons for her crotchetiness - she did miss her friends and relatives in Salwayash, after all, and particularly her ailing sister, Constance.

Raven was spared from defending his friendship with Molly further by the arrival of a tall if plainly dressed gentleman on horseback, coming from the opposite direction. The gentleman dismounted quickly from his large bay gelding on approaching them, and took off his broad brimmed hat with a flourish. His long black coat was of plain broadcloth, as were his unfashionable breeches, and his stockings were of coarse black wool, but it was a welcome change for Raven to see a gentleman who was not encumbered with yards of lace frills and bows, as were even sober men at court these days. Yet this man, for all his plain dress, was one of the wealthiest men in this part of England, as Raven well knew, and the sombre costume that he wore was in mourning for his lately deceased wife Margaret. 'Good day, Catherine,' the man said in greeting, turning to his more comely neighbour first. 'And to you too, Henry,' he added with an indulgent turn of his handsome head. 'I hope you will excuse me riding brazenly on your land, but this track is one of my favourite rides in the neighbourhood. After what happened to poor Margaret, I have not felt the urge to ride much lately. But this morning, with the sky so blue, and all this fresh spring greenery bursting forth, I felt a sudden need to blow away the cobwebs from my mind with a gallop.'

Catherine bowed politely in return but seemed momentarily flustered by the encounter. 'Err....of course...we would never refuse our hospitality to you, Ralph, and we expect you always to consider our land as your own...' As she spoke, her complexion seemed to her brother to turn momentarily even pinker than usual, which might perhaps have been due to the roseate glow of the morning sun stealing across the mist-covered fields below, or more likely, Raven thought, because of the personal charms of their wealthy neighbour. Ralph Warboys was the only surviving son of the late Oliver Warboys, who had been such a close friend of their own father, Thomas Raven. All Ralph's many siblings had died long ago, including his twin brother Geoffrey, who had supposedly been inseparable from him. Ralph remained an exceptionally handsome man, Raven had to admit, despite being past his fortieth year, with flowing black locks and well-chiselled features that seemed peculiarly resistant to ageing. In Raven's mind, Warboys seemed hardly to have changed at all during these last two decades while he and Catherine had been growing up, so that they now seemed almost to have caught him up by some strange quirk of time. They even shared the same unattached marital state with their ageless neighbour now, though in Warboys' case this single state had been renewed only recently, and by melancholy means. Warboys had been widowed only six weeks previously, after ten years of marriage. His wife Margaret had gone out riding alone early one February morning, despite the icy weather. Her horse had apparently put his foot down a hidden rabbit hole and rolled down a steep bank into a frozen stream, breaking Margaret Warboys' neck instantly. Warboys had found her himself, after he had sent out search parties to look for her, following her failure to return. His wife's death was an even sadder affair for him than would normally be the case, since she had left him no children to provide any solace for his loss, just a melancholy history of many stillborn babies.

Raven had returned to Dorset briefly for the funeral six weeks ago, and had found Warboys to be in the depth of a black despair. Yet he had apparently made a remarkable recovery from his distress by the time Raven and Catherine had next seen him — at the much happier occasion of their sister Mary's wedding a week ago. Ralph had seemed much more like his old self again at that happy gathering, though how much of this was merely an act to hide his continuing grief was hard to say.

Henry Raven had long suspected that his sister Catherine was partial to Warboys' manly charms, in the way that young ladies often hero-worship a handsome older man whom they come into regular contact with. But the fact that he was married had of course ensured that she had kept those feelings very much to herself.

The sad and untimely death of Warboys' wife had changed that situation abruptly, however, and Raven could not prevent his mind dwelling now on a new possibility. Because of the age difference between Warboys and his sister, and the fact that he had been so recently widowed, it had genuinely never occurred to Raven until this moment that he might now be a potential match for her. But that pink glow in Catherine's face made him suddenly acutely conscious of the deep physical attraction between his young sister and their distinguished neighbour, and he began instantly to assess the merits and disadvantages of such a match.

Warboys was still a relatively young man, and would no doubt want to marry again in the fullness of time, after waiting long enough to afford a due measure of respect to the memory of his late wife, of course. Given his newly widowed state, Raven thought that even Warboys himself must have acknowledged that his personal tragedy did have one positive aspect, at least — that it gave him some fresh hope of leaving an heir, in order to ensure that the Warboys' ancient lineage did not finally end with him. The Raven family were relative newcomers to this area by comparison, having only had possession of their estate for four generations, and that only because of a chance inheritance from a distant relative who had died childless. The Warboys family, on the other hand, could trace their ownership of their land back to the time of King Edward the First, and had, until the building of their new home Warboys Hall thirty years before, lived in a grand thirteenth century Norman castle, now a striking and romantic ruin on their estate.

It would certainly be a beneficial match from many practical aspects, Raven decided - for one thing, by connecting the two large neighbouring estates together, as well as keeping Catherine in the neighbourhood, and among the wild flowers and green vales that she loved. Yet, despite his well-preserved aspect and his prodigious wealth, Ralph Warboys was still old enough to be Catherine's father, so was he really such a wise choice for her, Raven wondered.

Warboys did have one other thing in his favour, though - a strong sense of humour that was most unusual in such a wealthy gentleman. Even after his recent melancholy personal history, there was still little of any stiffness or severity in his manner. So, given Catherine's pronouncement a few minutes ago concerning her preferences for her future partner, Raven decided that he was certainly a perfect match for her in the matter of character at least, as well as beauty and personal fortune.

Warboys squinted through the bare branches of the beech trees into the low bright sun. 'I can see why you two young people should be enjoying a walk together on this fine morning. The weather is wonderfully warm for so early in the year, is it not? And yet 'tis but a few weeks since the snow and ice finally released their grip even here in Dorset. A month ago I was still wondering if I would ever see the sun again, or feel warm again away from my own fireside. Yet here we are on April the first, the wild daffodils are already long finished, and the sun burns almost as warm as midsummer. It seems that nature is trying to make up for the hardships she forced us to endure last winter.'

'Ay, ye may well say that again, Ralph,' Raven agreed. 'In all honesty, I had wondered the same thing.' The winter truly had been an arduous one for Henry Raven, both because of the severity of the cold which had frozen the Thames solid for months, yet even more so for the dramatic events that Raven had personally had to face. Yet in retrospect he would not have changed things because those events of last winter had also been the means by which he had met his new love Molly, and achieved much happiness and contentment in his life as a result.

Yet the warm spring, though very welcome, had also brought new challenges for the country. Only a few weeks ago, the King had finally declared war on Holland. In truth England had been at war with the Dutch for several years now in everything but name, as their rivalry in the East Indies and the Americas had intensified. Conflict had simmered first between the English and the Dutch over the ownership of certain of the Spice Islands in the East Indies, and last year, in retaliation, the English had simply taken over the Dutch colony of New Netherland in the Americas and renamed the city of New Amsterdam as New York after the King's brother, James, Duke of York. So all-out war had perhaps been inevitable after that blatantly hostile action.

Yet Henry Raven was one of many English citizens who believed that this war was a reckless and ill-conceived venture, when England's true enemies were the ever scheming French across the Channel, and the powerful Spanish Empire beyond, whose baleful tentacles now spread all over the globe. Yet the King had made up his mind, and now there seemed nothing to be done about it except to fight this war with the Dutch to its bitter end. And only God knew where this unwanted war might lead, Raven thought with depression, or how many innocent and unnecessary deaths it would cause.

Warboys was still in full conversational flow, but Raven, caught up in his deep reflections about this unfortunate war with the Dutch, had failed to take in the meaning of his later sentences until he heard one particular word that filled him with foreboding...

'I am sorry, Ralph. What say you about the plague?' Raven interrupted him abruptly.

Warboys frowned. 'Only that I am glad that there have been no cases reported in England so far this year. I have heard reports of many deaths in Venice and Constantinople, and perhaps even some in Paris. Yet, thank the Lord, not here in England!'

Raven had his own particular reasons for fearing an outbreak of plague in England, and in London most of all, because an evil adversary with vengeance on his warped mind had warned him with his last breath last winter that he had unleashed a horde of plague-infected rats into the city. Ever since then, Raven had waited with dread for reports of the first cases in London. Now that unseasonably warm weather had arrived so early in the year, he had almost braced himself for the first calamitous announcement of a case of plague in the city. Yet Raven still lived in hopes too that this evil man's promise might have been a hollow one after all, or that, even if true, all those plague-infected rats might hopefully have been killed off by the severe winter. 'Ay, amen to that, Ralph!' he muttered. 'It would be a calamity indeed if plague reached the City of London. 'Tis the greatest city in the world, but also among the dirtiest and the most crowded. The plague would run through it like a...err...err...'

'Like the *plague* perhaps?' Catherine said with a smile, when she saw that her brother had found himself tongue-tied for once, and quite unable to come up with an adequate simile.

Warboys laughed heartily along with Catherine at Henry Raven's unusual difficulty with words – normally he was the most fluent of men. For his part, Raven immediately put his dark fears of the plague to one side for the moment as he recognized with surprise the secret intimate look that Catherine had shared with Warboys over her little joke. The depth of secret pleasure on Catherine's face quite startled him for a moment: perhaps he was wrong but it seemed from that shared moment of intimacy as if his sister and this gentleman were already well on their way to becoming lovers...

*

Raven and his sister had walked on after leaving Ralph Warboys, and within a quarter hour had reached the southern edge of the beech wood.

Crossing the meadow beyond, a sea of young spring grass and emerging wildflowers, they finally came to the boundary of their own land, beyond which lay a smallholding of several arable fields centred round a small copse of oak trees and a rustic cottage. 'That is Esther's cottage, is it not?' Raven said, glancing around. 'It seems deserted,' he added curiously, seeing no smoke issuing from the chimney, and a general air of dilapidation in the path leading to the front door.

Catherine nodded sombrely. 'That is one reason I brought you this far, Henry. I wanted you to see her cottage for yourself.'

They walked on to reach the copse of oak trees and then followed the track past an overgrown herb garden to the stout oak door of the cottage. Seen through the small leaded windows, the interior bore no signs of life at all, and the ragged thatch on the roof was badly in need of attention after the depredations of this last vicious winter.

'Where is Esther?' Raven asked his sister in perplexity. 'She always kept this little farm so neat and well-tended. Has something ill happened to her?'

Catherine grimaced. 'I think perhaps you have not heard that her brother Gideon was reported lost at sea last autumn.'

Raven took a long breath. 'Ah, I see. But 'tis not too surprising, given that he was a privateer of sorts on the Spanish Main, and lived a dangerous life in consequence.'

'Yet he was very dear to her.'

'As her only surviving relative, he could be nothing else.' Raven took off his wide-brimmed hat for a moment to feel the warmth of the morning sun on his face. 'Has Esther quit the place permanently then since her brother was lost? Does she intend to sell up and go elsewhere?'

'I know not, brother. All I do know is that she is presently in London,' Catherine replied, her face concerned. 'She wrote me a letter before she left, just after Candlemas, telling me that she had to go to London on the morrow, and intimating that she might have to stay there for several months to deal with matters of business.'

Raven frowned at this surprising news. Esther Linney was a local girl through and through, and he doubted whether she had ever been more than ten miles from Salwayash before in her entire life. She was the same age as Catherine, almost to the day, but her circumstances in life had been far less advantageous, and she had suffered great tragedies in her short life. As a babe, Esther had been sadly orphaned in the most terrible of circumstances, but her situation had at least improved later because she had been taken into the Raven household and treated kindly there, eventually becoming a virtual companion to Mary and Catherine. At the age of thirteen, Esther had however left the protection of the manor to keep house for her surviving elder brother Gideon, who had just returned home then from many years at sea, and with substantial Spanish prize money in his pocket - enough anyway to buy a small farm and cottage for himself and his sister. Henry Raven had seen little of Esther in the eight years since then, being settled mainly in London, but Catherine, now running the manor jointly with her sister Mary after the death of their mother, had stayed in close touch with her childhood friend.

'What business can Esther have in London?' Raven asked. 'I doubt that Esther was ever in London in her life before, or even knows anyone there. She has spent her whole life here in Salwayash, has she not?'

Catherine looked thoughtful. 'I was curious about her reasons for going there too, but she gave me no hint of the exact purpose in her letter, nor did she give me any address where I might write to her. She did say that she expected to return in the spring or summer, but I have heard no word from her now these two months.'

Raven peered through the dusty window again at the dark interior. 'It must be something serious to take her away from here, and to leave her fields neglected and unplanted. It must also have been a sudden decision otherwise she would surely have made arrangements for someone else to take care of her land. I do not like to see valuable crop land left to go wild.' He replaced his hat carefully over his long dark hair. 'Could her journey be something to do with her brother's loss? I suppose this farm must be in his name. Perhaps she has gone to lay claim in a court to her late brother's estate? Given his history as a privateer, who knows what wealth that young man might have secreted away in a London vault somewhere?'

'That would be a difficult claim for her to make because he was only lost at sea,' Catherine observed. 'His vessel, the *Hesperides*, went down in a mighty storm off the isle of Cuba with only a handful of survivors returned to tell the tale. So it is almost certain that Gideon Linney died a watery and unpleasant death. Yet whoever holds his wealth would want certain proof of the man's death before they would hand over any of it to his sister. She would probably have to wait for the mandatory period of seven years before her brother could be declared legally dead. So I doubt that her journey to London was anything to do with her brother, though I could be wrong…'

'Then could she have gone simply to get away from her sad memories here? She had always railed at the injustice of what happened to her mother here, so perhaps the loss of her only surviving brother had finally plunged her into a dark despair.'

Catherine blanched at the suggestion. 'If she was in despair, then surely she would have come to me for help? As for her concerns for her mother's fate, I hope Esther has put the memory of those evil times far behind her. Yet you may be right – she did seem melancholy of late, compared with the happy girl she had once been.'

Raven turned and scanned the quiet meadows around the house, his eyes taking in the quiet rustic beauty of the scene, the shifting pattern of sunlight, the thousand shades of green reflecting the light, the cascade of song from skylark and blackbird. 'It still pains me greatly that such terrible things could have taken place here. Most of these evil witch hunts took place among the more gullible people of Essex and Suffolk. I would have thought Dorset folk too sensible to indulge in such rabid superstition and hatred, but even here the madness was allowed to take hold.'

Catherine nodded solemnly. 'Most people here were indeed too decent to be tainted by such evil, yet a few succumbed. Do you know that Esther's mother, Meg Linney, was denounced by a local woman, who still lives brazenly in the village as if she has nothing to feel guilty about?'

'No, I did not.' Raven's interest was aroused because he had never known this particular detail of the story.

Catherine told him what she knew 'Yes, the name of this wicked harpy is Judith Pollock. I discovered this only recently: the Reverend Smythe pointed her out to me when we walked through the village together just last week. She looks far more of a witch than Esther's mother could ever have been,' she declared with most unusual venom for someone of her normally sweet disposition. 'I know not how this Mistress Pollock can live with herself. I could not if I had done such a wicked thing.' She relented a little in her anger. 'Though Mr Smythe says that we must show even people such as her Christian charity and forgiveness.'

They began walking back across the sunlit fields to their own land. Raven glanced at his sister as she strode forcefully at his side. 'Yet I have heard that Esther's mother was a strange woman by all accounts, so, in those hysterical times of twenty years ago, 'tis not too surprising that she would have attracted the unwelcome attention of the witch finders...'

Catherine continued walking, her long stride matching his with ease. 'What was so strange about her?' she asked moodily. 'Did you ever see her?'

Raven nodded. 'I remember her well from when I was a child of six or seven. She was a very tall and striking woman, with the blackest hair and the whitest skin, like Italian Carrara Marble. I believe she did have some Italian blood in her, which perhaps explains her appearance and her volatile temperament. She was a most unusual person to be the wife of a yeoman farmer – she had the look of an Italian aristocrat about her, a Borgia or a de Medici. Dora knew her particularly well – they were neighbours as children - and she remembers this sad business with great clarity.'

'What evidence did the witch finders uncover against Esther's mother?'

'Dora told me that Meg Linney was observed - in a fit of madness perhaps, or demonic possession - trying to bring her recently dead husband's body back to life with spells and incantations and weird shrieking. I suppose this Mistress Pollock was the main witness to this suspect behaviour. '

Catherine looked up sharply. 'If that be true, then Esther's mother needed help and Christian compassion, Henry, not to be accused of witchcraft.'

Raven reacted with surprise at her tone. 'I do not deny it, sister. You can hardly think me in favour of persecuting anyone, let alone a poor demented mother.'

'Of course I do not, Henry,' Catherine quickly reassured him. 'But my real concern now is for her daughter Esther. She is still like a second sister to me, so I feel an abiding urge to help her, even though she has not confided in me of late what troubles her.' Catherine sighed heavily. 'Perhaps this madness of her mother's runs in her blood too, and is driving her into morbid despair?' She recovered her equanimity with a visible effort and said in a much calmer voice, 'Will you try and find her whereabouts in London when you return there, Henry? And if possible, seek her out and discover if she needs our help in any way. I suspect she is in grave trouble of some sort, and that it may have something to do with the dark past of her family.'

Leaving the beech wood behind and entering a verdant meadow, Raven helped his sister over a rickety stile and then across a small gurgling stream where damselflies danced in the sunlight. Catherine pointed out to him the wide expanses of cowslips in the meadow that would soon be replaced by wonderful summer spreads of ox-eye daisies and rough hawkbit, of yellow horseshoe vetch and blue milkwort.

'I will try to find Esther, if that is what you wish,' Raven promised her, as she knelt down to examine an early spider orchid growing in the bank of the stream. 'But it will not be easy to find her – London is a vast city these days, three miles across from east to west, and home to three hundred thousand souls at least.'

Catherine reluctantly gave up her close examination of the orchid, and stood up again. 'I do have something that might aid your search, brother. Our neighbour, Lady Onslow, was staying in London a few weeks ago and swears that she saw Esther.'

'Where was this encounter?'

'In a street called Fetter Lane, I believe, which is somewhere in the city. If it was not her, then Lady Onslow said that Esther must have an identical twin.'

Raven took her hand to help her up the bank of the stream, then squeezed her fingers affectionately. 'Then I will speak to Lady Onslow before I leave Dorset again, and try and discover exactly where she saw her. It must be Esther, though – like her poor late mother, she is of striking appearance and not easily mistaken for another. And Fetter Lane would be the sort of street she might stay in London. 'Tis not a fashionable area but a place of artisans and book printers, and other small workshops.'

They carried on across the rough pasture land and came finally to the brow of a hill with a sweeping view over the River Simene. Across the valley rose an even taller hill with thick oak wood covering its flanks, but with a bare grassy plateau on top.

Catherine indicated the far hill with her hand. 'Imagine what Esther must have thought every time she looked at this same splendid view. To us it is merely beautiful, but in her it must have stirred all sorts of conflicting emotions. Perhaps that is why she has left Dorset...'

'Why so?' Raven asked curiously.

Catherine was pensive. 'Because that is Blackmore Hill where the Witchfinder General built his pyre twenty years ago and ordered the sentence of the court carried out on Esther's poor mother.' She shivered, despite the warmth of the day. 'Yes, that is the very place where Meg Linney was burnt at the stake. I have spoken to some who were there, and who were deeply affected by what they witnessed that sad day. They all said that it took many minutes for the poor woman to die. Yet the most surprising circumstance was that she died in complete silence – not even once did she call out or scream - even as the fire consumed her blackened flesh...'

# CHAPTER 1

Saturday, 8<sup>th</sup> April 1665

A week later, on a similarly warm spring day, Molly Titchen sat on a stool in the pit of the King's theatre in Bridges Street, and wondered what her lover Henry Raven might be doing at this precise moment. She surmised that his present circumstances were probably more agreeable than her own, suffering here in the stuffiness and heat of the theatre as she took a brief rest from rehearsals for a new play by the Earl of Orrery, called *Mustapha*. The only thing she actively disliked about this theatre was the unpleasant atmosphere on hot days – the packed hall could be suffocating, and ripe with the overpowering smell of stale bodies, powder and heady perfume. Yet she could blame no one but herself for this situation, nor - if she was pressed - did she truly want to change it, because she still loved striding across this wooden stage under that tall proscenium arch, and hearing the enthusiastic applause of the masses. At this particular moment however, breathing this stale warm air, and feeling an uncomfortable trickle of sweat under her heavy woollen skirts, she would probably have exchanged it gladly for walking down a green and leafy lane in the county of Dorset, arm-in-arm with her lover…

He had been gone these three weeks, and she had not known before how much she would miss his amiable presence in her life. Molly had never truly loved a man before, and even now she was not sure that what she felt for Henry Raven could honestly be called "love" - not the airy feeling that the poets described anyway. He had aroused no great simmering passions in her as yet. Deep affection certainly; much physical pleasure of course; also certainly gratitude for the many things he had done for her, and for the many things he had given her, including her own apartments in Bow Street. She lived a life of veritable luxury now compared to her impoverished situation just a few short months ago.

Yet she had to acknowledge, after three weeks separation, that she did feel almost a physical pain in her heart at his absence, and that she missed his familiar craggy face and the comfort of his arms around her at night. So perhaps this genuinely was love after all, even if she could not articulate the sentiment quite as she would have liked.

How her life had changed since this last terrible winter! Only a few months ago she had worked here as one of the orange sellers who stood at the front of the stage before the performance began, brazenly flaunting her duckies to the audience in order to sell as much of the fruit in her basket as possible. It was a cutthroat business, played out under the watchful eyes of their grim mistress, Mary Meggs, who ran her orange sellers with all the discipline of the King's guard. The orange sellers were invariably subjected to brazen attention and saucy wit from the audience, yet Molly saw now that this had been perfect training for her becoming an actress, and having the confidence and courage to face these noisy and lewd audiences, and to respond to their earthy comments with equally saucy ripostes.

Several of the actresses in the company had therefore graduated to acting from this hard school of selling oranges for a living, and Molly had no doubt that her precocious friend Nell – still only fifteen years old, but a knowing girl well matured beyond her tender years – would probably soon follow her onto the stage proper. Nell was a tawny-haired temptress already and certainly had the legs for breeches roles, as she was in the habit of regularly proving, by lifting her skirts to show them to all and sundry in the theatre, and particularly to the master of the company, Sir Thomas Killigrew.

The profession of actress was a new one, of course. Until five years ago, no woman had ever performed on stage, and the women's roles in plays had to be taken by pretty boys, whose balls had either yet to drop, or else seemed destined by nature never to do so. Yet now it was hard to remember a time when women had not performed on stage, and the public had certainly taken enthusiastically to the idea, even though the term "actress" had regrettably become virtually synonymous with "whore" so that, as far as the public were concerned, the two professions were completely interchangeable in common parlance.

Molly had to admit, though, that with many of the ladies in this company the public confusion of "actress" and "whore" was perhaps understandable. And, for that matter, many people looking at her own present situation might conclude uncharitably that she was little better than a whore too…

'You seem in a brown study, Molly…!'

Molly looked up sharply as she realized that Sir Thomas Killigrew, master of the company, had just joined her and had slumped his elderly body down onto a stool beside her.

'I am, sir, in a manner of speaking. I was thinking over my lines in the play, saying them silently in my head,' she lied.

'More likely you let your thoughts drift to Mr Henry Raven,' Killigrew said with a vulgar laugh. 'Does your heart beat faster at the thought of him, now that he is away? Or is it merely your private places that grow moist in anticipation of his return?' he suggested coarsely.

Molly wondered why she should still be so surprised at this gentleman's ability to read her thoughts so plainly, or indeed at his coarseness. She had recognized from the start of their acquaintance that Sir Thomas Killigrew was a shrewd and lustful devil, and every encounter with him merely confirmed her first opinion of him, and of those lewd habits. Yet there was more to Sir Thomas than a mere satyr, Molly had to admit. In the few months she had known him well, she had learned much of his interesting personal history. Killigrew was one of twelve children of Sir Robert Killigrew of Hanworth, who had been a courtier to the present King's Scotch grandfather, James I, and Thomas himself had become a page to King Charles I as a boy. Sir Thomas had confided to Molly directly that as a youth he used to volunteer as an extra, or "devil," at the Red Bull Theatre in Clerkenwell, so that he could see the plays there for free. The Court and the playhouse had been his schoolroom, he said, and he had started writing plays in his own right when still in his twenties - tragicomedies like *Claracilla* and *The Prisoners*, as well as his most popular play, *The Parson's Wedding*..

After the Civil War, Killigrew had willingly followed Prince Charles into exile in Europe and had later been appointed Charles' representative in Venice where he acquired a reputation for debauchery even among such libertines as the Venetians – a reputation deservedly earned in all likelihood in Molly's estimation, knowing that even now, at his advanced age, Killigrew had bedded every actress in the company, and even some of the prettier actors too. Killigrew's first wife had died many years ago, but ten years since, he had married a wealthy Dutch woman and fathered three children by her. Yet that did not seem to have blunted his appetite for other women in the slightest. Molly remembered with a blush of shame how she had been forced to "audition" for him in his private chamber upstairs in the theatre – this being the normal minimum price of admission to his company. However Killigrew had been more circumspect of late in touching her bum and grabbing her titties during rehearsals because he knew that her loyalty and bedding rights were now claimed by a wealthy man of business, Mr Henry Raven, who had been of great service to the King recently, therefore was not a man to be crossed lightly.

'I wish that I had nothing more to occupy my mind than mere thoughts of the flesh,' Killigrew went on piously, after it became clear to him that Molly was not going to grace his earlier tasteless remark with a reply.

'And what are these troubles that cause you such unquiet, sir,' Molly inquired coolly.

'Why, you must have noticed how difficult it becomes to fill this theatre now, no matter what fine plays and other diversions I offer the public. Last evening the pit was half empty even though we gave them a sumptuous production of Fletcher's *The Chances* with no less than Charles Hart in the role of Don John. This cannot go on: with the hall half empty, I lose money every week. If I am to maintain a company of this size, then I need to fill the hall every afternoon to bursting. I am frantic now to find new ways to entice people through the door. I need new plays and new playwrights to entertain them, it seems. Even your fine legs displayed in tight breeches do not seem sufficient for them any more. I require some new stars to add to the firmament of this theatre.'

'You think the crowd tire of me already?' Molly asked nervously.

Killigrew patted her hand solicitously. 'Of you, my child, no. No one could tire of you. But certainly of the sameness of the plays that we perform. Perhaps we must try and make the comedies a touch saucier.'

Molly did not know how the comedies could be made any saucier unless the actors shed all their clothes completely and made free sport on stage. 'Perhaps the audiences want less innuendo, sir, not more. And perhaps better plots and dialogue?' she suggested diffidently.

'Nay, it is tits and bums that this audience wants to see, and saucy dialogue to hear. We are all whores here in this temple to the Muses, giving the audience whatever base thing they want in order to hear a little pathetic applause in return.' Killigrew sighed emphatically. 'And what is this applause that we all yearn for, and would debase ourselves to get? 'Tis but a fart, the crude blast of the fickle multitude.'

'Perhaps the return of so many of your old company will change our fortunes, sir?' Molly said hopefully.

Molly knew that although Sir Thomas was a skilled actor and playwright yet he was also an incompetent theatre manager at best, and one who was constantly in dispute with both his actors and the playwrights who wrote for him. Many of his leading actors and actresses had eventually refused to work with him and had defected last year to Sir William Devanant's rival company in Lincoln Inn's Fields. Yet it seemed Davenant was an equally difficult taskmaster, so several of Killigrew's former actresses had recently returned to him – Margaret Hughes, Anne and Becky Marshall, and Elizabeth Davenport among them. Even better for Molly had been the return of several august actors to the company - Michael Mohun, William Wintershall, and, most particularly, the famed actor Charles Hart, who was not only remarkably handsome to look at, but also acknowledged to be the finest actor in London. And the young actor Edward Kynaston had also returned this week to the fold, a boy who was so beautiful to behold that he had only played ladies' parts until three years ago. Molly had heard that society ladies had often taken him riding in their coaches after a performance, still dressed in his female finery and looking like the loveliest lady among them, which ruse often fooled many gentlemen in their company, and provided the society ladies with much titillating entertainment at their expense...

'With the sad deaths of three of our youngest and brightest actresses last year, not to mention a very fine young actor too, there was clearly need to bring in fresh blood – or at least to welcome the return of some old blood. I hope their return will make a difference,' Killigrew said. 'Charles is a big draw for the ladies in the audience, of course. I think he must have sold his soul to the Devil because he seems not to have aged in twenty years. 'Tis not natural for a man approaching forty to be so beautiful. And Mistress Hughes was the first lady ever to perform on stage for me, which took some considerable courage on her part.'

'When was this, sir?'

'I know not the exact date, yet it was certainly less than five years ago – a production of Shakespeare's play *Othello,* at the old theatre in Vere Street. She played the role of Desdemona and made a most remarkable impression.' Killigrew leaned over and planted a meaty hand on Molly's right thigh. 'I think perhaps that we should try you on some of these darker and more tragic roles too, Molly. Thou art still very young, yet there is a depth to thy acting already that suggests great things ahead of thee.' He tightened his grip on her thigh with a suggestive smile. 'And such firm and lovely young flesh to display in those roles too! Ah, if only I was ten years younger...!'

Molly silently thanked God that Sir Thomas was not ten years younger otherwise she might have to use her knife on him to keep his amorous propensities in check. Yet she appreciated the compliment he had just paid to her developing acting skill, and she was excited about the possibility of working on bigger roles with these famous actors. Some of them had been in the business for over twenty years, and had tried to keep the art of performance alive after the Long Parliament, spurred on by Puritan opinion, had closed all the theatres down. For all his moral deficiencies, it had been Killigrew who had brought back theatre to England after the Restoration five years ago. The new King had rewarded his loyalty during his exile by making him Groom of the Bedchamber and Chamberlain to Queen Catherine, and, along with Sir William Davenant, had given him a royal warrant to form a new theatre company. Killigrew had beaten Davenant to a debut, at Gibbon's Tennis Court in Clare Market, and among the original members of that new King's Company had been these very gentlemen: Michael Mohun, William Wintershall and Charles Hart. Molly had heard the three of them reminiscing just yester evening over supper in a local tavern in Bow Street, and it seemed from the little she'd overheard that they had played for a time at the old Red Bull Theatre in Clerkenwell, until moving to this new King's theatre in Drury Lane two years ago.

Molly could only hope that the falling off in the theatre's audiences was a temporary setback, because the thought of not being able to perform here was almost more than she could bear.

She loved every intoxicating moment working here at the King's theatre. She loved the stage craft that could create such spellbinding illusions, she loved the plays (even the bad ones), the casting of spells on the audience that could take them away from their humdrum lives into an intoxicating make believe world. In Molly's opinion, there was much more magic to be found here in this theatre than outside on the streets of London, even in Spring Gardens or the new pleasure gardens at Fox Hall. This imagined world of the playwright was far more potent and enticing to her than the real world.

And where else in London could such a disparate audience assemble? From the commonest shopkeeper to the grandest courtier, from the lowest street sellers to fancy fops complacently combing their fine new curled wigs, this was a place where the coarse chatter of the pit mingled with the flutter of painted fans and the rustling of silk gowns from the white-bosomed court ladies in their private boxes. Molly thought that this theatre was the true heart of London where all its different elements and characters came together, to gossip and preen and brawl, the gallery and boxes constantly alive with the whispers of romantic assignations and scandal.

'What think you of this new play by the Earl of Orrery, *Mustapha*? Do you think the audience will take to it?' Killigrew asked.

Molly did not like the play at all, but knowing Killigrew's attachment to the playwright, decided to be politic in her answer. 'Tis a good play on the whole, but a trifle serious and dour, I fear, with little sparkle in the speeches to amuse an audience.'

Killigrew still had his hand on her thigh and he was now stroking it assiduously, making Molly feel a little warm. 'As ever, your judgement is impeccable, my girl. Those were precisely my thoughts too. But at least there will be no problem with tonight's offering, Mr Lacy's comedy *The Old Troop*. The audiences always like the base humour of Mr Lacy's work. And I must say you play the company whore with great accomplishment.'

Molly was not sure whether to take that as a compliment or not, though she did enjoy playing her part in this drama of corrupt Civil War soldiers billeted on resentful Yorkshire villagers. The play was full of Mr Lacy's usual bawdy jokes and made much fun of the French, featuring the character of the company chef 'Monsieur Raggou' who came out with much ludicrous mock French. Perhaps the accuracy of Molly's portrayal was due to the fact that she had based the character on her own foster mother, Celia Hornett, who ran a bawdy house in Whetstone Park. She knew of course that Killigrew was well aware of this fact and was patently teasing her for it.

What Killigrew did not know, though, was that Mistress Hornett was not her foster mother at all, but in fact her *real* mother. Molly herself had only discovered this startling fact a few months previously after a lifetime of deceit on her mother's part. Celia had been equally deceiving about the identity of Molly's real father, and the latest version that Molly had heard from her (which she did not believe in the slightest) was that her father had been an illustrious French nobleman. Molly knew full well the extent of the imaginative and romanticized fancies that her mother had often indulged in concerning her past life, and was content for the moment not to know the truth about her real father. The more likely truth was that he was a common criminal or ne'r do well, and Molly was in no rush to discover that her real father had probably been hanged as a sheep stealer, or transported for theft to the ends of the world....

'I am glad that you approve of my playing, sir, yet I know that I will have to look to my laurels. With the return of these other fine actresses to the company, there will be much more competition for parts.'

'You need have no fear in that direction, Molly. But others may fall down the pecking order, I fear.' Killigrew glanced significantly in the direction of Mary Pettican, who was still on stage talking with Christopher Malthouse. When Molly had first come into the company, Mary Pettican had been his leading actress and a personal favourite. She was undoubtedly a beautiful girl, Molly had to admit, yet her performances in recent months had grown lacklustre and jaded. As if understanding that she was under discussion, Mary flashed Molly an evil look in return. Molly had tried her best to get on with her fellow actress but, even when she was being superficially amiable, Mary still retained a coldness in her expression and a sharpness to her voice that had prevented them ever becoming true friends.

'Our northern friend Christopher too may have to yield the bigger roles now that Charles, William and Michael have returned to the fold,' Killigrew went on without much sign of regret. 'He is a good workmanlike actor, yet he does not have the stature of a true thespian.'

Molly thought this a harsh opinion given that Christopher worked so hard at his art. He did not have beauty on his side, of course, being a tall and gangly mouse-haired individual, yet he possessed a fine resonant voice that could electrify an audience on occasion. Molly chose however not to leap to his defence given the difficult situation in the theatre. Despite what Killigrew had said, she was sure that her own position was quite as vulnerable as those of Mary Pettican and Christopher Malthouse.

Sir Thomas excused himself. 'I have to go and rest these old bones upstairs in my chamber for a few minutes – age is finally catching up with me, I fear - but Charles will be in charge of the remainder of the rehearsal.'

Molly merely nodded in understanding, but privately wondered cynically who might be getting an "audition" in Killigrew's private chamber this morning...

*

An hour later, the rehearsal of the tragedy of Mustapha, son of Suleiman the Magnificent, was completed, and Molly was congratulating herself at having got through it safely in her role as a princess of the Imperial harem.

Molly thought that she had quite won over Charles Hart in her scenes with him in his own role as Mustapha. He had not formerly paid her much attention before, but today he was highly attentive and considerate to her in his directions, which had drawn angry looks from Mary Pettican in consequence. Mr Hart was most certainly a beautiful man, Molly concluded from her close examination of him, yet no painted effeminate fop. Her friend Nell (who knew everything about the intimate secrets of the company) had told her that Hart began his career as a boy player with the King's Men; then established his reputation by playing the role of the Duchess in *The Cardinal*, the famous tragedy by James Shirley, more than twenty years ago. Yet this pretty actor, who could imitate women so successfully on stage, went on to serve as a brave soldier in the Civil War, and was an officer in Prince Rupert's regiment of cavalry, seeing combat at the battles of Marston Moor and Naseby. Molly found Mr Hart's combination of prettiness and manliness to be an attractive quality, to say the least.

Hart had returned to acting after the war, and had been involved in an attempt to re-start the King's Men Company during the Puritan Commonwealth, which - not surprisingly perhaps – had failed in miserable fashion. Nell had heard rumours that he might even have been imprisoned briefly for violating the ban against theatrical performance, after being caught at the Cockpit theatre in the middle of a performance of *Rollo Duke of Normandy*...

Hart assembled the company on stage at the end of the rehearsal and thanked them all for their participation. 'Now you must all rest for an hour or so before we need to dress for this afternoon's performance of *The Old Troop*. Especially you, Molly,' he added, taking her hand briefly, 'since you have such a demanding role in today's play.'

'...As a whore, of course,' Mary Pettican whispered loudly at the back to one of her confidantes, 'which some may call perfect casting.'

Hart ignored the interruption and merely gripped Molly's hand more tightly, before finally releasing her with a languid smile.

Molly enjoyed this unexpected moment of intimacy, but could not help noticing that the young Irishman, Patrick Whelan, had flushed bright red on witnessing this moment of clear flirtation.

The company broke up into ones and twos, and Molly was not surprised to see Patrick follow her into a quiet corner off stage. She knew that this Irish boy was in love with her of course, or so he said anyway, and on balance she was prepared to believe his frequent declarations to be sincere. He had certainly been of great service to her during her serious troubles last year, and had it not been for her liaison with Henry Raven, she suspected that she would indeed have given in to his advances by now. He was young and muscular, and almost as beautiful as Charles Hart, therefore there was much about him to tempt her. Molly's little orange seller friend Nell believed Whelan to be a thief or highwayman in his past life in Ireland, though, and was of the opinion that he had taken to acting in order to lie low from the law. Such an interesting personal history was indeed a possibility for young Mr Whelan, Molly had to concede, because he did have a dark brooding presence and a devil-may-care attitude about him...

Patrick was fully aware of course that she was now the mistress of the wealthy Henry Raven, but that did not seem to have deterred him from further attempts to get her into his own bed at every opportunity. If anything, he seemed to have intensified his efforts of late. Molly in her turn did not mind some harmless flirtation with such a handsome man (as she did not mind similar flirtations with Charles Hart either), but was determined not to let any of it go too far.

'I hope your Mr Raven knows that you make cow eyes at the famous Charles Hart, Molly.' Whelan began with a breezy accusation.

'You have a powerful imagination, Patrick. What you saw was mere pretence on my part. 'Tis called "acting", sir,' she added cheekily. 'Ye should try it some time.'

Whelan only smiled in response.

The boy did have a very warm and genuine smile, Molly decided - a smile that could easily melt a girl's heart if she were not on guard against such evils. Therefore perhaps it was time to cool his ardour a little. 'If you will excuse me, Patrick, I have to go, and rest a little now.'

'Ah, yes, you are fortunate indeed that you now have sumptuous rooms so near in Bow Street, and can therefore return there and rest before the performance.'

''Tis true. I am fortunate indeed,' Molly freely admitted.

'Your lover is very generous,' Whelan said with a slight hint of derision.

'He is, and I am very grateful for his consideration.'

'Yet do you not crave to bed a real man, Molly – one who truly loves you?'

Molly blinked slowly. 'Mr Raven loves me truly, and I him.'

'I doubt not the first part, Molly, but I have sincere doubts over the second. Ye may love his money, but I do not believe that you love the man himself. He is a dry old stick for such a young man. I suppose it is a consequence of him having too much money, and too much unused time on his hands.'

Molly hid her anger. 'You misunderstand him, Patrick, and me. 'Tis not merely his wealth that attracts me. He brings me pleasure in all sorts of ways. He may not be so pretty as you, but he knows how to make me happy.'

'This is merely what you want to believe,' Whelan said with a shrug. 'But I could *truly* make you happy, if you would but give me the chance, young Molly.'

Molly merely smiled blandly at him. 'That vessel has sailed already, Patrick, and thou art too late.' She glanced around the theatre. 'But there are many pretty little yachts still berthed here in port, who would be only too happy to let you sail them away into the blue, Patrick. Why not give one of them a go and help them to slip their moorings?'

Whelan did not seem put out by her rejection. 'Ah, but my heart has sailed already with that pretty little vessel with the white sails and the entrancing little stern…'

*

Molly was still smiling to herself at her exchange with the persistent Patrick Whelan as she climbed the creaking oak stairs that led to Sir Thomas Killigrew's private chamber. She had been about to leave and return to her house in Bow Street until one of the theatre maidservants approached her at the main stage door and said that Sir Thomas wanted to see her briefly before she left.

Molly reached the door of his chamber but hesitated before knocking, not sure if it was safe to go over this threshold alone. It had been many months now since Killigrew had made any serious attempts to board her, but he was a licentious old rogue with enormous bodily appetites still. Fortunately his virility was no longer sufficient to match his appetite, therefore she reasoned that if he had already made some sport today with one of the other actresses, then she was reasonably safe from his advances.

She knocked diffidently, and heard a voice bid her enter. But it was not the raddled face and long white hair of Sir Thomas Killigrew that greeted her when she opened the door, but the pert and pretty face of her orange seller friend Nelly.

Not that Nell was presently equipped for selling oranges, being as naked as a baby, and admiring her own generous form in a full height wall mirror.

Nell shivered. 'Shut the door behind you, Molly. It may be April, but there's still a fierce draught from the corridor outside.' She giggled. 'And I might catch the cold to end all colds, dressed like this.' Sir Thomas's private chamber was a small oak-panelled room, with a fire burning cheerfully in the hearth. As well as the normal furniture of a parlour, it also contained a bed where Killigrew either rested before performances, or exerted himself, as the urge took him.

Molly could not help smiling. '*Dressed*, do you call it?' She glanced around uneasily. 'Where is Sir Thomas, Nell? Is he not here?'

'Oh, he has been and gone, and had his pleasure already. 'Tis the one blessing of making the beast with an old man – it does not last long. So worry not about him, Molly. It was I who wanted to see you.' Nell laughed and patted her plump belly. 'He is a randy old goat, though, to be sure. I was not five seconds in this room before he had me bare-arsed, and up against the bookcase there.'

'He is not coming back?' Molly asked worriedly, thinking that Sir Thomas might have ambitions of an enticing threesome.

'For seconds, mean you? I pray not.' Nell hesitated. 'I hope that I did not give in to him too easily or too quickly. Will he honour his word and let me into his company now, do you think?'

Molly was uncomfortable at such a question, which struck a little too close to home for comfort. 'He always has before...when dealing with others in the company, I mean. There is some slight honour in the man, I think – of a sort anyway. He would not take his pleasure with a maid and then not reward her in some way that would suit her inclinations. And I am sure he knows that you are desirous of performing on stage; I have mentioned it to him myself several times.'

Nell was relieved. 'Then I am heartily glad to hear it. It would be a pain to have gone through all that grunting and sweating for no reward. And the man has very ill breath, as you yourself must have noticed...' She reached for a pair of men's silk breeches lying on a chair and with a laugh slipped them on for size. 'I found these old silk breeches in Killigrew's wardrobe over there. They must be very old because he would never fit in them now. But they are just my size...see! Sir Tom says I have just the figure for breeches' parts.' She strained to see her own back view in the mirror. 'How looks my bum in breeches, Molly. Sir Tom says that it will likely bring the house down.'

Molly smiled. ''Tis lovely and firm, to be sure, Nell. But is this all you asked me up here for – to admire your sweet little bum?'

Nell became almost shy. 'Nay, that is merely an aside.' She seemed hesitant for a moment. 'You know that I am not a good reader, Molly, even though you have tried your damnedest to teach me. It will be very difficult for me to learn my parts when I cannot lift the words off the page with my eyes alone. I need to hear the sounds as well. Will you continue to help me, Molly? Read through my parts with me in private, and help me learn my lines when the time comes?'

Molly smiled. 'Yes, of course, I will. I am your friend still, am I not?'

'I hope so indeed, although I have noted that you have less time for me these days, now that you are the mistress of a wealthy and respected man. How goes that regular gallop with Mr Raven, by the way?' She pulled the breeches up with another giggle and stretched the silk until the waist came almost up to her breasts. 'I would not object to such an attractive arrangement myself. I believe I have a yen to find a wealthy lover of my own in time, just like your Mr Raven. Or - who knows - perhaps someone even grander? Quality not quantity shall be my watchword for the future, when it comes to gentlemen, Molly.'

Nell turned again to admire her front view in the mirror, then let her breeches fall slowly to the floor. 'That should not be too difficult to arrange, should it?' She placed her hands saucily on her hips. 'Given what I have to offer a gentleman, I mean,'

'Nay, not difficult at all.' Molly gave her cheek a little affectionate slap. 'But please stay well away from Mr Raven, or I shall have your eyes out,' she warned, only half-jokingly.

# CHAPTER 2

Henry Raven was one of those fortunate people in life who had never had to worry about where his next meal would come from. His mother had been the youngest daughter of an earl, after all, and his father, Thomas Raven, had been one of the largest landowners in Dorset. But Henry had nevertheless endured his share of unhappiness in his seven-and-twenty years of life.

His father, Thomas, a dour man of principle, had taken the Parliamentarian side in the Civil War (as had his neighbour, Oliver Warboys) and had died twenty years ago in the bloody carnage at Marston Moor, so that Henry barely remembered him. The Raven family had been well rewarded by Cromwell for their loyalty during the war and through the Interregnum that followed, even though his mother had not lived long past her fortieth year to enjoy this acclamation. Henry – the only son – had inherited everything at the tender age of nineteen.

Now that the Royalists had returned to power, aided by many former Parliamentarians who had judiciously changed sides after Cromwell's death, Henry had long been expecting to see his possession of his Salwayash estate challenged by the new power in the land. So far, though – perhaps because the land had been in his family's hands for many generations – no Royalist had yet appeared to lay any dubious claim to Henry Raven's estate or wealth...

Henry Raven had finally returned to London from his three-week stay in his home county of Dorset, arriving only late last night at his home in St Martin's Lane after a gruelling coach journey. The warm dry weather had finally broken yesterday and the heavens had opened in typically English fashion, turning the coach road on the sandy heathland between Winchester and Camberley into a quagmire and doubling the usual journey time.

Yet being a man of relentless personal habits, he found that he could not rest in bed on this Monday morning, but, with the sun returned, must make urgent steps to the Royal Exchange in Cornhill to deal with all the outstanding matters of business that had accumulated in his absence. His coal mines in the North had now vastly increased their production of late to over a thousand tons a month. England now produced the greater part of all the coal used in the world, and with the winters growing ever colder in recent years, the price of coal was rising to very profitable levels. English coal was burning in hearths and furnaces and kilns all over Northern Europe now, helping to stave off the terrible cold of a succession of winters of unparalleled bleakness and ferocity.

Much of this increased production at Raven's mines was due, no doubt, to the aggressive methods of his manager, Alexander Hicks, a young Northern man of direct speech and somewhat brutal manners. Raven had visited Newcastle last autumn to oversee the management of his recently acquired mines, and had been shocked to discover the backbreaking nature of the work, and the squalor and degradation of the conditions in which Hicks forced his miners to live. Although he desired to make a profit, Henry Raven had no wish to exploit his fellow men and cause them this much misery, so was determined to make beneficial changes to the working practices, and to the living conditions, of his miners. Yet Mr Hicks had proved unyielding in this respect, and had merely driven his workers even harder, somehow managing to achieve an increase in production even during this long hard winter just gone. Raven knew that he would have to travel to Newcastle soon to rectify the situation, and was sure that, given Mr Hicks' intransigence and his unwillingness to treat his workforce as human beings, he would have to replace him soon with someone more pliable to his will.

Henry Raven was an unusual employer in that he was prepared to sacrifice short term profit in favour of fair treatment of his workforce. He held the opinion that his workers would respond favourably to better conditions anyway, and that he might even see increased production and profitability in the end, with his men properly fed and clothed, and not being treated like pack animals.

As he went about his business in the Royal Exchange on this fine April morning, Raven cast frequent glances in the direction of his manservant Martin Gibney, standing patiently at his side, and wondered again about offering him the opportunity to take Mr Hicks' job. Although only four-and-twenty, and certainly having no experience of managing an enterprise on this scale, Raven's instincts told him that Martin would be the perfect person for the role, combining much good sense with a talent for figures and bookkeeping, yet also possessing a degree of humanity that was sadly lacking in Mr Hicks. Raven was sure that Martin did harbour ambitions to be more than a manservant or a book clerk all his life, although whether he would be willing to exile himself for many years to the North Country was another matter, of course. Already Raven thought of Martin as more of a companion and friend than a servant, and trusted him implicitly to keep his personal accounts in order. It would therefore be quite a sacrifice for himself too if Martin should agree to take up this challenge, yet perhaps the young man deserved this chance to increase his standing in the world. He had recently been paying court to a pretty maidservant in a nearby house in St Martin's Lane, and seemed likely to marry her in time. Therefore such an opportunity should perhaps be much more welcome to him than it would have been previously, although whether his pink-cheeked beauty would also care to exchange the vast city of London for the smaller city of Newcastle was another question. Newcastle was however a very fair city that had grown extremely prosperous because of the established monopoly over the Durham coal trade granted to the city merchants by the present King's grandfather. This legal monopoly was no longer in force since the Civil War, yet the city of Newcastle still held an effective monopoly because of its proximity to the coal fields and its unmatchable facilities for berthing ships. Raven for one would have loved to break this monopoly of the Newcastle merchants and perhaps export his coal through the rival ports of Hartlepool or Sunderland, which would have saved him a fortune in tariffs. Yet he would need to find some cheaper way of transporting coal across country than by ox wagon as at present if he wanted to make this scheme practicable. Martin was an ingenious young man, and Raven suspected that he might be just the man to come up with some workable ideas in this regard.

The central courtyard of the Royal Exchange was filled as usual on this sunny spring morning with haggling and querulous merchants, and the noise resembled that of a farmyard almost, more than a place of business. Each group of merchants had their own regular meeting point in the courtyard, while the upper floors arranged around the cobbled yard contained the finest shops in all England - apothecaries, armourers, milliners, booksellers, and goldsmiths. Raven had spent most of his time this morning in intense discussion with his shipping agent, a Mr George Vine, who, although an obnoxious man with unpleasing manners, was however scrupulously honest and fair in his financial dealings. Their main topic of conversation was the matter of the purchase of three new colliers for Raven's own fleet, which he needed to transport the increasing tonnage of coal being produced by his mines in Whickham, Winlaton and Heworth. Raven was already severely short of vessels for this purpose, having lost one collier last winter - the *Anne Raven* – which had been sacrificed in the service of the King, and for which he was still trying to get adequate compensation from the King's purse for his loss. Yet Raven could no longer go on hiring vessels at exorbitant rates from other ship owners, so he had charged Vine with ordering the construction of three new vessels from shipyards in Whitby and Hull. It seemed, God willing, that the first one would now be delivered in August, subject to Raven making the necessary payments.

After he had concluded his business, Raven pulled Martin aside into a quiet corner of the courtyard. 'I go now to enjoy a cup of coffee with Mr Vine in Jonathan's coffee house across the way, so you can return home now if you wish, Martin.'

'I would rather wait for you, Master.' Martin was always very conscious of his master's safety – particularly since the violent troubles he had suffered last winter – and did not care for his master's unusual habit, for such a wealthy man, of walking London's dangerous streets alone.

'No, 'tis better you do not. I may be some time, and there is something else I also need to do.' Raven was minded to go to Fetter Lane today, since it was on his way back from Cornhill to the West End, and begin those enquiries about Esther Linney that he had promised his sister he would make.

Martin accepted his master's decision, but with some considerable doubt written on his still youthful face. 'Are you sure that is your will, Master?'

'I am, Martin. I shall be back home by three o'clock this afternoon. There is something I need to broach with you. Can we talk this afternoon? I have a proposal to make to you to change your circumstances.'

'What is it, Master? Have I done something wrong in your eyes?' Martin looked more apprehensive than enthused by his announcement. Raven recalled that he had seemed distracted of late, and perhaps a little melancholy about something, but he had no inkling what the problem might be. Perhaps the ill feeling had arisen because he had left Martin behind in London with Dora Bagwell these three weeks while he had been away, although Raven had thought he had been doing his young manservant a favour by not taking him away from his lady love.

Raven put an affectionate hand on his shoulder. 'Nay, we shall talk later, Martin. This is not the right time or place. But concern yourself not – 'tis nothing ill that I have to say to you...in fact quite the opposite...'

Martin then bowed his head and took his leave, yet still cast a wary glance back at his master as he made his way through the milling throng in the sunlit courtyard of the Royal Exchange, and out into busy Cornhill.

*

Henry Raven's enquiries in Fetter Lane proved to be much simpler that he imagined. Before he left Dorset, he had visited Lady Onslow in her home near the village of Dottery and discovered that his elderly neighbour's apparent sighting of Esther Linney had taken place in the vicinity of a draper's shop in Fetter Lane, which the old lady described with remarkable detail.

Raven found the shop without difficulty from Lady Onslow's closely detailed description – a narrow old Tudor shop squeezed between a leaning tenement building and a small coaching inn and yard - and so began his questions with the proprietor of that shop, a wizened ancient sitting working behind a scarred oak table, who seemed to have barely any strength left in his fingers to cut cloth any more, or indeed the eyes to see where his scissors might be going.

The old draper knew nothing as it happened of any tall and striking young woman with black hair and pale skin, who might be living in this neighbourhood. 'Nay, I recognize not this young lady from your description, sir, but she could perhaps work in the inn next door, the White Lion. There are many pretty young maidservants there whose dainty looks and dimpled smiles might tempt a young man into wanton thoughts. Or even perhaps an old one...' he admitted with a tired smile.

Raven smiled back at the old man. 'You think I seek a temptress, sir?'

The old draper continued at his work, but did deign to glance up at his gentleman visitor at this point. 'It is what most men seek, if truth be known, sir...'

While making his way into the yard of the White Lion inn next door, Raven could not help his thoughts turning naturally to his own sweet temptress, after that conversation with the old draper, and he soon remembered that this was the very street where Molly came from originally. And from a draper's shop too, although it certainly could not be the one he had just visited...

Molly had told Raven very little of her origins but he had discovered this much at least – that as a babe in arms, she had survived a house fire in Bartlett's Passage, just off Fetter Lane, that had killed her real mother and father in their modest draper's shop. Molly had subsequently been taken into the care of Mistress Celia Hornett, who was no blood relative apparently, and of no great character either since she worked in a bawdy house. Yet there had been no one else willing or able to take the girl child, it seemed, so Molly had been brought up afterwards in various bawdy houses. Through knowing Molly, Raven had met Mistress Hornett several times, who was now the comparatively wealthy owner of her own bawdy house, and he had been pleasantly surprised by her ladylike manners. Yet he had noticed little warmth between Molly and her adoptive mother, therefore could not fully comprehend the true nature of their relationship. It seemed Celia had always treated her charge well enough as a child, yet not perhaps with the genuine warmth and affection of a true mother, Raven surmised.

These reflections about Molly soon filled Raven's mind with sentimental affection for her, and made him decide that he would go and see her this very evening at her apartments in Bow Street. Although Raven paid the rent for these rooms, and all the bills that came with them, he was scrupulous about treating the apartment as Molly's own private place of residence, and he never went there without sending her a note first to ask her permission. Although she was most certainly his mistress, Raven had no wish to take complete possession of her, body and soul, and preferred instead to have to continue to woo her in order to receive her favours rather than take them as a right. He hoped nevertheless that she was faithful to him, even when he was away for extended periods as he had been for these last three weeks. The good thing was that she was heavily engaged at the King's theatre six days a week, which gave her little time for mischief, although it also threw her into the way of many handsome young men, of course. Raven was a little suspicious of one young Irish actor in particular called Patrick Whelan who had professed love for her, and who seemed to enjoy Molly's particular regard as a result...

Having been denied the pleasure of her company for three weeks, Raven's sentimental reflections about Molly were soon augmented with some undeniably lustful thoughts too, so he now became determined to drop a note through her door on his way home presently.

At the White Lion inn, Raven spoke to the landlord, coachmen and all the maidservants he could find (many of whom were indeed just as comely as the old draper next door had suggested.) Raven soon found one among them in particular who believed she had seen a woman in the area matching Esther Linney's description. This was a plump young Irish kitchen maid who, although not matching her fellow maids in prettiness, did have a wanton look about her and a saucy smile. 'I believe I have seen the lady you mean, sorr...' – the girl had a thick Dublin brogue - 'I believe she has lodgings above the silversmith's shop at the corner with Fleet Street. Is she *your* lady, sorr, by any chance?' the girl asked with almost a snigger.

Raven wondered at the suggestive sound she made. 'Nay, she is an old friend who perhaps needs my help.'

'Then I hope you can help her, sorr,' the girl said with practically a wink.

Raven was mystified at the girl's meaning but said nothing.

The girl smiled awkwardly. 'I could show you exactly where she lives, if you like, sorr.'

'Nay, that will not be necessary. I believe I can find it well enough by myself,' Raven said quickly, giving this oddly forward girl a shilling, and hurrying off in the direction of Fleet Street.

The Irish girl was worth her expensive reward, though, because the silversmith, a bald man as thin as a rake, and of uncouth manners, soon confirmed that he had rented the rooms above his shop to a Mistress Linney from the county of Dorset...

*

As he climbed the wooden staircase at the side of the silversmith's shop and knocked on her door, Raven recalled more of the circumstances of Esther Linney's life. For a girl who had never strayed until now from her home county, she had led an eventful and often tragic life...

Her father, John Linney, had been a well-to-do yeoman farmer who had died when she was only a few months old, from a musket ball wound received fighting for the New Model Army in the siege of Taunton in Somerset. John Linney had been particularly unfortunate because his wound had not been sufficient to kill him outright, but merely enough to get severely infected and then consign him to a slow and agonising death over many days and weeks that followed. The drawn out death and suffering of her beloved husband had been the tool that had unhinged the mind of his pretty wife Meg, and led to an even worse fate for her.

After Meg had been found guilty of witchcraft and condemned to burn at the stake, the question had soon arisen as to what should happen to her baby daughter. Henry Raven's mother, Anne, herself widowed only the year before after the loss of her husband Thomas at Marston Moor, had taken pity on the infant and allowed one of her house servants in Salwayash Manor, a middle-aged and warm hearted maidservant called Doll Smurthwaite, to take the baby in. Esther had consequently grown up at the manor, being treated indulgently and eventually becoming more of a companion to the Raven children than a servant's child - and to Catherine in particular. She had in fact acquired the status of a foster sister to Henry Raven in everything but name, and it had only been his poor mother's long illness that had prevented that relationship being formalized in law.

There was more sadness in store for Esther, though, when she reached the age of thirteen, because both her mistress, Anne Raven, and her surrogate mother, Doll Smurthwaite, died that year within a few short weeks of each other.

Henry Raven was not twenty years old at the time and was still reeling with the sadness of his own mother's death, as well as the new responsibilities he had to bear, so had little time for Esther then. Yet, being so close to her, he had still expected her to stay on at the manor as a companion to Catherine and Mary. But Esther had chosen instead to leave at once, and keep house for her surviving elder brother Gideon, who had returned from sea with enough prize money from his privateering exploits to buy them a small farm and cottage. Raven remembered that he had been most upset when he had heard this news because he could scarce imagine Salwayash Manor without Esther's warm and comforting presence. And at thirteen she was already growing into a beauty to rival Catherine, and exciting his admiration in a way that Catherine, as a close blood relative, could not...

Raven got no answer to his first tentative knock, so banged again with his fist, this time much louder than he had intended, almost shaking the old wooden door off its hinges. The door finally opened, though, and the figure of a young woman stood expectantly in the dim light beyond. 'Mr Raven!' she exclaimed in surprise, as she belatedly recognized her visitor.

Raven smiled at her, pleased that he found her so easily. 'Surely there is no need of such formality between us, Esther. We are almost brother and sister, are we not - in feeling, if not in blood?'

Esther gave a little curtsey. 'I am honoured if you should think so, sir.' Having been brought up at the manor in close company with Mary and Catherine, Esther did still have a most ladylike way of speaking, which the years of hard work keeping house for her brother and running her small farm had not changed.

'Then please call me Henry, Esther,' he insisted.

Esther was reluctant to be so forward. 'I would feel uncomfortable treating you with that sort of intimacy, sir, when I have seen so little of you these last years.'

Raven accepted that, although a little hurt by her apparent coolness. 'As you wish, then. I truly meant to see more of you, Esther, but I am a busy man these days. I think that the last time we met was at the harvest feast last August, was it not?' It was the custom on the Raven estate to hold a feast and party for all the workers on the estate after the harvest was safely in. Last year they had held a combined party with the Warboys estate so that the celebrations had been an epic affair indeed that had gone on into the early hours. Raven recalled that he had drunk more ale than was good for him that night and had suffered a grim and enduring hangover as a result.

'Yes, I was there, sir, and we did talk briefly,' Esther agreed, but still without much visible warmth.

Raven hesitated. 'I was sorry to hear the sad news of your brother, Gideon. You have received no further news of him since his ship was lost?'

Esther shook her head dolefully. 'Nay, no hopeful news anyway. I have to assume that he was lost and that I am alone in the world again. I did not want him going to sea again and risking his life, but the lure of making easy money was too much for him. One of those privateering voyages could bring more wealth than a lifetime of toil on a farm, he said, and I could not dissuade him.'

'You shall not be alone in the world while any of the Raven family still draw breath, Esther,' Raven said firmly. 'That is why I came to see you. May I enter so that we can talk properly?'

Esther smiled apologetically and stepped back to let him enter her home. 'Of course you may, sir. 'Tis not a grand place, though, like Salwayash Manor.'

Raven held up a hand. 'Worry not, Esther. I have been in smaller homes than this, and I see that this one is pleasing enough.' It was indeed a comfortable little parlour with a patterned rug on the floor and even quaint pictures and ornaments on the plaster walls. Raven saw also that she kept it spotlessly clean as he would have expected of a hard working girl like Esther.

Esther bade him sit in the better of her two wooden chairs but remained standing herself in a dim corner of the room. 'What brings you here to my door, sir?'

Raven cleared his throat apologetically. 'Catherine was concerned about your sudden disappearance from Dorset and wanted me to find you and speak with you...

Esther turned briefly to adjust the curtain behind her and let a little more light into the room. Suddenly Raven flushed with embarrassment as he saw her figure from the side for the first time, plainly outlined against the rectangle of the leaded window behind. 'You are with child, Esther!' he blurted out. Suddenly the oddly suggestive behaviour of that Irish kitchen maid at the White Lion became all too clear – she obviously thought that *he* must be the father of Esther's child.

Esther reddened in turn at his accusatory tone, and Raven quickly excused himself. 'Please forgive me for my loud voice and bad manners, Esther. I did not mean to sound so accusing.'

Esther still said nothing, but the blush in her cheeks remained. Raven was struck as ever by the high-cheeked Italian beauty she had acquired from her mother, and her almost regal nature. She and his sister Catherine had made such an attractive pair as children, and both had grown to become remarkably beautiful women. Yet unlike Catherine, misfortune and disaster seemed to stalk Esther at every turn, though she was never deserving of it. Her life was like a disturbing dark mirror of Catherine's privileged life, strewn with trials and hardships waiting to test her, and showing how much of happiness in life was apparently down to blind chance rather than design.

'I suppose that this is why you left your farm and came to London...when the physical signs of your condition became obvious,' Raven went on briskly, trying to avoid any further note of censure in his voice. "Do you mean to have the baby here in secret? Is that it?'

"Tis no secret any more, sir,' Esther pointed out bleakly, 'now that you have found me here.'

Raven stood up and took her hand. 'It is *still* a secret, Esther, if you wish. I will tell no one, not even Catherine, if you prefer not.'

'Cathy will press you until she discovers the truth, if I know your sister,' Esther said with a near smile.

Raven smiled in return as he released her hand. 'I suppose that is true. Yet I could tell her simply that I have not been able to find you.'

'She will know that you dissemble, sir. She knows you too well, and I doubt that you could deceive her with any conviction. Deceit was not in your nature as a boy, and I am sure that it is the same now. You are too honourable a man for that, sir.' Esther had recovered her composure and she lifted her chin bravely to face him with calm grey eyes. 'No, you may tell Cathy the unfortunate truth, but no one else, I beg you. And also please ask Cathy not to spread word of this any further – she will honour such a promise to me.'

'Of course.' Raven paced the room a little. 'Then is there anything I can do for you during your confinement? You look as if you are close to your full term.'

'Indeed. The baby should arrive within six weeks.'

Raven could not help mentally calculating from that confirmation when she must have lain with her illicit lover. Today was the tenth day of April therefore Esther must have slept with the baby's father late last summer, perhaps at harvest time. There usually was a spate of illicit pregnancies incurred at the time of the harvest celebrations when much ale was drunk and many girls shed their normal inhibitions. Raven could not help but wonder if this significant event in Esther's life had taken place after the harvest celebration on his own estate. He tried to recall if he had seen Esther talking with any young man in particular at that happy party yet he could not remember much about the feast now, given the amount of ale he had himself incautiously imbibed. Yet such wanton behaviour was quite out of character for Esther, who was no silly or flirtatious serving girl but a sober and hardworking young woman of deep moral convictions.

'What mean you to do with the baby when it arrives? Will you keep it, or give it away to an orphanage or to a childless couple?'

'If I wish to return to my village and to the farm, then I can hardly bring the baby with me. I would be a marked woman, and so would my innocent child. But I cannot decide on my best course at present. I will give birth first, then decide later. Perhaps I will choose to keep the baby and go elsewhere to live, where no one knows me or my history.'

'Then do you need help?' Raven pressed her. 'A gift of money, or other material things? I could hire a maidservant to take care of you until you can look after yourself again. And I can find a physician to help you through the delivery, if you need it. I would be glad to support you through this trial, Esther.'

Esther was expressionless. 'Thou art very kind, sir, as always, but 'tis not necessary. I have enough support already.'

'From the father, do you mean?' Raven asked, wondering again at the man's identity. It had to be a local Dorset man, since no one else could have had access to Esther during the last harvest time. And if the incident had happened after his own feast, then there was a good chance that the father of the baby was one of the tenant farmers or labourers on his own estate.

Esther regarded him shrewdly. 'I can see you are wondering who the father of my child might be, sir. But please do not speculate in that regard. 'Tis my business, and mine alone.'

'As you wish, of course, Esther,' Raven reassured her. 'I have no wish to meddle. I merely want to help you, if you will let me.'

'Then I thank you kindly for your concern, sir, but the thing I want most now is to be left alone to have my baby in peace. Then I shall decide my own future without recourse to any other individual, even to the father of the child…'

*

Raven was still wondering at this conversation three hours later when he was at home in his library and waiting for Martin to appear.

Martin did eventually appear, knocking at the open door to announce his arrival. Raven could see his young kitchen maid Kate Soule lingering in the hallway outside, perhaps hopeful of hearing a little of their conversation. . She was a distant kinswoman of Dora's from Dorset too – a demure little thing, just sixteen, blue-eyed and golden-haired, if alarmingly pale and thin, who'd arrived last year in the household as a replacement kitchen maid. Raven suspected that Dora had brought her here from Dorset as much for her own company as for help with all the domestic chores in such a large house. It was common knowledge in the house that sweet little Kate now harboured a great passion for Martin, and was inclined to sigh and make cow eyes at him whenever he was about her. At one time Raven had suspected that Martin secretly returned this devotion but it seemed he was quite wrong in this supposition since Martin had lately taken up with the pretty maid Isabel at the nearby corner house in St Martin's Lane.

'You had better close the door behind you so we can keep our conversation private,' Raven said pointedly as he caught a glimpse of Katie's sweet little face peering through the crack in the door. 'And please sit down so that we can talk openly without any formality.'

Martin was still looking apprehensive as he took the seat by the fire next to his master, so Raven took pity on him and told him at once what he had in mind.

On hearing his master's unexpected proposal to change his life and career in this dramatic fashion, Martin was shocked at first into a complete silence, then, when he could finally muster an adequate response, his hesitant reply was undermined further by an unfamiliar stutter. Raven had not heard this old stutter of Martin's for many years, not in fact since Martin had first worked for him as a gauche young manservant of seventeen during his student days at Cambridge. 'M-me, m-master! As the manager of your Northern mines in place of Mr Hicks? Is this a j-jest? Why would you think that I am qualified for such a p-position?'

Raven could not conceal his disappointment with Martin's answer, and particularly with the lack of confidence it revealed. He had been hoping that Martin would react with enthusiasm and even joy at such an offer, but it seemed to have provoked only an unsettling unease in his young manservant. 'If you are unsure about it,' Raven said bluntly, 'then perhaps it is not the right position for you, Martin. Yet I had thought you might even be enthusiastic about it. I believe you have the necessary skills to make a success of this enterprise. You understand bookkeeping and you have a logical and precise mind. And you would bring some humane dealings to the management of these mines which Mr Hicks is simply not capable of doing. The miners are mere pack animals to him, to be worked until they drop.'

'But would I be able to exert the degree of authority that such a position would require? I am used to taking orders, Master, not giving them,' Martin reflected.

Raven regarded him with undisguised disappointment now. 'A man can soon get used to giving orders, if he is the kind of individual who can command the respect of his fellows.' He sighed heavily. 'I take it you reject the offer then, Martin.'

Martin wavered a little. 'May I have some time to consider, Master? It would be a wrench leaving you and everything I have known here in London.'

'Is it the pretty maid Isabel in the corner house who concerns you, Martin? You could marry her and take with you, Martin, to a new and prosperous life. Newcastle may be far from here, but it is a fine town, the third richest in all England after London and Bristol. You will find no hardship there, and you and she would enjoy a very comfortable life together, I believe, and perhaps even make your fortunes.'

'It is a generous offer, Master,' Martin admitted. 'But I shall not take Isabel anywhere. She has already spurned me for another.'

'Ah!' Raven understood now why Martin had looked so melancholy and distracted since he had returned from Dorset. Clearly Martin's courtship of Isabel had gone badly awry in the three weeks he had been away. 'Then I am sorry to hear it. But there is a positive aspect to this bad news: that there is nothing to tie you to this house any more.'

'Except my years of loyal service to you in Cambridge and in London, Master. I would never want to forget them.'

'Neither would I want to forget those good times, Martin. But time does not stand still, and you would still be serving me, and in a far greater capacity than at present. You should reflect that this may be the only opportunity you will ever have to take a step up in life. Even if the circumstances were to arise, I may not be disposed to offer you such a chance again. You have many talents, Martin, and I believe you are suited to a better life than merely as my manservant and bookkeeper. A new world awaits you if you have the courage to take it.'

Martin stood up, his face set in serious lines. 'Then I shall reflect deeply on it, Master, and let you know my decision. May I have a few days to think about it?'

Raven stood up too and put a reassuring hand on his shoulder. 'Take a few weeks if necessary, Martin. There is no need to make an instant decision. But I would like to have a new manager installed in that position before the autumn, and if it is not to be you, then I will need to find another candidate...'

*

At eight o'clock that evening, with just a lingering trace of dusk left in the night sky, Henry Raven entered the main entrance of the familiar house in Bow Street, and climbed the stairs at a gallop to the second floor where Molly lived.

Before leaving his own house tonight, he had told his housekeeper Dora Bagwell that he would not be home again before morning, and that she was to lock up securely before retiring for the night. As usual, he had noted the stern look of disapproval on Dora's face at this news – Mistress Bagwell knew exactly where he was going with such a spring in his step. Dora clearly disliked Molly even more than did his sister Catherine, and, in Mistress Bagwell's favour in the matter, her judgement was at least based on some personal acquaintance, if still very slight. No doubt Mistress Bagwell, like his sister Catherine, believed Molly to be a devious and manipulative hussy who would milk him for all that he was worth. Yet Raven knew this to be an entirely false charge – Molly was certainly pleased to enjoy some of the trappings of his wealth, yet she was far from being a mercenary girl, and he prided himself that he had genuinely won her affection too. There was a real warmth to their relationship that he could not possibly hope to explain to his sister, and he certainly felt no inclination to have to justify himself to his own servant. If Dora did not change her ways soon and become more agreeable again, then he was determined that she would have to go back to service at Salwayash Manor, which might be no bad thing for her either, since it might improve both her temper and her situation.

As he knocked at Molly's door and waited for her reply, Raven found that he already had a massive stirring in his loins at the mere thought of his temptress being so near. So that when Molly finally opened the door, dressed in a new gown of rich brocade, and wearing satin shoes decorated with rosettes of ribbon and lace, he simply lifted her off her feet and carried her to the bedchamber...

*

Raven was apologetic afterwards for his animal passion.

Molly, lying naked at his side, only smiled complacently. 'It would worry me more, my love, if you exhibited no passion at all after being away from me these three weeks.'

'Thou art still the amiable minx, I see,' Raven said with a smile.

'And you still love me for it,' Molly said. 'I wish only that some of your family and household thought better of me. I dare say your sisters think I am but a heartless whore trying to steal all your gold.'

'They do not know you, or properly comprehend your character,' Raven pointed out, choosing wisely not to deny his family's dislike of her. Molly was no fool, as Raven had soon discovered in their relationship, and was able to see through any evasions or dissembling on his part very easily.

Molly made a wry face. 'Nor will they ever comprehend my true character, when they will never meet me.'

Raven turned to look her in the face. 'Be not missish, Molly. I told you that you could come to Dorset with me and be a guest at my sister's wedding if you wished.'

Molly shrugged. 'I do not believe that you meant it as a serious invitation. I would have had to take leave of absence from the theatre, and with the present difficult situation there, might never have got my place back in the company again. And if I had travelled to Dorset with you, I would also have had to bear the snide looks of all your neighbours and family who would have enjoyed, no doubt, seeing the public humiliation of Mr Raven's little whore.'

Raven ran his hand down her soft pink flanks and gently stroked her firm buttocks. 'You seem out of temper, Molly. You yourself said you had no wish to marry me.'

Molly made a wry face. 'True. But you never asked me for my hand, and it might be nice to hear the words even if I intend to turn you down.'

Raven was aware that he had entered dangerous territory. 'Are you saying that you do want to marry me now, and want to carry all the responsibilities of being a wife? If so, you would have to leave the theatre for good. That is my only stipulation.'

Molly smiled uncomfortably, then took his hand and kissed his fingers tenderly one by one. 'Then you know I cannot accept that condition for the present, my love. I cannot forego the pleasure of performing on stage even to become your wife.' She laughed self-consciously. 'Yet we make foolish talk, Henry, do we not? I am not a fit woman to be a wife for you, as we both well know. We should just accept our happiness as it is for the moment, and not worry what trials and tribulations the future will bring us…'

# CHAPTER 3

Tuesday, 11th April 1665

After a fine warm day, a rainstorm had brewed up with unfortunate timing at seven o'clock in the evening, just as Molly was leaving the theatre. It did at least mean that there was not the usual number of camp followers and ne'er do wells lingering in the alleyway behind the stage door, whom she normally had to fight her way through, and from whose unwanted attentions she often had to run in order to escape.

The celebrity acquired by performing on stage was a powerful thing, it seemed, and Molly now found she received pestering attention from all sorts of rogues and misfits and odd fellows, who a year ago would not have given her a second glance as she left the theatre as a mere stripling orange girl. Molly had been most unsettled recently by the attentions of a tall dark-haired man of middle age whom she had noticed watching her with close scrutiny every time that she left the theatre. Though why his attention unsettled her so much she could not truthfully say, since he seemed a gentlemanly man by comparison with most of the lowly unwashed Londoners who gathered here at the stage door to pester and annoy her with their unwanted attentions and lewd praise. This man always stood at the back of the little crowd of onlookers and admirers – a head taller than most around him, and dressed well in Royalist cavalier fashion, with a lace collar at his throat and a fine long velvet coat to his knees. Molly, with her perceptive eye for fashion, had decided this coat could be in the French style, and therefore had mentally christened him the "sinister foreigner" because of that coat, and because of his unsettling gaze. Yet although he gave her long and penetrating looks, this mystery man never spoke a commending word to her about her performance, or even a lewd one (as did the rough fellows around him), nor did he ever smile, but always remained aloof and silent.

Perhaps that reticence to speak was why she found him so unsettling, and suspected some evil intent behind his odd behaviour...

Yet although the storm seemed to have deterred this foreign looking gentleman from waiting outside the stage door tonight, along with most of her usual admiring camp followers - something which Molly was grateful for - she saw from the fierce spattering of the rain on the cobbles that it was also going to mean a very wet walk back to Bow Street, so briefly considered sending the lecherous old doorman out in search of a sedan chair for her.

Yet something in her rebelled at the thought that she was now grown so grand and contrary that she could not even face a five-minute walk in the rain any more. So, brushing aside those few hardy admiring souls who had still congregated outside the stage door despite the driving rain, Molly set off with deliberate abandon, not even raising her umbrella but letting the rain soon flatten and destroy her elaborate hair style.

She had worn her hair on stage this afternoon in the fashionable *Hurluberlu* or scatterbrain style, elaborately curled at the sides and top, and with long ringlets draped around her low cut neckline, which was a style probably too elaborate for the common Yorkshire whore she was supposed to be, yet suited her well enough. The performance of *The Old Troop* had gone extremely well tonight, and Molly had enjoyed her brisk and playful scenes with the three famous returned actors, Messrs Mohun, Wintershall and Hart, who had all featured prominently in the play. From their virtuoso performances tonight, these three all clearly merited their considerable fame, but none more so than Mr Charles Hart, who had an amazing versatility and could turn himself into almost any character, it seemed, be it a stirring King Lear or a mere clown in a low comedy as in today's play. Molly thought immodestly that she had acquitted herself well too, though, and had certainly received particular applause at the end from the appreciative audience. The only black cloud over today's performance had been all the empty seats in the pit and the gallery. That old rogue Killigrew was right to be alarmed, it seemed, and the theatre was in serious trouble, no doubt of it. Six months ago, they would have had to turn people away at the door, and now they had almost to beg passers-by to come in...

The sun had not yet set, but the heavy rain and obscuring clouds made mockery of its power and had turned the street scene into virtual night anyway. Despite the near darkness, Molly soon began to enjoy the sensation of walking in the rain, as she often had as a girl, skipping over half-seen puddles and jumping over the open drains full of offal and dead rats that ran down the middle of the alleyways. Despite the present ill fortunes of the theatre, Molly felt happier inside than she had ever been. This inner happiness was mostly due to Henry's return of course, and his memorable arrival at her door last night.

Molly remembered suddenly what Patrick Whelan had called Henry a few days ago. *"Dry old stick" indeed...!* she said to herself with a smile, as she recalled Henry lifting her off her feet last night and whisking her away to the bedchamber.

Molly had been tempted to seek Patrick Whelan out today and perhaps make him eat his slanderous words by suggesting some intimate details of her night of exotic lovemaking with Mr Raven, but on further reflection decided it would be best not to goad him into further pointless advances of his own.

Molly wondered at her own brazenness, though, in bringing up the subject of a marriage proposal with Henry last night – it had been a naughty and presumptuous thing to do. Yet the astounding fact was that he did truly seem prepared to marry her if she would give up the stage. Even *she* did not believe herself ready for marriage yet. And she was also sure that, even if she had been prepared to sacrifice her stage career completely, she was still scarcely a fit wife for such a distinguished man as Henry Raven. The more she had learned about him the more she had become in awe of his standing in the world, and of his considerable achievements. As well as being a distinguished man of business and the owner of extensive lands and property, he had also studied medicine and was a member of both the College of Physicians and the Royal Society, the latter a group of gentlemen dedicated to the study of natural philosophy, it seemed, and to the application of that knowledge to improving the lot of humankind.

Yet the fact that Henry Raven was even prepared to consider her in this role of wife did leave a very warm glow in her innards, Molly had to admit to herself, and for the first time such a possibility did not seem entirely ridiculous to her. Her mother Celia, for one, would be overjoyed of course if such a miracle should ever happen...

Molly had reached the street door to her apartments by now, and was about to put the key into the lock when she became aware of someone skulking in the gloomy shadows across the street, his head hooded against the rain. For a moment she feared that it might be that mysterious foreigner from the theatre who had followed her home, and now intended her some harm. The hooded figure came forward from across the street with apparent reluctance, as Molly tried with increasing nervousness to open the stiff lock on her front door with the key. It was only when the man was a few feet from her, and he finally raised his hood, that a breathless Molly realized with relief that it was Patrick Whelan again.

Her relief soon turned to annoyance, though. He had often followed her home in the past like a loyal dog, but she hadn't noticed him much of late so she had rather hoped that he had given up this unfortunate habit.

'What is your business here, Patrick?' she demanded irately. He had not been performing in the play today so she had not seen much of him at the theatre, except in passing. She did notice that he seemed to be shivering a little, but perhaps that was just the rain.

She wanted simply to go inside and leave him here, but her innate good manners prevented her simply ignoring the man and closing the door in his face. After all Patrick did profess to love her, and had been of service to her in the past, so it would be ungenerous of her in the extreme to treat him without due courtesy. 'You are a long way from home, are you not, Patrick? You live in Red Cross Street still, do you not? That's a good mile and a half from here.'

'No, not any more, Molly. I was behind with the rent so the landlord turfed me out last week. I have been sleeping where I can since then. For the last few nights I found a nice billet in a builder's yard, but they did have rats the size of March hares lurking in the jakes.' He looked ruefully at his hand. 'I got bit by the devils two or three times.'

Molly's feelings were touched despite herself. 'You should have told me you were short of money, Patrick, and I would have helped you. But 'tis too late to go searching for new lodgings tonight.' She sighed. 'You had better come in with me. You seem not well, and my rooms are free of rats at least...'

*

Patrick was impressed with the spaciousness and style of her apartment, which consisted of no less than five rooms on the second floor of this well-appointed house – a sitting room, a kitchen and a wash room, and no less than two large bedchambers. He whistled softly at the opulence of the furnishings, the carpets on the floor, the silver candlesticks and the fine wainscoting. 'Indeed there are no rats,' he commented dryly. 'But do ye truly live alone here in this rat-free paradise, Molly?'

'There is a maidservant from Essex, Bathsheba, who comes every day from a nearby house to sweep the floors and do the washing, and another old serving woman comes in the evening from downstairs to make me a fire and cook me a meal if I need it.' She saw the look on his face. 'I did not ask for such help, but Mr Raven insisted that it be provided since I am so busy at the theatre.'

'You were busy before yet you had no skivvies to sweep and clean behind you,' Whelan pointed out. 'But I suppose Mr Raven, when he visits, does not want to be welcomed by roughened red hands and a body made tired by drudgery.'

'What is the point you make, Patrick? That I have sold my soul to become a rich man's whore? Why are you so convinced that there is no real love or respect between me and Mr Raven? I am not such a hypocrite that I can say that his wealth did not sway my decision at all to be his mistress. Yet I would not do it for a man I did not love and respect, Patrick.' Molly took a deep breath. 'And now, if you wish to stay the night here, Patrick, there will be no more talk of my relations with Mr Raven. Let us talk of other, less divisive, things like the theatre...'

*

After sharing Molly's generous dinner of cold game pie, they were seated together by the fire in the sitting room as a distant church clock struck nine. Whelan sank back in his high-backed chair and patted his belly. 'Thank ye kindly for dinner, Molly. And you are right; I have no right to meddle with your happiness, or make judgements about you and your wealthy benefactor. But I am a true friend to you, and I shall extend ye my help if you ever need it.'

'It is you who needs help at the moment, Patrick,' Molly pointed out tartly. 'No roof over your head, and you look very unwell, even by candlelight.'

'A little summer cold, that's all,' Whelan said. 'Yes, let us talk of the playhouse by all means. I watched the play this afternoon from the wings, and I thought you were wonderful in the part – bawdy yet vulnerable, funny yet sad. You acted Mr Hart completely off the stage.'

Molly hid her pleasure at this unexpected praise. 'What nonsense you talk as usual, Patrick!'

''Tis not nonsense. Mr Lacy watched with me from the wings, and, even though he be a great comic actor himself, he said that you played the part the best he had ever seen. He also said that if he could ever find such a woman as that, and one with such impressive bubbies, then he would never go home to his wife again...I think he referred to the character you played rather than you yourself, but I cannot be too sure given the foaming desire coming out of his mouth or the clear size of his erection as he watched you...' Patrick began to laugh heartily, but the laugh soon turned into a painful hacking cough.

'Shush your actor's nonsense, Patrick. I think that is more than a summer cold that infects you, Mr Whelan, so you had better away to your bed...and in *that* bedchamber over there,' Molly warned wryly, '*not mine.*'

'Are ye not scared that Mr Raven might still drop in unexpectedly tonight and catch me here?' Whelan said dangerously. 'It would not look good to him.'

Molly shuddered a little at the thought but hid her concern. 'Then perhaps I should kick you out of the door right now, Patrick, even though it be a windswept and rainy night. But nay, he never calls here without sending me a note in advance. And anyway, you shall be gone first thing in the morning and will not be allowed back, even if I have to pay for your lodgings myself to prevent it. And those lodgings shall be in distant Barnet, if I have anything to do with it,' she threatened with a laugh.

'By God's lid, you have become a hard, proud girl,' Whelan said in mock protest, but got up anyway to go to his bed.

44

*

On the morning after, Molly woke refreshed after a long dream-filled sleep. She stretched luxuriously as she saw sunlight peeping through the heavy wooden shutters on the window and realized that yesterday's storm was gone and that today was looking to be another fair and warm April day. She judged it to be about seven o'clock so decided that it would do no harm for her to lie here another half an hour more in blissful comfort.

It was then, though, as she turned over and put out her arm, and encountered something unfamiliar with her fingers, that she realized there was someone else in the bed with her – someone who should not be here! – someone large and naked and *male*...

She jumped out of bed and snarled at the figure lying under the sheets. 'Oh, ye villain! How could ye do such a thing, you ungrateful wretch, as to climb into my bed without permission! Ye lying, faithless toad!' She stopped for a moment to consider whether she might have been violated during the night without her knowing about it, but quickly dismissed that thought – there was no possible way that she could have slept on if this huge rutting rogue had penetrated her. Yet that didn't diminish her anger one whit...

'Oh, ye bucket of pigs' swill! Ye spotted, fornicating, false devil! Ye leprous rogue with maggot's breath! Ye...'

Molly stopped abruptly in mid-insult as she realized that Whelan had not moved, even though she had kicked him and whacked him hard with a straw-filled pillow. He could not be dead, could he? she wondered worriedly.

He had looked to have a high fever last evening, she recalled. Perhaps it was a case of sweating sickness? Or something even worse...?

She gasped in relief when finally he made a noise in response to her pummelling and her insults. But her relief soon turned to distress again when he pulled the sheets back from his head with a groan, and she saw his face covered in a waxy sheen, devoid of all colour.

Yet she still asked him abrasively, 'Why are you in my bed, Patrick?'

Patrick looked confused, as if not knowing where he was. 'Am I, Molly? Then I am most heartily sorry. I presently suffer from severe chills and muscle seizures, and my head spins fit to burst. I got up to vomit into a chamber pot during the night, and then I made my way back to the same bed I left. Or so I thought. My head was spinning so much, and my legs so weak, though, that I must have made a mistake. I beg your pardon if I have offended thee, sweet Molly...'

Molly's anger finally dissipated when she saw the genuine distress that Whelan was in. 'Well, there is no harm done...'

A fresh voice now interrupted her coldly from the door of the bedroom. 'That is a matter of opinion, Molly. What goes on here? Or is that a foolish question?'

Molly gaped in shock as she saw Henry standing in the doorway, his countenance turned to stone. In her great discomfiture, she began to gabble wildly. 'Patrick is very …err…sick, Henry. I was just…err…ministering to him.'

Henry remained icy and aloof. Molly had never seen him in such a cold and ugly mood, or with such a severe face. He seemed like a different man entirely to the one who had left this very bed yesterday in such a happy mood of contentment. 'Yes, but what need is there for him to be in your bed, Molly?'

Molly reddened. 'It was naught but a mistake, Henry. He got up in the middle of the night, and in his fevered confusion, came to my bed afterwards by mistake…'

Henry cleared his throat and looked disbelieving of this excuse. 'Then perhaps I should leave you to minister to your friend. My apologies for disturbing you without warning. I had left my diary somewhere, and I thought it must be here. I needed it urgently otherwise I would not have come without sending you a note. It is a large volume, handsomely bound in brown leather, and filled with my notes of business.'

'I have not seen it, Henry,' Molly said, biting her lip with embarrassment.

'Then I will leave you.' With that Henry Raven bowed his head formally, turned abruptly on his heel and was gone.

Molly watched him leave, and wondered numbly whether she would ever see him again...

*

Patrick was profuse with apologies for what had happened, but Molly made him desist as she rushed to the wash room to fetch another chamber pot for him as he seemed in danger of vomiting again.

She watched in distress as he vomited violently into the pewter chamber pot she had fetched for his relief. But her alarm only increased further when she saw the colour of his excreta.

'Your vomit is excessively bloody, Patrick,' she pointed out worriedly.

Whelan was trying to stand but swaying so wildly, and his legs shaking so much, that Molly made him lie down again.

He put his arms around himself to try and quell his shaking. 'That...does...not sound...good. Bloody vomit I can live with. But *excessively* bloody – that is something to bring fear to a man's innards.' He tried to smile reassuringly at her, but all she saw was a face devoid of colour and drawn into a painful rictus.

Given the unfortunate circumstance that had just happened to her, Molly imagined that her own expression must presently be something very similar...

# CHAPTER 4

Wednesday, 12th April 1665

''Tis no laughing matter, Anthony…'

Anthony Mawdsley regarded his friend Henry Raven with quiet amusement. 'Oh, but I believe it is. Did you truly believe that a girl like Molly would be faithful to you? By God's blest mother! The girl was brought up in a bawdy house, Henry! 'Tis a wonder you did not find *six* gentlemen in bed with her.'

Raven was in sombre mood. '*One* caused me pain enough, Anthony. If she had been romping with six, then I believe general disgust of her behaviour would have lessened any pain I might have felt. But to see her with one man in place of me, and a penniless actor at that…'

They sat together in the parlour in Mawdsley's little house in Axe Yard in Westminster, only a stone's throw away from King Street and Whitehall Palace. The address was a convenient one for Mawdsley because he was chief secretary to the Lord Chancellor of England, the First Earl of Clarendon, and therefore a young man close to the Privy Council and the heart of the King's government.

Mawdsley seemed to relent in his mockery a little, understanding finally that his friend had truly been wounded by what had happened earlier this morning. 'Did she make any excuse for her behaviour, Henry?'

Raven was reluctant to speak for fear of more mockery, but finally answered. 'She said that this man was sick and without a bed for the night, so she had let him stay with her.'

Mawdsley fought back a deep belly laugh. 'Forgive me for my cynicism, Henry. But taking a sick man into her own bed? Is that not taking hospitality too far, even by Molly's generous standards?'

Raven regarded his friend with cool disfavour, touched with some undoubted envy of his friend's beauty. Those long handsome curls and that chiselled jaw were indeed hard things for any young woman to resist so Raven was sure that Mawdsley never needed to worry about the faithfulness of his lady friends, of course. 'She said that it was a mistake,' Raven explained reluctantly. 'The man was feverish and climbed into her bed during the night by error, and the fact was unknown to her until she woke.'

Mawdsley frowned at this. ''Tis such a silly and feeble story that it could just be true, Henry. Have you considered that possibility? Did the man look sick?'

Raven was slightly reassured by his friend's opinion. 'Actually he did, now that I remember. My attention was fixed firmly on Molly, though, so I might have been deceived in that regard. His "sickness" might have simply been a rapid invention of hers in order to explain his presence there.'

Mawdsley was curious 'Who is this dastardly rival of yours, then?'

Raven scowled. 'His name is Patrick Whelan, a young Irish actor of the King's company.'

'Handsome?'

Raven shrugged. 'I dare say that most women would consider him handsomer than me.'

Mawdsley wrinkled his brow thoughtfully. 'Do you suspect some special regard between him and Molly?'

'She told me herself a few months ago that the man is in love with her,' Raven admitted hesitantly, as he waited for his friend to take yet more pleasure in his discomfort.

Anthony Mawdsley was Henry Raven's closest friend, if not his oldest, and they had both become acquainted with Molly last winter thanks to their regular attendance at the King's theatre. Mawdsley was the second son of a wealthy Royalist family who held a large estate near the village of Streatham, south of London in the green Surrey countryside, on the main coach road to Croydon and East Grinstead. Raven had first met him at Trinity College, Cambridge where they had both been students during the Protectorate – Mawdsley studying the law, and Raven medicine and natural philosophy - and they had soon become fast friends despite their divergent politics. Mawdsley's family had secretly supported Charles' court in exile with vast sums of money, so that they had prospered even more on the King's restoration, being given even more land and titles. Despite being so young, Mawdsley had soon won the coveted job of Chief Secretary to the Lord Chancellor yet, in truth, this appointment had as much to do with his fierce natural intelligence as with the King's inclinations to reward his family's loyalty. Mawdsley came from an even wealthier family than Raven, and had been the more prosperous of the two until recently. Yet Mawdsley's present career in politics had left him little time for increasing his wealth, while Raven's recent forays into the world of business and commerce – particularly his mining and shipping interests – had now helped him to surpass his friend in wealth, if not influence, for the first time.

Mawdsley deliberated for a while over Raven's love rival. 'Ah, well, if she is enamoured of this actor, then that does put a different complexion on things. She probably did fornicate with him in all likelihood. But is that a real concern for you, Henry? Even the King does not require his mistresses to be faithful to him... Look at Lady Castlemaine, to whom you are such a close friend and confidante these days.'

Raven objected half-heartedly to this absurd statement. 'I am not a close confidante of that lady. She has merely invited me twice to dinner parties at her own apartments in Whitehall Palace.'

Mawdsley gave a cynical shrug of his elegant shoulders. 'Has she made any improper advances to you? Has she shown you her silk garters? Have you slept with her?'

'With the King's mistress? Are you mad? I would lose my head.'

Mawdsley stroked his handsome pointed beard. 'The King is not so jealous of her these days as previously. Day by day she is losing ground to the King's new favourite, Mistress Frances Stuart. The King will eventually evict her from her apartments in the palace, and pension her off to a house somewhere in the country with her four Royal bastards. Or is a fifth on the way now? I have lost count. Castlemaine seems to pup with all the regularity of a bitch.'

'That is no way to talk of her, Anthony,' Raven reprimanded him. 'Such disrespect is unworthy of you. She is a lady of some character, I believe, and much maligned by her enemies. I am sure that they exaggerate her infidelities in order to weaken her influence with the King. '

Mawdsley was convinced of his own judgement now. 'Ah, you do care about Castlemaine! So why do you make such an issue of Molly having another lover? Did you ask Molly to grant you sole bedding rights? '

'Not exactly. And nor did I promise to be entirely faithful to her either. We both preferred an informal arrangement. There is nothing worse than formality for driving the romance from a relationship and turning it into an obligation. '

Mawdsley held up the palms of his hands expressively. 'Well then, there's an end to it! Molly has behaved properly according to the terms of your agreement, and according to her proper inclinations. So please do not punish the poor girl for it. You are happy with her, are you not?'

Raven sighed. 'I was.'

Mawdsley clapped him on the shoulder. 'Then you can be so again! Simply forget what Molly is doing when she is not with you. It is not your business. In any case, no man these days should expect fidelity from a mistress. It would destroy the whole fabric of our libertine London society if we were to begin taking a puritan's attitude when it comes to taking our pleasures. The two are quite incompatible.'

Raven could see his friend's point – perhaps he was indeed being hypocritical – yet the fact that he was deeply hurt by the thought of Molly being unfaithful did certainly mean that he had regarded her as being much more than simply a casual and short term pleasure. "The King might not expect fidelity from his mistresses,' he said. 'But he expects it from his queen, no doubt.'

Mawdsley took a deep breath. 'Ah, now I understand. You have been considering Molly as a wife in the making. This is where you make your mistake, Henry. I told you before that Molly is a lovely and vivacious girl, and if you were not bedding her, I would dearly like to take her to bed myself. But she is simply not a fit wife for you, Henry. It would merely bring unhappiness and misery for you both. Your family would shun her. Society would shun her if she ever presented herself to them as your wife.'

This was not truly the advice that Raven wanted to hear, but he decided that he had talked enough to his friend of his relationship with Molly, and certainly with more honesty and openness than he had intended. He had come here originally only to ask whether his friend would be coming to Gresham College this afternoon for a meeting of the Royal Society, at which the curator of experiments, Mr Hooke, had something particularly interesting to demonstrate.

Mawdsley regarded Raven with clear misgivings. 'I can see that you love your strumpet Molly, and that is why you cannot forgive her this transgression on your stubborn pride. I believe you intend to be bull-headed about this, and to discard her for it, despite the fact that you love her. Yet I am convinced that such a course would be a grave error on your part, Henry.'

Raven stirred resentfully in his chair by the fire. 'Why so?'

'Because I have never seen you happier than you have been these last few months, which must be mainly due to Molly's beneficial effect on you. She may not be a suitable wife for you, but she is the perfect mistress. Please do not reject her, and the happiness she brings you, over this…this…*trifle.*'

Raven felt wretched. "Tis no trifle to me, Anthony. I cannot forget and forgive so easily as you, because I had truly given my heart to that girl.'

'Then at least promise me that you will do nothing rash. A little time to reflect may soften your harsh judgement and restore Molly to your proper affection…'

Raven was about to agree with that sound advice but was interrupted by a knock at the door.

Mawdsley called out and bade the party at the door to enter; it turned out to be his long suffering servant Hannah.

Hannah was a big ungainly woman, forever given to straightening the white coif covering her unruly hair. 'I beg your pardon, sir, but there is a messenger here...' she began hesitantly.

Mawdsley interrupted brusquely. 'Is the message from my Lord Clarendon, Hannah?'

Hannah's slow train of thought was confused by the interruption. 'Nay, Master, 'tis not a message for you at all, but for Mr Raven. The messenger has been to your house, sir,' she went on, addressing Raven now, 'and your housemaid sent him on here, since it seemed to be urgent.'

Mawdsley interrupted again. 'Then you had better send him through, Hannah. Who is the messenger from?'

'He is from a Dr Croone, Master. He asks that Mr Raven should go and meet him in St Giles as soon as he can...'

*

The parish of St Giles was an area of ramshackle houses and shelters built recently on the rough grazing fields at the northern edge of the city to house many of London's new arrivals from the country, and its always generous supply of the poor and needy. The tide of life had washed these poor wretches up against the boundaries of the city, where they lingered like flotsam stranded on an ugly beach. The Gothic brick structure of the church of St Giles had been built in open fields thirty years before but now, surrounded by this swirling brown tide of poverty, had fallen into as disreputable a state of repair as the hovels and makeshift houses around it.

Fearing the worst after receiving Dr Croone's message, Henry Raven has rushed here from Westminster as fast as his feet could carry him. He had hoped that Mawdsley might accompany him to see the problem at first hand, but this hope was short-lived: a second later messenger (who arrived at Mawdsley's house in Axe Yard only a few minutes after the first and who, this time, did turn out to be from his Lord Clarendon) had sent Mawdsley rushing urgently to a more urgent appointment in the privy chamber of Whitehall Palace instead. Mawdsley had however promised Raven that, God willing, he would join him at Gresham College this afternoon to see Mr Hooke's promised new marvellous demonstration.

Raven found Dr Croone attending a family of ten, the Andrews, who lived in a miserable house of dilapidated appearance on the very outskirts of the city. It was a fine spring morning, yet neither the warm blue sky above, nor the glimpse of open fields beyond, could contrive to make this narrow street appear anything other than a grim refuge for human beings to have to live in and bring up families. The whole street consisted of leaning and patched hovels which seemed only to be standing by some miracle of providence rather than from any natural strength remaining in their walls of worn brick or their makeshift floors of salvaged timber. The alleyways on each side of the Andrews' house stank to high heaven, and had been turned to deep mud by last night's heavy rain, overfilling the open drains and cesspits and privies so that a sea of foul contagion lapped at the very doorway.

Dr Croone had appeared at the door of the Andrews' hovel, and smiled a grim greeting to his friend as he tried to step over the worst of the foul-smelling mire at the entrance. 'I am sorry to bring you to a place like this, Henry, but you did ask me to call for you at once if I came across any cases of the plague. And I believe, unfortunately, that I have found one, in the shape of the Andrews' little girl, Rebecca. She had been ill for a day or so with chills and a general malaise, according to her desperate mother. But now she is exhibiting all the classic signs of plague: the smooth and painful swelling in her groin and armpits. I can even see where the rats bit her in her sleep…'

Raven was distraught. 'Then if she has buboes already appearing on her body, there is no hope for the poor child.'

Croone agreed. 'Very little anyway, I fear, although some strong souls survive it. 'Tis not always fatal at this stage of its development. If the little girl begins to bleed from her ears, however, or her skin to blacken and rot, then we will know for certain that she is doomed to an early grave.'

Raven became aware of a group of slatternly women who had gathered in the foul street a few doors down from the Andrews' house, and who were talking in frightened whispers. Eventually one of them – a dirty-faced woman of thirty with a baby at her breast - plucked up her courage and spoke to the gentlemen visitors. 'Is it the plague, good sirs? Are we all to die here?'

Raven did not know what to say, but Dr Croone spoke up quickly. 'We are not sure yet, but we think it best that you keep away from this house. And I have seen many live rats in the ditches and drains here. You must send your menfolk out to catch them and kill them. And if they do, they must dispose of the carcases by burning.'

'Will that truly protect us?' the woman asked disbelievingly.

'In God's name, I hope so,' Croone said…

*

Raven went into the house with Croone and examined the little girl, who was in a state of terrible distress, and as clear a case of the plague as he had ever seen. He glanced around the interior of this hovel, which seemed overflowing with ragged dirty children, sucking their thumbs with wide-eyed innocence, and was consumed by a feeling of intense guilt that he had not done more to prevent this first sad case of the plague. Over the last three months he had tried his best to persuade local people to trap and kill any rats they could find in their neighbourhood, but most had little inclination to spend valuable time on such apparently futile endeavours.

Even worse for Raven, though, was the sensation of utter helplessness that he encountered when faced with an actual case of the disease. Such were the limitations of present medical knowledge that he knew he could do nothing to cure this little girl, or even alleviate her symptoms. Physicians now had a sound grasp of human anatomy, thanks to being able to dissect human cadavers and no longer having to rely on the ancient texts of Galen for their knowledge. And they could identify most of the common diseases and aliments that afflicted mankind, and understand the progression of symptoms in each case. Yet in the deepest sense they understood almost nothing of how the body worked, or of the living substances that made up human flesh and blood, so could do nothing to change the course of human diseases. Treatments were tried by an ad hoc process of trial and error, but Raven understood how hopeless this process was, without any understanding of the true nature of disease. Often the treatments were so bizarre and extreme that they simply made the patient worse...

It was hard to be sure in the dim light inside the house, but as he held the child's hand and felt the awful heat contained within, Raven imagined that he could see that her fair skin was already turning darker in places. What was patently clear was the appearance of the two large rat bites on her body, one on her leg, and one at her throat. Raven could not be sure of course that the rats living in the vicinity were some of those that had been deliberately released by that evil fiend Ingledew, but there had to be a high probability that this was not a natural outbreak of plague but had been contrived by the evil hand of that maniac.

Last winter this madman had conceived a wicked plot against the King and his navy, at the behest of his Dutch paymasters. Ultimately his scheme had failed, yet with his dying breath the man has cursed the City of London and, aided by his equally evil sister, had vowed to take revenge by releasing a horde of rats brought on a ship from Constantinople. Raven still blamed himself for not doing more to prevent this wicked threat.

Raven recalled what he knew of this terrible affliction that had caused so much human misery over the centuries. This particular plague was called bubonic plague, after the Greek word *bubo*, meaning "swollen gland". No one understood the agent of this affliction yet it was suspected to be carried somehow by rats. Raven's friend at the Royal Society, Mr Hooke, believed the true carriers of the disease to be the fleas living in the fur of rats, yet even Hooke did not comprehend the true agent of the disease except to say that it must be something exceeding small to be carried in the bite of a flea – so small that it was invisible even to his famous microscopes.

Raven looked up helplessly at his friend Dr Croone and saw that he was deeply affected by the suffering of this little girl too. Croone was a man some five years older than Raven but of a not dissimilar background, being the son of a wealthy merchant, and also educated at Cambridge – in his case Emmanuel College. He had been named Professor of Rhetoric at Gresham College at the age of only six-and-twenty, but his scientific interests were more wide ranging than mere rhetoric. As well as being a practising physician, he was now the Censor of the College of Physicians and the Registrar of the Royal Society. He and Raven had carried out many interesting experiments together at Croone's house, including attempts to transfuse blood from one dog into another. Yet Croone still found the time to visit the slum areas at the edge of the city, and freely dispense the physic that he made in his own basement from the herbs in his walled garden. He was a remarkable man, both in terms of his intellect and his humanity, and Raven counted him a very close friend, if one not quite on a par with Mawdsley. Raven needed to laugh and make merry with his friends sometimes, and the ever serious Dr Croone gave him very little cause for merriment, unlike Mawdsley.

Not that anyone would be in a mood for laughter in this city soon, Raven thought tiredly, if the plague was to take firm hold.

Raven took his leave of Croone, his mood as depressed as he could ever remember it. 'Shall I see you at the meeting of the society this afternoon, William? Perhaps the ingenious Mr Hooke can come up with some notion of how we may defeat this insidious enemy among us?'

Croone was sombre. 'I shall be there. Yet I fear that it will take even more than Mr Hooke's genius to save us this time. We are in the hands of God now, Henry…or perhaps the Devil's…'

*

The meetings of the Royal Society were normally held on Wednesday afternoons at three o'clock, and were invariably well attended, thanks to the society's principal attraction. This cynosure of the society was Mr Robert Hooke, the young Curator of Experiments, who was both a genius in his understanding of natural philosophy, and in his devising of clever experiments to unravel the astounding secrets of God's universe.

Henry Raven was seated in readiness in the second tier of seats in the lecture hall in Gresham College in Bishopsgate, and glanced around approvingly at the august assembly gathered here to see Mr Hooke's latest diverting demonstration. The elderly Dr John Wilkins was here as usual of course - as the founding father of this institution, he rarely missed a meeting. Lord Brouncker was in attendance too, a gifted man but also an infamous libertine, as well as a close confidante of the King. Raven recognized Dr Jonathan Goddard and Dr William Petty, both eminent fellow physicians, and the young astronomer and artist Mr Christopher Wren, who was a rising man in the society.

A wealthy man of business, Sir Paul Neile, was in deep conversation with that old rogue Sir Robert Moray. Both men were interesting in their own way: Sir Paul Neile planned to send an expedition in the next year or two to explore the frozen arctic waters of North America, and perhaps find a new way into the interior of that fabulous unknown continent, while Moray had reputedly a murky past as a spy for the French. Yet Moray was also very close to the King and had been instrumental in gaining royal patronage for the society, therefore Raven forgave him his many shortcomings.

Raven nodded a polite greeting to his younger businessmen friends Mr Abraham Hill and Mr Alexander Bruce, but could presently see no sign of Dr Croone or Anthony Mawdsley. Yet Croone proved himself a man of his word as usual, and did appear eventually, a few seconds before the nearby clock of St Helen's church rang out to signify three o'clock.

Raven managed with reasonable success to put the traumatic events of the last twenty four hours aside as he became absorbed in Mr Hooke's diverting lecture. Yet he could not help his attention wandering occasionally during the next hour: the memory of the suffering of poor little Rebecca Andrews kept intruding into his mind, as did the sweet face of Molly. He was now minded to overlook Molly's transgression as his friend Mawdsley had suggested. Perhaps it was simply not in her nature to be faithful, given her upbringing in bawdy houses. Even so, he was acutely disappointed with her. Yet he could not bear the thought of not seeing her again, so decided he must accept her promiscuous nature as part of the bargain. It would be punishing himself far more than her if he were to leave her for good. Yet her behaviour had certainly ended any brief thoughts that he might have entertained of Molly one day becoming his wife. Mawdsley was right in that respect too: she would simply never do as a wife...

With an effort, Raven roused himself from his reverie and returned his attention to the meeting. Mr Hooke's demonstration today required a complex assemblage of glass retorts and beakers and flasks and tubes, filled with various noxious chemicals, bubbling slowly over a series of hot braziers. Raven had seen him demonstrate something similar to him in private before but was still captivated as Hooke showed that neither charcoal nor sulphur would burn without the presence of air, but that saltpetre did so readily. These were, of course, the ingredients of gunpowder so it seemed that saltpetre provided some special explosive power to the whole mixture that was not provided by the charcoal and sulphur.

As he watched his friend perform these interesting experiments, Raven marvelled again at the man's commonplace appearance, wondering how genius could be so well concealed from general view. Hooke did not remotely look like a man of genius, nor even a man of society. He was wearing unfashionable breeches and doublet as usual, and his coarse woollen stockings hung loose on his spindly shanks. His bent posture was even more pronounced than usual as he worked away avidly at his demonstrations, so that it seemed as if his head had sunk into an even deeper depression than usual between his shoulder blades. Yet, despite his slovenly appearance, there was a feeling of exhilaration in glimpsing how this man's marvellous mind worked, and how it probed the intimate secrets of nature.

Hooke glanced up at his attentive audience at the climax of his demonstration. 'And what does all this mean, I can hear you ask?' He smiled. 'And how can I make money from it, I hear Sir Paul ask?'

Most laughed at Hooke's little joke – something very rare for him - but Raven saw that Sir Paul Neile himself was not remotely amused by it.

Hooke gave his attentive audience a grateful smile. "You know of course, gentlemen, that the society has just done me the great honour of publishing my work *Micrographia,* which splendidly printed book is a summary of my scientific researches to date in many fields. Among them in particular are my microscopic observations of both the natural and the man-made world....'

Raven had been privileged to read much of this book in draft as it was being readied for publication, and to see Mr Hooke's own splendid original drawings of the things he had seen through his microscopes - a glimpse of an unknown world that no one had suspected until now, the world of the very small. And who knew what even smaller things might be seen in time?

No one seeing those splendid drawings could sensibly doubt that Hooke had really seen these wonderful things with his microscopes, Raven thought. Raven had in fact made use of Hooke's microscopes to try and see the same startling images for himself, but with only moderate success. Yet Raven had seen enough through these lenses to know that the drawings in the new book were very real, and not just a figment of Mr Hooke's artistic imagination.

Hooke continued. '...In a chapter in the book, I show by further experiments that combustion in air is made possible only by a substance inherent, and mixed with the air. And my researches have proved that this substance inherent in the air is very like - if indeed not the very same - as that which is fixed in saltpetre...' Hooke paused for his audience to take in his words. 'Yes, gentlemen, I see that you have understood the implications of what you have just witnessed: that saltpetre contains a vapour within its solid form that is nothing but part of the air.' Hooke tapped the table in front of him emphatically. 'And this postulated part of the air is the most important constituent of all because I believe it is necessary not only to sustain combustion but also to sustain life itself...it is in fact the vital substance that we take into our lungs when we inhale.'

Hooke peered into one retort and studied the mysterious vapour arising inside with a penetrating eye. 'I believe we need to inhale this vapour in order to digest our food, which then provides us with the vital spirit that separates living creatures from the inanimate world.'

Dr Croone spoke up from the audience. 'So, Mr Hooke, your premise is that digestion of our food is naught but a form of combustion inside our bodies?'

Hooke raised his head from inspecting the bubbling retort. 'I think that "combustion" is as good a description as any, although of a very slow kind.'

'But what moderates this process and stops us exploding like gunpowder too, Mr Hooke?' Raven saw that Mawdsley had belatedly arrived at the back of the hall, and must have heard some of the lecture because he had come up with this amusing, if pertinent, question.

Hooke straightened his weak back with an effort. 'That is something I have yet to discover, but there must in the workings of the human body be contained many subtle and unknown substances that can slow down the speed of reactions. There is no such subtlety about gunpowder however, nothing to keep its burning in check. The destructive power of that substance seems simply due to burning too, but at such an extreme rate that the vapours produced soon exceed the capacity of any container in which the gunpowder is held. It is this frantic outpouring of vapours in a confined space that I believe gives gunpowder its frightening destructive power...'

The lecture ended after a few more pretty demonstrations of the burning of different substances from flowers of sulphur to resin of jalop.

The audience of distinguished men then gave Mr Hooke a warm burst of applause which Hooke acknowledged with a shy smile of gratitude. Raven, as ever, was astounded by the brilliance and unexpected revelations of Mr Hooke's demonstration and speculations...

*

Afterwards Raven sat supping ale in the first floor parlour of Mr Hooke's own comfortable quarters in the college, in company with his friends Mawdsley and Dr Croone, as they discussed the case of plague that he and Dr Croone had seen today. Late afternoon sunshine spilled into the room through the leaded window, which looked out onto a pleasant physic garden below. The pleasantness of the surroundings was at strange odds with the grim subject of their discussion.

Mr Hooke seemed a little discomfited in his unfamiliar role of host to three wealthy gentlemen, even though he had a manservant to take care of all the domestic duties for him. Raven knew that Hooke came from an impoverished background on the Isle of Wight, and was of a very retiring temperament, which unfortunate combination of circumstances had made him unsuited to the demands of society. He had been very grateful to obtain the demanding post of Curator of Experiments with the Royal Society (and more lately the title of Gresham Professor of Geometry) because this job and title had brought with them a salary of over a hundred pounds a year, and these pleasant rooms in Gresham College itself. Thanks to the good offices of the fellows of the society (and to Henry Raven in particular), Hooke now had a library, a parlour, and two smaller rooms on the ground floor at his disposal, as well as a garret above for his own servant. In these rooms the bachelor Hooke could carry out his clever explorations of the laws of nature at his leisure, and with no one to criticise his awkward manners, or the poor cut of his coat or the unfashionable colour of his breeches.

Mawdsley frowned on hearing Raven's bleak news. 'Are you convinced that it was a case of the plague, Henry?'

Raven nodded sombrely. 'I am sure that the poor child has the disease. I have rarely seen a clearer set of symptoms. She already had buboes forming in her armpits.'

Hooke nodded sadly in agreement. 'I concur with Mr Raven. From the symptoms, his diagnosis seems incontrovertible.'

Dr Croone spoke up. 'If I understand you correctly, Mr Hooke, it is your contention that the disease is not transferred through the bites of rats at all, but rather through the bites of infected fleas living in the fur of rats.'

Hooke stammered a little with nervousness at all the respectful attention trained on him. 'That is true, sir. Yet I have not managed to comprehend the true agent of the disease except to know that it must be something exceeding small. I have looked at smears of blood taken from fleabites, but I have not managed to see any agents of disease concealed within the fluid, even with my best microscope. '

Croone pressed him. 'But what is this infectious agent you look for?'

Hooke blinked defensively. 'Why, animal life, of course. But animals tiny beyond human imagination...*animalcules*, if you will...'

Raven interrupted. 'But if you have not seen these *"animalcules"*, Robert, how can you be sure that they exist at all?'

Hooke became assertive. 'Because I believe that someone *has* seen these agents of disease...'

'Who has seen these things?' asked Raven, astonished that some unknown person might have even better microscopes than Mr Hooke himself.

Hooke seemed reluctant to explain his statement at first, but finally spoke up. 'I have heard secret reports from my Lord Brouncker that this particular gentleman in question has discovered some means of making lenses even finer than my own. And with them he claims to see all sorts of miniature life – a teeming miniature world that lives all around us, and yet is something we fail to see with our inadequate vision. He has not yet however made public any of his wondrous discoveries...'

'Yes, Mr Hooke, but who is this gentleman you refer to?' Croone demanded acerbically.

Hooke looked up in surprise at Croone's rough tone of voice, which was quite unlike his usual polite manner. 'According to my Lord Brouncker, he is a mere tradesman, a draper from the city of Delft called van Leeuwenhoek...'

Mawdsley sniffed coldly. 'A *Dutchman?* Then he is presently our enemy.'

'Not mine, sir,' Hooke assured him stiffly, 'if he really has made such a momentous discovery as this. It could be the pathway to new treatments for disease, if we could but detect the real enemy that lurks within us all...'

# CHAPTER 5

Wednesday, 12<sup>th</sup> April 1665

Earlier that same day, Molly had sat in the tiny entrance parlour of her mother's bawdy house, located in one of the alleys of Whetstone Park behind Lincoln's Inn Fields, and poured out her heart to her mother in what was for her a most unusually frank manner. Mistress Celia Hornett had listened to Molly's story mostly in sympathetic silence (behaviour that was equally unusual and out of character for her), but had occasionally offered a word of comfort to her wounded daughter.

The true nature of Molly's often tempestuous relationship with Celia was difficult to describe, perhaps because of its odd history of three distinct phases. First had been her childhood up to the age of seven, when Molly had been devoted to the woman she thought to be her real mother, and had tried her best to earn her love and affection, if only with moderate success (Celia being sometimes impatient with the demands of the young child, and much more preoccupied with the needs of her business.)

At age seven, Molly had accidentally discovered the truth from a visiting gentleman at the bawdy house - that Celia was *not* her true mother at all, but that she was in fact the child of Samuel Titchen, a draper of Bartlett's Passage, and his wife Mary, who had both died in a terrible fire at their premises when she was still a babe-in-arms. This uncomfortable revelation had changed Molly's relationship with Celia completely: no longer did she do her best to please her foster mother, but instead to treat her with growing suspicion and resentment. From that time on, being a precocious and obstinate child, she had insisted on being known as Molly *Titchen*, not Molly Hornett.

A year ago, Celia had tried to persuade Molly that her best hope for finding a wealthy gentleman husband would be to learn the skills of a courtesan and then to practise those seductive arts in her house on the most select and wealthy of her clientele. Molly was not inclined to accept this demeaning course in her life, and her feelings for her "mother" had soon deteriorated from resentment into open hostility and rebellion. Eventually, though, she had accepted the inevitability of her situation, and had tried to comply with Celia's wishes. But this rapprochement with Celia had only lasted until Molly had taken violent exception to one gentleman's unnatural treatment of her, and had marked his manhood permanently in return with the blade of her knife. Shortly after, she had quitted the only home she knew, in favour of lodgings in a miserable cold garret in Coal Hole Lane, and uncertain work as an orange seller at the King's theatre.

The third phase of Molly's relationship with Celia had been the most unsettling in many ways because last winter Celia had finally admitted to Molly that she was in fact her *real* mother after all. Celia's story was that she had given birth to Molly when she was working in Paris seventeen years before, but that the father had rejected both her and his child. On her return to London a few months later, Celia had given the baby up to this childless couple, the Titchens, she being but twenty years old at the time, and with no knowledge of bringing up children. When the Titchens died in that terrible fire at their shop a few months later, it had seemed a miracle of providence to Celia that the baby Molly should survive, after being thrown to safety at the last minute from an upstairs window. So Celia had decided to heed this message from the Almighty (for such she took it to be) and to take the baby back into her care again.

Molly, for her part, was still not sure how much of this wild story to believe – for a woman who claimed to have lived three years in Paris, Celia knew remarkably little of that city when interrogated about it, nor could speak a single word of French (at least not any French fit for polite society.) But Molly had come to accept now that Celia was her natural mother, if only from the physical evidence of looking in the mirror every day. Molly could see, now that she had passed her seventeenth birthday and her face was maturing from that of a child into a woman's, that she began to resemble Celia more and more with every passing month. Not that this was anything to bemoan: for a woman of eight-and-thirty, Celia was still most presentable in appearance, with her hair still dark and lustrous, her skin smooth and creamy, and her bosom impressive and maidenly. But then she had never been able to bear children of her own after giving birth to Molly, which piece of ill luck had at least a beneficial side to it in that it had enabled her to avoid the rigours of endless child bearing suffered by most women, and therefore perhaps to retain some physical aspects of her youth. By dint of her natural intelligence and good business sense, Celia had soon gone on from being a mere working strumpet in a bawdy house to being the proprietor of a busy establishment of her own, which success had made her very comfortably off as she approached middle age, unlike most of her fellow workers in this difficult trade.

Today, as she had listened to Molly's story of the unfortunate situation that had occurred this morning, Celia was most motherly and comforting for once. They sat together by the fire in the snug parlour near the entrance to the house; despite the spring sunshine outside, Celia still liked to have a brisk log fire burning in the hearth to welcome visitors. Molly saw that, though it was only one o'clock in the afternoon, Celia's bawdy house was already enjoying a brisk trade, so much so that Celia had to break off frequently from consoling her daughter in order to deal with some new gentleman caller with an afternoon's lustful pleasure on his mind.

After Celia had returned from the latest of these interruptions to deal with a gentleman client, Molly voiced her worst fears. 'You understand how a gentleman's mind works, Mother. Do you think that Mr Raven will come back to me? Or will he reject me because he thinks me faithless, and cast me aside?'

Celia leaned over from her own chair and patted Molly's arm. 'Of course he will come back. It may take a little time, though, so you must be patient. A gentleman's pride is a fragile thing and is easily wounded. Yet I am sure that Mr Raven is a man of uncommonly good sense, and will soon see the folly of casting you aside over this misunderstanding... '

'Should I write him a letter and beg his forgiveness?' Molly suggested eagerly.

Celia shook her head firmly. 'Nay, that would be as good as an admission of guilt. You have done nothing wrong, child – you merely offered a friend in trouble a bed for the night...' Celia smiled wryly. 'Perhaps 'twould have been better if it had not been your *own* bed, of course...'

'I explained that circumstance already, Mother,' Molly re-joined with irritation.

'And I believe you, dear, as I am sure will Mr Raven also, in time. It is a remarkably lame story you tell, but then the truth often is. Therefore there is no need to prostrate yourself before your lover in order to win him back. I have seen the way that Mr Raven looks at you privately, which intimate look suggests to me a deep and binding affection for you. Therefore I believe he will not forsake you permanently over such a trifling matter as this.'

Molly was still downcast despite Celia's confident pronouncement. 'I doubt that he truly believed my story. From his face I am sure that he thought me a trull who had just made lusty sport with Mr Whelan.'

Celia lifted Molly's chin with her fingers and looked her in the eye. 'You truly have no special feelings for this young actor, then, Molly?'

'I have not.' Molly shrugged in acknowledgement. 'He is a pretty enough boy, and well-formed. *And* he professes to love me. If I had not met Mr Raven, then - who knows? - I might have fallen for Mr Whelan. Yet since I met Mr Raven, I have eyes for no one else - and not just because of his wealth, although few will believe me for that, of course.'

Celia sat back in her chair and tidied a loose tendril of hair from her smooth white forehead. 'After your altercation this morning, what happened to this young man, Mr Whelan?' she asked.

Molly roused herself and sat up straight again. 'I was worried that Mr Raven might return later and find him still there. So I am sorry to say that I forced him to leave, even though he was still obviously unwell.'

'I trust you did not do it in a heartless and unfeeling way, Molly. It would not become you if you had.'

'No, I believe that I was duly considerate of him. I found him alternative lodgings – a nice clean room in Bridges Street near the theatre, where he could recover by himself. I even paid a full month's rent for him, and hired a woman to bring him broth and physic should he need it. I thought it better in the circumstances that I should not do this duty myself.'

'That was wise.' Celia was satisfied. 'Then I am sure that your kindness will be rewarded, Molly. Mr Raven will return once he begins to miss you. Which, given your passionate and playful nature, cannot be long. He will not easily find a bed partner to rival you for beauty or tenderness, Molly, I am sure.'

Molly almost blushed. 'You truly think so?'

Celia stood up and kissed her firmly on the brow. 'I do, daughter…and now you had better hurry, or you will be late back at the theatre…'

*

Four hours later, Molly took her bows in the King's theatre with the rest of the cast at the end of the performance of today's play, Mr Dryden's *The Indian Queen*. This play had first been performed a year before, but Mr Dryden had now written a sequel to it called *The Indian Emperor*, and was desirous of seeing the first play performed again as a prelude to the coming of the new one next month. And Sir Thomas Killigrew had of course been only too happy to inculge his most prolific playwright, and stage a revival of *The Indian Queen*, particularly as the costumes and sets had still been readily available.

The play was an interesting historical one, being set in Mexico and Peru before the Spanish conquest of the last century, and featuring a Peruvian general, Montezuma, who had defeated Mexico, but who had fallen out with his own King Ynca after the king had refused to allow his young general leave to wed his daughter, Princess Orazia. A resentful Montezuma had then sided with Mexico against his own land, even though power in Mexico had been usurped by the evil and scheming Queen Zempolla and her accomplice, General Traxalla, an act of treason which had horrified even her own son Acacis, who had no wish to gain a throne that was not his by divine right.

Montezuma was portrayed by Mr Dryden in the play as a noble savage struggling to come to terms with the conflicting demands of passion and duty, of desire and honour. Eventually, by learning the restraints of civilization, and the need sometimes to subordinate his own wishes to those of his fellow men, Montezuma discovered that he was in fact the true son of the deposed King of Mexico, and overthrew Queen Zempolla and General Traxalla to win back his rightful throne.

Yet Molly was certain that the play was not truly about this man Montezuma at all, but was more likely a metaphor for the behaviour of their own monarch and his licentious court, of which Mr Dryden was privately very critical. Mr Dryden clearly intended the moral of the play – that Kingly power needs to be wielded with compassion and good sense - to be directed there, to the Palace of Whitehall.

Considering that she had been given so little time to learn the lines for her part as the fearsome eponymous queen of the title, Queen Zempolla, Molly was moderately satisfied with her performance, particularly since she was acting with most of the established actors in the company, with Michael Mohun playing her evil accomplice General Traxalla, and the beautiful Edward Kynaston her son Acacis.

In rehearsal, Molly had found it a little difficult to imagine herself with a grown-up son, and one moreover who was several years older than she was. It had made her wonder if she was equipped to be able to play a mature and dominating woman like Queen Zempolla. Yet when she put on the costume and the wig, and had her face painted in strong lines, she was amazed at her own physical transformation. Killigrew had intended that the part should be played today by the more experienced Anne Marshall but that lady had been indisposed at the last moment, and Molly was the only one of the other leading actresses prepared to take over such a severe and demanding role at short notice. It was a marked departure for Molly, though, since her usual roles were as smart talking court ladies or innocent country girls in saucy comedies. Molly guessed that the smirking Mary Pettican in particular had hoped that she would fall flat on her face and be humiliated today. Yet such a calamity had not happened, for which Molly was very grateful, especially as her rival, Montezuma, was being played by none other than Charles Hart. While Mr Hart was all solicitude and kindness when things were going well on stage, he was known to have a fierce foul-mouthed temper when things were going badly, as when an actress forgot her lines, or fluffed an entrance.

As they stood side by side to take their bows, Hart whispered in her ear. 'Well done, young Molly. You play the evil and powerful lady with great aplomb; I was quite aroused by your show of malevolent power. Now that you are your own sweet self again, you will no doubt be desirous of getting out of your constricting costume and wig as soon as possible, as I will also. I would be pleased to help you personally, if you wish...'

Molly blinked as she realized that she had just been propositioned on stage in full view of four thousand souls. 'Very obliging of you, sir, but I believe I can manage with my present dresser, who knows where all the hooks and buttons of this costume are hidden. I doubt very much that the Mexican queen really wore such a ridiculous heavy costume as this, though, when their land is such a hot one, is it not?' she added sweetly.

As she backed away into the wings with another bow, Molly came face-to-face with Sir Thomas Killigrew. The leader of the company had not performed today, so had instead been prowling offstage during the play, as was his habit, and looking worried at the poor size of the audience. She nevertheless expected to hear some words of praise from him for her hastily arranged performance, but, surprisingly, none was forthcoming. Instead Killigrew took her firmly by the elbow. 'I need you upstairs in my chamber right now, Molly.'

Molly blushed hotly again – *Men! - did they not think of anything but the pleasures of the flesh?* - and was trying to come up with some excuses why this would not be possible, when Killigrew eyed her with irritation. 'Tis not for my pleasure, Molly, much as I would like it.' He lowered his voice to a whisper so that even the other members of the cast, currently filing off stage in high spirits, might not hear what he had to say. 'It is young Patrick Whelan. He came to the side of the stage during the play, rambling about you in a most incoherent way. He seemed to think that he was due to perform in the play, and I believe he would have gone on stage if I had not restrained him and persuaded him to wait upstairs in my room. I am very worried for him. You have to come and help me deal with him...'

Molly immediately agreed, and within a minute the two were in Killigrew's private chamber, and looking down at the sad figure of Patrick Whelan, who lay tossing and moaning in distress on Killigrew's bed. Patrick's face was waxy and pale, and his dark hair was pressed flat to his brow with perspiration.

Molly put her hand to his damp brow. 'The poor boy burns up, Sir Thomas.'

Killigrew agreed readily. 'What know you of this, Molly? From his ranting speech at the side of the stage, I gather that you and he...err...'

''Tis nothing of the sort, sir,' Molly denied vehemently. 'At least not from my side. But Patrick is presently homeless, so he came to my house last evening. I saw that he was sick, and I had not the heart to turn him away, when I heard that he was sleeping in a rat-infested yard. So, against my better judgement, I let him stay the night, and this morning I helped him find a new lodging. That is all there is to it, sir. I know not how he came here. I had thought him to be improving, yet now he seems worse even than early this morning when he vomited some blood...'

Killigrew jumped in alarm. 'Vomited blood, do you say?' Immediately he began to unfasten the hooks on Whelan's doublet, and then to loosen his long shirt beneath. 'Help me undress him, at least his upper half anyway.'

Molly did as she was told, helping remove Patrick's shirt with much more care than the impatient Killigrew.

Killigrew pointed out the marks of several rat bites on Patrick's arms and chest. 'He did not lie to you, Molly, about the rats at least,' he observed worriedly. Then Sir Thomas lifted Patrick's arms one by one and began to examine the soft flesh in his armpit. He finally breathed a sigh of relief. 'The Lord be praised. I feel nothing there.'

'What do you search for, sir?' Molly thought that Killigrew behaved most curiously.

'I feared from the rat bites and the bloody vomit that Patrick might have caught the plague: blood in the vomit is one common symptom. I am no physician but I have spent considerable time in the city of Constantinople and seen plague victims there. And one of the other unmistakeable later signs of the plague is a swelling in the armpits or the groin. Thankfully Patrick has no swelling in the armpit so I am reassured that he suffers not from the plague as I feared.'

Molly spoke up reluctantly. 'Should we not also then check his...err...*groin*...sir? 'Tis better to be completely sure, is it not? And he has been bit most sorely by rats, has he not?'

Killigrew grunted. 'You have a most disconcerting direct way with you sometimes, Molly. But you are right. We must check.' He relented a little in his rough tone. 'Although, in deference to you and your feminine sensibilities, this is perhaps something that I should do myself.'

'That is most considerate, sir,' Molly said with heavy sarcasm, before adding with a tart look, 'As I remember, you were not so considerate of my feelings and my feminine sensibilities when you "auditioned" me in this very chamber a few months ago, Sir Thomas. But, regardless, you can hardly believe me a blushing virgin, sir, who has never seen a man without breeches.' With that she started immediately to loosen the buttons and hooks on Patrick's breeches, and had them off in ten seconds.

'I see that you have indeed done this before,' Killigrew said with a wry smile. But his smile faded rapidly when he saw the unpleasant sight that confronted him. 'By God's blest mother! He has buboes in his groin that are already the size of spring onions.' Killigrew sank down onto a stool at the side of the bed. 'This will be the end! A case of the plague here in the theatre! They will close us down immediately...'

Molly was greatly distressed for Patrick, and regarded Killigrew angrily. 'Sir, is not a more important question what we need to do for this poor boy?'

Killigrew put his head in his hands. 'If you say so...'

'I do indeed say so – most vehemently!' Molly cried.

Killigrew looked up in alarm at her tone of voice and thought rapidly. 'You said that you had a lodging room for him? Is it nearby? And private?'

Molly was suspicious of his meaning. 'Yes, it is no more than a hundred paces from the theatre door,' she finally admitted with reluctance. 'And it is private too; I thought that he would need his own room since he was unwell.'

Killigrew squeezed her hand. 'God bless you for that kind thought, Molly; it might be the saving of the theatre. Then you and I must get Patrick back there as soon as we can. And then deny that he was ever here...*should anyone in authority ask, I mean...*' he added lamely.

Molly was doubtful. 'We can hardly do that, sir, when he is an actor with the company.'

Sir Thomas sighed. 'No, I suppose not. Yet we can deny that he has been here since he got sick. But that will only do if you will help me get him back to these lodgings you have kindly provided him with, and in secret.'

Molly looked down at her extravagant costume as Queen Zempolla, and felt the weight of her imposing wig. 'I am hardly dressed to help you carry Patrick to his lodgings, sir.'

'No, and it would not be fitting even if you were. I will need to trust one more person in the company to help. And that person must be highly discreet, which narrows down the possibilities somewhat.' Killigrew sighed even louder in frustration as he went through possible names in his head. 'Actually it narrows down the possibilities to nought, I fear. Apart from you, Molly, there is not an actor or actress, nor servant, in this place whom I could trust not to spread this wretched news all over London by next morning.' Sir Thomas had another thought, though – and clearly a better one from the more hopeful expression on his face. 'What of your kind Mr Raven, though? Would he not help us move Patrick? He is also a physician so he could give this poor boy whatever care and attention is possible to a victim of the plague.'

In her present circumstances, Molly was desperate not to have to ask Henry for such a dubious favour. 'He would feel it is his duty to inform the authorities of a case of plague, sir,' she pointed out, which was at least the truth.

Killigrew nodded resignedly. 'Ay, true enough, no doubt, for such a civic-minded man as he. Then we need someone of Mr Raven's intelligence, but without his refined conscience. Do you think his friend Mawdsley would help? He works for the Lord Chancellor so certainly knows how to keep an embarrassing secret. And Mawdsley would not want to see the playhouses closed down for one case of the plague...'

Molly shook her head dolefully. 'I do not think that will do either, sir.

Mr Mawdsley may like to see the theatre stay open, but even he cannot overlook a case of the plague, and keep news of it from his master, Lord Clarendon.' Molly gritted her teeth. 'It will have to be me alone, sir, as your helper. Allow me a few minutes to get out of this cumbersome costume, and then I will help you take Patrick to his lodgings. But I do this more for his sake, than for yours, Sir Thomas, if I may be frank...'

Sir Thomas was not offended, and his eyes almost twinkled. 'Thou art a good girl, Molly – too good for this place, and for me, if I be truthful.'

Molly was still thinking rapidly. 'Perhaps I will have to stay with Patrick this night and minister to his needs...? I did hire a woman to bring him food and physic from the apothecary, if he needed it, but I did not know then that it was a case of the plague. I cannot let this woman be subject to the risk of contagion.'

Killigrew looked much alarmed. 'Nay, Molly, that would be foolish indeed, and far beyond the call of duty when young Whelan is no more than a fellow actor of yours. He will spread the contagion to you even as he dies.' He took her hand. 'I cannot afford to lose another dear actress from this company. But you can release your woman drudge from her duty. I will find someone else to take care of Patrick tonight, and will reward the man well to keep his tongue. In fact, I wonder why I did not think of this individual before. He is a strange man, but knows many arcane and wondrous things about the workings of the human body, including how to treat the symptoms of plagues. He lives close by, so I shall go and summon him now while you rush to the tiring room and change from your queenly costume. What think you of that plan?'

'As you say, sir,' Molly agreed resignedly, wondering who this strange individual might be.

*

Bassam the Moor was an even stranger individual than Molly could reasonably have expected. Yet it seemed that he and Sir Thomas Killigrew were friends of a sort, which strange meeting of minds had to be a most unusual conjunction of humankind.

Molly had never met a black man of any sort before – not to speak to anyway - so had naturally been intrigued to encounter this individual who Sir Thomas had fetched to aid their cause. Molly had recently played in a performance of *Othello* in which William Wintershall had played the troubled eponymous hero, yet she saw now that Wintershall's performance as a Moor – which she had thought at the time to be so convincing – was but a crude mockery of the real thing.

Molly had taken only five frantic minutes to wash the paint off her face, and to change from her stage clothes into her plain old servant's dress of coarse black wool, before rushing back to Sir Thomas's private chamber. Fortunately most of the other actresses had already changed and left, so she had to face no difficult questions about her unseemly haste tonight. On the way back she had encountered Charles Hart in a dark passageway, but he, fortunately preoccupied with some deep thoughts of his own, did not even glance at her in her plain servant garb, and passed by without a word.

On knocking at the door of Killigrew's chamber again, Molly was quickly admitted, and there came face to face with this exotic black creature from the Barbary Coast. Sir Thomas introduced them, and seemed pleased at the effect that his strange visitor had on young Molly. 'This is Bassam Abdul Latif, Molly, who is a famous apothecary in his own land. I met Bassam in Venice many years ago, where he saved my life by the application of his curative skills. His fame and skill are such that he has ministered to emperors and kings, as well as to common people.'

The Moor bowed low to her. 'I am honoured, Mistress.'

Molly curtsied in response while she took in the man's powerful build and dramatic appearance. Although his skin was undoubtedly brown and a little coarse, yet he possessed a handsome enough face for a black man, with a fine aquiline nose, full lips and short wiry hair, threaded with silver. He was perhaps of a similar age to his unlikely friend Sir Thomas, but there all resemblance ended. He was dressed in plain European style, yet overlain with a certain Oriental exoticness in the rich colours of his cravat and shirt. He spoke English with great accuracy and precision, but also with extreme slowness as if he was practising every word in his head before he said it.

'Bassam has just made an examination of Patrick's condition, and he regretfully concurs with me that it is indeed a case of plague,' Killigrew said, becoming instantly serious again.

The Moor acknowledged that with a doleful nod of his handsome head. 'Indeed so. Is this gentleman a good friend of thine, Mistress?'

Molly hesitated. 'Nay, I cannot say that truly. Yet he is my fellow actor here, and a man of good character, I believe.' Molly tactfully drew a veil over any hints of Patrick's darker past, which according to the well-informed Nell had included a spell as a lawless highwayman in his native Ireland.

Bassam gave her a dignified appraisal. 'Regardless of his good character or not, I promise that I shall take good care of him. He has a lodging room nearby, I believe.'

Molly felt the Moor's piercing brown eyes on her, which seemed to her in her fancy capable of seeing right into her very soul. 'Yes, in Bridges Street, no more than a hundred paces from the theatre – 'tis the house with the red door at the corner with Drury Lane. The room is on the third floor, I am afraid.' She indicated the key lying on a table. 'That is the key to the outside door: Patrick had it in his pocket. The room itself will be unlocked, I believe. The servant should have brought clean bed linen today, and scrubbed the floor.'

The Moor took a deep breath. 'Then I think that Sir Thomas and I can carry this sick young man there by ourselves, Mistress, and put him to bed.'

Molly realized gratefully that she was being released from any further part in this sad drama. Yet she looked at Sir Thomas quizzically, seeking his confirmation.

Killigrew took her hand. 'Yes, indeed, young Molly, you have done enough. There is no further need to trouble yourself over this matter. As Bassam says, we can manage this duty between the two of us.'

Molly was now reluctant to go. 'You will take proper care of Patrick's needs, will you not? Not merely leave him alone to suffer?'

The Moor nodded. 'I promise thee to give my best attention to thy friend, Mistress. The affliction is well advanced, though. My treatment needs to be applied early if it is to succeed, so it may already be too late for this young man. Still, I will do what I can for him, and – God willing – he may yet come through it.'

Molly felt comforted by the man's dignified manner and his clear honesty. This was no mountebank or coney man, she was glad to see. 'Then I will leave you to your work, sirs,' she said simply.

Killigrew saw her to the door, and said confidingly to her as she left. ''Tis no welcome thing for me to admit, Molly, but my acquaintance with Bassam began when I was laid low with the pox in Venice. And he cured me completely of this affliction of Venus, so a simple case of the plague should be easily within his abilities to cure.'

Molly could only nod in apparent agreement with this, before hurrying down the passageway, and then down the stairs to the side door of the theatre. Fortunately the alleyway at the stage door was deserted now because of the lateness of the hour – all of the other actresses and actors had already departed for the evening, and only the servants and cleaning maids were left in attendance in the building. Nor was there any rain like last evening, so Molly turned gratefully in the direction of home.

On the way she could not help but wonder at her change in fortune since last evening when she had made this same walk home in the rain. Yesterday her happiness had been complete and her mood one of quiet joy. Now her happiness seemed threatened on all sides. She tried to put thoughts of Patrick's suffering to one side at least – there was nothing she could do to aid his situation except pray for him tonight. She thought instead of her own situation with Henry Raven, which in the distress of discovering that Patrick Whelan had the plague, had fortuitously slipped her mind this evening. Now her darkest fears over the fate of her friendship with Henry returned. She wondered if he would ever be truly reconciled to her now, and if his feelings for her could ever recover to what they had once been.

She doubted that many gentlemen of his standing would readily forgive the slight of finding another man in their mistress's bed. Most would even evict their former mistresses from their rooms without any ceremony, and it did cross Molly's mind for a bleak moment whether Henry would have had the locks to her rooms changed during the day, and that she would return now to find herself homeless.

But she dismissed this unworthy thought – Henry was not such a petty man as that. Even if he did not come back to her, he would give her enough time to make other living arrangements…

Hurrying through the darkened and malodorous alleyways, Molly suddenly became distracted from these sad thoughts, as she realized that she was being followed yet again…

Since the dramatic events of last winter, Molly had become more conscious of her safety when walking alone, and force of habit now often made her turn her head to see if she was being followed. And tonight there was little doubt of it, as she glimpsed a shadowy cloaked figure in the street behind her.

She increased her pace as she got to the corner of Bow Street, almost breaking into a trot to get to her front door. Now would certainly not be the best time to discover that her trust in Henry's generous spirit had been misplaced, and that she was indeed locked out.

As the figure approached closer behind her, Molly inserted the key hurriedly in the lock of the street door to her building and tried to turn it. For a moment it would not turn at all, and her heart raced, and her breathing became ragged and laboured. But then she forced herself to display a measure of composure and tried a second time. And on this occasion, with a satisfying click, she felt the key engage the stiff lock properly and turn the mechanism smoothly.

She did not dare to look back, though, but opened the door quickly and locked it behind her, her heart fluttering wildly with anxiety. Then she mounted the stairs to the first floor at the double, entering her own rooms and then rushing to the window of the parlour overlooking Bow Street to see if she could catch a further glimpse of this individual who had apparently followed her here from the theatre.

She was just in time to see a cloaked figure disappearing down the street, outlined for a moment by a weak glow of candlelight from a window. Although he was more than fifty paces away by now, Molly was almost convinced from his height that the man was none other than the mysterious foreign gentleman who waited most evenings for her to appear outside the stage door of the King's theatre.

This man seemed to have some peculiar fascination with her, a situation that Molly found most unsettling…

# CHAPTER 6

Thursday, 13th April 1665

On this warm spring afternoon, Esther Linney waited nervously in her parlour in Fetter Lane for her visitor to arrive.

She dared not imagine what he had come to say to her. She could have no expectations that his circumstances had changed, of course, so had to be content with the notion that he came merely to inquire after her wellbeing. Yet when she received the letter two days ago saying he would be calling this afternoon, she had been overjoyed that he would take the risk of coming here to London and being seen with her. The tone of his letter suggested that he did still have a genuine affection for her as he had once claimed, and also hinted at the possibility that, had he not been married already, he might have been prepared to take full responsibility for his impulsive act of passion and marry her, despite the difference in their social stations.

As she waited, pacing nervously back and forward for the appointed hour of two o'clock to ring from nearby St Paul's, she thought back to her other surprise visitor from three days ago.

Henry Raven had grown into the fine man that she had always known he would become. It had shamed her beyond measure, though, for him to come here and see her like this, carrying another man's bastard child. She had grown up in his home and always been treated affectionately and considerately by him – truly almost as another sister, as he said. Yet by the age of thirteen, her feelings for him in return had been anything but sisterly. Henry was not a *very* handsome boy, yet she had never met anyone with such a sweet nature and an understanding heart. One day, she had happened to catch sight of him writing a letter at his desk by an open window, quill pen in hand, and a thoughtful expression on his face. Dressed all in black that day, and with his hair long and curling over his lace collar,

72

she had felt such a wrench in her heart at this secret glimpse of him that she realized for the first time how much she loved him. When he left the manor to go to Cambridge to study, his absence from her life for months at a time was like a knife in her side. And when he came back finally, her happiness had overflowed. For that last year that she had lived at Salwayash Manor, each day had been a mixture of breathtaking joy and agonizing pain. The joy was something she felt every time he came near her; the pain came from the realization that she could never declare her true feelings to him. It would have been gross ingratitude on her part to have thrown herself at Henry, both to his sister Cathy - who, Esther was sure, had no inkling of the deep feelings she had for her brother - and to Anne Raven, his stern Puritan mother. She, after all, had not invited Esther into their house as a child with any expectation that one day she might marry Henry and become mistress of the manor. Anne Raven had been fond of her, Esther believed, but not so fond that she could have imagined a union between someone of her unfortunate background and her only son.

And there had never truly been any chance of success anyway for Esther's unattainable daydream: she could tell that Henry, for all his liking of her as a sister, would never be able to regard her as a lover and a future wife.

When both Henry's mother and her own adoptive mother, Doll Smurthwaite, had died within a few short weeks of each other, Esther was desolated and had no idea of what to do, or where to go. The return of her brother Gideon from sea a few weeks later had been a welcome excuse for her to leave the manor household, even though Gideon was truly a stranger to her, while the Ravens were the only family she had ever known...

A gentle knock at the door made Esther jump and woke her from her sad reverie. She took a deep breath, composed herself, and then went to answer the door.

Her visitor did not smile at her, but bowed formally. 'Good day, Esther. I trust you received my message, and that this visit is not an unpleasant imposition on you?'

She curtsied in response, before showing him through into the tiny parlour. 'I did receive your letter, of course, sir, since you sent it by personal messenger. Yet even if you had come unannounced, it would still have been a pleasant surprise to me, not an unpleasant one.'

He bowed again, more awkwardly this time. 'You are very good to treat me so politely when I hardly deserve such consideration,' he said.

'Will you take a seat, sir? You have travelled far and must be tired from the coach journey.'

'Nay, I have been sitting long enough since yesterday, so prefer to stand.' He smiled at her engagingly. 'The Winchester coach is as badly sprung as ever, and the roads still badly rutted from the severe winter, so I am a mass of private bruises.'

Esther kept her voice calm and her expression distant, though inside she felt the urge to scream aloud to relieve some of her deep emotional wounds. 'I am sorry to hear it, sir, so appreciate the trouble you have taken to come and see me even more. And I make no complaint of my treatment at your hands, sir. I was as much to blame as you for what happened, and you have since been kind enough to support me during these difficult months.'

He looked around the room, then went to the window where, beyond the mass of dirty gables and moss-covered rooftops, the Thames could just be glimpsed, with its sparkle of water and its teeming river traffic of wherries and barges. And further beyond were the green hills of Surrey on the south side of the river, dominated by the forested slopes of Sydenham Hill, whose proximity made the countryside seem reassuringly within reach. 'You did well to find such pleasant lodgings in the city, Esther. Is the money I gave you sufficient for your needs until the baby is born? Or do you need more?'

'I do not need more, sir – you have been more than generous already.' Esther hesitated. 'Yet I fear I may have to move again before the baby comes. The silversmith and his wife below in the shop are tolerable enough as landlords. But the neighbours here are not so amiable as I thought, and they begin to make trouble for me, and point me out in the street, now that they see I am with child, and yet have no wedding ring.'

Her visitor frowned and ran a hand through his long sleek, black hair. Esther marvelled again at his boyish beauty, which seemed remarkably untouched by time. He was close to his fortieth year, she knew, but he seemed hardly to have changed in the last eight years. For most of that time, he had been no more to her than a local gentleman of great consequence, and she had never done more than to curtsey in acknowledgement to him at his regular passing by her cottage. Last year, though, he had taken to regularly dismounting from his horse, and exchanging a few pleasant words with her as she worked in her herb garden at the front of the cottage. After a while she had begun to suspect that he might have formed some partiality for her, since many people had observed that she had grown of late from a thin and unnoticed girl into a tall and well-built woman of striking colouring. His attention had certainly seemed more marked than mere friendliness anyway, and he had occasionally even discussed intimate details of his life with her. Yet he was a married man of great wealth and prestige, and therefore it would have been far beyond the bounds of propriety for her to have encouraged him. Yet Esther could not deny that she had found his attentions a pleasant compliment, and had looked forward every day to seeing his mounted figure appearing on the wooded track leading to her cottage.

It was only on the afternoon of the harvest feast at Salwayash Manor, with his wife absent from the celebrations for some unexplained reason, that he had finally declared his true affection for her. Yet even then his behaviour had been most circumspect, and he had not even tried to hold her hand secretly under the table.

It was only later that evening at her cottage, when he had appeared at twilight without warning and forced his way in, that he had finally lost control of his good sense...

He seemed now to have reverted entirely to that polite and distant gentleman who had passed by her cottage on horseback every few days. 'Can I help you find other alternative lodgings, then?' he offered solicitously. 'I have an acquaintance in the village of Little Chelsea, west of the city, who owns a pretty cottage by the river. It could be made available for you, if you wish. It is a more salubrious place than here, with clean air and fresh meadows around, full of buttercups and daisies, therefore much more like the home you are used to. I could also hire a servant woman to take care of your needs, perhaps one with experience of midwifery duties.'

Esther nodded gratefully. 'Then I would be pleased to accept your kind offer, sir. I want the baby, be it a boy or a girl, to be born healthy.'

Her visitor frowned. 'You mean to keep the child, and bring it up yourself?'

At his harsher tone, Esther felt the beginnings of a tear in her eye, and turned away for a second to hide it. 'I have not decided yet, sir. But I believe that I may, despite the stigma of my child having no father.'

The man fell silent for a second, before speaking up again. 'As you wish. 'Tis your decision to make, Esther. But please reflect on the difficulties and responsibilities of raising a child alone, especially now that you have lost your brother Gideon. 'Tis hard enough bringing up children even in a normal family.'

Esther regarded him coldly, sure of his real meaning. 'Whatever happens, sir, there will be no embarrassment to you, or to your good wife. If I choose to keep the baby, then I doubt that I will return to Dorset to suffer fresh opprobrium to add to that endured by my mother, but will instead make my life elsewhere. My brother Gideon had some money secured in a London vault which I should be able to claim in time...'

He stepped forward. 'Ye need never worry for money, Esther. I shall always make sure that you and the child are provided for. I trust you understand that.'

Esther nodded dutifully. 'If you say so, sir, then I must believe it, and be grateful for it.' She sighed. 'How is everyone in Dorset? I miss my friends and neighbours sorely.'

Her visitor became wary, clearly not wishing to increase her melancholy at her isolation from the county of her birth. 'Mary Raven has recently married, and gone to live in Kent. But you must have heard of those forthcoming nuptials even before you left at Candlemas. Her brother was home for several weeks in March, both for the wedding, and to deal with matters on the estate. He has become quite the London man of business these days, with some influence at court even. They even say he has an actress as a mistress...'

Esther blinked in surprise at that latter statement, which sounded most out-of-character for Henry Raven, if it were true. 'And your family life at Warboys Hall, sir? Is everything well?'

Ralph Warboys seemed evasive for the first time. 'Much the same. Everyone in my household is well.'

An awkward silence ensued, and all that Esther wanted now was for Mr Warboys to leave forever. Yet she could not help finally saying something of her real feelings. 'I make no criticism, sir, but I still do not fully comprehend your behaviour last August...'

He held his hands up in exasperation. 'I can say nothing to justify myself, Esther...I am a weak and susceptible man...that is all...'

Esther would not be denied a fuller explanation however. 'At the feast in the afternoon, you were your usual restrained self, even though you claimed a real affection for me. Yet when you came to my cottage later, and burst through the door, you seemed almost an entirely different man.'

Warboys' face stiffened to an uncomfortable mask. 'Who can explain or justify such disgraceful behaviour? I cannot, in truth. All men have two sides, the light and the dark, the human and the inhuman. I gave in to my baser side that night, Esther, for which I truly beg your pardon yet again. But 'tis difficult for a man not to give into lust, when so much stirring beauty is before him.'

Esther flushed bright red. 'I truly did not expect you, sir. I was washing myself before retiring, not in expectation of you bursting through the door.'

Warboys nodded. 'I know that it was no deliberate ploy of yours, Esther, but your natural beauty seduced me nevertheless.'

Esther turned her back again to hide her burning cheeks. 'Yet I gave in to lustful behaviour too, sir, so you are not entirely to blame. If I had ordered you to leave, I believe sincerely that you would have gone. But I did not; instead I responded to your passion with equal passion of my own...'

'I am not so sure of that, Esther. Yet it does you credit that you take part of the blame on yourself, when in truth you were blameless,' he said huskily. Stepping forward Warboys took her hand and kissed the back of it. Then he put his arms around her waist, feeling the swell of the baby inside, and pulled her towards him. 'Truly I am sorry for the bestial nature of all men towards the gentler sex,' he said, weeping. 'Forgive me, Esther.'

She lifted his chin and put her fingers to his lips. 'Then say no more. I do forgive you...'

*

Henry Raven examined the body lying stretched out on the stone slab, and wondered if he was up to watching a dissection in his present severely depressed mood.

Dr Croone noticed his discomfort. 'This gentleman is no fine physical specimen, to be sure, but I had thought you would be more interested to see his innards exposed, Henry.'

They were alone together in the stone-flagged basement of Dr Croone's fine house on the Strand, apart from the company of a pair of Croone's sturdy manservants, Will and Jeremiah, who stood in attendance to one side, dressed in leather aprons to help with the bloodier duties of the dissection.

Raven looked at the man on the granite slab – a thin man of middle age, with a stringy white body and a balding head. 'I *am* tolerably interested, I assure you, despite my many preoccupations at present. Who was he, William?'

Croone looked at his notes. 'His name was Ezekiel Painter, and he was a carpenter in life, and a most mild-mannered and God-fearing man from all accounts. Never argued with his neighbours, never cheated his customers, and always attended both communion and evensong every Lord's day.'

'Most mild-mannered men do not end their lives at Tyburn, hanging from a gibbet like this Mr Painter,' Raven pointed out bleakly.

'No, indeed. After a lifetime of doing nothing remarkable or noteworthy, Mr Painter had a mild row with his wife over some trifling domestic issue, then calmly slit her throat, then those of his six young children, one by one...'

Realization dawned on Raven. 'Remarkable indeed. So *this* was the man who went mad and murdered his entire family but two weeks ago! I saw an account of it in a newssheet on my return from Dorset this week, but had quite forgotten the sad case with everything else that has happened. '

Croone nodded and got back to removing the man's intestines and spleen. 'Yes. And our infamous hanging judge, Matthew Holinshead, lived up his reputation as usual, and dispatched Mr Painter to Tyburn after a trial of no more than one hour, despite the man being clearly mad. Yet Judge Holinshead does provide me with more corpses for dissection than any other judge in the city, so I should not complain too much but make the best of his generosity to further the study of natural philosophy. I am interested to discover if there are any abnormalities in Mr Painter's organs that might explain this sudden aberration in an otherwise blameless life. And particularly to examine his brain of course...'

Raven nodded with as much enthusiasm as he could muster, still hardly in the mood for this examination despite the interesting tale that was attached to it. Yet it was always difficult to get hold of fresh corpses suitable for dissection, and Croone was one of the few men in London who had ready access to them, so Raven knew that he should be grateful for this further opportunity to see at first hand the inner workings of the human body.

Croone was, like Raven, a convert to the theory of Drs William Petty and Thomas Willis that the seat of human intelligence and behaviour was to be found in the brain, not elsewhere. Aristotle had thought the brain merely an organ for cooling the blood, yet Willis had argued in his recent book, *Cerebri Anatome*, that the complexity of its construction, and the degree of protection given to it by the solid bony skull, all suggested a much greater purpose than that. Dr Petty, his collaborator, had once studied in Caen in Normandy under the great Descartes himself, therefore was a man of considerable reputation in his own right.

Croone stopped probing with his knife for a moment, and held up the spleen to examine it minutely. 'I take it from your sour disposition, Henry, that you received no great support from the King today when you went to tell him of the case of the plague in St Giles.'

Raven stepped back from his friend, not wishing to get any of the blood spattered on him, even though his clothes were protected too by a leather apron. In truth he had never had much taste for the bloodier duties of a surgeon, which was why he had never practised as a physician except on rare occasions. 'You are right as always, William. Mawdsley obtained for me a half hour private audience with the King and the Lord Chancellor this morning, but they both said there is nothing the Privy Council can do, except hope that this is an isolated case. There is simply no money available for demolishing slums, clearing drains and moving people away from the source of infection.'

Croone sighed. 'I guessed what they would say. "The people will have to take their chances...we are fighting a war with a ruthless enemy, and all our resources must go into that...etcetera...etcetera" '

Raven shrugged wryly. 'I did not think you could hear into Whitehall Palace from here in the Strand, yet it seems you must from the accuracy of your recall.' His voice rose angrily. 'It seems that our fleet will be assembled at Harwich next month to take the war to the Dutch, and that this operation will likely bleed the exchequer dry of all its remaining funds.'

'You do not approve of this war, Henry?' Croone said, more of a statement than a question.

'I do not,' Raven stated flatly. 'I dislike wars at any time, but particularly when they are against our natural allies. 'Tis the French and the Spanish we should be fighting, if anybody, William.'

With all the pressures in his life, plus the added unhappiness of his betrayal by Molly, Henry Raven had truly given little thought of late to the war with the Dutch. Yet it did now seem to be building up to a real conflict, with such a mighty English fleet being assembled at Harwich to wage battle in the North Sea.

There was no doubt that the Dutch were a new emerging power in Europe after finally ridding themselves of their Spanish colonial masters half a century ago (even though most of the Southern Netherlands still remained under Spanish rule, while other Southern provinces had been lost to the opportunistic French.) Since the end of the Thirty Years War in Europe between Protestant and Catholic nations, the Dutch Republic had grown rapidly in this welcome interlude of peace, and experienced a remarkable flowering of scientific and artistic thought. Yet the changes went further than mere culture: there had been a major political shift in Holland too. Independence from Spain had set the Dutch irrevocably on the path to becoming a major world power in their own right, thanks to their talent for trade and their incomparable skill as navigators. Although they had formerly been close Protestant allies of England in their resistance against the dominant European powers of France and Spain, the newly ambitious Dutch had now inevitably become yet another powerful competitor to the English too, who were involved in their own search for new trade routes and overseas colonies.

Yet, like the English, the Dutch had internal struggles and divisions of their own to distract them from their foreign enemies – in their case between the Royalist supporters of the House of Orange and those more republican-minded supporters of the Regents of the States-General, who were determined that Holland would stay a republic. The Dutch republicans, fearful of the power and popularity of the House of Orange in some quarters, had vowed that the office of *stadholder* would never be given to William, Prince of Orange, particularly as he was the nephew of King Charles of England. This opposition to his fifteen-year-old nephew from the States-General had been one of the King's secret reasons for declaring war, Raven was sure – Charles was determined that his late sister Mary's son, William, would one day rule Holland.

'I agree with you, Henry,' Croone said. 'The Dutch are so much like ourselves in their search for knowledge, and in their remarkable voyages of discovery to the East and the Americas, that it seems truly that we fight our brothers, while our real enemies look on in grateful amusement.' He paused. 'In fact I visited Amsterdam and The Hague recently and was met only with cordiality and civility. I saw much of their fine art, and even met their famous Meneer Huygens. You have been there yourself, I know. Have you ever seen a painting called *The Anatomy Lesson of Dr Nicolaes Tulp* by their Meneer Rembrandt, which depicts the late Dr Tulp dissecting a criminal's forearm? It is a wonderfully observed scene. Meneer Rembrandt made this painting some thirty years ago, and there has been much speculation recently among men of science in Holland as to why that dissection began on the forearm, which is something no anatomist would do these days. Yet the artist himself is an old reclusive man now and refuses to discuss his work with strangers, so no one can be sure whether Dr Tulp actually performed dissections in this way, or whether this is some artistic license on Meneer Rembrandt's part...'

Raven interrupted. 'I have indeed seen this painting for myself, William, on a visit to Amsterdam last summer. And I doubt that Meneer Rembrandt would invent such a thing. Was the dissection not done that way because medical thought at that time, thirty years ago, was concentrated on recent observations of the lymphatics and 'the white veins?' There was, of course, a popular anatomical text recently published then on this subject by our own late Dr Harvey, called *Exercitatio Anatomica de Motu Cordis et Sanguinis in Animalibus*, which prompted much of this interest in the anatomists of the time...'

'Yes, indeed,' Croone added eagerly, 'and it was later expanded and corrected by the great Malpighi. I believe that you may be partly correct in your supposition, Henry, that Dr Harvey's excellent text may have excited this fascination with the lymphatics.'

Raven nodded. 'And yet we still have not the slightest comprehension what the lymphatics are for, do we, William?'

'No, indeed,' Croone admitted.

'When I studied the painting in detail,' Raven went on, 'I could not help but observe that the dissection room seems a little crowded by our standards, certainly by comparison with our modest dissection here today. Even these days, it seems that the Dutch still treat anatomy lessons as a social event, and hold them in *theatres* of all places, with students, colleagues and the general public permitted to attend on payment of an entrance fee, as it they had come to see a play...'

'Then I foresee that every hospital in England will one day require a special "theatre" in which to perform acts of surgery,' Croone suggested with a smile.

'Ay, no doubt,' agreed Raven.

Croone smiled. 'You yourself would have made a fine anatomist, if you were not so taken with the business of commerce, Henry. But I commend you for the time you have spent this week on this case of the plague, which must keep you presently from pressing business matters of your own.'

Raven frowned. 'Commerce and business will suffer too, if the plague takes hold on this city, William. So my actions in this matter, such as they are, are not entirely altruistic. Regardless of my motives, though, I intend to do what I can to fight the spread of the plague to the best of my ability. We may get little help from the King and his Privy Council, but the people of London can do much by their own efforts to alleviate the spread of the affliction.'

Croone clapped a bloodied hand on his shoulder. 'Well said, Henry. And I too shall do my part. But for the next hours, shall we delve into the organs of Mr Painter here and see what we can discover about this man that might have driven him to perform such a terrible deed as infanticide…'

# CHAPTER 7

Friday, 14<sup>th</sup> April 1665

Molly was but half way through the third act of the Friday performance of *The Indian Queen* when she began to feel unwell. The feeling began with no more than a sense of general malaise, but soon she began to feel intense cramps in her stomach muscles, and a severe chill, even though the atmosphere in the theatre had felt close and stuffy not minutes before.

The discomfort became almost unbearable as she reached the middle of a long speech as the fearsome Queen Zempolla that disparaged her rival Montezuma's quaint view of his personal honour. "*Honour is but an itch in youthful blood, of...*' - she faltered briefly, seized by a sudden pain that rippled through her body and made her flinch - '*...of doing acts...extravagantly good.*"

Yet Molly was a seasoned performer after only five months on the stage, and she shook off this ill feeling by simple force of will, and went into her next line with reasonable fluency, so that the audience certainly knew nothing of her inner turmoil.

Her fellow player in the scene, though - Charles Hart - was heavily attuned to her character by now, and to the little nuances of her performance, so she was sure that he at least must have noticed that something was amiss with her. Yet Molly's debilitating weakness soon passed, and her muscle cramps to ease a little, so she was gradually able to lift her performance again through the remainder of the act, and to complete it with reasonable normalcy.

Offstage, at the end of the act, Hart approached her with a concerned look. 'Molly, are you quite...*yourself?* If I may be critical, your speeches lack their usual crispness and flair today.' He examined her closely, his handsome face concerned. 'Perhaps you suffer some bodily incapacity or distemper?'

Molly denied his suspicions vigorously. 'Nay, sir. I am in rude health.'

Hart looked doubtful. 'If you say so, Molly. Yet, even with your face painted, I can see that it has a sickly pallor quite unlike its usual rosy glow, and you seem to tremble with cold, despite the warmth of the theatre. If you feel unwell and cannot continue for the final two acts, then 'tis better to admit it now during the intermission. Mary Pettican is standing by to take over your part, and your costume, should you need her to.'

Molly glanced over to a dark corner backstage, from where Mistress Pettican regarded her with an expression of barely concealed malice. That look of evil intent only served to make Molly even more determined to see through the performance to the end than she had been previously. She would not give up her role now, no matter if she were dying - which she most certainly was not, she told herself forcibly. 'Mary is kindness itself, sir, and I appreciate her gracious offer,' she said with mock sweetness. 'But truly I am well, so will continue...'

Molly did pause momentarily in her speech, as she wondered with a shiver of apprehension whether she might possibly have caught the plague too, like poor Patrick. Yet she was sure that she had not been bit by any rat recently - which was the only known way of catching the plague, was it not? - so was soon reassured that she worried herself unnecessarily.

Hart nodded, still not entirely convinced of her veracity, but prepared to give her the benefit of the doubt.

Molly escaped from him, and went to a quiet corner offstage to try and recover her composure. Good health was something she had always taken for granted, and it was disturbing for her to discover that her always healthy body could be subject to the same aches and afflictions as other less fortunate people. Yet Molly's search for a little peace and quiet was soon disturbed by the whirlwind arrival of Nell. Young Nelly was in boisterous mood because Sir Thomas had made good on his promise to reward her for allowing him to take liberties with her earlier this week, and she had been given a walk-on part in the play today as a naked female slave.

She was attired in a close fitting costume of thin brown wool, which did make her appear almost naked on stage under the light of a hundred burning candles. Yet she did not seem to mind wearing the revealing costume, only complaining rather that it was not even more revealing, and that it itched excessively against her nipples.

Molly for once found Nell's bright chatter almost unbearable, and snapped at her in uncharacteristic fashion. 'Then take it off altogether, Nell, if it pleases you, paint yourself brown all over with vegetable dye, and parade in your natural state. That will doubtless stop your nipples itching, while the audience will be equally appreciative too, no doubt.'

Nell was taken aback for a moment, thinking Molly to be serious. 'Would Sir Thomas truly allow such forwardness, though, Molly?' she asked doubtfully.

'When word got out of the naked girl on stage, it would almost certainly fill all of the empty seats at the next performance of *The Indian Queen*,' Molly said. 'Therefore Sir Thomas would most likely be overjoyed at your initiative.'

'Oh! I had not thought of that.' Nell narrowed her eyes suspiciously. 'But I see now that you mean it not. You merely jest with me.' She frowned as she examined Molly's face as well as she could in the dimness at the side of the stage. 'Does something ail you, Molly? You seem not your usual composed self.'

'Tis but my time of the month, Nell,' Molly lied, but then instantly regretted it with a girl like Nell, who was an odd mixture of youthful naivety and extreme worldliness.

'I thought your menses flowed but two weeks ago,' she said suspiciously. 'You must have a most strange cycle.'

'I do,' Molly claimed desperately. 'And I would appreciate a little quiet before the next act starts, if you will allow it, Nell.' Actually, Molly's body was most regular in its natural cycle, so that she knew exactly when she had to avoid her lover if she did not want to conceive, which she most certainly did not want to at present, even for such a fine man as Henry...

Nell was a little hurt by Molly's brusque manner, and responded coolly. 'Of course I will leave you be, if that is what you wish. I thought that you would be happy to see me get my chance to shine on stage, but it seems not...'

*

Molly found the final acts to be torture, as she did her best to play Queen Zempolla convincingly, while struggling with pain, dizziness and increasing nausea. It was only the sight of Mary Pettican gloating in the wings at her distress that made Molly determined to see the play through to the bitter end. That and her pride as an actress not to let down the rest of the company.

Molly could see that Charles Hart was no longer deceived, and knew her to be suffering in some severe way. As the good company actor that he was, though, he did his able best to cover for her lapses in her speeches, and her occasional mental confusion.

By the end of the play, Molly was desperate to reach her death scene so that she might be carried off stage. As she gave her last speech before killing herself, her eyes fell accidentally on someone sitting in the nearest box to the stage. For a moment, she thought that she knew whom it must be, sitting back in the shadows of the box – this was Henry's usual box after all! - and was overjoyed momentarily to think that Henry had forgiven her that lapse of judgement and had come to watch her again. But her ailing eyes had deceived her: when the man leaned forward over the edge of the box, she saw that it was none other than the foreign gentleman who she believed had followed her home last night. From the penetrating looks he gave her, this mysterious man did indeed seem to be in the grip of some unhealthy obsession with her.

But Molly was in far too distressed a state by now to worry whether this intense-looking individual truly meant her harm, or if he was simply taken with her as a performer.

It was with a deep sense of relief that Molly was finally carried off stage on her bier, where she struggled unaided to her feet, and tried to behave as normal, despite feeling a most powerful urge to expel the contents of her stomach.

Her vision was beginning to blur increasingly too, and she felt quite as dizzy as if she had imbibed several stone flagons of the strongest Kent ale. But she nevertheless made her way to the passageway leading to the tiring rooms, so that she could get out of this constricting costume. She could not even bear to wait to take her applause at the end as was customary; the weight of this costume, and the heaviness of the wig, were much more troubling than usual in her weakened state, and felt like a suit of armour.

On stage, the play continued without her to its conclusion when General Montezuma took his rightful place as Emperor of Mexico. Which conclusion was fortunate for Molly because it meant that the tiring rooms were almost deserted so she did not have to suffer too many difficult questions about her ill performance.

Yet Molly had barely sat down in the tiring room before Sir Thomas Killigrew appeared behind her. 'You should not be in here, sir,' she chided him gently. She glanced back at the old reprobate's face, and even with her presently blurred vision, she saw at once that he suffered with some distress of his own.

Killigrew sighed heavily. 'Bassam the Moor has returned with some sad news, Molly...'

Molly saw the tall black man emerge from the shadows in the passageway outside, and she made to stand up to greet him. But her head spun alarmingly, and her legs to wobble under her, so that she was forced to keep her seat.

Bassam came forward into the room. 'I regret to inform thee, Mistress, that thy young actor friend has gone to meet his maker. May God have mercy on his soul!'

Molly was numb. 'When did the poor boy pass away?'

Bassam was sombre. 'Not an hour since. He seemed to recover a little yesterday, so I retained some hope that my treatment would be efficacious in relieving his affliction. But this is a most virulent sort of plague, and an unforgiving one, and the poison eventually swept through his body and consumed him. I have never felt a man so hot and feverish; 'tis a wonder he did not scorch the bed linen.'

Molly nodded, trying to make her voice sound normal. Yet she could hardly tell what was normal any more; even this familiar room seemed strange and unnatural to her now, and filled with strange demons lurking in the shadows, waiting to devour her.

She tried to ignore the evil faces forming from the mist, knowing they must be created in her own weary head.

Bassam tried to take her hand, but she snatched it away in alarm.

'Excuse me, Mistress,' he said. 'I did not mean to be forward. I merely wanted to feel thy hand for warmth. You seem feverish too.'

Killigrew stepped forward in alarm.

'Nay, Sir Thomas, concern yourself not,' Molly said with as much emphasis as she could muster. 'I am merely distressed to hear the sad news of Patrick's passing; he was a good and kind-hearted man, I believe…'

'And would have been a capable actor in time, I am sure,' Killigrew said. Even in her feverish condition, Molly could see that Killigrew was genuinely moved at his loss. 'Yet another young actor from the company dead! This is almost more than I can bear,' he said bleakly.

Molly turned back to the mirror and looked at the cruel face of Queen Zempolla reflected in the polished metal. 'If you will excuse me, Sir Thomas, I must call my dresser and change from this costume to go home. I cannot bear to go back on stage for the audience's applause. It would ring hollow tonight.'

'Ay, Molly,' Sir Thomas agreed. 'You should indeed go home and rest tonight…'

*

A quarter hour later, Killigrew stood in the passageway with Bassam and watched Molly leave in the other direction, on her way to the stage door.

Molly had washed the paint off her face, and had changed from her Queen Zempolla costume into her plain old servant's dress of coarse black wool, so that she seemed like the sweet and unsophisticated Molly of old. Killigrew was reminded of the first time he had noticed her last year, when she had worked in the theatre as a lowly orange seller and drudge. Even then her beauty was hard to miss, and she had shone out among her companions like a bright sparkling candle among so many smoky and ordinary flames.

'Does Molly suffer the plague too, Bassam?' Killigrew whispered to his companion, as he watched Molly's unsteady walk down the passageway, with eyes grown suddenly moist with emotion.

Bassam nodded, towering over him. 'I fear so. I felt her skin briefly, and it simmers like molten iron.'

Killigrew grimaced, careless of the tears staining his withered old cheeks. 'Poor dear girl! I have heard that she has had some falling out with her lover too, Mr Raven, so there is no one presently to look out for her except me...'

Bassam looked interested. 'Is that Mr Henry Raven, the famed natural philosopher, of whom you speak?'

Killigrew watched Molly finally disappear from sight at the other end of the passageway. 'It is, although I know him more as a man of business. He is a leading exporter of coal from the North of England, and also has large estates in the county of Dorset. Do you know Mr Raven?'

'I know *of* him, by reputation. He and his friends, Mr Hooke and Dr Croone, are lauded all over Europe for their scientific researches, even in the salons and drawing rooms of Venice and Constantinople.'

'I had no idea that Mr Raven was held in such esteem,' Killigrew said. 'But given his estrangement from poor Molly, he will not be of much help to her, likely.' Sir Thomas craned his neck to look into the liquid brown eyes of this imposing black man. 'Can you do what you can for her, Bassam? I will pay you a hundred pounds in gold if you can save that girl's life. She is worth that much to me as an actress.'

'I see that she is more to you than a mere employee though, Sir Thomas. You have warm feelings for her.'

'I admit it readily. She is among the best young actresses in the company. Her performance last evening as Queen Zempolla was remarkable enough for any actress. But for a seventeen-year-old girl to play that fearsome and evil matriarch with such conviction was truly astounding!' Sir Thomas ran a sweaty hand across his forehead. 'But she is also a sweet soul who gives me much pleasure in my life. And innocent pleasures at that – as well as the occasional lusty thought too, of course,' Killigrew admitted. 'She would leave a huge void in my life if she were to fly with the angels long before her time.'

Bassam gave a dignified bow. 'Then of course I accept your offer of the hundred pounds, although I would have tried to save Mistress Molly for nothing, sir. Yet I am not such a wealthy man that I can refuse your offer, and it may spur me on to even greater efforts to keep young Molly from crossing the River Styx just yet...'

\*

In her feverish nightmare, Molly's world had dwindled to a circle a mere ten paces across. Outside the circle was only mist and darkness, but she could hear wild beasts snarling just beyond the line of her vision, waiting to tear her limb from limb should she fall to the ground. So she stumbled on in near blindness, desperate to keep her feet.

One small voice in her head told her that this enveloping fog was merely imagined, as were the hungry beasts, yet that voice of reason soon became a dwindling one, overpowered by the silent screaming in her head, as she stumbled along the dirty alleyways back to Bow Street and her own front door. Finding her way home tonight was as difficult as finding a way through a maze in the outer reaches of Hell, and the walk seemed as endless.

A doorway finally loomed before her, and something seemed familiar enough about it for her to retrieve her key from her bag and try to open that high imposing door. But even opening her embroidered linen bag seemed a task entirely beyond her in her present distressed state, and as she tried to unfasten the iron clasp, she dropped it clumsily to the ground. When she tried to retrieve it, the world spun around, and she found herself lying on her back on the cold wet earth, as helpless as a new born babe.

She could hear the monsters approaching from all sides, gnashing their teeth in triumph, slavering with delight at their forthcoming feast. But before the monsters could take her, she was lifted off her feet by immensely strong and comforting arms.

'I am here, Molly,' Henry said.

Henry found the key in her bag with ease and opened the street door. Then he carried her swiftly up the stairs and into her own apartments, where he found her bedroom and laid her gently on the bed.

She could see nothing at all now; the circle of mist had closed around her completely so that she was virtually blind. Yet it mattered not, now that Henry had come back to her. She could die happily now, in his arms, the way it was meant to be.

'Forgive me,' she said woozily.

'*Il n'y a pas de quoi,*' Henry said.

Molly shook her head to try and clear the mist. 'What say you, Henry?'

'*Je ne suis pas Henri, Ma'mselle. Mon nom est Philippe. Ne vous inquiétez pas vous-même, je vous aiderai. Je dois aller maintenant pour porter un médecin. Restez calme jusqu'à mon retour.*'

Suddenly the fog in her mind cleared a little. Molly realized the bitter truth - that this was not Henry at all, but instead the mystery foreigner from the theatre. Yet, in her awful disappointment that Henry had not come back to her after all, she cared not any more if this man intended to slit her throat and take her money, or even whether she lived or died.

If this man slit her throat now, it would be a relief only...

# CHAPTER 8

Friday, 28<sup>th</sup> April 1665

For the last two weeks Henry Raven had worked like a Trojan in the dismal slums of the parish of St Giles in an effort to prevent the spread of the plague. But in the end, despite his best efforts to have all the street drains cleaned of offal and carrion and excrement, and to wage war against the vast population of sleek well-fed rats who infested the back alleys and open privies, his work had proved as futile as King Canute trying to halt the incoming tide with a Royal command.

The poor girl Rebecca Andrews had died of course within two days of Raven seeing her; he was only surprised that she had lingered as long as that when her frail little body had been ravaged so severely by this devouring black monster. The second case – a little boy – had followed three days later. By the second week, there had been at least ten cases, and it had been impossible after that to isolate the sufferers from the rest of the slum dwellers of St Giles. Now, more than two weeks later, there were a hundred known cases, and the numbers were rising daily.

Yet Raven had still formed the sanguine hope that he and the parish authorities might be able to contain the outbreak within the area of St Giles by controlling the passage of people in and out of the area. Yesterday had come the depressing news, however, of two cases among seamen in the dock area east of the city, so Raven had known then that it was only a matter of time before the plague reached the city itself. And there, among that vast and densely packed population, it would spread no doubt like wildfire. Raven understood now that the City of London was facing a catastrophe greater than any it had known in three hundred years.

His concerns now were increasingly for those who were dear to him. If the plague became widespread, as he feared, then he was determined that he would move his household back to Dorset and would stay here alone in the city to do what he could to alleviate the people's suffering. Dora Bagwell had already gone back to Dorset permanently, which was one personal problem solved for Raven, though her request to return to Salwayash Manor had been motivated less by her fear of the plague than by her wish to be near her ailing sister, Constance.

Raven had been so occupied with his endeavours against the plague for the last fortnight that he had been forced to neglect Molly entirely, though he had sent a note of reassurance to her in Bow Street saying that all was well between them, and that he would return to her when he had some time. He could perhaps have found some time to visit her still, yet it worried him that he might unknowingly bring the agent of this terrible disease into her home, which was of course the last thing he wanted, so had chosen to stay away deliberately.

He had decided by now that he should offer Molly the chance to escape from the plague too, either staying at his manor house in Salwayash, or, if such a drastic move was not acceptable to her (as it probably would not), to a cottage in some quiet country village a safe distance from London, like Kensington or Chiswick. She would not want to go, of course, especially if the King's theatre was still open. Yet if the plague outbreak became bad enough, then the theatres would certainly have to be closed for fear of contagion, so Molly might then be more amenable to such a proposal.

Raven had also been concerned for the fate of Esther Linney, who lodged above that silversmith's shop in the city, and expected the arrival of her fatherless child within a month. Although he had neglected his business affairs along with everything else during his battle against the spread of the plague, Raven had made one brief visit to the Royal Exchange last week to deal with the mass of outstanding business documents needing his signature, and on the way back by coach had called at Fetter Lane to warn Esther of her imminent danger. But Esther was gone from her lodgings already, and her former landlord – an uncouth and ill-tempered rogue of a silversmith – was either unwilling, or unable, to be of any help to Raven in telling him where Esther might have gone. Raven could only hope that she had moved out of the city of her own volition anyway, perhaps to a more salubrious and fitting place for the birth of her child.

Now, on this fine Friday morning in late April, Henry Raven dozed at home in his library, being still greatly fatigued from an arduous late night assisting Dr Croone in treating plague victims. The essence of Croone's treatment was to isolate the victims as much as possible into clean and dry conditions where they might resist the infection themselves, and to supply them with what remedies he could. Croone placed no store on the various quack medicines that proliferated throughout the rest of Europe to fight the plague – Venice Treacle, Celestial Waters or Dragon Waters. Yet he had remedies of his own that he could try – one an extract from the stems of white willow that could relieve pain most efficaciously, while the other much rarer physic was an extract from the bark of the Jesuit's tree from the Americas that had proved most effective in reducing fevers. Yet Croone had only a tiny amount of this latter precious bark available – at least until the next vessel from the Spanish Main put into the Pool of London...

Raven thought again about the severe trials of this last week as he looked around his library from the comfort of his favourite new reading chair, one built for him recently by a cabinet-maker in the Strand from English maple, but in the French style. This was a chair taller, more slender, and more elegant of form than the squat English chairs of old. The stretcher especially was a work of art - an exceedingly graceful semi-circular ornament connecting all four legs, with a vase-shaped knob in the centre. This decorative style of chair had only recently been brought to England by the courtiers who had been in exile with the King, and who had returned with their heads full of French style and manners – which details were mainly to be admired, yet also including unfortunately the abominable new habit of wearing periwigs...

Raven was suddenly beset with shame that he should even find the time to think such inconsequential thoughts as these when outside, no more than a mile from where he sat in splendid comfort, the wretched poor of this city were succumbing to the plague, and dying in droves.

Raven roused himself at a loud knock on the door, before his manservant Martin entered the room tentatively. Martin had reflected for two whole weeks on the opportunity Raven had offered him to replace Mr Hicks as the manager of his Northern coal mines, but had in the end decided he was not suited to such a great responsibility. Raven was now sorry that he had offered Martin the post at all because it had introduced a measure of doubt into their previously stable and comfortable relationship. On Raven's side, he wondered if he had perhaps overestimated Martin's capabilities after all, and that perhaps Martin himself was a better judge of his own limitations than he was. And Raven sensed on Martin's side some unease at having to disappoint his master. So, all in all, there was some unease and disappointment on both sides, and Raven thought it might be some time before circumstances returned to their previous stable and contented level.

Yet Henry Raven had presently more pressing matters to deal with than smoothing his strained relationship with his long time manservant, even though he still believed at heart that Martin had made a poor decision regarding his own future. On the other hand, young Kate Soule was overjoyed that Martin intended to remain with the household, so one person at least was happy at the fruitless outcome of these deliberations. Yet Raven was sure that Martin had not made the decision to stay with the household because of any inclinations for her – despite her sweet waif-like charm, Raven was now sure that Katie meant nothing personal to him at all, which was another source of disappointment to Raven. He would have liked to see Martin courting young Kate because they seemed so well suited to each other, and as a couple could eventually have moved to the estate in Dorset to live out their lives comfortably.

Martin could still not look Raven in the eye quite as frankly as before. 'Excuse me, Master, but you have visitors at the front door. Are you ready to receive them?'

Raven sat up and yawned. 'Yes, of course. Who calls so early on this fine Friday morning?'

'It is the gentleman manager from the King's theatre, Sir Thomas Killigrew, and a servant.' Martin frowned. 'I *assume* this man is a servant since he was not introduced to me, though he carries himself mighty haughty, and dresses exceeding well, for someone with such a black face.'

Raven blinked in surprise. '*Black* face?'

'I believe the servant is a Moor, Master, although I cannot swear to it, having seen their likenesses only in paintings up to now.'

'Then please show them through, where we will discover if you are right in your suppositions.' Raven wondered what Killigrew might have come here for. The leader of the King's company of players had never called here before, and their acquaintanceship, such as it was, was merely polite at best, therefore this personal visit to his home was a surprise. Nevertheless Raven stood up to greet his unexpected visitors.

In a moment Sir Thomas breezed into the room, accompanied by a tall foreign man of Moorish appearance. Raven had made several voyages to the Barbary Coast of North Africa, and to Spain, so had seen Moors and Berbers at first hand. This gentleman was most decidedly of Moorish appearance, but dressed in the style of a conservative English gentleman, which because of his imposing size required perhaps twice the area of broadcloth that would be needed normally. Unlike Sir Thomas, the Moor had at least not given in to the current excessive fashion for canions and other lace frills to his coat and breeches, for which sensible decision Raven duly gave him an unspoken measure of respect.

Sir Thomas bowed in courtly fashion. 'Please excuse me for calling without an invitation, Mr Raven, but I felt it my duty to make you aware of unfortunate tidings.'

Raven felt a shiver of apprehension as he wondered if this visit had anything to do with Molly. Sir Thomas knew of course that Molly was his mistress; Raven had made a point of informing him personally in order to hopefully persuade him to keep his hands to himself as far as Molly was concerned. Killigrew was well known for his licentious and lewd behaviour towards the comely young actresses of his company, and Raven intended by this deliberate action to warn him off from taking any further liberties with

Molly.

'Is this something to do with Molly?' Raven asked abruptly.

Killigrew inclined his long mane of white hair. 'Indeed so, sir. I regret to tell you that she suffers from the plague...'

Raven felt his heart lurch. 'Are you sure? Has a physician examined her?'

Sir Thomas indicated his companion. 'My worthy acquaintance here, Mr Bassam Abdul Latif, is treating her...'

'So she lives still?' Raven cried in relief.

The Moor spoke up. 'Ay, indeed, sir. And she should now hopefully continue so for many years more, *insha' Allah*, although 'twas a close run thing. She came as near death as I think a human can come, and yet draw back from the brink. She has an admirable constitution, and immense reserves of strength within that slender feminine body.'

Raven had a thought about this man whose name struck a chord in his memory. 'Are you perhaps the famed apothecary of Venice, sir? Are you Bassam the Moor?'

Killigrew interrupted. 'He is, sir, and therefore young Molly could not have been in better hands.'

Raven stepped forward and offered the giant Moor his hand. 'Then I must shake the hand of the man who has saved Molly's life, sir. I only regret that I was not there to help you, yet I had no inkling that she was sickening.'

The Moor took his hand gratefully. 'And I must shake thy hand in return, sir, and acknowledge the famous Henry Raven, whose diverting experiments with Dr Croone have made both you gentlemen famous all over Europe. I have read many of your own accounts of these experiments, sir, and even translated some of them into Arabic and Turkish for wider dissemination.'

Raven was surprised to learn that his minor published accounts of those experiments appeared to have spread far beyond the lecture room at Gresham College, and the Royal Society. ''Tis a modest enough contribution to human knowledge, sir, and not on a level with your own achievements, by all accounts.'

'Perhaps my talents have been rated more highly by my acquaintances than they should,' Bassam suggested deprecatingly. 'Yet of all the people I have nursed through the plague, I take most pleasure in saving Mistress Molly, for her talents and her youthful beauty make her special indeed. I am happy to say that I believe her now to be out of mortal danger.'

'Then I thank you again, sir. But how and when did Molly catch the plague?' Raven cast an irritated eye in Sir Thomas's direction. 'No one saw fit to inform me.'

Killigrew spoke up apologetically. 'I do beg your pardon, sir. But I had been told by one of my other actresses of the company – Mary Pettican –

that there had been some falling out between you and Molly, so I was not sure that I should take it upon myself to tell you of her condition. And to be honest, she seemed so close to death that I was barely able to think clearly of my duty, sir. It has been a most trying time.'

Raven was apologetic in return. 'Then please pardon me, sir, for speaking out of turn. It is clear to me that you have done your duty by Molly, as both her employer and her mentor, while I have failed in my responsibilities towards her. I should not have neglected her, but, contrary to this lady, Mistress Pettican, this was not due to any falling out between us. Of late, I have been fully occupied assisting with the treatment of the many other plague victims in St Giles. I have deliberately stayed away from Molly these last few weeks because I worried about bringing the agents of the plague into her own home. Had Molly visited St Giles, do you think? It is close to Whetstone Park where her mother lives. Does that perhaps explain how she contracted the plague?'

Killigrew shook his head dolefully. 'I think not, sir. I believe she caught it from one of her fellow actors, Mr Whelan. *He* may perhaps have visited St Giles of late.'

Raven frowned when he heard that name. 'Is that *Patrick* Whelan you mean?'

'Indeed so. He succumbed first a fortnight ago, and now the poor boy lies mouldering in the churchyard of St Katherine Cree in Leadenhall Street.'

Raven's mind was distressed as he remembered the circumstances of his last meeting with Molly. So that young actor had truly been sick after all...

It seemed then that Molly had told the truth about that, but that did not mean of course that she had not also done the deed with him. The fact that she had apparently caught the plague from Whelan suggested the possibility that they might even have been intimate together for some time. Raven frowned as the full implications of Killigrew's information dawned on him. 'Yet I have heard no reports of any plague cases in the city. Why was Whelan's case, and Molly's, not reported, sir?'

Killigrew became defensive. ''Twas a mere lapse on my part, sir. I should indeed have reported this, but in my urge to save Molly, all else slipped from my mind.'

Raven made no issue of this, but was convinced that Killigrew's reticence to report this case of plague among his company probably had more to do with his desire to keep his theatre open as long as possible. 'You are sure that Molly has the plague, and not another ailment? 'Tis unusual enough for anyone to survive the plague, and especially this virulent strain. There have been a hundred cases in the parish of St Giles, and a hundred deaths to follow.'

Bassam answered with authority. 'Believe me, sir, it is certainly the plague that she had; I have seen enough cases of this cursed affliction in my time. I am sure also that although my compounds and potions certainly aided Molly in her fight against this infection, yet the real victor was Molly herself, who seems to possess a strong innate resistance to the disease.'

'I am sure that she would be most appreciative of a visit from you, sir, even though she is still very weak, of course,' Killigrew added. 'Yet I do not doubt that she will be back on stage in the theatre before very long, for which everyone will be grateful. Already she talks of returning to see her friends at the theatre.'

'I will go and see her this very day,' Raven promised. 'And I must thank you both again for your care and regard for Molly. I should have performed this duty myself, if I had but known. Yet it matters not, provided she is come safe through this ordeal...'

*

Esther Linney was glad indeed that she had left the City of London many miles behind, and now lodged in the green tranquillity of the riverside village of Little Chelsea, away from all the noise and dirt of the town. And particularly to escape from this severe and frightening outbreak of the plague in the parish of St Giles, which had caused such panic and unrest in the city during the last two weeks. Esther had managed to leave the city just before a first mass exodus of worried citizens had begun, and so her journey here had been both uneventful and unremarkable. Trundling along in an old ox-cart on the road to Fulham Palace, the journey had even been almost enjoyable at times, if sometimes made uncomfortable by the hard rutted surface of the Middlesex roads, which, in her delicate condition, gave her some cause for alarm. Although her baby was not due for another five weeks by her reckoning, something about the lusty movement of this child within her womb told Esther that this active baby was clearly anxious to see the world as soon as possible, therefore might not choose to wait for the full natural term. She was half-convinced now from the baby's vigorous movements that she carried a boy child, and had already begun to think of possible names for this new arrival to the world. She toyed with the idea of calling him Ralph after his father, but soon dismissed that notion when that father was certain to be missing entirely from the boy's life...

Yet Esther could not complain of her new situation. Mr Warboys had been as good as his word, and had provided her with a sweet and spacious thatched cottage at the end of a dusty lane, all to herself. It was not as beautiful as Dorset, of course, yet it was still a pretty place, located on the edge of the village, with a vegetable patch full of cabbages and turnips in front, and hedges of blackthorn and downy rose growing in profusion all around. Beyond the hedges, the Thames wound its sun-speckled way through lush water meadows, and presented an entirely different aspect here to the busy and crowded thoroughfare it was at London Bridge.

Esther had quickly grown to enjoy the morning hush of this rustic place, the lengthening spring days with fresh greenery bursting forth from every bough and branch, and the wondrous breathless sunsets over the river, filled with circling swallows and a painter's palate of colours,

Esther was less appreciative, though, of the woman whom Mr Warboys had hired as her helper and midwife. This was Mistress Bernadette Worme, a stern young spinster of Puritan dress and manners, who lived in a house close by in the village, and who had some knowledge of delivering babies. Esther was grateful for the physical help from Mistress Worme of course, because the more arduous tasks of housekeeping – fetching water from the well, washing clothes by the stream, or keeping a fire burning in the hearth – were all hard things to manage when carrying a lusty child in your womb. Yet Mistress Worme, though still young enough at five-and-twenty to remember her own childhood without difficulty, was not an amiable woman, nor did she regard herself as a servant to Esther, but as someone superior to her in both social status and moral authority.

Perhaps the moral aspect of this superiority stemmed from Mistress Worme's clear disapproval of Esther's unwed state. Esther had been tempted to lie to her and call herself a young widow, yet deceit was unnatural to her, and she preferred people to know her truly for what she was.

Despite the fact that Mr Warboys had paid her so well, Mistress Worme did not seem obliged by that generosity to extend any great warmth or womanly compassion to the object of her endeavours, but instead rather to act as Esther's unwanted muse and relentless conscience.

Yet Esther in her turn was in no mood to be judged so harshly by a woman who knew so little of her history, so was equally cold in return. Esther did not mind being judged severely for her own actions, yet she was defensive of the innocent child who resided in her womb, and who deserved no such sanction from anyone.

On this warm Friday morn, Esther was tending to her newly planted carrots, which were already sprouting feathery green leaves in the late April warmth. She did not know how long she would live here, yet old habits died hard, and she had always sown carrots at this time of year, and then fought a long summer battle with the predations of the indefatigable carrot fly.

Mistress Worme was in the cobbled yard at the side of the cottage, scrubbing the stains from a stubborn bed sheet in a wooden tub, and eyeing Esther with apparent disdain from time to time. In return, Esther gave her equally cold answering looks, although grateful that she did not have to wash that stiff old bed sheet herself. For all the woman's pretensions to gentility, and her superior manner, Esther was prepared to acknowledge that Mistress Worme did know how to wield a scrubbing brush and was no shirker when it came to housework.

Esther had felt queasy this morning, although it was many weeks since she had suffered any regular morning sickness. Then after breakfast she had started to feel regular muscular pains that seemed to come with increasing frequency as the morning went on. Esther told herself that she worried without cause – her baby had been much quieter of late, with less kicking and jostling inside her womb, so seemed resigned now to stay within its dark prison for the allotted term, still a full three weeks more. It was true that Esther had no direct experience of being with child on which to base this judgement, and that her knowledge of the process was predicated more on the habits of cows than on humans. Yet she had been reluctant to inform Mistress Worme of the pains she experienced today, hoping that they would simply go away by themselves.

Now the contraction pains were coming so frequently that Esther could no longer deny the truth to herself. The baby was coming today, there was little doubt of it, and Esther knew she would have to ask Mistress Worme soon for her assistance in the matter. If Mistress Worme had been a more amiable woman, and less of a termagant, then Esther would, no doubt, have told her already of her condition. But now the pains were so bad, and came so quickly, that Esther knew that there was no other recourse but to turn to this harridan for help.

But even as she called out to Mistress Worme for assistance, Esther knew that she had left it too late already, because with a sudden rush, her waters broke…

*

As he was about to knock for admittance at the street door of the now familiar house in Bow Street, Henry Raven met Mistress Celia Hornett just departing. Celia was a most handsome woman, and was dressed today in the height of fashion, therefore did not look like anyone's common expectation of what a bawdy house keeper should be. If he had not known of her profession and merely chanced on her in passing in the street, then Raven was convinced that he would have taken Mistress Hornett for a lady of moderately high society.

She curtsied civilly enough to him, but there was a glitter of disapproval in her eye, and her manner was colder than it had been on their previous meetings. To Raven's inquiry after Molly's health, she answered with bleak severity. 'I see that you have heard this unwelcome news, Mr Raven. I am glad that you finally show your face here again, sir; your presence has been sorely missed of late while Molly has been laid low with this dreaded affliction. It was fortunate that Sir Thomas Killigrew proved himself a *worthy* friend to Molly, and found this renowned Moorish apothecary to minister to her. Sir Thomas may have many deficiencies of character, yet it seems that in the fundamentals, he is very sound. Unlike *other* of Molly's friends, who have been so neglectful towards her…'

Raven was cool in response, not liking to be lectured to by this bawdy house madam, even though she was Molly's foster mother. 'I have been occupied excessively of late, Madam, and I truly did not know Molly was taken with this sickness until today.'

Celia sniffed. 'I doubt not that a more considerate gentleman than you would have been attentive to her, and would have discovered the truth earlier, sir. Molly was close to death scarce more than a week ago, and sore distressed that you did not come to her in a spirit of conciliation…'

Raven frowned. 'Conciliation, Madam?'

Celia raised her parasol against the warm morning sun that bathed Bow Street in an unfamiliar golden glow. 'I know that you and she had a lover's tiff over her young actor friend, Mr Whelan, sir. But that gentleman is now sadly deceased, and nearly took Molly to the grave with him.' She hesitated. 'I hope that I do not give the impression of anything untoward between this young actor and Molly, sir. I trust you understand that there were never any foundations for the suspicions you might have had of Molly's conduct. Molly has always been most loyal and principled in her devotion to you, sir.'

'I am sure that she is, Madam,' Raven assured her, although his conviction on that point was less than certain. There was no doubt that his view of Molly had been jaundiced a little by his friend Mawdsley's opinions of her likely promiscuity, and that he could not bury his suspicions of her conduct entirely, even now.

Celia lowered her voice to a whisper, and took his arm in a most forward manner. 'Before you ascend to her rooms, sir, I should warn you that you will find her beauty a little faded by the ordeal of the last two weeks. Yet the dark apothecary is confident that she will recover the glow in her cheeks quickly enough. And I am confident too, sir, now that you are returned to her.'

Raven bowed to her awkwardly, now feeling some considerable guilt over his conduct to Molly, and acknowledging his sin of neglect…

*

Molly's homely young maid, Bathsheba, let Raven into the apartment.

'The mistress s…sleeps p…presently,' she said to Raven with a pink-cheeked stammer.

Raven gave her his hat. 'Then I shall just sit with her awhile, Bathsheba.'

Raven crossed the sitting room and entered Molly's bedroom as quietly as he could. She was indeed soundly asleep, as Bathsheba had said, her hair a dark moist tangle of curls on the feather pillow. But her unconscious state did at least give Raven a chance to sit by the bedside and examine her face at leisure. It was true that her skin presently looked dry and unhealthy, he had to admit, and that she had lost the glorious pink bloom in her cheeks. Yet to Raven, her sickness had made her more beautiful than he remembered, not less. The girlish plumpness in her face was gone, and revealed startlingly fine cheek bones, as well as emphasizing the beauty of her large blue eyes and her sensuous mouth. And he fancied that the present ghostly whiteness of her skin did give her the look of a Renaissance beauty in a painting by Raphael or Titian. Yet was she truly Raphael's *Madonna of the Meadows*, he wondered, or perhaps more of Titian's *Salome*? Saint or temptress, which was it? She could surely be no saint, though, with her upbringing…

Yet he chided himself for such an unworthy thought. As Mawdsley had said, what did it truly matter if she had been unfaithful to him with this actor Whelan? He told himself that he should just be grateful that the Lord God had chosen to spare her…

Raven saw Molly stir. Then suddenly she was awake, her huge eyes fluttering open. Even with black circles beneath, those wondrous eyes were enough to haunt any man. She blinked in surprise to see him there at her bedside, then smiled weakly. 'I am so happy to see you again, Henry.' She tried to sit up a little as she said this, but he bade her lie still.

'It does seem a long time since we last met, Henry. Long for me because I worried that you had left me that day with an ill opinion of my conduct.'

'I have no ill opinion of you, Molly,' Raven said uneasily. 'I take your character as it is, and like you very well for it.'

'Yet you still believe that I have been unfaithful to you; I see it in your eyes.' Molly looked hurt by the thought.

'It is of no matter whether you have been faithful or not,' Raven argued unconvincingly. 'You made me no such promise, and I in turn sought no such assurance from you.'

'I doubt your sincerity, Henry. It is clearly important to you. And I want you to understand that I have been entirely faithful to you over the past months, and will continue to be so, as long as you want me.' Molly glanced around the rich furnishings of the bedroom, at the wall hangings of Tyrian tapestry, the fine linen on the four poster bed, the pewter wash basin and plates on the oak table, and the cypress chests full of her new gowns. 'I would rather have your good opinion than all of these other fine things you have given me.'

She reached out her hand and he took it at once, warmed again with affection for her, and now convinced by her hurt manner that she spoke the truth. 'Then I believe you, Molly, and we will speak no more of it. In any case, my absence from this house was not done in a fit of pique. I have been occupied the whole of my days with the outbreak of the plague in St Giles, which has killed a hundred innocent souls so far, and will kill many more before it is done. You and Mr Whelan are apparently the first cases within the city itself, yet it can only be a matter of time before it spreads properly to the city. Then thousands may become afflicted.' He squeezed her hand, then felt her brow. 'The apothecary was right, though – you have no trace of fever remaining. You are exceeding fortunate to be breathing still, Molly, when so many others have succumbed.'

Molly stirred a little. 'Perhaps it was not the plague that I had, but some lesser disease, despite what the excellent Bassam says. I am sure that I was never bitten by any rat…'

'But you have been bitten by many fleas, as we all have in this city during the warmer months,' Raven pointed out. 'No, it was most certainly the plague that you had. You suffered the buboes under the arms, but your skin did not then waste away and blacken as with most other victims. It seems you must have some special resistance to these little animals that cause this disease.'

Molly blinked in surprise. '*Little animals*? What are these, Henry?'

Raven patted her hand. 'These are postulated only, therefore no one can truly say whether they exist or no. According to my friend Mr Hooke at the Royal Society, though, diseases like the plague are caused by tiny animals that enter the blood stream through a flea bite or something similar, and then proliferate inside your body, like an invading army.'

Molly smiled. 'Your friend has a powerful imagination to imagine such tiny animals burrowing inside me.'

Raven shook his head. 'Perhaps it is not merely an act of imagination, Molly. According to Hooke, these animals have even been glimpsed by a Dutchman with some magic instrument that can make the infinitesimal appear large.' Raven looked into her eyes, marvelling at their brightness still, despite her suffering such a debilitating affliction. 'Since you have such resistance to these tiny animals, my friend Dr Croone will no doubt wish to study your body in intimate detail to see what is so special about it.'

Molly smiled back engagingly. 'I would gladly accept your close scrutiny of my body, Henry, but I draw the line at being studied by your friends of the Royal Society, worthy gentlemen though they doubtless are.'

Raven laughed with her. 'There is one good thing in all this suffering you have endured, Molly. In view of the coming outbreak of the plague, I did think to send you out of the city a safe way, perhaps to Kensington or Chiswick…'

Molly shook her head vehemently. 'So far, Henry? I will not go.'

Raven gave her a wry look. 'I thought you would say as much, Molly. But 'tis no longer strictly necessary for your health to leave the city, although it might still be a wise thing to do, since living conditions here will become difficult soon, no doubt. As far as your health is concerned, you are now the safest person in this city. Because the one certain thing about the plague is that, if you suffer it and survive, then you can never catch the affliction again.'

Molly was amazed. 'Truly? Then that is welcome news indeed. Yet I can hardly celebrate this fact when I fear for all my friends in the city who are at risk. And what of you, Henry? Are you not at a severe risk of catching the plague, either from me, or from these poor victims in St Giles?'

'Yes, I am most certainly at risk,' Raven admitted. 'Yet I have begun the habit of bathing once a day in a large tub, and administering the oil of a certain Mediterranean herb that is meant to discourage flea bites.'

Molly smiled. 'I think that I smell it on you, Henry. It is quite pungent, and may deter more than fleas from coming near you. Yet if this balm does keep you safe, then I shall welcome it despite its strong aroma, and may even help you apply it, if you wish it...'

Raven and Molly were interrupted in this increasingly intimate conversation by the sudden arrival of an unexpected visitor, who entered the room after only the slightest of knocks at the bedroom door.

Raven stood up in surprise at the manner of this gentleman's entry. Clearly this was no stranger, but a regular visitor to this bedroom by his confident swagger. Raven took in the man's tall stature and fine clothes: baggy Rhinegrave breeches decorated excessively with *canions,* a long velvet coat of Continental cut with silver buttons, and fine lace French *cravate* around his strong muscular neck. He carried no sword, but instead a mahogany walking stick, and fine calfskin gloves.

Raven turned in perplexity to Molly to explain the presence of this handsome middle-aged dandy in her apartments.

Molly obliged, but uneasily. 'Henry, this is M'sieur Philippe Desargues of Paris. He is an acquaintance from the theatre, and has been of great service to me during my sickness.'

Raven turned to Desargues and bowed, but his voice remained cool and suspicious. 'Then I am infinitely obliged to you, M'sieur. *Je suis heureux de faire votre connaissance.'*

The man bowed coolly in response. 'Ah, you speak French, sir. That is most thoughtful of you, sir, but perhaps we had better converse in your language for sweet Molly's sake.'

'You speak excellent English, M'sieur, and with no accent at all,' Raven noted with surprise. 'That is unusual for a Frenchman.'

M'sieur Desargues agreed. 'It is *most* unusual, sir. But then I am a most unusual fellow...' – he laughed – 'who must also confess to having an English nurse as a child, who stayed with me for many years, and made me a pronounced anglophile.'

Raven glanced at Molly, who still looked most discomforted by her visitor's unexpected arrival. 'It seems that Molly has had the blessing of many friends to help her through her affliction.'

Desargues came to the opposite side of the bed from Raven, and took Molly's slightly resisting hand. 'And why should she not? Such a pretty creature deserves the devotion of her many friends, does she not?' He leaned down and kissed the back of her hand. 'And what an actress she is, sir. Why, I saw her play Queen Zempolla in *The Indian Queen* just two weeks ago, and she was...*formidable...*'

*

A few minutes later, after Henry had left, Molly turned testily to M'sieur Desargues. 'I am most grateful for your continued support, M'sieur, but now that I am recovered, it is not appropriate for you to simply march into my bedroom unannounced.'

Desargues bowed extravagantly. 'I beg your pardon, Molly. I have visited you here daily during your sickness, and always been welcomed by the Moor who was caring for you, so I had not thought to change my behaviour. Your maid Bathsheba let me in today; she is used to see me here, and knows me to be your true friend.'

Molly's ill temper was mollified a little by this disarming apology. 'I do not wish to appear ungrateful, M'sieur. I thank you again for all your help and your concern, particularly when we are truly so little acquainted. But I really...'

'Ah, but I feel that I have known you a long time, Molly,' Desargues interrupted, disarming her even more with a warm smile. 'On stage, your performances reveal your own character in intimate detail to the audience. I for one feel that anyway, Molly, and have become very close to you because of it.'

Molly's vision was getting back to normal after her illness, and she could inspect her visitor's face clearly today for almost the first time. In the warm glowing light of a spring day, he no longer seemed the sinister figure that he had once been when waiting nightly at the stage door for her to appear, but instead the epitome of charm and affability. Yet there was still something a little unsettling about him, although now for different reasons. He clearly wanted to bed her, she was convinced of it, perhaps as some sort of challenge to his ageing manhood. That seemed the only plausible reason for all this attention she had received from him. Henry had certainly thought the same of this French dandy, judging from his renewed peevishness as he left. Molly could see regretfully that the visit of this man had revived Henry's suspicions of her conduct – no doubt he now thought Desargues to be yet another of her many lovers from the theatre.

'You truly do not wish me to visit you again, Molly?' Desargues asked disappointedly. 'Are you concerned that I might frighten off your lover Mr Raven?' He tut-tutted. 'Oh, do not deny that he is your lover, my sweet, and the provider of these splendid rooms. I see everything with these experienced eyes. There is nothing you can tell a Frenchman about the art of love and seduction; we understand the pain and pleasure all too well.'

It would have been the politic thing to do, of course - to bar this gentleman from any future visits, in order to allay Henry's suspicions of her conduct. Yet Molly had grown a little impatient with Henry and his doubts over her faithfulness by now. If he really thought her such a wanton trull as all that, Molly wondered peevishly why he even tolerated her. She was not minded therefore to go further out of her way to silence his suspicions now; he would have to accept her word that she was entirely faithful.

And M'sieur Desargues was a most handsome, witty and worldly man, and probably wealthy too, so Molly decided that she could not afford to reject his friendship out of hand, not when her own future was so uncertain.

Finally, after long reflection, she laid her head back on the pillow and said, 'No, M'sieur Desargues. I do not wish you to stop visiting me. Please continue to come and see me, if it pleases you...'

# CHAPTER 9

Saturday, 29<sup>th</sup> April 1665

The nearest large town to the Raven family's Dorset estate at Salwayash Manor was the town of Bridport, which had a bleak claim to fame that was at odds with its picturesque setting at the confluence of the River Brit with its tributaries, the Simene and the Asker. Bridport had been famous since the Middle Ages for the manufacture of rope, which did noble service for the King's navy in holding aloft the fluttering sails of its warships. But this same rope also performed a more dubious function in the service of the hangman - so much so that the phrase 'stabbed with a Bridport dagger' was commonly used to describe someone who had been hanged. The local rope was of such superior quality that, two centuries before, King Henry VII had decreed that all hemp within a five-mile radius of the town was to be reserved for the navy. Yet, perhaps unsurprisingly, the hangman had never seemed to run short of rope as a consequence...

Yet Henry Raven's sister Catherine was glad that her home county was also noted for many pleasanter things than the 'Bridport dagger' - for one, the production of extremely fine cloth. The village of Blandford for example was famed for its unequalled bone lace, and Stalbridge for its stockings that graced many a society beauty's leg.

The village of Salwayash had no such special claims to fame as Blandford or Stalbridge, although there was now a small establishment owned by the Raven family in the village that employed several local women and produced linen of an increasingly fine quality under Catherine's patronage. Catherine was today wearing a fine linen petticoat made in that very establishment, and reflected on this fact with quiet pleasure as she enjoyed the green tranquillity of the beech woods on the Salwayash Manor estate, in company with Dora Bagwell.

Catherine was quietly pleased to have Mistress Bagwell back at the manor. Dora's husband Nathaniel had been a fine man and a loyal servant of the Raven family in Dorset for thirty years, and his death two years ago had been a great blow to Dora. Last spring, childless, and finally alone, she had declared her wish to get away from the constant reminders of her sad loss and so had taken up the position of housekeeper to her brother Henry at his London town house. But being a country woman through and through, Dora was ill-suited to city life, and, according to Henry, had soon begun to miss the quieter pleasures of a country life, and the society of her surviving sister and her other former servant friends. So when Dora had recently expressed a wish through her master to return to Dorset, Catherine had been only too content to accept this change to her household.

Apart from the benefits to Dora herself, Catherine had reasons of her own to welcome Mistress Bagwell back into the fold. Since Dora had left for London a year ago, the manor had suffered the deaths of two more elderly servants – a married couple, Joshua and Edith Witcombe - who had been the backbone of the household for twenty years, and who had held it together through many trials and tribulations - even through the traumatic times of the Civil War, and then the deaths of their former master and his lady. The final departure of the Witcombes from this mortal coil, within a few weeks of each other, had left the Raven household with only young and callow servants to stand in their places, because those few mature servants who remained at the manor were either too decrepit by now, or too ill-suited by nature and character, to take on a more leading role. This had left the household as a whole suffering from a lack of proper leadership and discipline, a problem which had been exacerbated by the departure of Catherine's stern-tongued sister Mary to Kent a month ago as a married woman. Mary's regular tongue lashings had long kept the idle and baser inclinations of the younger servants in check, but Catherine, being a gentler soul, was not able to imitate her departed sister in this regard with any conviction, so the situation had deteriorated since her departure. As a consequence, Catherine was sorely in need of a mature and controlling authority in the house, and Dora was the perfect choice to fit such a role, having both the severe presence and the determined character to make the other servants jump to her commands.

On this fine Saturday morning, Catherine had invited Dora to walk with her on the estate. This was partly to discuss the new servant arrangements in the manor in private, but also because Catherine wished to question Dora discreetly about Henry's private life in London, particularly his relationship with this importunate young actress Molly Titchen, about whom Dora should by rights be a mine of useful further information.

Catherine had not intended the walk to be so long, but her discussion with Dora over the situation of the household was so long and interesting that, before they were hardly aware of it, they found themselves beyond the steep sheep pastures, and deep within the beech wood. As usual Catherine had stopped to examine every wildflower of note on the way: the dark green arum leaves of lords-and-ladies hiding in shady places, early gentian just showing its vivid blue flowers on the chalk slopes, while stars-in-grass (which some locals referred to coarsely as bastard toadflax) was flowering a month early on south-facing hillsides. Not that Catherine could teach Dora anything about the local herbs and flowers: Mistress Bagwell still recognized all the wild plants of Dorset like old friends, and knew of their use as palliatives and cures for various ailments. Dora had long been known locally for her healing arts: her father had a deep knowledge of country herbs and their uses in curing maladies, and he had passed much of this learning on to Dora as a girl. Yet the year she had spent in London had taken some physical toll on Dora, Catherine could see; she was clearly not used to such long enervating country walks up hill and down dale any more, and Catherine noticed with concern that Dora was puffing greatly after an hour's hard walking, and also looking very red in the face.

Catherine decided to slacken her pace her little as a consequence, and also acknowledged to herself that it was perhaps time to turn again for home once they reached the southern edge of the beech wood. As they walked on, their feet trailing through the remnants of last year's decaying leaves, Catherine inquired politely after the condition of Dora's sister, who lived close by in the village of Limbury, and who suffered greatly from dropsy and swollen limbs.

'Constance still suffers severely from shortness of breath and palpitations of the heart, though she seems a little improved in health since Christmas, Mistress,' Dora answered politely.

'Perhaps she is simply glad to have her only sister back in the neighbourhood, and able to visit her regularly?'

'Perhaps so,' agreed Dora, still perspiring, and red in the face, despite the slower pace. 'And I am content to be back too, even though I had to leave young Kate behind in London with the master. It would not have been right to deprive the master of another servant, until he has time to find a proper replacement for me. In any event, Kate truly does not want to leave London; she is much enamoured of young Martin and wants him for her husband.'

Catherine made mental note of that. 'Ah, is that so? Well, he is a handsome and hard-working fellow, and she a pretty waif-like thing, so perhaps it is not unexpected. And does Martin return her affections?'

'Not so as you would notice, Mistress. He was walking out with a pretty maid from a nearby house in St Martin's Lane, but this girl has now rejected his advances, I believe.'

Catherine reflected. 'Then perhaps there is still hope for Kate in pursuing her troth. The whole of my brother's household may have to leave for Dorset anyway, if the plague takes hold in the city, so both Kate and Martin may have to come and stay here for some time. And perhaps in these pleasant vales and hills, Kate may be able to inspire Martin to a greater degree of affection than in the town. '

'Tis not a matter of *if* the plague comes to the city, Mistress, but *when*,' Dora declared bleakly. 'Or so the master said anyway. He has worked exceeding hard to try and halt the spread of this affliction, and keep it confined to the poor parish of St Giles. In fact his dedication to this task has made him quite the lauded hero in the city. Yet even he says that the task is beyond any mortal man — he told me that he feels like Sisyphus, or some such name like that which I never heard before - and he is sure that the plague will soon spread to the city, despite all his efforts.'

Catherine had not known before that her brother took such a leading role in the fight against this worrying outbreak of plague, and she felt a brief spasm of alarm. 'And what of his own health? If he mixes with these plague victims, will he not also succumb himself?' The thought of losing her brother to the plague was almost more than Catherine could bear. He was still a stalwart figure in her life, as much like a father to her as a brother, and she could not imagine life without his comforting and mature presence.

Dora stopped walking for a moment to catch her breath properly. 'There is that danger, of course. Yet the master is sensible of the risks to his own health, and takes what precautions he can to avoid the contagion.'

Catherine frowned. 'Precautions? What precautions can save you from the plague? There are none.'

Dora looked uneasy. 'Perhaps so. Yet 'tis possible at least to discourage fleabites, which my master believes is the method by which the contagion is spread. At his request, therefore, I prepared for him a pungent extract from a certain Mediterranean herb that is most hateful to fleas. Your brother bathes every day after breakfast now, and anoints his whole body with this powerful smelling oil.'

Catherine frowned even more deeply. 'And has it truly protected him from fleabites? How are his limbs and chest?'

Dora seemed to blush a little at this question, though with her face already so ruddy from the walking, it was difficult to say to what degree. 'I cannot answer for certain, of course, since Martin supervises his bath these days,' Dora said. 'Yet from what little I have seen of the master's body of late, there were no new flea bites.'

'Then I can only hope that my brother is right about the cause of the plague.' Catherine was still deeply concerned about Henry despite Dora's pronouncement, since she knew how contagious and virulent the plague was. Three hundred years ago, the Black Death had first come to England, probably landing in ports very near to Salwayash along the south coast, including Melcombe Regis near Weymouth. That then busy port had, according to local legend, been one of the first towns to experience the epidemic, which then went on to wipe out a third of the population of the country...

Dora began walking again, apparently eager to be on her way. 'Please do not fret too much over the master, Mistress. He is a most sensible young man, as you know, and will not risk his own health without good reason.'

Catherine pursed her lips tightly at this remark, and decided that this was the perfect opening to allow her to turn to another disagreeable matter: that of Henry's young actress mistress, Molly Titchen, who, although perhaps not as serious a threat to Henry's wellbeing as the plague, was nevertheless a malevolent influence on him. 'My brother does not have good sense in everything, though,' Catherine complained with an artful sigh. 'If only he showed as much good sense and decorum in his choice of female companion as he does in all other aspects of his life.'

Surprisingly, Dora was not as critical of her brother's choice as Catherine had expected her to be. 'Perhaps he cannot be blamed entirely for his natural inclinations, Mistress,' Dora said thoughtfully. 'The master is young, after all, and most young men are susceptible to female beauty, are they not.'

Catherine was surprised to hear that particular word, "beauty", mentioned, though perhaps she should not have been, given that this new profession of actress was already famed as much for the charm and bewitchment of its practitioners as for their licentious behaviour. *'Beauty?* And is this young actress really so beautiful?' she asked suspiciously.

Dora nodded regretfully. 'I dare say she is considered so, with her fortunate attributes. Dark lustrous curls, a swelling white bosom, and quite a sweet face for someone with her background.'

'She must be a silly girl, though?' suggested Catherine hopefully. 'Empty-headed and vain, and endlessly preening before a mirror, no doubt?'

Dora wavered a little before answering, as if considering her answer with great care. Finally she said, 'I think Molly Titchen is not so stupid as that, Mistress. There is some considerable intelligence in that girl, and perhaps some assertive ambition too. I did see her once in the master's library, reading one of his heavy tomes – something to do with the workings of the human body – and she seemed most engrossed.'

'Scarce suitable reading for a young woman,' Catherine suggested darkly, 'and most likely a simple ruse to entice Henry further and make him think her more intelligent than she really is.'.

'Perhaps so,' Dora agreed reluctantly. 'Yet it did not seem like an affectation. Molly Titchen did seem truly engrossed, and later asked the master some deep and searching questions about philosophy which I could not follow at all.'

Catherine shook her head in bewilderment. 'You make his choice of bed mate seem almost commendable.'

Dora blinked slowly. 'I truly did not like Mistress Titchen at all when the master first brought her into his house, yet I admit that she comported herself well with no great airs or graces. And I believe that she has made the master a happier man. I have not seen him so content before, therefore must acknowledge her part in this.'

This was not truly what Catherine had wished to hear. 'You were not so complimentary of this maid when we spoke at Christmas.'

Dora acknowledged that. 'Yet I did not know her so well then,' she explained, 'nor did I understand what beneficial effect she would have on my master.'

They had finally emerged from the beech wood now, and into the meadow beyond, and the boundary of the Salwayash manor estate. Yet Catherine broke her silent promise to herself and did not turn for home at once, as she had planned to, but carried on a little further. She continued walking across the arable fields beyond, until she caught sight of Esther Linney's cottage, looking even more forlorn than it had a month ago, with the untended herbs in front even more overgrown.

Catherine walked up the narrow track to the front door of the cottage, with Dora trailing a few steps behind her. The interior still bore no signs of life, and the ragged thatch on the roof was now showing some incipient holes which needed urgent repair.

A puzzled Dora asked Catherine why she had come here.

'I thought that I had better send some of our men to repair this roof. Esther will be most displeased if she comes back and finds her precious home open to the elements,' Catherine explained.

'Where is Esther, then?' Dora asked, bemused.

Catherine was surprised. 'You must have heard that she left her cottage nearly three months ago, and is believed to be living in London now?'

Dora shook her head in puzzlement. 'I had not heard such a thing. Why would young Esther Linney go to London? What business could she have there?'

Catherine walked around to the side of the cottage, examining its walls of wattle and daub. 'I know not the reason,' she called out behind her. 'But I was concerned for her, so I asked Henry to try and find her if he could.'

Dora was still perplexed. 'The master never mentioned this to me, Mistress.'

Catherine thought it odd that Henry had never mentioned this matter to Dora, but perhaps he had been too preoccupied with other matters. She continued her circumnavigation of the cottage, and sighed heavily as she returned to the front again. 'No matter, Dora. Henry could not find her, otherwise I am sure he would have writ and told me of it. Perhaps he has had no time for such distractions, what with the demands of his business, and with this outbreak of the plague.' She regarded Dora with interest. 'You knew Esther's mother well, did you not?'

Dora nodded uneasily. 'Yes, we played together often as children. Her father was a smithy, and they lived close to the farm where I grew up. We made a strange pair as children, though – she so white and beautiful and tall, and me so skinny and stunted and freckled.'

Catherine looked around, seeing again with distress the wild and untended state of Esther's fields. This farm would revert quickly to wilderness, if something was not done to cultivate these fields again, she thought. But all she said was, 'Esther has grown up to look exactly like her poor mother, I believe.'

Dora nodded. 'Ay, there is a striking resemblance...but then there often is between mother and daughter,' she added dryly.

Catherine glanced at her curiously. 'You were living here at the manor when her poor mother was burnt for witchcraft, were you not?'

Dora swallowed uncomfortably. 'I was, and I attended the trial too, though I could not bear to watch the burning on Blackmore Hill, of course.'

'I have been told that Meg Linney was denounced by a local woman...'

Dora looked contemptuous. 'Yes, her name is Judith Pollock. She looks such a sweet grey-haired old spinster, but her heart must be as cold as ice.'

'Yes, the Reverend Smythe pointed her out to me a few weeks ago after Evensong. I was surprised that I did not know this woman before. I had thought that I knew most of the villagers,' Catherine said thoughtfully.

'She has no family, other than a nephew called Jacob Shawn...'

'Not the same youth who has recently joined our household at the manor?' Catherine said in surprise.

'Ay, the very same boy, I believe, Mistress. Yet he is a well-mannered youth from all accounts, and would not deserve to be censured merely because he is related to that ogre of a woman.' Dora's brows darkened. 'If ever a woman deserves to die a horrible death for her sins, 'tis that evil scheming woman. She claimed to have spied on Meg and seen her trying to bring her dead husband back to life with spells and incantations.'

'You think her evidence was a lie?'

Dora shrugged. 'Nay, it was probably the truth. Meg worshipped her poor husband, and the pain of seeing him die slowly in terrible agony was more than her mind could bear. Yet she was no witch; she merely suffered from a sickness of the soul...'

Going finally on their way home again, Catherine and Dora crossed over an ancient stile and then a languid limpid stream before entering another verdant meadow, where bees droned above the dense mass of flowers. The cowslips of early spring were gone now, Catherine saw, but the meadow still blazed yellow with lush expanses of meadow vetchling and toothed medick.

Given the rural tranquillity of this county, it was difficult for Catherine to credit the savageries that had taken place here during the Civil War, a mere twenty years ago. She knew that Dorset had contained a number of key royalist strongholds, such as Sherborne Castle and Corfe Castle, which were completely destroyed in the war. Corfe had been successfully defended against an earlier attack in '43, but an act of betrayal during a second siege in '46 had led to its final capture and the butchering of its Royalist defenders. Yet Parliamentarians had suffered grievous losses too, Catherine knew: the residents of Lyme Regis had been staunch supporters of Parliament and had paid a high price for their political loyalty, being put to the sword three times by Royalist armies. Catherine had heard however that the greatest massacre in Dorset had not been of Cavaliers or Roundheads at all, but of "Dorset clubmen", a group of angry dissident civilians who held allegiance to neither side and who were merely annoyed by the disruption caused by the war. Their clubs and staffs had been no match for the swords and muskets of the Parliamentarian army which had routed them, though, and left the chalk hills of their native county stained red with their blood...

Catherine and Dora left the hills and the open meadows behind, and were soon in a stretch of low lying oak wood near the manor, where many of the trees were even more stately and ancient than in the beech wood, and the forest floor was carpeted by bracken and bramble, and spotted with drifts of bluebells, ramsons and dogs mercury. The onion smell of the ramsons was particularly ripe and strong, as it always was at this time of the year. Some of these trees were hundreds of years old, and one even went back to King Alfred's time, or so it was claimed. Catherine's eyes turned from the track towards one familiar venerable giant that had a trunk so thick and so encumbered with giant boils and blisters and warts that it did seem from a distance like some diseased old leper. Catherine frowned as she noted something odd about the tree today, an additional protuberance from the gnarled old trunk that she had never noticed before.

From this distance, and half obscured by the trees in between, this odd protuberance in the trunk looked for all the world like the outline of a human figure hanging from a bough above. Catherine stared in bemusement, wondering why she had never noticed this strange apparition before. She must have looked at this tree from this same footpath a thousand times or more, yet had never seen this appendage before, which bore such a convincing likeness to a figure with a rope around its neck. Then Catherine's throat became suddenly dry as she began to realize the terrible truth...

Without even a word of warning or explanation to Dora, Catherine turned off the footpath at once, and made her way through the tangle of brambles and bracken towards the giant oak, careless of the thorns that cruelly scratched her hands and tore at her skirts.

Yet, even suspecting the worst, she was still not prepared for the awful sight that met her eyes as she reached the clearing in front of the old oak tree. Catherine's eyes followed the line of the rope that led up from a massive dead trunk anchoring it to the ground, to a thick bough on the living tree and then down to an elaborate noose. Dora had followed close behind in Catherine's steps, and she shrieked aloud in shock when she saw the figure hanging from the noose for the first time.

It was the body of a young fair-haired maid of fifteen years or so, entirely naked, and swinging slightly in the scented breeze...

*

That evening, Catherine sat at home in the wood-panelled parlour of Salwayash Manor and tried to compose herself after the tribulations of this awful day. The sun had still not set, even though it was after seven o'clock, and the warm flood of evening sunlight bathing the room in golden light was a gross contradiction to the grimness of her mood.

After cutting the rope and lowering that poor maid to the ground, and then finally releasing her from the noose, Catherine had left Dora to keep guard over the body until help could be brought from the house. Catherine had wanted to ensure that no fox or badger disturbed the body, nor any carrion crow or magpie allowed to peck the poor child's blue eyes out.

Catherine had not recognized the girl, but Dora believed she might be a milkmaid from a tenant farm on the Warboys estate.

After rushing back to the manor, Catherine had dispatched two of the more capable manservants to relieve Dora and take charge of the body, while she sent young Jacob Shawn on horseback to Bridport to report the incident to the local magistrate Sir Malcolm Batcock. Jacob, although only seventeen, was the best rider in the household, and a mature and capable young man for his age. On receiving the urgent message, Sir Malcolm had immediately sent two of his constables to the scene to investigate, and to take charge of the corpse.

One of the constables, a young man of plain and sober appearance called Adam Drew, had later called at the manor to question Catherine about what she knew of this sad business, which was little enough. Dora too had returned to the manor house in the afternoon after her ordeal in guarding the body, and confirmed that the maid was indeed young Lorna Wanless from the Warboys estate, as she had thought...

Now, at seven o'clock in the evening, one of the young maidservants at the manor entered the parlour and coughed loudly to gain Catherine's attention. This was a new girl to the household, Ruth Pilcher, who, Catherine now realized with a surprise, bore quite a strong and touching resemblance to the dead girl in the oak wood. Catherine was so taken with this thought that she was quite bereft of speech for a moment. Eventually, though, she recovered from her surprise and said, 'Yes, what is it, Ruth?'

The pretty girl curtsied. She looked pale and nervous, as did everyone in the house at the grim discovery of a body so near to the manor. 'Mr Warboys is in the hall, and wishes to speak with you if you have the time and composure, Mistress.'

Catherine got to her feet. 'Yes, of course, Ruth. Please show him through.'

Within a minute, Ralph Warboys strode purposefully into the room. Even in her preoccupied and nervous state, Catherine felt her spirits stir at this man's presence. She saw that he had finally abandoned his mourning clothes for his late wife Margaret, and was sporting gaudier clothes than she had seen him wear of late, which was perhaps unfortunate timing, given the death of a girl from one of his tenant farms. Yet it mattered not how he was dressed; the beauty of this man always shone through no matter what clothes he wore. She noted again the perfect masculine arrangement of his features, his thick and lustrous hair, and his tall and manly figure, and felt the colour rising in her face as a result.

He bowed to her, then stepped forward and took her hand in intimate fashion, causing her heart to race further. 'I am so sorry that you had to be the unfortunate person to find that poor girl, Catherine,' he declared awkwardly.

Catherine sighed. 'Someone had to, and better it was me than one of the more impressionable young girls on the estate. It seems the dead girl is a milkmaid from one of your tenant farms.'

'Ay, indeed. And clearly a troubled girl.'

Catherine blinked as she took in the implication of his words. 'You think Lorna Wanless took her own life, Ralph?'

Warboys released her hand, and stepped back a pace in apparent surprise. 'Do you not? The constable sent from Bridport, Mr Drew, certainly seems to think so. And, having been to the scene, I concur it is the only sensible explanation – the girl had no doubt been jilted by a sweetheart, and in her distress took the ultimate melancholy decision…'

'Yet the noose was made in a most professional manner,' Catherine argued. 'Would a simple maid like Lorna be so accomplished in that direction, Ralph? And how did she get herself up the tree with a heavy noose around her neck, though she be a girl of little strength, judging by her slight body?'

'From what I hear, you managed to lower her down easily enough, Catherine, so I see no reason why Lorna should not have been able to do the same in reverse…'

'But I had the doughty assistance of Dora on the ground, who managed to cut the rope from around the anchor on the ground,' Catherine persisted.

Warboys was equally insistent, though. 'Lorna's clothes were found nearby, so it seems that she decided to leave her life exactly as she came into it. She must have tied one end of the rope around that dead weight of wood on the ground, then ascended the tree some twenty feet to that first thick bough, then jumped off with the rope noose looped around her neck. What other plausible explanation is there?'

Catherine had to admit it was a possibility at least. Yet her instincts told her that the true story of what had happened to poor Lorna Wanless might contain some element even darker than the sad tale that Ralph had described. Though it was hard to believe, she half-suspected that some devil must have done this to that poor girl – an inhuman devil who roamed these green woods and meadows around her beloved manor house, and who had murder in his heart. Yet she found herself unable to express such suspicions directly to Ralph, who was clearly disbelieving of such an unlikely notion, and would no doubt think her to be a wild and undependable person if she should suggest such a fanciful alternative.

Instead she said simply, 'Of course you must be right, Ralph. There can be no other sensible explanation.'

Ralph nodded, apparently reassured by her subdued acquiescence. 'I hope your unpleasant experience today will not cause you any permanent distress, Catherine. Our petty lives must always bring us into contact with death and human tragedies from time to time - 'tis the nature of existence, after all. But we must take consolation in the many joys and pleasures of life, which good must outweigh the bad when measured over a lifetime.'

Catherine smiled at his eloquence and was rewarded with a handsome smile in return. That warm and engaging smile of his was certainly one of *her* secret pleasures in life, if truth be known.

He took his leave of her, though, with yet more disappointing news. 'I am afraid that I must decline your kind invitation to dinner next week, as I must go to London again.'

Catherine failed to hide her disappointment. '*So soon*, Ralph? Were you not there but a fortnight ago?' She began to fish a little. 'One might suspect that you have a new attachment there?'

He looked her frankly in the eyes, making her go a little weak at the knees. 'No, quite the contrary, Catherine. My attachments are all here in Dorset, as I think you well know.' He took her hand again and bent down to kiss the back of it, which Catherine was heartily glad of, because it spared her from trying to hide from him the flush of pleasure that burned her cheeks so brightly.

# CHAPTER 10

Monday, 1st May 1665

On this fine Mayday, Henry Raven was in no mood for any springtime celebrations, being engaged on a further depressing tour of the plague-ridden parish of St Giles with his friend Dr Croone. And his mood was soured even further by the jarring memory of seeing that ageing French dog Desargues hanging around his lady Molly like a rampant old bull, and she openly flirtatious with him in return, despite her weak condition.

Yet the spread of the plague gave him little time for such jealous reflections, or for taking precipitate action over the matter, which was perhaps as well. The situation in the city with regard to the outbreak was now critical. There had been near three hundred reported cases of the plague by now, and many of them were increasingly outside St Giles, so their hopes to keep the outbreak confined to that parish had already been dashed. There had still been no cases reported within the old city walls as yet, but that seemed only a matter of time now when new cases were sprouting up in different locations all the time.

As far as Raven knew, though, Molly was the only person who had caught the disease and survived, so there was indeed something notable about her constitution that merited scientific study, as well as the treatment used by the Moorish apothecary, which also clearly deserved close examination. Yet Raven acknowledged that he was hardly the right man to undertake an objective study of Molly: in regard to her, he was blinded both by love and by his increasingly morbid jealousy. In any case, he could hardly make public the fact that Molly had survived the plague: yesterday, when he had visited her at her home again, she had expressly asked him to keep her affliction secret because she wished to return to the theatre to work, and thought rightly that the rumour of her carrying the taint of this disease might hinder that return. And despite his now uncertain relations with

Molly, Raven found that he could not deny her this consideration.

Anthony Mawdsley had told Raven that the court was already making plans to leave London should the contagion spread to dangerous levels. The King and his family and court would likely leave for one of the outlying palaces, at Richmond or Hampton Court - or if that was not far enough from London to be safe, perhaps even for Oxfordshire. The aldermen and the majority of the other city authorities had however opted to stay at their posts while the Lord Mayor of the city, Sir John Lawrence, had also pledged to stay and support the people of London, no matter what happened. Yet businesses were already closing as wealthy merchants and professional people fled the city. Raven suspected that if the plague raged through the city proper only a small brave number of clergymen, physicians and apothecaries would choose to remain to care for the welfare of their fellow citizens. Raven had however met a casual acquaintance from the Navy Office in Seething Lane, a Mr Pepys who was the Clerk of the Acts there, who had declared his intention, like the Lord Mayor, to stay and ride out the storm, no matter how bad it became. His selfless dedication had convinced Raven that he must do the same, and stay no matter how distressing things became.

Plague doctors now traversed the streets of London, diagnosing victims by the dozen, although Raven knew that many of these gentlemen were unqualified physicians and purveyors of pure quackery, or even outright coney men. Several public health initiatives were now in force to try and halt the spread of the disease, but most had proved ineffective. Physicians had been hired by city officials to advise them on the conduct of their campaign, and burial details had been organized to find and bury corpses discreetly. But in the panic now spreading through the city, these discreet burials had soon been abandoned, and many of the victims were now being hastily buried in mass graves to the north of the city. The city officials had also ordered a cull of dogs and cats, a perplexing decision which Raven had done his best to dissuade them from, since those animals - the cats especially – were the best means to keep the population of rats in check. Fires were now kept burning night and day in houses all over London, despite the warm weather, in vague hopes that the air would be cleansed of contagion by the smoke. Substances giving off strong odours, such as pepper, hops or frankincense, were also being burned in an attempt to ward off the infection, and many physicians recommended the smoking of Virginia tobacco as a preventative measure...

As Henry Raven left yet another hovel where a child had died, he had trouble fighting back a tear, which unusual display of emotion his friend Dr Croone discreetly ignored.

'What think you of this notion of tobacco as a cure to the malady, Henry?' Croone asked almost in desperation, as they made their way down a muddy lane between the lines of wretched houses and hovels that passed for homes in St Giles. The streets were silent now and mostly deserted, no longer enlivened by the sounds of children playing at games, or by the vociferous calls of street traders come to mend pots or sell their wares. Today might be Mayday, but there was no spring joyousness to be found here, only misery, tragedy and death.

Raven glanced at the miserable hovels on each side, with windows shuttered, and wood smoke issuing from makeshift chimneys. 'I think nothing of Monsieur Nicot's poisonous smelling plant. There is no evidence of its efficacy in preventing disease; the smoke is so pungent and distasteful that it may even *cause* disease for all that we know, rather than relieve it.' He sighed heavily. 'No, William, prayer is the only thing that can save these poor people now. We physicians are as helpless in the face of this threat as the most shameless coney man...'

'You are harsh on yourself, and on our profession, Henry,' Croone said mildly.

Raven smiled bleakly. 'I take no pleasure in the fact, William. I merely state the truth as I see it.'

'Yet some people do survive the plague,' Croone pointed out. 'Therefore the body must have some natural means of defence against the agents of disease, be they little invisible animals as Mr Hooke thinks, or some miasma in the air that passes into our bodily fluids, as I believe. If only we could have the opportunity to study a plague survivor in detail, then who knows what we might discover – perhaps some way of improving the body's natural defences. '

'Presently we know too little of the workings and matter of the human body to make such a study worthwhile. Therefore we would do better to leave any fortunate survivor to her...' - Raven corrected himself quickly – 'or *his*...good fortune. We physicians are in the position of explorers landing on the shore of an unknown continent, and catching vague glimpses of forests and mountains in the interior, but of having no comprehension of what life and wonders might exist therein.'

Croone gave Raven a shrewd look. 'Have you encountered a survivor of this epidemic, by any chance, Henry?'

Raven did not want to lie to his friend, but his promise to Molly was the greater imperative in this case. 'No, William, I have not...'

*

On this same sad Mayday, Molly was still weak from the debilitating effects of the disease she had suffered, but had now risen from her bed and was trying to return to the normal routines of her life. At eleven o'clock on this melancholy May morning, she was pleased and touched to hear from her maid Bathsheba that her mentor Sir Thomas Killigrew was at the door below and wished to call on her. Molly immediately bade Bathsheba to bring him up to her sitting room, and stood up formally by the fire to await his arrival. She would have been even more pleased to have seen Henry again, but he had only called once since finding M'sieur Desargues here in her apartments three days ago, and that for only the briefest of times. M'sieur Desargues himself had however called every day since and although his gallantry and charm were a little wearing at times, Molly had still welcomed him warmly, and even flirted mildly with him. Yet she had no intention of ever inviting this elderly gentleman into her bed - not unless she was desperate for his patronage anyway - and for the present he remained no more than a comforting diversion to her while she waited for Henry to return to her in better spirits than of late.

Greeting her, Killigrew was overjoyed to see her up and about. 'I trust you did not find my interference in your private affairs officious, Molly,' he said apologetically.

Molly was not sure of his meaning. 'Interference, sir? What interference?'

'Only that it was I who took the trouble to inform Mr Raven of your condition, when I was not certain that you would have wished me to,' Killigrew explained. 'Mary Pettican had given me to understand that you had broken with Mr Raven, yet I was sure that she must be ill informed.'

Molly reassured him. 'Oh, that she certainly is, Sir Thomas. No, I did not resent your interference, such as it was. And Mr Raven has been to see me here several times as a result, and was most solicitous.'

Sir Thomas beamed his approval. 'Then I am happy that all is resolved between you, and that Mary was quite wrong in her suppositions. You and Mr Raven truly make a most affectionate and suitable couple.'

Molly nodded, but said nothing to encourage further enquiries from Sir Thomas on this sensitive subject. After the awkward silence that followed, Killigrew coughed in embarrassment before continuing. 'I am happy indeed to see you looking so well, Molly, though your bosom is a little thin and sagging, and your face very white and pinched. '

Molly sat down again on her settle by the fire and glanced down at her breasts which were indeed a little sadder in form than usual. 'I thank you for coming, Sir Thomas. And I hope my bosom will soon perk up and recover its former plumpness, and my cheeks their pink glow. If they do, then I have you to thank for it, sir, and your esteemed friend Bassam too, for his kind and efficacious treatment.'

Killigrew bowed in acknowledgment, then stood by the fire, even though it was a warm day. 'I could not stand aside and do nothing. 'Tis a pity he could not save young Patrick too, but if there had to be but one survivor, then I am glad it is you, young Molly. Patrick was a most ordinary actor compared to thee.'

Molly thought sadly of Patrick, who had been a sweet-natured boy at heart, and who, she was now convinced, had held a genuine affection for her. 'I doubt that the Almighty God takes such trivial things as acting ability into consideration when deciding someone's fate,' she said in a melancholy voice.

Sir Thomas was annoyed by this aspersion on his profession. '*Trivial* thing, do you say? Why, we players are the abstracts and brief chronicles of our time – what other profession can lay claim to such a role? A man would better have a bad epitaph than have our ill report while he lives, or so a greater man than I once said. And that is why I have come to see you, Molly. I want to know when you will be well enough to return to the theatre.'

It was the welcome news that Molly wanted to hear. 'You want me to return, sir, even though I have been afflicted with the plague?'

'I do, but perhaps 'tis best not to report to the rest of the company that you have been ill. The theatre remains open for the present, but I cannot afford to have any reports of plague cases in the theatre itself, or else the authorities will close us down. I explained your absence to the company by telling them that you had to leave the city to visit an old friend in the country. I knew in my heart then that you would recover and come back to us in time, although even I did not expect quite such a miraculous deliverance as this.'

Molly inclined her head in grateful ladylike fashion. 'That was most thoughtful of you, sir, not to label me with the stigma of the plague. But will not my thin and pasty appearance give me away anyway?'

'Not at all, young Molly. In another week or so, you will be returned to your full youthful vigour, I have no doubt of it. And to prove my belief of it, I want you to play the Emperor Montezuma's beautiful daughter, Cydaria in Mr Dryden's new play *The Indian Emperor.*'

Molly laughed. 'Then that truly will require some great feat of acting on my part. Only three weeks ago I was Montezuma's rival, the old queen Zempolla in *The Indian Queen*. And now I am to be Mr Hart's daughter? Well, perhaps our true ages match better with this disposition of roles…'

''Tis of no account, since Mr Hart will not play Montezuma this time. You must remember that *The Indian Emperor* is set some twenty years after the rivalries of *The Indian Queen*. Montezuma is now an ageing emperor, and faced with the greatest challenge to his empire, the arrival of the Spaniards under Cortez. In our planned production, Mr Mohun will play the Emperor, while Charles will take on the role of his nemesis Cortez. Young Kynaston will play Guyomar, Montezuma's younger son; and William Wintershall will essay the role of his eldest son, Odmar. The play, as I think you know, is about the conflict between love and honour. Montezuma refuses a chance to save his kingdom from conquest, for personal reasons: "*But of my crown thou too much care dost take; That which I value more, my love's at stake…*",' Sir Thomas quoted with a flourish. 'Cortez takes the opposite course, turning his back on his love for Cydaria to obey the orders of his king, even though he acknowledges that those orders are flawed. Montezuma gets the worst of their conflict, of course; he is tortured by the Spaniards, and the play ends finally with his suicide.'

'Are there no other women's roles?' Molly asked. 'I have only seen a draft of the script, but I seem to recall there are several interesting women in the play.'

Sir Thomas looked her frankly in the eyes. 'Anne Marshall will play Almeria, consort of Montezuma, but I want you for Cydaria. None of the other actresses will do for this role.'

Molly was suspicious of his insistence since it seemed to her that any number of the company actresses could play the part as well as she - Margaret Hughes, or Becky Marshall, or Elizabeth Davenport would all easily suffice. Perhaps even that scheming strumpet Mary Pettican could have a tolerable stab at it, which was the best possible reason for Molly to accept the part, to thwart her malignant ambition. 'Is there something wrong with the play, Sir Thomas? Do you fear the public might not like it, therefore hope that my return might distract some of the criticism?'

Sir Thomas was still standing warming his ample backside by the fire but now he crossed the sitting room and sat finally by Molly on the settle. He patted her hand in fatherly fashion. 'I can see that your illness has not dimmed your intellect, Molly. You can still read me like a book – being the frayed and tattered old manuscript that I am. Yes, you are quite right. I do indeed have some doubts of the play. 'Tis a good play full of rich and wondrous dialogue. But it is also exceeding complicated in plot, so I fear the audience may not warm to it without some pleasant distractions. And we have created such a wonderful costume for the character of Cydaria, a gown resplendent with feathers and jewels and gold, and with the front cut very low…'

Molly nodded, finally understanding. 'Ah, now I comprehend your concern about my shrunken bubbies.'

Killigrew made an expressive gesture. 'I told you once before, Molly, what the audience wants to see. 'Tis tits and bums that our people want to ogle at from the pit, and saucy dialogue to hear.'

'Then of course I will display my bubbies if that is what it takes to fill the theatre again,' Molly declared with a smile. 'And in the meantime, I will eat myself back into plumpness so that our patrons are not too disappointed.'

'Yes, the plumper the better,' Killigrew said frankly. 'Because of the complex nature of the plot, Mr Dryden is determined that on opening night he will distribute a program to the audience, to explain the connection between this play and his earlier *The Indian Queen*. I have tried to dissuade him from this foolishness – it will merely perplex the audience even more. But never fear, when you step out on stage under those bright candles, with all your feathers, and your painted face and legs on display…'

Molly frowned. '*Legs* on display?'

Sir Thomas blinked innocently. 'Did I not say? That the costume only comes to above the knees…'

Molly's frown deepened. 'And what is below the knees?'

Killigrew smiled roguishly. 'Why, nothing much at all, but coloured silk stockings and pink garters.'

Molly laughed out loud with delight. 'Then how can I possibly refuse?'

*

Esther Linney had been a mother for only three days, yet that state now seemed as natural to her as breathing to keep her own body alive. She had still not recovered from the sheer physical wonder of her baby, though, and of the miracle that she could have produced from within her womb such a perfect little human being. Her baby's early birth had not caused him any physical problems as far as she could see – he seemed as perfectly formed and healthy as any full term infant.

She had not made any arrangements to have the baby christened yet – perhaps that might be impossible in the village church given her unmarried state, and the stern and disapproving looks of the local parson, a young man who seemed to take a positive joy in threatening his parishioners with hellfire and damnation. Yet, christened or not, Esther had already resolved to call the baby Henry after her own first love. It was true that Henry Raven had been far from beautiful as a boy, while her own baby son was both perfect and beautiful. Yet although the baby only looked blankly at her presently with his big blue eyes, Esther fancied she saw something of Henry Raven's amiable character in that sweet little face.

Mistress Worme had been a great comfort to her during the delivery, being so familiar with the process, and a calm reassuring presence throughout. For once, her severe character had been a blessing, because her concise commands during the birth had been devoid of emotion and therefore the epitome of clarity, so that Esther had borne those commands and the pain of childbirth with equal detachment and determination. Even in the three days since, Mistress Worme had been a blessing, teaching Esther many things she would otherwise have merely had to guess at, and inducting her rapidly into the art of motherhood. Mistress Worme might not be a mother herself, yet she seemed to understand all the intimate secrets and needs of a three-day-old human being with unerring precision.

On this warm Mayday, Esther stood above the makeshift cradle in the parlour of her cottage, and smiled again at her baby's sleeping form. But then she frowned as she heard what sounded like a distant clap of thunder. Baby Henry did not stir even faintly at the noise, though, deep in slumber.

Esther went to the front door to investigate the weather. This morning had been uniformly fine and dry with scarce a cloud in the sky, so she wondered whether the noise was truly thunder, or whether it was perhaps the boom of a cannon. Yet who would be firing cannon near the village of Little Chelsea on this holy day? she wondered uneasily. Could it perhaps be some sort of warning about the worsening plague in the city to the east?

Esther was soon reassured, though, to see that it must have simply been thunder that she heard after all: the sky was overcast to the west now, filled with billowing storm clouds, shot through with angry streaks of black and grey. The wind was blowing hard too, flexing the tops of the willow trees across the way, and sending swirling gusts through her vegetable patch. So it seemed that there was a thunderstorm on its way after all, despite the fine start to the day, which was perhaps no undesirable thing given the bone dry state of the soil after a month with almost no rain. Above the noise of the rising wind, Esther also heard the sound of an unseen carriage passing by behind the tall and rampant hedgerow at the front of the cottage, and was curious to see who this might be. There was never very much wheeled traffic at all on this dusty lane that passed the cottage, as it was only a side track from the main street through the village, and one moreover that went nowhere but to a few isolated cottages. Mistress Worme herself lived in one of those nearby cottages, yet she had no carriage of course, nor even a cart, and walked everywhere, like all of the villagers.

Her curiosity piqued, Esther walked quickly through the vegetable patch in front of the house and poked her head through the gap in the hedgerow that led to the lane, but was only in time to see the carriage – a grand coach-and-four from its ornate rear - already disappearing around the next bend in the road. Esther was not so curious, though, as to chase after it to see who its grand occupants might be, especially with her baby lying untended indoors.

She retraced her steps back up the path to the front door of the cottage where she glanced up at the thatched roof with some degree of affection. Esther was firmly attached to this place now, and was minded to stay here as long as Mr Warboys would continue to pay the rent for it. It was bigger than her own cottage back in Dorset, and in better repair too, with three rooms, a kitchen, a bedchamber, and a parlour of sorts, all with stone flagged floors and glass in some of the windows.

The front door that led directly into the parlour was still open as she had left it, and the wind now whistled through from the side door that led through the kitchen to the yard and the outside privy. Esther could not remember opening that kitchen door, but assumed that the rising wind must have blown it open, perhaps when she had gone out through the front door.

Or else perhaps Mistress Worme had arrived today to begin her work, and entered the house that way? She did normally come at noon to begin her afternoon's work, yet she did not usually enter the house directly from the side yard, but rather at the front door where she habitually knocked on the heavy oak timbers to announce her presence. A quick look around the cottage showed no sign of Mistress Worme's presence, though, so a slightly concerned Esther went back to Henry's simple wooden cradle, which was in a sheltered corner of the parlour, but also near a window for good light.

A quick glance showed her that all was well, and that baby Henry was in exactly the same posture as when she had left him three minutes ago.

A reassured Esther smiled to herself, and then went through to the kitchen to check on a pot of stew that was bubbling over the cooking hearth. But as she stirred the pot, Esther's feeling of unease returned, and she retraced her steps rapidly to her baby's cradle. Was it her imagination, or did little Henry's face have an unfamiliar blue tinge? She put her hand near the baby's nose to feel for his gentle breathing, and then had a moment of sheer panic as she felt nothing at all. She felt for his little pinched chest, yet could feel no comforting heartbeat.

In desperation she shook the baby to hopefully wake him, yet nothing happened, and the baby flopped lifelessly in his cradle. She began to shake him ever more violently, hoping that the action would jolt the baby's heart back into life. Yet there was no joyous sound of wailing from that little mouth, nor angry resentment at being woke from sleep, only the same dead baby.

Esther began to wail and moan as she picked up the baby in her arms, pinching and kneading the baby's skin to force life back into that poor little body...

Suddenly the baby was wrenched from her grasp by a pair of strong wiry arms.

'What evil have you done here?' Mistress Worme demanded, staring at the dead white face of the child.

In her abject distress, Esther did not answer her but tried to recover the baby from the stupid woman's iron grasp. Yet the snarling woman would not let the baby go, and backed away to the door, clutching the dead child to her chest. 'Ye shall not have him, you deranged harlot! You have killed your own child, you wicked creature...!'

# CHAPTER 11

Tuesday, 9th May 1665

The chamber in which women prisoners awaiting trial were held at Newgate Prison was supposedly a haven of civilized peace and tranquillity compared to the quarters in which the male prisoners were kept. Yet to Esther Linney this seemed more like a place of interment for the dead, rather than somewhere fit for the living. This long stinking chamber, with its low ceiling constructed of dripping brick arches, and its cold stone-flagged floor, did indeed resemble some ancient sepulchre, down to the niches and alcoves in the walls.

Even the behaviour of its occupants reinforced that impression, since they were slouched in such a well of despair and dejection that most of them could easily have passed for dead. Every square inch of the chamber's floor space was occupied by women prisoners, who were of every age and condition – old and scheming, sick and hungry, young and vicious, bewildered and lost - and some even with babes and small children at their breast, who seemed, though, to be infected with the same deathlike malaise as their parents.

The chamber was half-buried below the level of the press-yard outside, and a line of tiny barred windows at the tops of the walls let the only natural light into the room, as well as a few tantalising sounds from the outside world. To most of the women incarcerated here, that small glimpse of the press-yard was a precious thing because it led to Newgate Street and the world beyond – a world that had been a hard and demanding school for all of these women, yet was still infinitely to be preferred to their present situation. Because of the worsening outbreak of plague, though, Newgate Street was presently unnaturally quiet so even that small contact with the world of the living was presently denied to these imprisoned women. For her part, Esther had found that she welcomed even the discordant sounds of creaking springs and iron shod wheels of passing coaches on Newgate Street, or the occasional distant call from the dwindling number of street criers on Old Bailey: these distractions were a small reassurance to her that the world still continued outside these four miserable stone walls.

Most of the women on remand in the prison were pickpockets, thieves, or whores caught stealing from their customers, but several were accused of murder like Esther, and these individuals simply mingled with the rest, and were treated like the rest, without any evidence of any particular prejudice against them. This benefit was of limited value to Esther, though, given the bleak conditions for everyone here, conditions unrelieved by any semblance of compassion, humanity or comfort. The only real advantage of being a woman prisoner in Newgate was that females were not subject to being permanently manacled or shackled – but that benefit was not given from any humane consideration, but only a practical one. It would have cost the gaolers much time and trouble to have to lock and unlock so many heavy chains, and was hardly necessary when the limited strength and weak physical condition of the women prisoners made escape impossible for them anyway.

The majority of the women occupied damp straw mattresses on the cold wet floor, but a few privileged prisoners – thanks to having the wherewithal to pay the venal turnkeys in this awful place – had the luxury of stone benches along the dripping stone walls to sit on, or even their own little alcove to themselves.

Esther was not so fortunate, though, having a less than select position on the floor near the privy, which was no more than an iron grille over a buried drain. At night, rats came up into the chamber from the drain, and her sleep was often disturbed by the sounds of their feet scurrying across the stone floor, or the cry of a baby as it was bitten.

Esther had been brought here a day after Mistress Worme had reported her suspicions to the local Middlesex parish constable, and he in turn had requested the London city magistrate to deal with this case since he was not equipped by either inclination or temperament to deal with such a heinous crime as infanticide. Esther had begged to stay in Middlesex and not be sent back to London, where the plague was taking hold, but her appeal fell on deaf ears, as did all her attempts to send a letter to Mr Warboys informing him of what had happened. Mistress Worme could have informed Mr Warboys, of course, since she must have some form of regular contact with him, if only through an agent who paid her wages. But Esther was convinced that she had not informed Mr Warboys of this terrible news, otherwise he would certainly have come to her aid by now, after a full week of this enduring nightmare. In desperation, Esther had written a letter to her friend Meg Bulstrode in the village of Salwayash, and had given the letter, together with all her remaining coins, to a woman pickpocket who was being freed from Newgate for want of evidence. Esther was almost sure that the woman would merely pocket the money and throw her letter in the river, but it was better doing something rather than nothing.

Esther had been in Newgate for six days now, yet it seemed more like six years of unending misery. Had the sun really risen and set only six times while she had been trapped in this terrible place? Had it really only been eight days since her sweet baby boy had been taken from her so cruelly? Time played curious tricks with her tortured mind so that sometimes, waking in a dislocated mood from a nightmarish sleep, she could no longer quite remember what was real and what was imagined any more. Sometimes – perhaps as a form of escape from her distress - she became convinced that all this had happened to her long ago, and that she had been incarcerated here for a lifetime. If she could but look at her face in a mirror, she imagined that she would only discover the visage of a bitter old woman staring back at her with resignation...

In her moments of greater clarity, though, she had been tempted to try and get word of her plight to Henry Raven, who lived within a mile of Newgate and who, she was sure, would come if requested. Yet the pain of him coming here and having him see her in this even further degraded condition was more than she could bear. She had decided she must take the full blame for baby Henry's death and plead guilty, since his death must have been due to some neglect or ill action on her part. She had no true comprehension of how or why her baby had stopped breathing, but it seemed almost like a punishment from God for her wanton and lustful behaviour. It was true that Mr Warboys had forced himself on her initially, yet she had quickly given into him, and in the end had indulged her passions just as wantonly as him, so perhaps deserved this punishment from the almighty.

Whoever's fault it truly was, Esther's despair at the death of her baby was such that she scarce wanted to live any more, and a quick death seemed to her almost a mercy now. Her world had been reduced to the extent of one damp straw mattress, one chamber pot, and a few other pitiful possessions. Yet even such pathetic properties as these were a temptation to the vicious young pickpocket lying next to her, who was constantly trying to steal her things while Esther slept.

On this sixth day of her captivity, Esther was roused at noon from her torpor by a rough old turnkey called Buttle, a cruel man with the body of a whale and the raddled face of a regular drunkard. 'Thou hast a treat today, dearie – a meeting with Marshall Weaver,' he said with heavy sarcasm. He pulled her roughly to her feet, deliberately groping her breast as he did so, then gave her a stern whack on the backside with his turnkey's bludgeon. He continued to direct her in this cruel and demeaning way even when they were in the dripping stone corridor outside. The main block of Newgate

Prison was a bleak quadrangle of blackened stone, two stories high, arranged around a square stone-flagged yard next to the old city gate. Still prodded roughly from behind by the old turnkey, Esther climbed a set of worn stone steps up to ground level, and then followed a passageway leading to this central yard. As they left the main building and crossed the yard, Esther was momentarily blinded by the brightness of the high May sun, and felt dizzy with all the light and movement around her. Even in this drab place, the sunlight lit up the brickwork and the cobbles, revealing to her a world of forgotten colour and texture, while, overhead, darting swifts twisted and turned across a sky of brilliant blue, and filled the yard with the sound of their high-pitched squeals.

The turnkey led her to a room on the opposite side of the yard, a bare parlour with dirty lime-washed walls, and a single high window, and furnished only with a battered table and two crudely made chairs. Yet this grim little parlour was a veritable paradise compared to the stinking chamber where she had been imprisoned for a week. Esther was suddenly conscious of the rancid stink of her own body, the filthy state of her clothes, and the itching lice in her hair.

The fat turnkey pulled himself to some sort of attention, and tried to suck in his vast gut, as a second man entered the room behind them.

The newcomer moved to one side of the table and indicated the chair on the other side with the palm of his hand. 'Sit down, Mistress,' he ordered, though without any trace of warmth or humanity in his voice. He was a thin, sour-looking individual of forty years, dressed in Puritan black. His shorn hair was the colour of old straw, and his lips were thin and bloodless, and clamped permanently into an expression of distaste. His skin was startlingly white and drawn, as if he had shunned the warming balm of sunlight for many years.

Esther tried to clear her still spinning head. 'I prefer to stand, sir. I have been sitting too long this last week.'

'As you wish, Mistress Linney.' The man had a manner as cold and unfeeling as a piece of carved stone. 'As for me, I prefer to sit, as this may take some time.' With that he took his seat, scraping the legs of the chair on the stone-flagged floor as he did so, then regarded her with grim satisfaction for a moment. 'My name is John Weaver; I am the City Marshal to the City of London. My authority in regard to the law is unassailable within the walls of this city. Even the King has no power of proscription over my decisions,' he added with pride. 'I am answerable only to the Lord Mayor and aldermen of this great city…'

'I have committed no crime within this city,' Esther declared boldly, angered by this man's cold and insulting manner, and finding some inner reserve of strength again.

The man seemed momentarily taken aback by this unexpected

interruption but did finally deign to answer. 'Ah, if you think that strategy will constitute a valid defence, then you will quickly be disabused of that notion. The county of Middlesex presently defers to the laws of this city in regard to selected serious crimes, therefore any such matters referred to me fall under my legal jurisdiction too...'

'I have committed no crime in the county of Middlesex either,' Esther interrupted. 'My baby simply died a natural death.'

Weaver looked at her with disdain. 'That is for *me* to decide, at least initially. And the suspicious circumstances of your bastard child's death lead me to conclude that you do indeed have a case to answer. Therefore I wish to inform you that you will appear before Judge Holinshead in the court next door to plead your case with him...'

'When must I appear?' Esther demanded.

'The new London Sessions begin this very week. Judge Holinshead and his fellow court officials will sit in judgement on several cases on the morrow, including your own...'

'On the morrow!' Esther exclaimed.

Weaver sniffed coldly. 'If you are as innocent as you claim, Madam, then I am sure you will have no difficulty in persuading the judge and his jury of your veracity...'

*

Anthony Mawdsley stretched indulgently in his seat. 'Ah, Henry, 'tis good to be back in our old box in the theatre, is it not, and with the prospect of seeing a new play by Mr Dryden in the offing. What with all the pressing demands imposed on me by my Lord Clarendon in regard to the war, and with all the uncertainties caused by this outbreak of plague, I have been a very dull fellow of late, with no time at all for either pleasure or sin.'

The delightful Mrs Behn raised an elegant eyebrow in disbelief. 'Forgive my inability to keep a straight face, Anthony, but the notion of you as an ascetic man denying himself all pleasure is a hard one to contemplate without amusement.'

Henry Raven laughed at his friend's discomfiture for once. 'Well said, Mrs Behn,' he complimented her. 'You have learned the true measure of Mr Mawdsley very quickly.'

Mrs Behn inclined her head in acknowledgment to him, her eyes sparkling. This was the first time that Raven had met this vivacious young lady, who had appeared here with Mawdsley as his other guest. Mawdsley had sent a messenger to St Martin's Lane inviting Raven to this afternoon's performance at the King's theatre, and he had been only too happy to accept after the last few weeks of unrelieved misery in his life. This afternoon he wanted only to forget the plague epidemic that now raged through the city almost unchecked. And he had a second ulterior motive in coming here because Sir Thomas Killigrew had mentioned to him at a chance meeting in King Street in Whitehall yesterday that Molly had returned to the company and was due to perform today. Conscious of his further neglect of her over the last week, Raven had decided that he would renew his advances to her after the performance, and try and mend the rift between them caused by that young actor Whelan, and more lately by that Frenchman Desargues. Raven had begun to see that, even though his working day was now consumed by the fight against the spread of the plague, yet it was foolish of him to neglect Molly any more. She would eventually take his neglect for a loss of interest in her, and nothing was further from the truth than that. His absence from her had reinforced his affection for her, if anything, and turned that affection into something deeper and more passionate. Therefore it was foolishness indeed to allow that old French dog to steal his way into Molly's bed while he, out of feelings of stubborn pride, did nothing to prevent it.

Mawdsley had introduced his other guest to Raven as Mrs Aphra Behn, but so far Raven had learned little of her history other than the obvious fact that she was a beautiful young woman of exotic appearance. There was certainly no sign of a Mr Behn, so Raven was soon convinced that Mawdsley was bedding this enticing female. When she disappeared to powder her already beautifully powdered nose, Raven begged to know some of Mrs Behn's personal history, which turned out to more exotic than even he had guessed.

Mawdsley was quietly pleased with the stir that his new lady friend had caused. 'Aphra is an exquisite creature, is she not? I have done my best to discover the facts of her life but she is extremely secretive about revealing her origins. However I have made discreet enquiries with some of her acquaintances and I believe her to be from Canterbury, and the daughter of a Mr Bartholomew Johnson, a barber, and his wife Elizabeth. It seems her mother was employed as a nurse to the wealthy Culpepper family who lived locally, so Aphra grew up with the family's children, almost as a foster sister. Her history took a surprising turn two years ago, however, for she set sail for the English sugar colony on the Surinam River, on the coast east of Venezuela...'

'That young lady has been in South America?' Raven exclaimed in disbelief.

Mawdsley nodded. 'I believe so, particularly as she makes no great issue of such adventures, yet clearly knows much of that continent. During her sojourn in this place called Oroonoko, she told me that she met an African slave leader, whose interesting story she intends to commit to print if she can ever find a publisher for it.'

Raven laughed cynically. 'A woman writer? I never heard of such a thing! And what of her husband? Where is Mr Behn?'

'Ah, she is even more reticent in talking of him. But I believe him to be a gentleman of German or Dutch extraction, a wealthy merchant whom Aphra met on her travels in Europe, then went with him to the Americas. She claims to be a widow now, although I am far from sure that this Mr Behn is truly deceased. I believe he simply left her.'

'Or else he never existed at all, and he is a simple figment of this lady's imagination to justify her with the more dignified status of widow? As is perhaps her trip to South America too?' Raven suggested dryly.

Mawdsley gave his friend a reproving look. 'Nay, both her husband, and her trip to the Surinam River are real enough, I am convinced. I know for a fact that she has lent Sir Thomas Killigrew the use of a gorgeously feathered Indian cloak for use in this production by the actor playing Montezuma, Mr Mohun. And where else could she have acquired such a thing except in South America? ' He dropped his voice to a whisper. 'Perhaps her husband found her risqué habits unacceptable, and left her in consequence, but I make no complaints in that regard.'

'*Risqué habits?*' Raven was intrigued, despite his normal distaste for salacious gossip.

Mawdsley smiled. 'Shall we say that Aphra is as happy with a female partner in bed as a male one? Perhaps even more so, which is therefore a compliment to my own powers to please even such a demanding Amazon lover as her...'

'What compliments are these that I have paid you, Anthony?' a voice interrupted sharply. Mrs Behn appeared suddenly behind them in the box, and neither of the red-faced gentlemen was sure just how long she had been standing there listening to their idle gossip. Raven was deeply embarrassed, but Mrs Behn herself most certainly was not, and sat down complacently between them without so much as a murmur of complaint.

They talked a little more as the preparations for the play began on stage, and the benches in the pit below began to fill up with more people. There was only half an hour to go to the start of the play at three o'clock, yet there were still many vacant seats, Raven noticed, though whether this was because of the deterring effect of the plague outbreak, or because of a general disinterest in Mr Dryden's new play, he did not know. He did learn a little more about Mrs Behn, though, as she charmed him and his friend Mawdsley with anecdotes of her surprising life.

'...Yes, Mr Raven. I was brought up as a strict Catholic and was designed by my father for a nun. Yet despite my sympathy for Catholics, I believe I would have made a poor nun, and would no doubt have corrupted the entire nunnery given half the chance, so 'tis as well I took a different course in life. And what of you, Mr Raven? Are you married?'

Mawdsley laughed. 'In a way, he is indeed. He has given his heart to a pretty strumpet from this very company of players.'

Mrs Behn pouted. 'Really, 'tis an *actress* who has claimed your heart, Mr

Raven? I thought such a serious gentleman as you would have a more refined taste than that. But do not tell me which – let me watch the play and decide for myself which of these painted hussies would most attract a man of your sensibilities.' She turned her pretty head to Mawdsley. 'I wager ten shillings, Anthony, that I can pick out the right lady.'

Mawdsley laughed. 'Agreed, though I doubt not your talents to read Henry's inclinations precisely, so I know that I may as well give you the ten shillings now.'

Mawdsley looked around as a richly dressed young courtier came into the box, and then approached him to whisper a discreet message into his ear. Mawdsley smiled weakly at Raven and Mrs Behn as the messenger withdrew. 'It seems the King is in attendance in his Royal box this afternoon, and has seen that you and I are here, Henry, so we are all invited forthwith to sit with him and Lady Castlemaine to watch the play.' He patted Mrs Behn's petite gloved hands. 'However I suspect that the King is less interested in the company of Henry and myself – which is no novelty to him at all - and much more interested to see at close hand our delightful female companion.'

Mrs Behn took her fan and fluttered it enticingly. 'Then I hope that I am not a disappointment to him, when studied at close quarters,' she declared innocently...

*

Backstage in the tiring room, Molly made some last minute adjustments to her costume and face, then stood back to inspect herself in the mirror. When she saw how short the skirts were on this costume, she began to regret her impetuous decision to agree to wear such an outrageous ensemble as this for her role as Princess Cydaria. She could not believe that the Emperor Montezuma's real daughter had ever truly worn such a preposterous and revealing costume. Her bubbies were almost completely exposed while the skirt, decorated with feathers and garish colours, barely covered her thighs. Not only that, the skirts were so light that the lightest breeze would lift the hem, so if she made even so much as a slight twirl on stage, she would end up showing her bare bum to half of London. Yet it was too late to change her mind now. The playwright, Mr Dryden, was already going among the audience personally, and distributing his program explaining the relationship of this new play *The Indian Emperor* to his former one, *The Indian Queen*...

Molly turned sharply as she felt a cold hand rest firmly on her buttocks.

Sir Thomas laughed at her reaction. 'Now, now, do not pretend that you do not like me putting my hand there, Molly. And, in truth, 'tis but a mark of my esteem and respect for you.'

Molly regarded him cynically. 'A mark of esteem and respect, is it, sir? I doubt that truly.'

Killigrew walked around her and smiled his approval at the way she looked. 'You have been as good as your word, Molly, and eaten yourself back into plump and healthy vigour in the last week...'

'Not too plump, I hope, sir,' Molly said worriedly, checking her figure again in the mirror.

'Nay, not too much. Just enough to be infinitely pleasing to any sane man, Molly, including this white-haired old gentleman before you.' With that, Killigrew was gone to the other end of the tiring room to have similar encouraging words with Nell. Molly had been a little shocked on returning to the theatre last week for rehearsal to see that Nell had been promoted from a mere walk on part as a slave girl in *The Indian Queen* to the role of Alibech, the sister of Almeria, in this production. This was a part almost as large as her own, which gave her some cause for consternation, and perhaps a little annoyance at seeing Nell rise quite so quickly in the ranks. And Nell's costume was even scantier than her own so Killigrew was clearly taking no chances of not pleasing the audience this afternoon. Yet, to give Nell her dues, she was quite good in the role, therefore not there merely to give the audience an eyeful of her sweet little body. And Molly much preferred that Nell had gotten the role in place of Mary Pettican anyway, so this was a second reason to be happy for her.

After Killigrew had departed to check preparations on stage, Nell came up to Molly, and they compared costumes with a laugh. 'What larks, eh, Molly? I feel such a draught up my bum in these short skirts! We are a couple of naughty girls to wear such things, are we not?' She giggled again, even louder. 'Yet, unless the audiences pick up, I fear that even this will not be enough, and Sir Tom will have us both stark naked on that stage by the end of this summer, in order to bring the crowds back to the theatre.'

'Nay, I shall draw the line long before that,' Molly said with a smile, as they made their way down the stairs to the side of the stage in preparation for the start. All of the actors were assembled there in costume, ready to make their entrances as required. Michael Mohun looked most impressive and regal as the Emperor, while Charles Hart made an impossibly handsome Cortez. Hart smiled at Molly, but then smiled even more broadly in Nell's direction, so Molly was suddenly suspicious that Nell might have made a further conquest that might explain her recent elevation. Edward Kynaston looked most pretty as the Emperor's son, Guyomar, Molly saw — he was quite the prettiest person in the company, she thought, even including the actresses. Nicholas Burt was saying his lines to himself as Cortez's army commander, Vasquez, William Wintershall was a calm Odmar, William Cartwright was completely in character as the High Priest (which was a remarkable feat of acting for such a rake, Molly thought), while Anne Marshall preened herself as the beautiful Almeria, daughter of the old Indian Queen, who becomes Montezuma's consort yet does not return his love.

Molly exchanged a word of greeting with Christopher Malthouse, who was playing Orbellan, son of the late Indian Queen by Traxalla, and brother to Almeria and Alibech. In the play, Molly's character of Cydaria was forced to marry Orbellan against her will by her father, the emperor. Molly did not find the plain Christopher even remotely attractive which was a great aid to her in her role, since she could easily imagine what pain Cydaria must suffer to be ordered to marry a man she did not love...

Molly was looking forward to the start now, and prayed for a great success to lift the spirits of everyone in the theatre. Mr Dryden had spiced his play with features that could not fail to please a discerning audience, including incantations and conjured spirits, and an elaborate grotto scene with a real fountain spouting real water. Yet the question remained whether it would all work for this first performance. Molly could only hope that the fountain at least would work, because it most certainly had not during their dress rehearsal...

Nell came up beside her again and pointed out the Royal box. 'Look, Molly, the King is in attendance today. 'Tis good fortune indeed, for we shall be hard to miss in these revealing costumes. And I see that your Mr Raven sits with him. You sly dog! You did not say that he would be here today.'

Molly was overjoyed to see Henry in the King's box, together with his friend Mawdsley and other courtiers, but she kept her voice deliberately calm. 'Oh, he told me that he would not miss this play for the world.'

As she peeped out from behind the stage to take another furtive look, Molly could not fail to see that M'sieur Desargues was also in attendance in the crowd, since he waved to her gaily from the gallery and blew her an exaggerated kiss that everyone in the theatre must have seen. Swiftly, a mortified Molly ducked back out of sight again, and felt her burning cheeks.

Nell gave her a sharp dig in the ribs. 'You truly are a sly dog, Molly, I see! Not one lover in the audience, but two.'

Molly glanced pointedly at their fellow players gathered behind them, and at Charles Hart in particular. 'Then I still have far fewer lovers in this house than you, Nell,' she retaliated.

Nell was not put out by the remark but only smiled. 'There's no hiding anything from you, is there, Molly?' she said admiringly...

*

Barbara Castlemaine was most attentive to Henry Raven after Mawdsley and his small party had joined the King in the grand Royal Box. Raven guessed, though, that this was as much in retaliation for the King's obvious flirtations with Mrs Behn as because of any genuine affection Barbara might have truly held for him. Mawdsley was the disgruntled loser in all this, Raven decided, as he saw his friend Mrs Behn monopolized by the King,

133

and realized perhaps that his own days as Mrs Behn's lover might be numbered as a result.

Raven enquired politely after the health of the Queen, and the King responded graciously. 'The Queen is lately gone to Tunbridge to take the waters, Mr Raven. But I am glad that she is gone, with the plague now raging in London and seemingly out of control, despite your best efforts to halt it. I have heard of your sterling work in St Giles and elsewhere from Mr Mawdsley and I only wish there were more public-minded citizens like you in this city. Nevertheless, if things worsen, the whole court will have to move to safer climes for the good of the country, though it would grieve me to have to go, and leave my subjects here in the city to suffer alone...'

While the King was saying this, Barbara Castlemaine had secretly put her hand on Raven's thigh under the cover of her large fan, and now stroked his leg assiduously.

The King regarded him worriedly. '...You seem in high colour, Mr Raven, with your cheeks most flushed. I hope this is not a sign that you are sickening.'

Out of sight, Raven took a tight grip of Barbara's hand to ensure that it went no higher. 'Nay, your majesty, I am in rude health.'

'Not even any stiffening of the joints, Mr Raven?' Lady Castlemaine asked innocently. Barbara finally withdrew her hand and fluttered her fan delicately in his face. 'That will cool you down, Mr Raven, and quell the blood rushing where it should not.'

The King, who seemed merely amused by this exchange, read the program that Mr Dryden had handed to him personally when visiting the Royal Box a few minutes before. He turned to Mrs Behn, who was sitting attentively at his side, and behaving in a similarly shameless manner, Henry Raven suspected, to the way that Barbara Castlemaine was favouring him. 'I am somewhat bemused by the plot of this play, and Mr Dryden's program notes seem more designed to confuse me, than to instil any true conception of his plot.'

Mrs Behn laughed delightfully. 'I could not agree more, your majesty. Still, we must not prejudge the issue, and perhaps all will be clear once the players are on stage. As I told you, I have travelled in these regions of the Americas myself, and I would much enjoy the opportunity to write a play of my own on the history and culture of those romantic lands.'

The King coughed in disbelief. 'A woman playwright? It is difficult to comprehend of such a thing.'

Surprisingly, it was Barbara who came to the defence of Mrs Behn. 'It was difficult to comprehend of women actors until a few years ago. But now it would seem preposterous for men to be playing women's parts, Charles. Therefore I am sure that there will be women playwrights too before too long, and that the pretty, witty Mrs Behn, with all her many *interesting* experiences, may well be one of them.'

Mrs Behn was compelled to say to Barbara, 'You are most kind, Madam.'

Mawdsley finally interrupted, his good mood apparently restored by this banter. 'It seems, your majesty, that the sisterhood still finds reasons to close ranks when it suits them. And, with regard to the play, why, I do not see that the plot is *so* difficult to comprehend! It is simply about a great king who loses his throne because he allows his personal weaknesses and desires to destroy his good judgement and his sense of duty to his subjects...'

The King frowned but said nothing in response. A long stony silence then ensued as Mawdsley apparently realized the full enormity of his mistake. But he was rescued from his deepening red-faced embarrassment by the noise from the pit below as the players came on stage for Act 1, Scene 1, "*set in a pleasant Indian country...*"

When Molly first appeared in the temple scene in Act 1, Scene 2, the King's mood improved perceptibly. He turned to Raven and whispered deafeningly in his ear. 'Is that not your lady, Mr Raven, playing Cydaria? Is that not Mistress Titchen in the part?'

Raven heard Mawdsley curse mildly under his breath, and Mrs Behn give a little shrug of satisfaction, as she discovered the identity of Raven's lover without any effort at all. Raven was tempted to dissemble, but found that he could not deny his feelings for Molly even in this august company. 'It is, your majesty.'

'You are a fortunate man, then, to enjoy so much beauty. She looks most fetching in that costume, I must say. And with legs of such perfect and delightful form.' The King turned his attention to another scantily clad actress on stage. 'The girl playing Alibech is a lot shorter than your Mistress Titchen, yet she has exquisite legs too. Old Tom Killigrew knows how to pick a pretty girl for his company, I will say that for the old rogue.'

Mrs Behn turned to Lady Castlemaine and said coolly, 'Perhaps if you and I were to wear such revealing costumes as those, my lady, then our legs might receive equal complimentary remarks.' With that she brazenly lifted her skirts to show her silk clad legs to the King.

The King laughed. 'You have a winning argument there, Mrs Behn.'

Raven was hardly listening now, though, to the flirtatious chatter around him, his attention concentrated entirely on Molly's performance in the play. She was sensual and exciting in that daring costume, yet also touching and vulnerable as a sad princess forced to marry against her will.

As the play went on, and his affection for her filled his heart even more, he determined that he would indeed go backstage afterwards to see her. And if she wished, he would go back to Bow Street with her and spend the night again. From here in the Royal Box, she seemed entirely restored to all her former health and beauty, which seemed entirely remarkable given that she had nearly died of the plague barely three weeks ago. She was a remarkable girl in more ways than one, and her constitution had to be as unique as her personality and her beauty.

Raven had of course seen that old French dog, Desargues, wave at Molly before the play, but had been content that she had not waved back. Instead she had looked a second time in his direction in the Royal Box, and smiled a greeting at him, which gave him much cause for renewed happiness.

*

The play came to its final conclusion with Montezuma's sad suicide, and the destruction of his empire, which drew loud and sustained applause from the audience, even though many were confused by the complexities of the plot and dissatisfied with the play as a whole.

Raven begged leave to go at this point, and the King laughed heartily. 'Perhaps you go to help Mistress Titchen out of that scanty costume, sir. If so, I do not blame you in the slightest, so please take your leave with my blessing.' The King however took a firm hold of Mrs Behn's hand as she seemed about to get up too. 'But I am sure this lady will favour us with her presence a little longer, will you not, Madam?'

Mrs Behn was only too happy to stay despite some sullen murmurings of displeasure from Barbara Castlemaine, but Mawdsley too decided it was time to leave and got up to join Raven, having apparently seen that he had no hopes of bedding Mrs Behn this night as he had clearly hoped.

In the candlelit passage outside, Mawdsley held Raven's sleeve for a moment. 'Can I have a brief word, Henry, before you rush off to Molly's arms?'

Raven halted in his tracks. 'Of course, Anthony. What matter concerns you?'

Mawdsley hesitated before replying. 'Err...the fact is...I have...err...*volunteered* to join the fleet at Harwich, and take my part in the forthcoming battle with the Dutch.'

Raven frowned. '*You*, Anthony? Why? You are no seafaring man. Or fighting man, for that matter. You are a lawyer and a statesman, a thinker not a doer. You will be as much use on board a man o' war as your master, Lord Clarendon.'

Mawdsley sighed heavily. 'Nevertheless I must go. Many gentlemen of the court have volunteered, and it would not be politic for a young man like me to stay behind in the comfort of the court when so many are offering to risk their lives.'

Raven sniffed suspiciously. 'Who else has volunteered, Anthony?'

'Why, Charles Berkeley for one. He is the King's favourite, and a coming man. He will no doubt be Lord Chancellor one day, and I must try and curry favour with him. My Lord Clarendon's unchallenged position as

Lord Chancellor will not last forever; and if the war goes badly – as I suspect it might against such formidable opponents as the Dutch - he is no more immune from censure than anyone else. Arlington and Buckingham are only waiting like vultures for him to falter, and then they will peck over his corpse, and try and take his place.'

'So you must prove your courage by an act of vain self-sacrifice, if you want to keep your position at court?' Raven observed with a wry shake of his head

'Just so. Even those young libertines, Buckhurst, Sedley and Lord Rochester, are considering to go with the fleet and make a name for themselves,' Mawdsley added moodily.

Raven grimaced. 'Then things must be grave indeed for this country, if we need those three disreputable young gentlemen to carry our standard. Sedley is a disgraceful reprobate, and John Wilmot, Lord Rochester, though not yet twenty years, is the worst of the lot. I would not let my sisters within a mile of that amoral young devil.'

'I would not disagree, Henry. I would not even let Wilmot near my female servants, never mind my sisters.' Mawdsley clapped a hand on Raven's shoulder. 'But will ye not join me anyway, Henry? You are a useful man with a sword, and a seagoing man to boot, as well as being a physician and surgeon. And 'tis safer for you to go with the fleet than staying here in the city to suffer the plague. That battle is already lost, Henry, but there is still a battle at sea that might be won for this nation.'

Raven was lost for words for a moment at this unexpected and unwelcome invitation from his friend. But he was saved from making a quick dismissive reply by the arrival of his manservant Martin in the passageway. Raven had walked here to the theatre on his own this evening, so was naturally surprised that Martin should now have followed him from home.

Martin was even more hesitant in his manner than of late. 'I am sorry to disturb you, Master, but this letter arrived for you not an hour since from your sister in Dorset, with a request from the messenger that it be read at once. So I thought it better not to wait until you had returned home tonight, but brought it to you at once. I trust that I did right.'

Martin was still much troubled of late about the continuing awkwardness in his relations with his master, so Raven swiftly put him at his ease. 'Worry yourself, not, Martin. I am sure that you did right.' Raven broke the wax seal on the letter, and took it over to where a sconce on the wall provided a useful pool of light. Even though he suspected the letter must be important, he gasped, though, as he read the letter and took in its full meaning.

Mawdsley was curious at his severe reaction. 'What is it, Henry? It seems to be exceeding bad news from the grim set of your visage.'

Raven nodded. 'Indeed so. A friend of mine - a lady called Esther Linney – has been taken into custody over the death of her child.' He looked at his friend in concern. 'Esther was almost a foster sister to me when I was young, as your friend Mrs Behn was to the Culpepper family. Esther is presently incarcerated in Newgate, it seems.'

Mawdsley grunted loudly. 'Then the Lord help her! This letter is from her?' he asked, not having heard properly what Martin had said earlier.

Raven shook his head. 'Nay, 'tis from my sister Catherine in Dorset. As regards the content of the letter, Catherine had heard some rumour of this sad story in the local village of Salwayash, and wished me to know of it. It seems Esther wrote a plea for help to someone in the village – an old friend of hers, a farmer's wife called Meg Bulstrode – and word then spread among Mrs Bulstrode's friends and acquaintances.'

'What are the circumstances of Mistress Linney's alleged crime?' Mawdsley asked in puzzlement.

Raven deliberated. 'Catherine does not know the precise circumstances. Excuse my rudeness, Anthony, but there is no time to deliberate further. I must leave for Newgate at once, and see what I can do for Esther tonight. She is to be tried tomorrow, it seems.'

Mawdsley acknowledged the urgency. 'Then you must indeed go. If I can be of help, please let me know, Henry. I have a barrister colleague, Richard Sherbrooke, who is a member of Gray's Inn, and a most useful advocate for those accused of criminal offences. But what of Molly – did you not intend to see her tonight?'

Raven sighed regretfully. 'I fear that Molly and I will have to wait a little longer to be properly reconciled. I must go at once.'

*

Backstage, Molly listened with one ear to Killigrew's warm congratulations on her performance. But most of her attention was elsewhere, as she waited eagerly for Henry to appear. She was sure from his manner that he would come backstage to see her tonight; he had given her a very warm smile from the Royal Box as she took her bows with the rest of the company, and seemed fully restored to the amiable Henry of old.

Yet her mood plummeted when he did not appear within ten minutes, and she sank onto a stool in a dark corner off stage, heavy again with woe. She looked up sharply, though, as someone coughed to gain her attention, and her heart leapt again with renewed hope as she recognized Henry's young manservant, Martin. She was convinced that the sober and serious Master Gibney did not like her one jot, and certainly did not regard her as being a worthy lady for his master. Yet he was always unfailingly polite to her, as he was again tonight. 'My master sent me to tell you that he wished to dine with you this evening, Mistress, but that unfortunate circumstances prevent his wishes from being fulfilled. He will call at Bow Street soon and

138

pay his compliments to you then.'

Molly was intensely disappointed, but hid her feelings well, like the accomplished actress she was. After Martin had bowed and left, Molly was still ruminating on the true meaning of Henry's message, when M'sieur Desargues appeared from nowhere at her side, full of enthusiasm and *joie de vivre* as usual. '*Ma chérie*, your performance was a triumph tonight. After you have changed out of that naughty and revealing costume, Molly, and taken all that paint and powder off your sweet face, may I take you to the Will's Coffee House in Russell Street so that we can celebrate the success of your performance properly.'

Molly was half tempted to refuse any more of this ebullient gentleman's attentions, which were as much an irritant to her as a blessing. But out of the corner of her eye, she caught sight of Nell giggling intimately with Charles Hart, while all of the rest of the company seemed to be paired off happily too. Even Mary Pettican was engaged in flirtatious banter with Edward Kynaston (though whether it was wise for a woman to make eyes at a man who was so much prettier than herself was a debatable point, Molly thought cattishly.)

Molly had however spent too many nights in her own company of late to harbour any real feelings of resentment against her fellow players for their flirtations. Tonight she was badly in need of some flirting of her own to sweeten her life, even if it did not come from as welcome a source as she would have wished. So she smiled at M'sieur Desargues engagingly. 'I shall be honoured, sir, if you can but give me twenty minutes to make myself beautiful.'

Desargues bowed gallantly. 'You can take all the time you want, Molly, but you have no need of it in the pursuit of beauty. Beauty shines through you always like a ray of hot sun...'

# CHAPTER 12

Wednesday, 10<sup>th</sup> May 1665

Henry Raven's heart had fallen instantly when he had discovered the identity of the judge who was to preside over Esther's trial on the first day of the London Sessions.

*Judge Matthew Holinshead...*

This was the same Judge Holinshead, of course, whom William Croone had mentioned to him a few weeks ago – a man noted for the sternness of his judgements and for the lack of any apparent willingness to listen to any evidence that contradicted his natural prejudices.

Despite the worsening effects of the plague in the city, the epidemic had not deterred the usual ghoulish and querulous spectators from attending the first day of the new London Sessions, and the public gallery of the Sessions House, located immediately next to Newgate Prison on Old Bailey, was jammed to bursting with a jostling crowd of a hundred people or more. The scarlet-robed judge sat on an imposing dais at the far end of the courtroom from the public gallery, surrounded by his coterie of officials and lackeys. The jury of twelve men sat to one side of the bench, blinking in the bright afternoon sunlight from the two high windows on the opposite wall. Despite the sunlight, the clothing of the judge was almost the sole bright spot of colour in this drab room, which was wainscoted from floor to ceiling in a dark and gloomy wood that seemed as black and unreflective as coal. Even the spectators seemed to have settled for the drabbest elements of their wardrobe today, comprising a dreary assembly of black and brown that matched the tone of these proceedings perfectly.

Esther stood in the central dock on her own, while the barristers sat with their helpers at tables on each side of the chamber, engaged in whispered consultations with each other. Their rough-hewn tables were strewn with documents, parchments and writing materials, and their ancient surfaces scarred and scratched with the deliberations of many previous generations of barristers. Raven was seated at the back of the public gallery behind Esther, so had not had the opportunity yet to catch her eye and let her know that he was here in court to support her.

Mawdsley was not with him as he had hoped, having been called this morning to an urgent meeting of the Privy Council in Whitehall Palace to discuss some pressing matters of state. Raven guessed that the war with Holland was taking increasing precedence over everything else - even over the conduct of the fight against the spread of the plague in the capital, which was a major source of regret to him. Raven had no doubt where the Privy Council's priorities should really lie – in protecting the lives and welfare of their own citizens from a far more invidious enemy than the Dutch, rather than indulging in vainglorious wars overseas. Yet it seemed few in the corridors of power in Whitehall Palace agreed with him on that point.

Raven had not been able to gain personal access to see Esther last evening in Newgate Prison as he had hoped, although, by bribing a fat old turnkey called Elias Buttle, he had managed to send a written message to her telling her that he was aware of her plight and was arranging for an experienced barrister to speak for her today. At first light this morning he had paid a visit to Mawdsley's barrister friend Richard Sherbrooke to solicit his services for Esther. Sherbrooke was a gentlemanly individual of thirty, with a fine house in Bishopsgate, though Raven suspected that the possession of this prestigious Tudor mansion owed more to the wealth of Sherbrooke's merchant family, than to any particular success he might have found as a lawyer. Mawdsley's close acquaintance with Sherbrooke went back to Cambridge when they had both studied the law together at Trinity College. Raven had been at Trinity at the same time, studying natural philosophy and medicine, and had met Sherbrooke on occasion then, but without forming any great attachment to the man, perhaps because of their very different interests in life. According to Mawdsley, though, Sherbrooke had gone on to become a most able, even brilliant, advocate after gaining admittance to the Inns of Court, and Mawdsley was confident that if anyone could sway Judge Holinshead from his implacable determination to find the accused guilty, then it would be Mr Sherbrooke.

Sherbrooke, though similar to Mawdsley in so many respects - of background, wealth and intellect - had however none of Mawdsley's extravagant physical beauty, being a plain young man with fiery red hair, prominent teeth, and a distressing surfeit of freckles. Yet despite being physically unprepossessing, Raven had taken to the man during their early morning meeting much more warmly than he had during their former brief acquaintance as students: on proper acquaintance Mr Sherbrooke seemed a most amiable and capable man, and certainly the best hope that Esther had of gaining acquittal, Raven guessed.

Raven could not of course give any credence to these disgraceful charges against Esther, which had to be either malicious, or simply a dreadful mistake. The thought that Esther might have harmed her own baby after carrying it dutifully for the best part of nine months seemed quite incomprehensible to him. As a physician, Raven knew that some women became moody and unstable after giving birth for reasons that no one could yet fathom (though Raven suspected there were hidden physical reasons behind this behaviour and that it was not simply due to any natural weakness in a woman's constitution.) Even if Esther had succumbed to this dark mood, though, no one who truly knew her could believe that it would cause her to abandon her kindly and humane nature to the point of murdering her own child.

Raven was sure that the identity of the baby's father would no doubt have to come out in the course of the trial. Henry Raven was a man with no taste for idle gossip or slander, yet even he was curious to know the identity of Esther's secret lover. He had no idea whether the man was still in contact with Esther, but it seemed likely since he had apparently been giving her financial help. This in turn pointed to the father being a local Dorset man of reasonable wealth, therefore more likely a neighbouring farmer than a mere labourer. The fact that he had not married Esther suggested that he was married already, but that did not narrow the field of suspicion down significantly – most of the local yeoman farmers on the Salwayash Manor estate, and the surrounding estates, were married men, of course.

*Did this man, whoever he was, even know that his child was dead?* Or if he did, then did he care what had happened, or was this tragedy simply, for him, a convenient end to an inconvenient problem...?

The barrister who spoke for the Lord Mayor and his Marshal in the case against Esther was an elderly gentleman called Leonard Puttergill, although awarding him the title of "gentleman" was an overly generous compliment in Sherbrooke's view, since Puttergill was known to be a dissolute old rake who spent more of his time indulging in bawdy houses and carousing in alehouses than in dealing with matters of the law. Yet it seemed he was an unlikely friend and confidante of the stern and puritanical City Marshal, John Weaver, therefore was paid a retainer by the Lord Mayor to present the evidence against those brought to trial for criminal offences.

As the preliminary formalities for the case against Esther began, and the charge against her was read out by the court usher, Raven found time to glance around the chamber. His attention soon fixed on the striking white visage of the City Marshal, John Weaver, who was watching proceedings from a high gallery to one side of the court bench with all the rapt attention of a bird of prey. Raven had previous acquaintance of this Mr Weaver, from various other criminal law cases in which he had been peripherally involved, and had found him to be a most unsettling individual. Weaver seemed as grim of expression as usual, as he watched from his high perch, but there was perhaps a gleam of satisfaction in his eyes, since Judge Holinshead had already presided over the conviction of two men for robbery this morning, on the flimsiest of evidence provided by Weaver and his undermarshals, and condemned them to hang at Tyburn. The Judge's compliant jury comprised a reluctant selection of craftsmen and merchants who seemed to have been taken off London's streets on a whim and dragged unwillingly to court to fulfil the due process of law. Judging from their expressions, Raven thought, they all clearly wished to be elsewhere, and rather looking to their own businesses than being here in court sitting in judgement on their fellow citizens. Jurors were supposed to be impartial and independent of the judge, of course, but Raven's experience of criminal trials, such as it was, suggested that - in this court at least - jurors were bullied and cajoled into giving the decisions that the judge expected from them. Therefore he doubted that Esther could afford to place any hopes on such a jury weighing up the evidence dispassionately, or, even more so, of ever overriding the Judge in his decisions. If Esther was to be acquitted, then Holinshead himself would have to be convinced of the doubtful nature of the evidence against her, which would be no easy thing to achieve, even for someone of Mr Sherbrooke's considerable powers of persuasion and exposition. Sherbrooke's ability to defend the case was already in considerable question because he did not know more than a rough outline of the case against Esther, nor had he been informed yet what individuals might give witness against her.

Not being able to see her face from his seat in the public gallery, Raven was unsure how Esther was facing up to the testing circumstances of this trial. It must be a hard enough torment for her to lose her baby to a natural death, but then to be accused of the child's murder must have made that suffering a hundred times worse...

A temporary hush had fallen over the assembly as the judge called for Mr Puttergill to give the case against Mistress Linney. A babble of noise then erupted again from the spectators in the public gallery, which disturbance drew a stern rebuke and call for order from the court usher, and also induced Esther to turn her head for a moment to look behind at the gallery. Immediately her eyes came to rest on Henry Raven, who gave her a warm smile of encouragement. But his smile seemed only to distress Esther further rather than to encourage her, as her face crumpled and she was forced to wipe away a tear from her white cheek. But she recovered her composure quickly, Raven saw, as she turned her head again to hear the evidence against her.

*

Mistress Bernadette Worme was the first person to bear witness against Esther. This stern young woman told her story calmly under sympathetic questioning from the judge and Mr Puttergill, but Raven could sense an underlying venom and hatred of Esther in her restrained manner. He wondered what could have provoked such hatred for a sweet-natured girl like Esther from a member of her own sex.

Puttergill puffed himself up into an exaggerated image of effrontery. 'So there is no doubt in your mind, Mistress, that Esther Linney shook her own poor child to death in a rage.'

'None, sir,' the woman answered dutifully. 'I saw her do it with my own eyes. It gives me no pleasure to give evidence against Mistress Linney,' she added piously. 'But she must be a wicked creature despite her quiet ways...'

Mr Sherbrooke leapt to his feet to speak to the judge. 'My Lord, I can bring forward many witnesses to testify to the good and unblemished character of Mistress Linney. So why should we give countenance to this lady's deluded views of her...?'

The judge raised an imperious eyebrow. '*Unblemished*, sir? How can you make such a preposterous claim? She has given in to the lust of her body, and had a child out of the holy state of wedlock. How can such a woman be unblemished?'

'We have no evidence that Mistress Linney was a willing partner in this illicit conception, my lord,' Sherbrooke said, barely concealing his anger.

Judge Holinshead glowered beneath his thick mane of grey hair. His was a face defined completely by hard lines – horizontal furrows in his high brow, long creases at each side of his beak-like nose, and deep lines that divided his drawn cheeks from cheek bone to severe jaw. 'Have we not?' he enquired caustically. 'Then perhaps we should put this question to her, since you raise it?' He turned to the tall figure of Esther standing erect in the dock. 'Mistress Linney, would you care to name the father of your child?'

Esther spoke up resentfully. 'His identity is not a concern for this court, sir.'

Judge Holinshead bristled like a bantam cock. 'I order you to give an answer to my question, Mistress.'

Esther remained defiant. 'You cannot force me to give such an answer. It is not pertinent to this case.'

Judge Holinshead gave her a knowing look. 'You wish to protect this man's privacy, then?'

Esther gave a resigned shrug. 'If that is the way you choose to see it, sir.'

'It is indeed the way I choose to see it, Mistress, because there is no other sensible interpretation.' Holinshead turned triumphantly back to Sherbrooke. 'You see, sir, she protects the father. She would scarce do that if she had not been complicit with this man in her wanton act.'

'I did not kill my child!' Esther raised her voice, and pleaded directly with the jurors, who in response avoided her eye uneasily. 'He had stopped breathing, and I was merely trying to shake his poor little body back into life.'

The judge sniffed dismissively. 'Why should a baby simply stop breathing?'

Raven stood up abruptly in the public gallery. 'My Lord, if I may interject.'

Judge Holinshead fixed him with a beady eye. 'With what purpose, sir?'

'I am a physician, my Lord, and have some knowledge of breathing irregularities in infants.'

'You are also a friend of the accused, I believe, sir,' Puttergill sneered, 'and your evidence will therefore scarce be dispassionate or objective.'

The judge frowned. 'Is that true, sir?'

'Yes, my Lord,' Raven admitted. 'I have known Mistress Linney since childhood. But I make this statement only in the interests of justice and truth. I have seen several instances of babes who simply stopped breathing in their cots, particularly in premature infants like this one.'

'Why? What is the physical cause?' Holinshead demanded irately.

Raven glanced briefly at Esther who had turned to look at him with gratitude in her eyes. 'No one knows the cause, my Lord. Our knowledge of the workings of the human body is still at an elementary level in this regard.'

The judge grunted loudly in derision. 'Is that really true, sir? Why, I have seen anatomical texts in which the organs of the body are drawn and described in extraordinary detail.'

Raven bit back a sharp reply. 'Yes, my Lord, that is true – we do understand the anatomy of the human body much better than in former times. Yet it is also a fact that we do not understand even the smallest thing about the materials that constitute human flesh and blood, or the processes that control our bodies. And we know even less of the diseases and ailments that afflict humankind, and interfere with the proper regulation of the bodily processes…'

Holinshead gave him a stony look in response. 'What you say may have some validity, sir, and I will give you the benefit of the doubt that you give this information in good faith. Yet the only personal witness to what happened is Mistress Worme, and she says that she saw Mistress Linney shake her baby to death with her own eyes…'

Mr Sherbrooke spoke up. 'Mistress Linney has explained that, my Lord. She went outside for a moment on hearing a peal of thunder. When she came back after no more than three minutes, she found her baby no longer breathing, and tried to revive him with force. Mistress Worme's evidence merely confirms Mistress Linney's own story…'

Mistress Worme spoke up resentfully. 'It does not, sir. I know what I saw. She murdered her own child in a fit of rage.'

The judge dismissed her with a grateful look. 'We fully comprehend your evidence, Mistress, and thank you for your time. You may leave the witness stand now.'

In the hubbub that followed her dismissal, Mistress Worme left the chamber, giving Esther a sullen look of triumph as she passed the dock.

Judge Holinshead addressed Mr Puttergill. 'Do you have any further witnesses to give evidence, sir?'

Puttergill nodded emphatically. 'Yes, my Lord. And bearing in mind the discussion of Mistress Linney's true character, the evidence of this witness may be most pertinent. I call on Mistress Judith Pollock to give witness.'

Raven frowned as he wondered where he had heard that familiar name before. But when he saw Esther's strained face and distraught mood at the announcement of this second witness, he remembered at once where he had heard that name. This was the woman whom his sister Catherine had mentioned to him on his last visit to Dorset, the same woman who had denounced Esther's mother as a witch and caused her to be burned at the stake...

*

His sister Catherine had called Mistress Judith Pollock a wicked harpy, which insult had naturally formed some unfavourable physical impression of the woman in Henry Raven's mind. Yet the reality was somewhat different, and Mistress Pollock presented in person a far more sympathetic appearance than Raven had suspected she might. Raven would not have gone so far as to describe her face as kindly, yet she seemed on the surface an amiable grey-haired spinster of quiet disposition, and not the type of woman to denounce a neighbour of witchcraft without good reason.

Mr Puttergill addressed the woman firmly, after first confirming that she came from the village of Salwayash in Dorset. 'You have some acquaintance with Mistress Linney, I believe, Mistress?'

The woman nodded. 'Yes, I was in fact present at her birth, and helped bring her into the world. Her mother was a neighbour and friend...'

'You were no friend of my mother, you wicked, deceiving creature!' Esther called from the dock.

Judge Holinshead was outraged. 'Silence! You will hear this lady's evidence, whether you like it or no, Mistress Linney,' he added balefully.

Puttergill waited for the sudden babble of noise in court to die down before asking Mistress Pollock to continue her story. 'I swear that I *was* a true friend of Meg Linney. She was a very tall and handsome woman, with raven hair and white skin. Many people suspected she was a secret papist because of her mother's Italian ancestry, yet I knew her to be a true adherent of the protestant faith. Yet when her poor husband came home from the war with terrible wounds incurred at the siege of Taunton, Meg began to dabble secretly in witchcraft and sorcery in order to try and save him. Perhaps her foreign ancestry explains this weakness, and her refusal to accept the will of Our Lord. Standing over her dying husband, I heard her openly renounce her faith and then blaspheme against Our Lord for allowing her husband to suffer in this way. After that our intimacy was over, of course. Yet I felt compelled to observe her behaviour afterwards – for the good of her own immortal soul, I mean. When her husband died a few days later, she made no attempt to send him for Christian burial but kept the body in her house for a week afterwards, even though it was high summer. It was then that I observed the worst sin of all. I saw her - through an open window, on a late summer's eve...' - here there was catch in Mistress Pollock's voice, almost like a sob of pain – '...trying to bring her dead husband's body back to life with witches' spells and incantations.'

'So you reported this wicked behaviour to the parish priest?' Puttergill asked.

Mistress Pollock wavered a little before answering. 'How could I not? I feared for her mortal soul.'

'And the parish called in the witch finders to judge the woman's guilt?' Puttergill continued.

Mistress Pollock could not meet Esther's accusing gaze from across the chamber. 'Yes. And they duly found her guilty and condemned her to burn for her witchcraft.'

Puttergill approached the woman. 'Did you attend the burning on Blackmore Hill, Mistress?' he asked in a quieter voice.

Mistress Pollock glanced briefly at Esther, who stood in a silent rage. 'I did, because I hoped that Meg would renounce the Devil before she died, and embrace again her true faith before it was too late. Yet she went to her death without a sound, and burned as if she enjoyed it. I was sore distressed to see her go to eternal damnation...'

'It is you that shall suffer eternal damnation, ye wicked woman,' Esther said under her breath, yet the words still carried to the jurors.

The judge did not silence her this time, but seemed tolerant of her outburst on this occasion, conscious no doubt of the murmurs of dismay among the jury, who did seem shocked by Esther's bitter words.

Mr Sherbrooke stood up to question Mistress Pollock. 'Please study the face of the accused lady who stands in the dock, Madam. Do you seriously believe that this quiet and well-mannered lady, Esther Linney, is a witch, as her mother was supposed to be?' he asked derisively. 'Is this what you truly suggest with this sad evidence you give about her mother?'

Mistress Pollock was uneasy. 'I know not her true ways. She is very like her mother in both looks and temperament, that much I can say, therefore could bear her mother's evil stamp. Yet I had heard only good reports of

Esther as she grew up, therefore I had hopes she was not tainted by her mother's blood.'

'So you had heard only good reports of Esther Linney, Mistress?' Sherbrooke leapt on that one positive statement.

Mistress Pollock looked momentarily confused. 'Yes, until now…'

Judge Holinshead did not apparently like the way this questioning of Mistress Pollock was rather favouring the accused, and chose to intervene at this point. 'That is precisely the point, Mr Sherbrooke. By her clear act of infanticide, Mistress Linney has finally revealed her true nature, and the taint of her blood. I know not whether she has indulged in such wicked acts as her mother previously, yet I do see a most troubling aspect in her eye as she stares at me.'

Sherbrooke was amazed. 'You accuse Mistress Linney of witchcraft too, my Lord? On what evidence?' He turned to the jury in desperation. 'I beg you, good sirs, not to be swayed by this superstition and innuendo. Mistress Linney is neither witch nor murderess. She is simply a mother who has lost her child in sad and distressing circumstances. You must not blame her, and curse her further than she has already been cursed by ill fortune.'

Henry Raven could see from the aspect of this jury, though, that the talk of witchcraft had struck home with them, and one or two of them, in regarding Esther uneasily, had even crossed themselves surreptitiously…

\*

Afterwards, in the now empty court chamber, a deeply shocked Henry Raven consulted with Mr Sherbrooke at his table over the verdict and the grim sentence.

Sherbrooke was most effusive in his apologies but Raven quickly silenced him. 'There was naught that you could sensibly do against such a bloody-minded judge as that, sir. Yet I cannot comprehend that even such a judge as he could sentence Esther to hang on such flimsy evidence as was presented here today.' Raven put his head in his hands and fought back a tear. 'Is there naught else that we can do to save her, sir? Is there no power of appeal?'

'Not here in the city, sir. This court is already considered to be the supreme court for criminal cases.' Sherbrooke put a consoling hand on Raven's shoulder. 'Can our good friend Mawdsley not do anything for her, Mr Raven? Only the King can save Mistress Linney now, and Mawdsley has much influence with His Majesty.'

'Can the King simply overturn the verdict of this court?' Raven asked hopefully.

Sherbrooke looked doubtful in response. 'He could in exceptional circumstances, but I suspect that he will not dare to interfere in the jurisdiction of the Lord Mayor over such a case as this. The King could however grant her a Royal pardon if he so wished. That would be much less contentious as he has that authority. Yet he has not taken such precipitate action for any other common criminal case since he came to power, so the likelihood of such a thing is not promising.'

Raven stood up abruptly. 'Even so, I will speak to Mawdsley, of course, to see what he can do to persuade the King. The King owes me some considerable favours for my past services, as well as the cost of a collier of mine that was destroyed in the service of the Crown last winter.' Raven hesitated. 'Is there naught else to be done, Mr Sherbrooke? We have only two days to save Esther. Is there no way to spirit Esther out of Newgate before she is due to hang on Friday?'

Sherbrooke hesitated. 'As a barrister-at-law, I cannot give you any formal advice in this matter.' He lowered his voice to a conspiratorial whisper. 'I have heard however that the turnkeys in Newgate are not averse to well-placed bribes on occasion, yet I know not whether they would stretch their venality to the point of allowing a prisoner to escape. Yet, even if it were so, I could not recommend such a course of action to you, sir. I believe that it would be a terrible risk for a person of your standing to attempt such a reckless act. If you were caught in such a practise, then you might hang with Esther, sir, even though ye be a friend of the King.'

'Yet if that is the only way to free her, then I must give it serious consideration, no matter what the risks to myself,' said Raven grimly...

# CHAPTER 13

Friday, 12th May 1665

Henry Raven suddenly awoke naked in bed, with a blinding headache and a foul dry taste in his mouth. His limbs felt leaden and unresponsive, and his mind confused and troubled. He also realized that he had no comprehension of where he was, or what time it was.

Or even what day it might be, come to think of it, such was his mental confusion...

For a moment he had a moment of blinding fear as he realized that he must have finally succumbed to the plague and must be suffering its initial effects. It would not be too surprising, after all, since he had spent much of the past month in the plague-ridden parish of St Giles. Perhaps the unguent prepared for him by Dora Bagwell to discourage the bites of fleas was less effective than he thought, and one of those insects had finally penetrated his defences. Yet Raven was certain that he had not been bitten by any fleas for several weeks – his body reacted unfavourably to such bites as a rule with swelling and itchiness, therefore he usually knew exactly when he had been bitten. Presently he had none of such itching symptoms, so if fleas truly were the carriers of the plague, then his present bodily weakness could not be ascribed to that cause...

Raven glanced around the unfamiliar bedchamber where he lay, as he looked for some means to slake his powerful thirst. It was a small room, with rough-hewn oak beams for a ceiling, and cracked plastered walls, yet the four poster bed was comfortable enough, with a thick feather mattress and rich brocade covers. From the angle of the sunlight penetrating the cracks in the shutters, the day was already well advanced. Raven tried to concentrate his confused mind on the last things he could remember.

He recalled Esther's trial on Wednesday, of course, and, at that melancholy thought, other memories came flooding back. Immediately after the trial, Martin had driven him in his carriage at breakneck speed along Fleet Street and the Strand to Whitehall, so that he could speak with Mawdsley, in the hope of petitioning a Royal pardon for Esther, or at least reducing her sentence to transportation to the American colonies for life. Esther had been condemned to hang at Tyburn on Friday at noon so there was not a second to waste if he hoped to save her life.

Afterwards Raven had gone back to his own home to wait for the outcome, favourable or otherwise, of Mawdsley's deliberations with the King. When no messenger from Mawdsley had come with the dawn on Thursday, Raven had gone secretly to a rooming house in Cheapside where a certain turnkey from Newgate called Elias Buttle lodged. This portly old rogue had already shown himself to be amenable to bribery, since he had agreed to take secret messages to Esther in her condemned cell for a price. Raven had begun the delicate task of negotiating with the man, and seeing how far Mr Buttle was prepared to go in the name of personal greed. At the end of their meeting, Raven was sufficiently encouraged to believe that a deal might be struck with this man. For the sum of ten pounds in gold, Buttle had suggested that he and his various gaoler accomplices would be able to spirit Esther away from the prison during the night before her planned hanging, though he would not divulge any details of how this daring escape might be achieved until he had the money in his hand.

Raven had then gone at once to his bankers to arrange the illicit payment to Mr Buttle through a trusted intermediary. Yet, although willing to pay, Raven still did not trust the old gaoler entirely. Despite the man's ready promises, Raven was not convinced that the old turnkey could truly deliver what he had promised, which was to bring Esther out of the prison in the dead of night, and to deliver her safely to Billingsgate Wharf, where Raven planned for her to leave in the early hours of Friday for refuge in Holland, on board one of his own vessels – the collier *Thomas Raven* – which was currently berthed there.

At noon on Thursday, Raven had returned to Whitehall Palace to see Mawdsley and discover whether there was any lingering possibility of a Royal pardon for Esther. This was still the preferred solution to save Esther's life, of course, if Mawdsley could but accomplish it. Raven had no prior appointment arranged with Mawdsley, though, and found that his friend was presently engaged in lengthy private discussions with his master Lord Clarendon and other officials of the Privy Council, so he had been forced to wait patiently in an antechamber to the Great Hall for Mawdsley to appear.

Those next few hours of waiting had been an agony of frustration and mental torture for Raven as he saw Esther's life slipping away while he waited here in this dull chamber for a positive answer from his friend that might never come. When Mawdsley had finally appeared at the conclusion of his meeting with Clarendon, Raven had seen immediately from the grim cast of his features that he had been unsuccessful in his endeavours.

Raven had planned to leave immediately for Cheapside again and his final meeting with the venal turnkey Buttle, as this now seemed the only possible way to save Esther, risky though it was. Yet Mawdsley insisted first that Raven should walk across with him to his home in Axe Yard, where he would explain why the King could do nothing in this particular case.

Raven had been reluctant to go when time was so pressing, but had accepted the invitation because he hoped that there might still be some possibility of the King changing his mind and granting a legal reprieve of some sort for Esther, even if it was only to spare her from hanging.

Raven remembered that he had been sitting in the parlour of Mawdsley's pleasant little house in Axe Yard, and taking a little ale while Mawdsley had told him more of the details of his discussions with Lord Clarendon and the King over the fate of Esther Linney. *And Raven now realized that this was the very last thing he could remember...*

Suddenly Raven understood with a panic that he was still in Mawdsley's house, and that this must already be Friday. Even worse, it must already be near noon...

Despite the leaden feeling in his limbs, Raven struggled out of bed, and climbed slowly to his feet, as he realized with an aching heart that Esther must already be on her way in the hanging cart to the village of Tyburn. There would already be a savage jeering crowd milling around the cart, which would in turn be guarded by a ring of constables, so there was no possibility now of obtaining her escape from her awful fate. Raven was desolated that he had failed Esther in the worst way possible. He must have simply got drunk with Mawdsley on Thursday night, and then, in that weak and inebriated state, thought no more of Esther's fate...

Suddenly the door to the bedchamber opened slightly, and Mawdsley peered in cautiously. When he saw that Raven was standing up naked in the middle of the room, he came into the bedchamber properly, yet in a most uneasy manner.

Mawdsley was wearing a very fine indoor *banyan* dressing gown of painted Indian cotton from India, and Raven was deeply irritated for once by his friend's peacock devotion to such expensive fashion when there was so much suffering and poverty in the world. 'What goes on here, Anthony?' Raven demanded hoarsely, as he began to dimly suspect that his friend had deceived him in some way.

Mawdsley was full of contrition. 'Lie down again on the bed, Henry. I believe that I gave you too much of that sleeping draught in your ale last evening, so I have been worried sick that I might have killed you, or at least done some permanent damage to you. Yet it seems you have the constitution of a bull after all, for which I thank the Lord most heartily...'

Raven was livid with his friend, but still reeling and dizzy too, so he was forced to take Mawdsley's advice finally and sit again on the bed. 'You gave me a sleeping draught? In God's name, why? I thought you were my friend...'

Mawdsley looked distraught. I am indeed your friend, Henry, and that is precisely why I did what I had to do.' He hesitated. 'I know of this madcap scheme you had engaged in to try and effect Mistress Linney's escape from Newgate. I had to save you from such foolishness – it would not have saved the woman, and it would have ended in disaster and imprisonment for you at the very least. Even I could not have saved you if you had entered formally into this plot, which would have constituted treasonous behaviour. More likely than imprisonment, you would have ended up swinging from the gibbet at Tyburn too...'

Raven tried to clear his befogged mind. 'How did you know of the plan, Anthony?' he asked suspiciously.

Mawdsley went over by the shuttered window, then turned to face Raven. 'I should not tell you this, Henry, but the Privy Council has a network of spies and informers all over this country who study their fellow citizens for signs of dissent and anti-Royalist sentiment. And Turnkey Buttle is one of our master agents in the city of London – he spends more of his time spying on his fellow gaolers and the visitors to the prison than he does in guarding the inmates. If you had gone ahead with your plan, you would have been swiftly arrested for treason. Imagine what joy it would have been for Judge Holinshead if you had fallen into his malignant clutches!'

Raven shook his head in bewilderment. 'If you had but persuaded the King to grant Esther a pardon, then such a wild plan would not have been necessary,' he complained angrily. 'Does the King not owe me some gratitude for the wild deeds I did on his behalf last winter. Did I not save his life, and his ships at Deptford from destruction at the hands of a madman?'

Mawdsley tried to quell Raven's rising anger. 'The King does indeed owe you a considerable debt of gratitude, Henry, and is sore distressed that he was not able to repay that debt on this occasion.'

Raven gritted his teeth. 'Why not? Why could he not release Esther? What does the fate of one poor girl matter to his vast kingdom?'

Mawdsley looked down at his feet in embarrassment. 'The Star Chamber has long been abolished, Henry, and the absolute power of the King is now severely proscribed. The King simply cannot afford to subvert the legal powers of the Lord Mayor and overrule his decisions without a compelling reason. The City of London has always been full of religious and political dissenters, and any attack on the independence of the city's courts would be seen as a provocation and an attack on those dissenters.

Also you must be aware of the depth of feeling that the case of Mistress Linney has aroused in the city. She is now widely cursed as a witch who murdered her own child in an act of demonic possession...'

Raven groaned dismissively. 'That is mere superstitious nonsense, as ye well know...'

Mawdsley sighed heavily. 'Yet the people believe it, and there have been newssheets and pamphlets published in the city in the last days accusing her of causing this outbreak of plague.'

Raven gasped at this mass stupidity. 'That is madness, indeed.'

Mawdsley hesitated. 'Of course it is. Yet, given the depth of feeling against Mistress Linney, the King would make himself a most unpopular figure if he were to overturn the judgement of the court and to pardon her.'

'So you and your Royal master will do nothing for Esther?' Raven said bitterly.

Mawdsley went to the window and opened the wooden shutters to let in a flood of sunlight. 'There is nothing I can do, Henry. She is due to hang at noon today, which is but a quarter hour away. There is nothing anyone can do for Mistress Linney now.'

Raven put his head in his hands. 'Then God forgive us all, Anthony, for what we are about to do to that innocent young woman...'

*

At first light this morning, Esther had been woken in her condemned cell by her regular gaoler. For whatever perverse reason, condemned criminals were accorded much better treatment in Newgate Prison than those merely suspected of crime. In the last two days, Esther had been repeatedly offered the solace of food and drink for her body, and spiritual balm for her soul. The chaplain of the prison, an earnest young man called James Hughes with the smooth face of a child and a naïve belief in redemption for even the wickedest of human souls, had barely left her side during these hours as he tried to offer her every consolation in his power. More to rid herself of his attentions than anything else, Esther had agreed to receive the sacrament from him, since the young chaplain, although he clearly thought her guilty of infanticide, was nevertheless convinced by her desolate manner that she must have sincerely repented of this wickedness.

Esther knew of course that she was entirely innocent of her baby's deliberate murder, yet she nevertheless felt some intense guilt at not taking better care of his young life. She must have done something terribly wrong in her motherly duties, she decided, therefore deserved to be punished for this neglect. To be hanged for such a thing was a severe punishment indeed, yet the truth was that Esther no longer truly cared whether she lived or died. There was in truth nothing left for her to live for – her child was dead; her brother too; and the only man she had ever truly loved was lost to her forever. Yet she was troubled that she was going to her grave with her reputation so tarnished.

She had been in two minds about Henry Raven's attempts to save her. Half of her mind had been intensely grateful for his intervention and the fact that he truly seemed to care for her still, and believe in her innocence. Yet the other half of her simply wished that Henry had never learned of this trial, and that she could have gone to her fate quietly without him ever knowing anything of it. His was the one good opinion in the world that she had always craved, and, despite his assurances in his written messages to her in prison that he believed in her innocence, it grieved her bitterly that he must now harbour some doubts over her true character, and perhaps at heart believed her to have murdered her own child.

Apart from this regret, though, Esther Linney was going to meet her maker with remarkable equanimity. In fact, despite her outbursts of anger at the trial, Esther held no real hatred for the two women who had borne witness against her and brought her to this desperate situation. No doubt Mistress Worme truly believed the evidence of her own eyes that Esther had choked the life out of her own baby and, misguided though that belief was, was merely trying to get justice for the dead infant.

Mistress Pollock was a more difficult person to forgive, perhaps, because of the damning evidence she had formerly given against her mother. To participate in the persecution of two generations of the same family suggested that she had some particular hurt to avenge. Yet she too had no doubt expressed the truth as she saw it. Esther had been a babe-in-arms at the time this earlier event happened, therefore could not know whether her mother had done the unsettling things that Mistress Pollock had suggested. Yet her evidence, as repeated at Esther's own trial, had seemed plausible. Esther could only wonder at the degree of anguish her mother must have suffered from the death of her beloved husband, an anguish that had induced her to abandon her faith and seek solace in the dark arts of witchcraft...

From her cell, Esther had been able to glimpse a section of Newgate Street and to see the crowds gathering to get a look at her. She did not understand the reason for the particular venom of this crowd, though – after all, a middle-aged carpenter had murdered his wife and six children only a few weeks ago, and suffered much less abuse from the mob than she was getting. When Esther had asked Chaplain Hughes to explain why this was so, he had gone red in the face with embarrassment as he clearly dissembled over the causes of the mob's particular hatred of her.

At ten o'clock, Esther was given a white linen shirt to wear over her own simple gown, and a cap to put on her head. Two men had been hanged at Tyburn earlier today, but the prison authorities had decided that Esther would travel to that village on her own cart since there was much public interest in seeing this evil villainess. At eleven o'clock, she was finally brought out from her cell into the press-yard and lifted onto the back of the cart where she was trussed hand and foot, with her back to the horses' tails. Then, surrounded by constables and other police officers on horseback, each armed with a pike, the gates of the press-yard were swung open and the cart trundled out into Newgate Street. Esther was shocked by the vastness of the crowd assembled outside, and the sudden violent eruption of noise as she appeared. Perhaps the fine weather had encouraged them onto the streets in such numbers despite the threat of the plague; the sun shone down from a sky of unsullied blue, and scarcely a breath of wind stirred the flags on the surrounding buildings.

She heard foul curses and insults directed at her from the mob, even from children – 'Witch! - Harlot of Satan! - Whore of Babylon!' Then she heard one hideous old woman shout to her from an open window – 'Thou art an evil witch to bring the plague down on our poor heads!'

Esther finally understood now why this mob hated her so much – because of the history of her mother, these people truly believed that she was a witch who had inflicted this curse on their city, and therefore was not merely the common sort of evil doer.

Chaplain Hughes, walking beside the cart, looked up at her with sympathy. 'Be brave, Mistress. The crowd is not so multitudinous as it may appear, so you will not have to suffer these barbs and insults all the way to Tyburn.'

Which statement proved to be correct: by the time the cart and procession reached the main thoroughfare of Holborn, the crowd had thinned to odd groups of stragglers, although ones still potent enough in their hatred for all that. Then, once out of the city and across the open fields on the Oxford Road, the watchers were reduced to the odd passer-by or labourer in the fields. Esther tried to retain her composure throughout, but it was difficult not to break down and weep occasionally when she could see the end of her sad and meaningless life approaching so rapidly before her. As the cart approached the crossroads in the village of Tyburn where the gibbet stood, Esther almost fainted with the terror of the moment. Yet somehow she found the resolve to keep standing and facing the accusing mob, despite the darkness enveloping her. Her most overwhelming sadness was of course over the death of her baby son, yet she also felt an overwhelming melancholy that she would never see Dorset again, or the beautiful flower-filled meadows and sunlit woods in which she had grown up.

At the gallows, a large crowd had gathered in jubilant mood, as if the death of this one woman would solve all their earthly problems in one fell swoop. Or perhaps it was just the sight of someone suffering an even greater misery than themselves that drew the citizens of London in such numbers and in such a difficult mood. Esther thought she even recognized some of the faces from the earlier confrontation outside the prison, so these bloodthirsty people had obviously rushed ahead of the cart in order to find a good place to view her final demise.

Chaplain Hughes spoke up again with a word of comfort as the cart bumped to a halt next to the gibbet. Esther was surprised at the appearance of the gallows, which was a simple wooden frame with a platform below reached by a ladder, and much lower than she had expected for such an infamous instrument of execution. The executioner too seemed less fearsome than she had expected, being a common balding man with the appearance of a mere tradesman.

A constable mounted the cart and untied Esther's feet so that she could walk to the ladder unaided. There was a fierce cheer from the swelling crowd when she was prodded by the executioner in the small of the back and made to climb the rickety ladder up to the narrow platform, which was truly more of a wide beam than a proper floor. The chaplain followed her up the ladder, steadying her swaying body with his hand, and then a hush finally fell over the mob as he said a prayer and then sang a few verses of the Psalms.

Esther had no relatives or friends on hand to come and say their farewells at this point, as with most of the condemned at Tyburn. Even her accusers, Mistress Pollock and Mistress Worme, were not here to celebrate their triumph, as far as she could see. Or had their consciences been finally pricked by a seed of self-doubt so that they preferred to stay away...?

Esther had half expected that Henry Raven would have come to see her at the end, yet was glad that he had not. Perhaps he had finally tired of his vain attempts to save her from the hangman, which suggested perhaps that he would not waste too much time in idle grieving for her, for which Esther was heartily grateful. It was better for Henry that he should simply expunge her unfortunate life from his memory...

After five minutes of prayers and supplications from the chaplain, many of the mob were growing impatient in the hot sunshine, and wanted to see the rope placed around Esther's slender white neck. Finally the chaplain got down off the gallows and gave Esther a reluctant bow of acknowledgement, before the executioner covered her eyes with a blindfold...

*

Molly Titchen was amongst the crowd at Tyburn, in company with M'sieur Desargues, though her presence here was certainly not from choice, merely the fact that their carriage had been caught up in all this press of people as they approached Tyburn from the road to Edgware.

After their evening dining together at Will's Coffee House in Russell Street, Molly had expected that M'sieur Desargues might well try to worm his way into her bed that very night. He had been a most amusing companion during dinner, with a wealth of stories, some very rude and vulgar, about his life at the French court. He was also very funny in his mockery of the other actors in her company, whose foibles and affections he could mimic with surprising accuracy from his slight knowledge of them, even those of the ladies. Molly had barely been able to conceal her giggles when M'sieur Desargues had given her his unerring impression of Sir Thomas Killigrew and his haughty English accent. Molly was astute enough to know that when a gentleman spent this much time and effort in entertaining her that he would expect some physical pleasure in return. And in her mood of continuing annoyance with Henry over his failure to visit her, she had been half-tempted to allow M'sieur Desargues to finally indulge his pleasures if he wished it. If Henry truly believed her to be a heartless harlot, then perhaps it was time to live up to his expectations, and perhaps also make him mightily jealous in the process.

Yet, surprisingly – and perhaps a little disappointingly by this point – M'sieur Desargues had been a perfect gentleman afterwards, and had merely walked her back to her front door in Bow Street and bade her good night with a flourish of his wide-brimmed hat, and a deep bow of gratitude.

After the performance on the following day, though, he had again invited her to dinner, and then today, he had arrived at her door at ten o'clock in a fine coach-and-four and suggested a scenic ride in the country before her performance began at three o'clock. On such a glorious May day, it did seem perverse to want to stay indoors in the hot theatre rehearsing her part in a play that she already knew to the letter. So putting on her fine new satin gown, and with her hair freshly washed in spring water, she accepted his invitation at once.

'Is this your own carriage, sir?' she asked him politely, as she stepped into the back and inspected the rich velvet cushions and painted wood inside.

'Alas, no, Molly. I am not a wealthy man. In fact I am virtually penniless. But fortunately I have some wealthy friends, who indulge me in many ways, and will even lend me the use of a fine carriage like this on occasion.'

Molly tried to hide her disappointment at this frank announcement, as she made a fresh evaluation of this gentleman and decided he would have to be firmly rebuffed now if he ever tried to board her. While he was presently a welcome and amusing distraction to her, she was certainly not going to risk her future with Henry Raven by lying with a man of no fortune. 'You are *penniless*, then, M'sieur?' she asked tentatively, hoping that perhaps he was jesting.

'Sadly, that is almost true. I came from an ancient and noble family of considerable wealth and influence, yet we have been cursed by generations of feckless and imprudent young men who frittered away the family's land and fortune. Of which, I regret to say, I was one until recently. Yet I have hopes of changing my impecunious situation. There is a new world of opportunities in the American colonies, and that is where I intend to remake my fortune in time. I realize that I am not in the first flush of youth, yet I am not so old either, so believe I still have enough time on my side to accomplish this goal. What I do need, though, is a good woman at my side...'

Molly fell silent after this, as she wondered whether this gentleman offered her the chance of a new life in the Cape Colony or Virginia, which unexpected notion did give her some considerable pause for thought, as her mind dwelled on visions of wild mountains and rugged forests and painted red savages...

The countryside north of London was not so rugged at this mental image in Molly's mind, yet the meadows and fields and wooded copses still looked their best in the warm spring sunshine. The carriage ride took them along dusty highways lined with green hedgerows dense with cow parsley, and filled with the perfume of downy rose and honeysuckle. M'sieur Desargues was once again wonderfully entertaining as the carriage went north through the flowering fields, skirted Primrose Hill and its bleating sheep, passed through the quiet village of Hampstead and crossed the heathland. Molly was worried for her safety in such a notorious place where highwaymen and footpads were known to congregate, and M'sieur Desargues himself carried no sword today as far as she could see. But when she raised her concerns on this point, the French gentleman spoke up with quiet assurance. 'Worry not over such things, Molly. Any villain who would dare to accost this carriage will soon feel the taste of a pistol ball. Our driver is armed with two pistols, which should be enough to frighten any of the miserable footpads who frequent this heath.'

Molly felt reassured by this gentleman's words. M'sieur Desargues might be a man excessively taken with fashion, yet he was no fop, and looked a gentleman well able to take care of himself in a quarrel. Even so, Molly was glad when the carriage finally turned south for the city again, and towards the distant tower of St Paul's standing proud above the rooftops. However, approaching the village of Tyburn near noon, the carriage soon became caught up in an immense crowd gathered on the road before them, and was eventually brought to a halt in a swirl of dust by all the people and carts in front of them.

Molly realized at once what the cause of the commotion was. ''Tis a hanging in the village of Tyburn ahead, sir,' she explained in answer to M'sieur Desargues's question. 'I had forgot that there was one today.'

M'sieur Desargues was intrigued to see how the English dispatched their criminals, although Molly was less keen, having seen one hanging a few years ago as a child, and not particularly wishing to enjoy such a sad spectacle again. Yet there was no avoiding it now, as there was no room to turn the carriage around and find another way back to the distant city.

The armed driver of the coach-and-four – a talkative and chirpy young fellow called Jack - eventually found a way through all the sightseers and farm carts to a slight hillock near the crossroads where he pulled the steaming horses to a halt under an ancient oak tree. By joining the driver up front, M'sieur Desargues was able to get a good look at proceedings at the gallows and relay them down to Molly, still sitting inside the carriage.

'It seems the condemned is a young woman,' Desargues called down to her. 'And a most decorous and handsome young woman too from her manner, and from her fair skin and fine features, even though I have to judge their quality from fully fifty paces away, therefore may be deceived.'

Molly now remembered the broadsheet she had read yesterday at the theatre concerning this young woman. Quickly she opened the door of the carriage and stood up on the steps on tiptoe to catch a glimpse of the woman. Molly was just able to get a brief view through a fortuitous gap in the crowd of a tall and elegant young woman, who seemed remarkably composed in these horrid circumstances. Molly took her seat again, not wishing to see what terrible thing would follow to that beautiful woman. 'Her name is Esther Linney, M'sieur. She was accused of murdering her own child, and is also believed to be a witch and to have brought the plague to the city.'

Desargues leaned over the side of the carriage and caught Molly's eye with a sad shake of his black curls. 'I did not know you English were so backward and superstitious. Witches indeed!' He glanced back dismissively at the gallows. "They have just put the rope around her neck now, and covered her head, so it cannot be long now. That looks a most inhuman way of hanging anyone, though. That drop is not enough to break the victim's neck quickly when she falls, so that young woman will no doubt suffer great agonies before she dies.'

Molly spoke up reluctantly. 'Ay, sir, 'tis true. I have been told that you often see friends and relations tugging at a condemned man's feet so that he should die quicker and not suffer a slow strangulation.'

'Yet this poor lady seems to have no one at hand to provide this compassionate service to ease her suffering. I would like to do it myself, but there are too many people in front of me.' Desargues leaned over the side of the carriage again. 'What happens to the bodies of the condemned, and to their possessions?' he asked Molly curiously.

Molly listened to the sound of the mob, rising like a great storm around her, as the executioner made ready to send Mistress Linney to her fate. 'I believe, sir, that the bodies and clothing of the dead belong to the executioner; relatives must, if they wish, buy them back from that gentleman, and unclaimed bodies are usually sold to surgeons to be dissected. I have heard that there are often fierce confrontations between the family and friends who do not wish the bodies to be cut, and the messengers who have been sent by their surgeon friends to buy the bodies on their behalf; blows are often given and returned, and sometimes in the turmoil the bodies are quickly stolen by the family and buried secretly.'

Desargues grunted sadly. 'Yet this poor lady seems to have no family to fight for her, merely a jeering mob all around her, so she will no doubt end up as a carcase for some bloodthirsty surgeon to dissect...'

Desargues's further words were drowned out by a great roar from the crowd as Mistress Linney was finally pushed off the gallows, to turn slowly in a sudden violent wind that had sprung up at the crossroads in Tyburn, as if the Lord God himself was angry with these sordid proceedings...

*

At one o'clock, Henry Raven banged loudly at the door of his friend Dr Croone's house in the Strand.

He had come here directly from Mawdsley's house in Westminster as soon as he felt fit enough to walk. He cursed Mawdsley again, not only for giving him that sleeping draught against his will, but administering such a dose that it had rendered him unconscious for nearly eighteen hours, and had left him now with a raging headache and a general weakness in his limbs. There was not even time to send a servant to summon Martin from home with his carriage, so he had set off on foot directly for his destination rather than wait for a contrite Mawdsley to provide him with transport. After a while, his continued weakness made him wish that he had taken a sedan chair after all, yet he persevered on his way down the Strand until his head cleared in the fresh spring sunshine and he felt more his usual self again. The Strand, though, seemed but a shadow of the normal busy thoroughfare it was; on such a fine May day as this, it should have been filled with life, with street sellers and carriages, and all the limitless characters who normally populated London's streets. Yet the pavements were almost empty of passers-by, and the carriages and sedan chairs of the wealthy were gone, replaced by doleful carts and processions of mourners in black.

Yet Raven was too preoccupied with his own business today to worry about the continuing effects of the plague. There was nothing he could do now to save Esther Linney's life, of course, yet he could still do one important service for her and give her a decent Christian burial. Once he had recovered a little from the sickening realization of Esther's brutal and untimely death, it had suddenly occurred to him that, with no one to claim it, her corpse would almost certainly be sold to his friend Dr Croone for dissection...

Which fact explained his urgency: Dr Croone liked to take personal delivery of any freshly hanged corpse and begin his dissections within two hours of the victim's death, before the tissue had any time to deteriorate and rot. Raven arrived at the door of Dr Croone's tall and narrow Jacobean mansion just as the churches in the Strand were ringing out one o'clock, their different peals echoing plaintively in the unusual quiet of the city. Raven thought that he must be in time because even Dr Croone would be unlikely to take possession of a body from Tyburn within an hour of a hanging. Raven was confident therefore that, once the situation was explained to him, Dr Croone would decline to use his knives and scalpels on this particular corpse and would willingly give the body into his care for proper burial. Raven had the idea that he would try and take the body back to Dorset where Esther might be buried with proper respect in a green churchyard with views over the valley of the River Simene, which she had loved so well. Or if the church forbade that because of her supposed crime, then Raven would find some pleasant green spot on his own land where she might be interred to rest in peace.

A manservant answered the door and Raven instantly recognized him as one of the servants who habitually aided Croone with his dissections. He remembered the man's name – Will - and tried to keep his voice calm as he noticed the ominous signs of fresh bloodstains on the man's apron.

Surely he could not be too late, and Dr Croone was already at work dismembering poor Esther's body…?

'Is your master at home, Will?' Raven asked urgently.

Will was a sturdy young man with the powerful hands and forearms of a blacksmith. 'He is, Mr Raven, but he is presently engaged in a dissection in the basement…'

Raven pushed past him at once without explanation, and found the worn stone steps leading down into the basement. He came to a sudden halt, though, when he reached the main cellar room and saw Dr Croone standing with his other servant Jeremiah over a dismembered corpse, and holding a bloody liver to his eye for close inspection.

Croone turned and saw Raven's distraught face. 'Why, Henry, what ails thee? You seem to see a ghost.'

Raven pointed to the fresh liver in Croone's hand. 'Is that a newly delivered corpse, William?' he asked hoarsely.

Croone regarded the liver with admiration. 'Yes, but a few hours dead. And he had a most magnificent liver, did he not? I have rarely seen better.'

Raven felt a flood of relief. '*He*? 'Tis a man that you dissect?'

'Indeed so. Yet I am fortunate today, because I was able to obtain *two* freshly hanged corpses in one day, and the other is a young woman who has recently given birth, which is something rare indeed to find.'

'You have not started with her yet, William?' Raven demanded.

Croone was puzzled by Raven's questions. 'Nay, she lies over there on that other slab, covered by a shroud.' He pointed to the corner of the room. 'I doubt that she has been dead even an hour yet, so I do wish to start on her as soon as I can, though.'

'I fear that you cannot do such a thing, William,' Raven said apologetically, then went on to explain briefly the close connection of Esther Linney to his own family, and her sad recent history.

Croone regarded the shroud-covered corpse with clear regret, and sighed in exasperation. 'Of course, if this lady was a friend of yours, then I cannot possibly dissect her. It would not be respectful or proper, although I may never get to see such a perfect female specimen as this again...' Croone suddenly went white with shock, and his jaw dropped.

'What is it, William?' a startled Raven asked, looking around.

'It must have been a trick of the light, but I could have sworn that I saw that sheet move.' Croone turned to his manservant Will. 'Is there some draught in here, perhaps?' But then Croone cried out in alarm as the corpse on the slab emitted a wailing noise from her throat, then raised herself slowly to a seating position.

Will and the other servant, Jeremiah, ran from the room in terror, but Croone was exultant as he pulled back the shroud fully and saw the woman struggling to get her breath. 'We seem to have a miracle, Henry! *This woman lives still...*'

# CHAPTER 14

Friday, 12<sup>th</sup> May 1665

It took a full three hours for Esther Linney to recover any coherent voice, although she was able to move her limbs, and even hold a stoneware cup in her hands to take a sip of water, within a few minutes of her miraculous rebirth.

'Lazarus rising from the grave could not have caused a greater shock to those who witnessed it than I have just experienced,' Croone declared, still in a state of bewilderment several hours after Esther had come back to life. 'I never thought to see such a thing as a hanged woman brought back to life.' He gave Raven a wry look. 'Perhaps she truly is a witch...'

Raven too was in a state of considerable confusion, but his mental state was mixed with elation as well as wonder. 'I doubt that is a serious proposition you make, William,' he chided his friend, not wishing to make any such unnatural connection to Esther, even in jest.

Croone blinked in embarrassment. 'Nay, of course not, and forgive my weak attempt at wit. I beg your pardon for impugning this lady's reputation when you clearly know her better.'

Raven looked at Esther, who was now, at seven o'clock in the evening, sleeping in a comfortable bed in an upstairs bedchamber. The servants Will and Jeremiah, after recovering from their fright, and still a little pink with shame, had soon carried her from the cold stone slab in the basement to a soft feather bed in an empty bedchamber on the first floor. After her miraculous reawakening, Croone had given Esther some hot cordial and brandy to revive her, and Croone's maidservant Rose had then cleansed Esther's body from head to foot with hot steaming towels, though Esther was still not yet able to utter anything very meaningful in response. 'If we must look for unworldly explanations in all this,' Raven said, 'then perhaps this is more a case of the Lord God taking pity on this innocent woman and righting a terrible wrong.'

Croone said nothing to that, and Raven understood why, of course. Being a most rational man of science, Croone had no taste for invoking miracles as the cause of strange and unexplained events, but preferred always to look to the laws of nature for an explanation. Raven too thought that the most likely explanation was that the executioner had simply botched the hanging, and that Esther had been taken down while still just alive. He wondered in fact whether Croone's own agents might have been partly responsible for this, since they knew that the good doctor always wanted his subjects for dissection to be as recently dead as possible. Was it possible, then, that, in their eagerness to obtain a fresh corpse for their client, his agents had simply taken the body down before it was truly dead? Raven suggested this notion to Croone who nodded in agreement, happy to be given some credit in this interesting business, if only a passive one.

'But even if that is true, this is still a remarkable circumstance, is it not? Perhaps even unique...' Croone collected his thoughts as he bent down to examine the sleeping Esther again in wonder. 'My agents who obtained this supposed corpse for me said she had been hanging for a full fifteen minutes from the gibbet and showed no signs of life. Look at the marks of the rope on her neck! - she will likely carry those deep scars for life. Perhaps she is simply blessed with a very strong neck, and the muscles were somehow able to keep her breathing passages part open while she hung from the gibbet. '

'Yet she has a very slim swanlike neck, so that explanation seems doubtful to me,' Raven murmured. 'Perhaps she has the unconscious ability to slow down her bodily functions to such an extent that she merely seemed dead. But, even allowing for that, I know not how someone can survive for nearly an hour without apparently taking breath.' Raven bent down to feel Esther's brow, which still felt remarkably cool. He felt the pulse in her wrist, and found that also to be remarkably slow in comparison with his own. Although he was elated at her improbable survival, Raven had been a little concerned from Esther's vacant look earlier that her intelligence and wit might have been irreparably impaired by the severe terror of what had happened to her. Yet later in the afternoon he believed that she had recognized him, even though unable to make any intelligible response to his questions at the time. 'We must let her sleep now, and try and recover by herself from the terrors of this day, William...'

'Indeed so,' Croone concurred.

Neither Croone nor Raven had any faith in the efficacy of bloodletting to restore health, therefore they agreed instead merely to keep Esther warmly swaddled in hot bandages and plied with hot water for the next few hours, under the constant watch of his servants for any signs of distress. For all his amiable nature, Croone was a strict disciplinarian with his household, and Raven was not surprised to see the way his servants jumped to attention as he issued them some orders at the door.

Fortunately Croone's talkative wife, Mary, was presently away from home visiting relatives in the country, so that was one potential difficulty removed. Yet Raven still had concerns about this remarkable story getting out. 'Are your servants discreet, William?' he asked his friend later, when they had retired to Croone's immense library on the ground floor. 'We must keep this strange happening strictly to ourselves.'

Croone deliberated, as he glanced out of the window of his library at his private knot garden, which basked in strong evening sunshine. 'Will and Jeremiah will say nothing of this, if I ask them. And Rose and Flora will no doubt try to obey my orders in this regard too, although I am less trusting of their good sense and their ability to hold their tongues. But do we truly need to keep Mistress Linney's remarkable resurrection a secret? She has been tried and hanged for her crime already; she cannot surely be hanged again for the same offence.'

Raven was pensive. 'Yet these scurrilous newssheets accused her of being a witch, and her survival of hanging will seem rather a confirmation of these superstitious beliefs rather than a denial. You made light of this, but other more gullible people will seriously believe her to be in league with the Devil. Even if we restore her to full health again, we must therefore never let it be known that she has survived.'

Dr Croone made a wry face. 'Then what do we do with her?'

Raven was forthright in his opinion. 'The first priority is to get her away from London, which has been a most unhappy place for her.'

'Where would you take her, Henry?'

Raven had already given that some thought. 'After her trial two days ago, I did attempt to bribe her gaolers to release her, and I was then of a mind for her to emigrate to Holland and start a new life there. But perhaps such a drastic step is not necessary yet. In the meantime, I will take her back to her native Dorset where she can hopefully recover fully in mind and body from these terrible events. Then we will decide what to do for the best.'

Croone frowned. 'Is that not more dangerous for her than staying in London? Will she not be recognized there?'

Raven had thought of that difficulty too. 'Yes, there is that risk. I think she will therefore need a disguise of some sort, and certainly when travelling. But in the longer term, she may be able to return to the kind of life she knew as a girl, perhaps in a different part of Dorset.'

'Does she have any family, Henry?'

Raven shook his head. 'Her only brother is likely dead at sea, so my own family is the nearest thing Esther has to relations. Esther lived in our house as a child, and was very close to my sisters when they were growing up.'

'And the father of her child – the man who caused all this trouble for her – what of him?' Croone asked curiously.

Raven deliberated 'I know not who this man is. But perhaps Esther will divulge his identity to me in time, and, if the man is not already married, I may then be able to take some steps to uniting them properly. I suspect, though, that the man *is* married, otherwise surely he would have married such a desirable woman as Esther already.'

Croone cast him a shrewd look. 'I see there is also some close bond between you and this maid, Henry.'

'She was almost like a third sister to me,' Raven admitted. 'So I do feel some shame at my neglect of her.'

'A *sister*? Truly? Are you certain that your feelings for her were brotherly ones, and not something different?'

Raven was surprised by such a direct question from the staid Dr Croone of all people. Yet he found that he could not answer it with complete frankness, since it was true that his feelings for Esther had not always been precisely those that he felt for his sisters, but had at one time been something rather different…

*

M'sieur Desargues had to return the grand coach-and-four that he had borrowed for the day to the stables off Holborn where his unknown benefactor kept his horses, yet was reluctant for some reason to name this generous individual. Molly surmised that this person might be some wealthy acquaintance from Paris, perhaps someone who preferred to remain anonymous. There were many French émigrés in the city now, Molly knew, but they made no great show of their presence here, many of them still fearing for their safety, having been persecuted in their own country for one reason or another, usually to do with their politics or their religion. For some reason, these displaced Frenchmen were now among the more visible patrons of Molly's mother's discerning establishment in Whetstone Park, and, as a consequence, Molly knew that Celia had tried to introduce a little Parisian style into her bawdy house of late, as well as employing girls of more refined appearance and manners to suit her Continental visitors, who had a more demanding taste than Englishmen when it came to courtesans. Molly had cast a shrewd glance at M'sieur Desargues at this point in her secret musings, and wondered again what had motivated this particular French gentleman's interest in her. Now that she knew him to be a relatively poor man, she was inclined to be even more suspicious of his attentions towards her, thinking that he had perhaps cultivated her acquaintance with some nefarious purpose in mind…

Molly was still deeply upset to have witnessed the hanging of that poor woman, Mistress Linney. Even if she truly was a murderess, she did not deserve such dreadful punishment as that. And she was, most likely, innocent as she had apparently claimed – she certainly did not have the appearance of someone who would murder their own child. Molly was also certain that she could be no witch as the news pamphlets and posters had claimed. Surely no witch could be as sweet of countenance as that sad young woman...?

M'sieur Desargues walked with Molly from Holborn to the theatre in Bridges Street, through streets that seemed almost deserted in the afternoon sun. Molly was uneasy at the strange emptiness of the streets, and particularly of Drury Lane which was usually bustling at this time of day, with a play soon to start. Yet today even Drury Lane seemed abandoned and forlorn, which Molly could only ascribe to worries over the plague.

However Molly knew something more particular was wrong when she drew close to the theatre itself, and saw not a single individual waiting outside. The crowds had been thinning outside the theatre for some time of course as the outbreak of plague had worsened, yet even yesterday there had been a sizeable crowd waiting outside in anticipation of the start of the play at three o'clock.

It was no great surprise to Molly, then, when she saw the poster pasted over the main doorway of the building. She sighed heavily and turned to M'sieur Desargues. 'The theatre is closed until further notice because of the plague, M'sieur. It seems that I did not need to hurry back from Hampstead Heath for this performance after all.' Molly tried to be light in manner, yet she was severely upset by the news, even though it was hardly unexpected.

She went around to the stage door, with M'sieur Desargues following obediently at her heels, but that too was boarded up. The theatre truly looked a dismal place with its doors barred, and no light inside. *What were they all to do now?* Molly wondered emptily. So many livelihoods were tied up in the business of that building, so much pleasure and gaiety for the citizens of London too, and so much of the needs of her own life in particular. The theatre was in Molly's blood now, and she could not conceive of a future where she could not perform on stage for the delectation of the public. It occurred to her that this need to perform was the most important requisite of her life, as great as her need to eat and sleep and make love – perhaps even greater than her need for the companionship of Henry Raven, if she was being absolutely truthful.

Now all that purpose in her life was gone, if the theatre was going to remain closed for some considerable time. The poster over the front door had made no mention of how long the closure might go on for, but Molly doubted now if the theatre would reopen until the plague had run its course, which might not be until the colder days of autumn. Sir Thomas would know more of course, but she could hardly go to his house directly and ask him. Killigrew did not allow anyone from the company anywhere near his household, probably for fear that news of his philandering at the theatre might reach the ears of his long suffering but wealthy Dutch wife, Charlotte. Molly now cursed the fact that she had missed rehearsal and gone off on that frivolous coach ride to Hampstead Heath. If she had gone to rehearsal, then she would probably have discovered how long this closure might go on for.

At least she still had a roof over her head, courtesy of Henry, which she was sure would continue for the near future at least. Although she was no longer so sure of Henry Raven's permanent commitment to her, yet he was an honourable man and would not turn her out of that house in Bow Street at short notice. Yet living there might be a hardship once the plague had taken hold and emptied half the city. Molly had never thought of leaving the city before, but that was entirely because of her commitment to the theatre. Without that pressing need to stay, Molly now considered whether it might not be better to quit the city for a more favourable place to ride out this storm. If what Henry had said was true, then she was safe from any recurrence of the affliction now, yet it might soon be impossible to get food and other essentials here, with so many businesses and shops closed.

Standing in the alleyway outside the stage door, a dejected Molly now turned to M'sieur Desargues with slight displeasure and wished only that this man should be gone from her life. With such serious matters going on, his apparent pursuit of her was no longer an amusement to her but a mere distraction that she now wished to do without.

M'sieur Desargues was not so easily put off by her cool dismissal, though, and made a sensible suggestion that Molly could hardly object to. 'Before you finally go home, Molly, why not join me for some food at the Cock Inn, which is at the end of your own street, is it not? The taverns and ale houses in this city are still open, I am sure – knowing the English, they will be the last thing to close. And even though English ale has a disturbing resemblance to horse piss, both in appearance and taste…' – here he smiled charmingly – 'I will suffer it gladly for a little more of your sweet company.'

Molly could not help but laugh at this remark, so it seemed that she did need M'sieur Desargues's company after all, even if only to lighten her present dark mood. Yet she could not help saying, 'But you still have no sword, M'sieur, and now no armed coachman to protect you either. Are you sure that you can protect me, if we should be accosted in the Cock Inn, which is a well-known place of ill-repute?'

M'sieur Desargues took her gentle mockery with good humour. 'I promise you that anyone who accosts you or insults you, Molly, will feel the blow of a steely French fist to his jaw. Is that not enough reassurance for you, young Madam?'

They did indeed find the Cock Inn to be still open for business, yet any hopes that Molly might have had to see some of her fellow players engaged there in drowning their sorrows were soon dashed. Even this usually boisterous coaching inn was a melancholy place today, which was perhaps an unfortunate portent for the whole of London. Nevertheless, Molly shared some bread and cheese and light ale with M'sieur Desargues in a corner of the tap room, which was a welcome enough repast after a trying day.

'So this is what French horse piss tastes like,' she suggested mischievously to M'sieur Desargues, as she took a sip of ale. ''Tis not so bad, then. I must get myself a French horse if he can make ale like this from water.'

M'sieur Desargues smiled in return. '*Bonne idée*...provided he is a big powerful stallion, of course...' His smile faded. 'What will you do, Molly, now that the theatre is closed?' he asked more seriously.

'I know not, sir. Perhaps I must return to my mother's house,' she said, only partly in jest.

M'sieur Desargues nodded. 'Ah, Mistress Hornett's delightful establishment for entertaining gentlemen. I hope that you do not see your future to be that of bawdy house keeper too, even though it has made your mother a wealthy woman by all accounts...'

Molly blinked in surprise at that. She was certain that she had never informed M'sieur Desargues of the name of her mother, and certainly not of her mother's type of business before, so her earlier suspicions of this gentleman were aroused even further now that she knew him by his own admission to be penniless. Perhaps this gentleman had picked her out for particular attention from all the other actresses at the theatre because he had heard of her connection to Madam Celia Hornett? Molly had no idea how much money her mother might be worth, yet she suspected - given the recent success of her mother's businesses (Celia now owned several other more legitimate businesses than the bawdy house, including a bakery and a milliner's shop), and given also her miserly refusal to waste any money - that her mother must have amassed a goodly sum of money of late. Perhaps M'sieur Desargues had heard of this and was desirous of finding a way to get to that fortune...

Molly deliberately avoided saying anything of her mother, though, to see if that might draw out M'sieur Desargues further, but he too seemed reluctant to say more on that subject, which led to an awkward hiatus in the conversation. Molly finally broke the silence with an enigmatic remark of her own. 'Or perhaps I too will sail off for the American colonies, as you intend to, M'sieur, and make my fortune there,' Molly said with mock seriousness. 'Do the colonists in Virginia and New York have theatres yet, do you think? Could I make a living there as an actress?'

M'sieur Desargues leaned across the table. 'I doubt that such serious folk as those English Puritans have much interest in frivolous things like playing. What those colonists are badly in need of is some fresh European blood to enliven their society, and to bring some civilization and enlightenment to brighten their dull lives…'

'Yet that is not the main reason why you go there, M'sieur, is it?' Molly teased him. 'You go to re-make your fortune, do you not?'

'I do indeed. There truly lies a virgin and virgin land across the ocean whose riches are just waiting to be explored and exploited, and we Frenchmen must not be left behind in that race.' He put his hand on top of Molly's, and patted it comfortingly. 'Perhaps we should explore its virgin wonders together, Molly? Together we would bring some joyous life to these stern English colonies, would we not?'

Despite herself, Molly was enticed at the thought and did not remove his hand from hers immediately, but let him hold it there for some time while she daydreamed of this new world across the great ocean. In the end, they stayed for much longer at the Cock Inn than Molly had intended, and she was a little merry with drink by the time she and her mysterious Frenchman left the establishment. She saw with surprise that it was already grown dark so must be past eight o'clock in the evening.

But M'sieur Desargues would not leave her even then, and insisted on walking with her back to her front door further up Bow Street. Molly was concerned by now that he would want to come in and take his pleasures with her, and, if so, she was presently in no condition of body or mind to resist him, even if she wanted to.

But soon her worries were diverted to a more particular problem than M'sieur Desargues's amorous propensities. As she stepped over the foul open drain that ran down the middle of Bow Street, Molly glanced around in the dusky light and glimpsed a figure behind her, the tall figure of a man who ducked swiftly out of sight into a doorway on being observed…

Suddenly wary that she was being stalked yet again, Molly regarded her companion with instant suspicion as she recalled that this gentleman himself had certainly followed her home from the theatre on at least two previous occasions. *Could that man behind be an accomplice of M'sieur Desargues, who now intended to join him in forcing their way into her home and taking everything she possessed?* Was that the truth about M'sieur Desargues – that he was a common thief after her money? Yet that seemed an unworthy thought when she remembered how this man had saved her the night she came down with the plague. She might have died in the street that night if it had not been for him. And also, if he *was* a mere thief, then he had already had numerous opportunities to steal from her, yet had taken nothing…

These thoughts flashed through her head in but a moment, and so she decided to warn M'sieur Desargues of the man behind them, of whom he must surely be unaware. But even that short time she had chosen to equivocate proved to be too long. Before she had time to utter a warning, a cloaked and hooded figure appeared from nowhere and knocked her roughly to the ground. After a bewildering flurry of movement, Molly saw from her dazed position on the ground that the newcomer had forced M'sieur Desargues against a wall, and now held a vicious-looking dagger to his throat.

'I have no money, sir,' M'sieur Desargues protested to his attacker, 'so I regret that you have waylaid the wrong person if it's riches that you seek.'

The man spoke in a guttural whisper. *'Il n'est pas votre argent que je veux, mais votre vie...'*

Molly could not understand the words, but recognized the language well enough, so knew well that this could be no common street robber. Molly could see little of M'sieur Desargues's assailant behind his cloak and hood, but she got rapidly to her feet in order to help the Frenchman fight off this sinister individual. Molly instinctively reached through the secret pocket in her skirts to get at the knife that she always carried there for her own protection, strapped to her thigh.

*Except that it was no longer there...*

Molly cursed to herself that she had given up this useful habit of carrying a knife for protection under own skirts, since her rise as an actress and a wealthy man's mistress. Henry had thought the knife a most unladylike thing to find when she undressed in her bedchamber, and so she had given up this vulgar habit to please him. And in truth, she moved in different and more exalted circles these days, and rarely walked the streets alone at night like the old days, so the knife had hardly been necessary any more – *until tonight anyway...*

M'sieur Desargues could not speak properly with the knife pressed so hard against his throat, but now seemed to recognize who this sinister individual might be. With difficulty he whispered, *'Usted podría matarme aquí a sangre fría, Señor de Santiago?'* For some reason M'sieur Desargues spoke not in French but in a language that sounded to Molly's inexpert ear like Spanish.

The man himself responded in English, though, if heavily accented. 'And very slowly and painfully, sir. I am flattered that you finally recognize me, though I wish you had not spoken to me in that cursed Spanish tongue when I am Catalan, born and bred. My employer has asked that you not be dispatched too quickly or painlessly, but must first suffer a little fear and anguish before leaving this world. He asked me therefore to cut out your lying tongue while you still live, so that you would be properly repaid for all the misery that you have caused him with your lies and deceit.'

M'sieur Desargues seemed remarkably unafraid. 'I am unarmed, sir. Would you not care to give me the chance of a fairer fight? Or do you doubt your ability against me, when not given the advantage of surprise?'

Then Molly became aware of yet more figures approaching them in the rapidly fading light, and for a moment she thought worriedly that this villain who had accosted M'sieur Desargues must have accomplices of his own.

But the newcomers were only a poor woman with the plague, stumbling along with a child in tow. The woman's face was covered in dreadful black pustules, and blood seeped from her ears in a slow trickle of impending death. Yet she seemed still a young woman to Molly, though it was hard to tell in truth. The woman did not seem to even notice the two men pressed up against the wall at first, but spoke only to Molly. 'Please, sister,' she begged with outstretched arms, 'I need some money for my child. I will be...dead by morning, and she has...no one to take care of her.'

Molly stepped back instinctively from her to feel inside her purse, and the woman, thinking her plea for help was to be coldly ignored, now turned her attention to the two men pressed against the wall. Molly realized that the poor woman must be nearly blind, as she herself had been on that grim night when the disease had taken hold of her. The woman's trembling outstretched hands found a surprisingly tenacious grip instead on the cloak of M'sieur Desargues's assailant.

This villain was still so engrossed in holding his knife to M'sieur Desargues's throat that he had ignored the begging woman up to now. But now he finally turned his head in exasperation to see who tugged softly at his cloak, then pulled back in immediate revulsion as he saw the disease-ridden face floating before him in the half-light.

The woman kept a tight grip on the man's cloak, though, impeding the villain's movements considerably, and this allowed M'sieur Desargues finally to break free from the pressure of his dagger. The woman apparently saw enough to realize that it was a man that she clung to now. 'Have some pity, sir. I am stricken with the plague, sir, and need money for my child.'

When the woman put her blackened hands to the villain's face by accident, the man gasped in horror, then turned and fled into the descending gloom with a parting curse for M'sieur Desargues. 'Have no fear, M'sieur. I will be back in time to cut out your tongue, as I have promised...'

After the man had disappeared into the night, M'sieur Desargues breathed a sigh of relief and turned to the plague victim. 'Madam, take everything in my purse, though 'tis little enough. You have saved my own poor life.'

Molly too had emptied her purse of coin, and now she embraced the woman. 'Take this too, sister. I wish that I could do more for thee.'

The woman tried to smile through bleeding teeth. 'I pray only that the Lord will take care of my soul, because my...earthly worries will soon be over. Thank thee kindly, Mistress. This money...will be enough for my girl here to leave the city and live for a while.'

Molly was uneasy as she glanced at the child, a girl of ten or eleven, who did seem mercifully free of the plague. ''Tis little enough that I do for thee, sister,' Molly said, again embracing the woman despite the reek of death on her.

The woman and her child pocketed the offered coins and stumbled away into the darkness, while Molly felt the tears pricking at her eyes.

M'sieur Desargues was more business-like, though. 'That was good fortune for me indeed that this plague woman came along. It was even better fortune to discover that my enemy has an Achilles heel – he is sore afraid of the plague, it seems, and has gone to try and scrub his face and body clean of the contagion of that woman's touch. Otherwise I would be a corpse by now, and a tongueless one at that. Yet that man will be back for me soon, as he said, and will not be distracted a second time, I fear.'

'He was not a common footpad, then?' Molly said, though it was hardly a serious question.

M'sieur Desargues laughed humourlessly. 'By no means. The gentleman who held that blade against the base of my neck is, I believe, the most dangerous assassin in Europe.'

Molly gasped. 'Have you encountered this villain before tonight, then?' she asked in wonder.

'No, I know him only by reputation, but that is enough to cause me great disquiet. I had been warned by friends that there was a man recently come to London to murder me, and that it might be this individual, though foolishly I chose not to believe this wild story. Yet, regretfully, it seems to be more than a rumour after all,' M'sieur Desargues added dryly. 'This gentleman is, I believe, a Catalan from the city of Barcelona, and he uses many names in his dealings, including the French name Jacques Pailler. However the world knows him best as Francisco Nunez de Santiago. I have heard many reports of this man's evil deeds in France in the service of wealthy and important men.' M'sieur Desargues grimaced. 'Although I offered to fight him fair, it would not have made any difference to the outcome. I am an accomplished swordsman myself but that devil, de Santiago, could dispatch me like an unarmed child.' He looked into Molly's eyes, and she was disturbed by the shiver of fear she saw there. 'If I do not get away from London soon, Molly, I am as good as dead. Even the plague is not as implacable and relentless an enemy as that villain, once he is on your scent.'

Molly glanced around nervously, and began walking immediately towards her own front door again. 'For what reason does he persecute you? Is this the result of a personal feud?'

M'sieur Desargues kept up at her side. 'It is indeed a personal feud that has brought this man here in pursuit of me. Yet not with him directly; he is but the agent of another man's retribution.'

'What did you do to excite this other man's hatred?' Molly asked

174

suspiciously.

M'sieur Desargues sighed. "Tis enough for you to know that I fear for my life, Molly.' He glanced in the direction taken by the plague woman and her child. 'I wonder that you embraced that woman, Molly. Do you not fear these sufferers of the plague still?'

'Do you not fear them too, sir? Yet you came to see me often enough when I was stricken with the contagion.'

M'sieur Desargues shrugged. 'That was different. I have some special regard for you, Molly. And even so, I did not embrace you as you did that poor woman.'

Molly finally reached her front door with a sigh of relief that the villain with the dagger had not returned. 'Worry not for my welfare, sir. According to Mr Raven, who is most knowledgeable in these things, being a trained physician, I am safe forever from the plague, having caught the disease once and survived.'

M'sieur Desargues was surprised. 'Is that so? I have not heard that before.'

'Perhaps that is because so few survive the affliction, for which mercy I must be heartily grateful.'

'I say Amen to that too, Molly, since your life is very important to me.' M'sieur Desargues stood awkwardly at the door. 'I hesitate to ask this great favour, Molly, but may I stay with you here tonight.' He saw her expression and added quickly, 'Not in your own bed, of course. I will be happy in another bed, or even on the floor.'

Molly was sceptical. 'That is a poor ploy, sir, and one beneath you, to take advantage of tonight's circumstance to try and gain access to my bed.'

M'sieur Desargues was affronted. 'Indeed not, Molly. You misjudge me indeed if you think that I lust after your body. That would be most improper, even for a Frenchman. I truly believe that if I return to my lodgings in Fleet Street again, I will not survive until morning. This assassin, de Santiago, likely knows my present lodgings by now, and will be waiting there for me to return.'

The desperate tone in his voice made her finally take him seriously. 'Then you had better come in, sir. But mark it well, M'sieur, this is not an invitation to my body. I like your company well enough, sir, but 'tis no more than that...'

*

Late that night, Raven was finally able to talk to Esther, who had woken and recovered enough by this late hour to be able to speak coherently again. Dr Croone's other maidservant, Flora, had volunteered to lie in the same bed with Esther and warm her with her own bodily warmth throughout the evening, and this human contact seemed to have improved and speeded Esther's recovery.

Raven took her hand. ''Tis a wondrous thing that thou art still alive, Esther. The Lord God took pity on you and saved you.'

Esther stared vacantly into his eyes, though he knew well that she recognized him. 'Then I would rather…that he had not…bothered. I would rather be…dead, sir. In fact I feel…dead.'

Raven took a tighter grip of her hand. 'Then we must bring you back to life, Esther, and give you proper reasons to appreciate the world again.'

Esther did not move her hand in response to his, and seemed sunk in a deathly embrace still. 'What reasons…do I have to live now? Where can I go…and what can I do …to escape from this…cursed life of mine? '

Raven had not expected her to be the same Esther he remembered, of course, after such traumatic happenings, yet he was disappointed at this defeatism. 'You can come with me to Dorset, Esther. You can see again the glory of the meadows and hedgerows in May, and you can renew your close acquaintance with my family and household.'

Esther sighed. 'Word will soon get out…that I am there, sir. Will they not…come for me again?'

'I think you have nothing more to fear from the law. They cannot hang you again for the same supposed crime. But we will hide you from common view for the present, and my household will be sworn to secrecy until such time as we resolve a plan for your future life, Esther.'

'Then, I shall do as you say, sir. You have been…most kind. I thank you…for your support during the trial, and your…attempts to free me.'

'There is no need for thanks, Esther. You are my sister, and in truth I should have done more for you. Not only during your trial, but in previous years. I have always held a special regard for you, Esther, but I have not always been capable of showing you that affection…' Raven fell silent, not sure how much note Esther was taking of his words. 'Please never call me "sir" again, though, Esther. I shall be "Henry" to you from now on, or nothing. Is that clear?' he added with mock seriousness.

Esther finally tried to smile. It was a weak attempt but at least it showed that her spirit had still survived this terrible ordeal. 'I would like to return to Dorset…Henry…but I still fear that I will excite…attention…if I go there. Everyone knows my face.'

Raven smiled back, trying not to let his eyes linger on the cruel rope burns around her slender neck. 'Well, 'tis true that it is a very special face, so we will have to disguise your beauty in some way.' He hesitated. 'I hesitate to suggest this, but would you be prepared to sacrifice your beautiful hair in order to gain some anonymity?'

Esther blinked slowly, and a tear trickled down her pale cheeks. 'Why not? I have sacrificed everything else…'

# CHAPTER 15

Saturday, 13th May 1665

At first light on Saturday, Henry Raven walked over from St Martin's Lane to Anthony Mawdsley's house in Axe Yard to apologize for the intemperate language he had used to his friend the day before. Raven found him in his kitchen, partaking of a little breakfast of goose flesh scavenged from the remains of his previous night's dinner.

'So you understand that I acted in your best interest, Henry,' Mawdsley said with relief, as he continued to eat.

Raven had taken a seat at the same table in the kitchen, but had declined to join his friend in breakfast, having presently no appetite at all. 'I understand it well, Anthony. You acted in my best interest, if not in Mistress Linney's.'

Mawdsley paused in his eating, with a large slice of goose breast impaled on his knife. 'I would have saved Mistress Linney too, if it had been in my power, Henry. But it was not; I have no authority in such matters, and have to rely on my powers of persuasion with the King, which in this case were insufficient for the purpose.'

Raven nodded. 'I know that well too, and that you tried most heartily to win a pardon for her. Yet Mistress Linney is sadly dead now,' he lied, 'and we must put this miserable business behind us now, otherwise our friendship might be permanently tainted.' Raven had no intention of telling his friend the truth of the matter; and in fact his visit here this morning was as much concerned with discovering whether Mawdsley had heard any rumours that Esther might have survived her execution, as with his need to secure his friendship. As far as Raven knew, only he and Dr Croone's household knew of Esther's improbable survival so far. The household had been sworn to secrecy of course, and Raven had promised Croone's four servants twenty five pounds each to keep the secret forever. Croone's two

177

young manservants, Will and Jeremiah, were honourable young men who would no doubt fulfil this bargain, but Raven was less sure of the ability of the two maidservants, Rose and Flora, to keep this secret. They were not scheming girls by nature, yet neither were they equipped with much intelligence, therefore could easily spread the story with loose gossip to the servants of neighbouring houses. And from there the story would soon spread all over the city, and beyond...

Yet Raven could see that Mawdsley had certainly heard no such rumours so far about the fate of Esther Linney, and he must be remarkably well informed about gossip on the streets of London, given his network of agents, spies and informers. Therefore, for the present at least, it seemed that Rose and Flora must have held their tongues, and the secret seemed to be holding.

Raven had further news to impart to his friend. 'I came also to tell you that I have decided to take your advice and leave the city.'

Mawdsley was curious. 'Why this sudden change of heart, Henry? When we spoke of this on Tuesday at the King's theatre, you seemed determined to stay in the city and help the plague victims.'

Raven swallowed uncomfortably. 'You said yourself that the battle against the plague is already lost. There is nothing more that a single physician can do. New cases are now a hundred a day; soon there will be thousands infected. Normal business will then be impossible in the city, Anthony, as you well know, and it will be difficult to get food with all the bakers and butchers gone. Even my fellow members of the Royal Society, Mr Wilkins, Mr Hooke and Dr Petty, have decided to leave Gresham College and take up residence in Lord Berkeley's house at Epsom, and I have reluctantly concurred with their decision. I believe that those citizens who are not infected, and who have the means, should leave the city, while those without the means must unfortunately ride out the storm, and simply stay off the streets as much as possible. Yet many of those ordinary people who cannot afford to leave for the country are nevertheless abandoning their homes and moving out into encampments of tents on the north edge of the city. Last night I walked home along the Strand, and it was most disconcertingly quiet with no rattling coaches or street cries...'

Mawdsley agreed dolefully. 'Yes, 'tis strange indeed to see the streets so empty. Yesterday the King ordered that the theatres should be closed until further notice, which is not a step that His Majesty has taken lightly when he loves the art of playacting so much. The King feels greatly for his subjects in this trying time, and is doing all he can to help them.'

Raven simmered resentfully. 'Which is not much, by all accounts! The city authorities have entirely given up treating victims, as far as I can see, and now merely want to identify them quickly and move them outside the city to die, where they can be swiftly buried in mass graves.'

Mawdsley put his slice of goose down on his pewter plate, and looked at it distastefully, his appetite now apparently gone too. 'What else can the Mayor and his aldermen do?' he argued uneasily. 'But I thought there were still plague nurses operating on the streets, who try to offer succour to victims when they find them?'

'Not that I have seen,' Raven answered harshly. 'No one wants to do this dangerous work any more, not even old women, even though the pay is a shilling a day. The same women can now make that much as so-called "searchers" by finding but three corpses, which is no difficult task these days, and a much quicker way of earning a shilling.' Last night, on his way home from Dr Croone's house to his own home, Raven had seen several gangs of these old women who were employed by the city now to go from door to door looking for corpses at four pence each. He had found them a most disconcerting sight with their ancient witchlike faces and their black dresses and sinister white sticks. They had seemed to him more like vultures come to feast on the rich pickings than angels of mercy.

Mawdsley had nothing to say to that, and a gloomy silence pervaded the kitchen, broken only by the sound of the bubbling pots of stew and water over the open fire.

Finally, Raven spoke up again. 'I came also to tell you, Anthony, that I will volunteer to join you and the fleet at Harwich at the end of this month.'

Mawdsley was delighted that his friend would come and support him. '*You will*? That's splendid news, Henry. Yet you sounded so doubtful of the idea when I suggested it at the theatre this week.'

Raven made a wry face. 'I am still doubtful of the sense of this war. But if I have to leave the city anyway, I would not be comfortable enjoying my leisure on my estate in Dorset when other Englishmen are risking their lives in the service of their country. Especially since some of those Englishmen are such idlers and wastrels as Sedley, Buckhurst and Rochester. If such as they choose to go, then it would be difficult for me to stay behind in safety, sleeping comfortably in my bed.'

Mawdsley agreed. 'Those were my feelings too. Yet are you sure of this, Henry? I have other compelling reasons to go, unlike you. I will enhance my reputation at court by going, but there is no such profit in this for you.'

Raven smiled. 'Now you seek to talk me out of it, after arguing so persuasively for it but four days ago? Yet I have made up my mind to go, unwise though it might be. I want no commission in the navy, though,' he warned. 'I want only to serve as a civilian volunteer, and only for the duration of this campaign, which I trust will not be for more than a matter of weeks.'

Mawdsley clapped him on the shoulder. 'Then of course you shall, Henry. Your medical skills will be a great boon when the fleet is so short of surgeons. You may find that you have to saw off many a shattered limb, though, and piece together many a bloodied body, in the course of your work, which I know are tasks distasteful to you. So I cannot tell you how much I appreciate this sacrifice you make, Henry. I will try and get you aboard the *Royal Charles* with me and Charles Berkeley. After all, you saved that vessel from destruction in the dry dock at Deptford last winter, so it seems only right that you should be on board the flagship of the fleet. You know that the fleet will sail from Harwich before the end of May to take the fight directly to the Dutch? We do not intend to merely sit in port waiting for them to come to us.'

'I do know it, Anthony. And I will be in Harwich in good time. But first I have to go back to Dorset, to put my affairs in good order, and take proper leave of my sister.'

'Of course. How is the fair Catherine coping at the manor on her own, now that Mary has married and left home?'

'Well enough, I believe. I would not be too surprised if she married soon.'

Mawdsley looked a little crestfallen at this news. He had met Catherine on several occasions when she visited London, and Raven had suspected some partiality on his side, if not hers. 'And who is the fortunate gentleman?'

Raven coughed in embarrassment. 'I should not have spoken of it, since nothing is settled. But I believe that our neighbour Ralph Warboys has some ambitions in her direction.'

Mawdsley narrowed his handsome eyes. 'Is not that gentleman married?'

'No longer. He was sadly widowed three months ago.' Raven was even more apologetic. 'Which is why I should not have spoken of it. Even if I am correct in my thinking, it would, out of decency, be some considerable time before they could marry, of course.'

Mawdsley put a friendly hand on Raven's arm. 'And what of Molly, Henry? Have you made it up with her? '

Raven shook his head. ''Nay, I have had no time this week for Molly. But I doubt that she is too upset at my absence; she seems to have found herself an old French dog to play with.'

Mawdsley grunted in exasperation. 'If she has, 'tis only because you neglect her so wilfully, Henry. She is a lusty young vixen, and if you do not choose to pleasure her twice nightly, then there are numerous rivals who will, I have no doubt.' He waved an admonitory finger at his friend. 'Make sure you see her before you go, and pleasure her until her bum is sore. Then she will welcome you back with open arms when you return as a hero from our adventures at sea...'

\*

Raven was not disposed to argue with his friend, as he had every intention of calling and seeing Molly before he left for Dorset, although he doubted that he would have time to pleasure her in quite the vigorous way that Mawdsley suggested. He planned instead to take her to Dorset with him, if she would go. But following his early morning meeting with Mawdsley he first went on foot to the city of tents in the fields north of St Giles to meet Dr Croone again and see what little he could do to separate any plague sufferers from the rest of this fresh exodus from the city.

And almost the first person Raven saw when he entered the tented area where those identified with the plague were sequestered was the young woman who had given witness last week against Esther - Mistress Bernadette Worme. She was lying on a straw mattress within one of the large canvas tents, and looked distressingly near death.

Raven had seen her in the court at Newgate only three days before looking perfectly healthy, yet now her face was covered in weeping black sores and her armpits swollen with buboes. Yet he had no doubt that it was the same woman.

He tried to get her to drink some hot cordial but she was too weak even for that. The speed of advancement of the disease in her case had been remarkable. As a rational man, Raven was reluctant to believe in miracles or curses, yet the fact was that Esther Linney had somehow miraculously survived being hanged, while her accuser here had been cursed with this awful affliction. It was difficult in this case not to see the hand of God operating to apply proper justice, where the human variety had proved so inadequate.

It was just as well that no one else knew of this, Raven thought, or many would conclude that Esther Linney was indeed a witch...

The woman was trying to say something to him as she lay writhing in pain on her straw mattress on the hard ground.

'What is it, Mistress?' Raven asked, trying again to get her to drink something.

The woman was wild of eye, and half mad now. 'Get away from me, all of ye who fear for your soul!' she screamed. 'For I am cursed by that evil witch...!'

*

Just before ten o'clock, Molly was standing at the window of her parlour overlooking Bow Street when she saw Henry Raven in the distance, striding purposefully towards her front door. She had no doubt that he was headed in this direction, and would be here within half a minute. She gave a sigh of frustration as she glanced behind at M'sieur Desargues, reclining comfortably in her best chair. ''Tis Henry finally come to call on me. And you are here yet again, sir, to excite his jealousy, damn you!'

To be fair to M'sieur Desargues, he had kept his word and behaved most properly during his stay overnight. He had slept dutifully in the other chamber, and made no attempt to enter her own private bedchamber. Nor had he attempted any intimacy with her at all, not even trying to steal a kiss over their shared breakfast this morning. His behaviour was most bewildering to Molly since she was sure that he had lustful intentions towards her. Yet he had enjoyed several opportunities now to satiate his lust on her if he wished, and had taken none of them, therefore he had left Molly entirely perplexed, and perhaps a little frustrated too. Until he made that ultimate move to get into her bed, Molly was not at all sure how she would react when the moment came. M'sieur Desargues was certainly a handsome and amusing fellow, and, if Molly was being frank, it was probably only her continuing loyalty to Henry that had caused her to be so discouraging to him thus far.

Yet it would be a disaster if Henry should find this gentleman here in her apartments yet again; he would never believe that the Frenchman's presence here could be entirely innocent.

Molly had other worries too today: her maid Bathsheba had not arrived this morning from her nearby lodgings, and usually she was here promptly at seven o'clock so Molly worried that she might have succumbed to the plague too.

M'sieur Desargues had leapt to his feet on hearing Molly's announcement. 'Please do not let him in, Molly. I am sure my enemy is even now watching this house for a fresh opportunity to gain access.'

Molly glanced through the window again. 'I see no one in the street who resembles that man who accosted you. Remind me again - what did you say his name was?'

'*Francisco...Nunez...de Santiago,*' M'sieur Desargues said, enunciating each word with precision. 'De Santiago is too clever to expose himself to view in the street. But at the very least, he will have left someone to watch this street, after last night's events. When I did not return to my own lodgings last night, he will have guessed that I stayed here with you.'

Molly was alarmed. 'Yet he cannot know my name, or where I live, can he, sir?'

M'sieur Desargues gave an enigmatic shrug. 'I would not be too confident of that, Molly. Knowing this man by reputation, and his thoroughness, I suspect he may well know your name by now. He may have been observing me for several days before he struck last night, so would have seen you with me too. You are a pretty and well-known actress now, so it would not be too difficult to discover your name, and even where you live, if he had someone watching you too. I am sorry indeed to have embroiled you in my troubles too, but 'tis better that you know the truth so that you will watch your step now.'

Molly was most uneasy at the thought of agents of this unknown Catalan assassin possibly watching her every movement. She decided that she would most certainly revert to her previous cautionary habits, and would carry a knife again from now on to protect herself. 'Do you really fear that he will try and get in here, M'sieur?'

M'sieur Desargues was grim-faced. 'If I stay here for long, I am sure he will try. I need to get away from here, Molly, for your sake as well as mine. Yet no matter where I go in this country, that gentleman will be my shadow from now on until his job is done. That man knows neither fatigue nor pity. He will hunt me all over England, no matter how long it takes. Somehow I must get away to the New World, if I wish to survive.'

Molly still had considerable doubts over the veracity of this story, half suspecting that it was a mere ploy to insinuate himself with her, while keeping Henry away from her. M'sieur Desargues's motives in pursuing her were still somewhat of a mystery when he made no obvious attempts to seduce her, yet Molly could still see no other reason for his interest in her.

Molly jumped involuntarily as she heard Henry's loud knock on the door below, and then his equally loud call. She moved towards the door of the parlour in preparation to go downstairs, determined to answer his call.

Yet the look on M'sieur Desargues's face halted her in her tracks. This gentleman truly was in fear for his life, or else he was the best natural actor in the world...

Molly stopped and retraced her steps reluctantly to the window. From the concealment of the shutters, Molly watched helplessly as Henry, his face more pensive than angry, finally turned away after getting no response, and made his way back towards Covent Garden.

'Thank you, Molly,' M'sieur Desargues said. 'You have saved my life again by that noble act.'

Molly watched Henry disappear into the distance. 'Then I hope your life is worth the price I have just paid, M'sieur,' she declared coldly.

*

At two o'clock in the afternoon, Henry Raven and his party were already well advanced on the first leg of their journey to Dorset. Because of the difficulties of getting seats on any of the regular stage coaches leaving from Charing Cross today, Raven had decided to use his own old coach-and-four for the journey. He used this coach, which had belonged to his father, only seldom now because of its heaviness and its difficulty of manoeuvre in London's narrow streets. For transport in the city, he preferred to use a new light carriage of his own design, which was usually driven by Martin for convenience sake. Today, though, Raven had hired two skilled old coach drivers  for the journey because Martin had no experience, either of the long road to Dorset, or the physical difficulties of controlling this cumbersome and heavy boneshaker of a vehicle.

Yet with the roads dry and hard after the recent fine weather, and with the two old coach drivers proving their worth, they had made good time, and by early afternoon they were on the highway to Southampton and had just rattled through the village of Camberley. Soon they were traversing the Surrey heathland of pines and heathers to the south of the village.

Raven was still distressed that Molly had not answered his knock this morning when he had gone to Bow Street. He was almost sure that she must have been at home: the theatre was now closed, after all, and most shops and businesses too, therefore there would not be much reason for her to be abroad on the streets this morning when everyone else in the city was avoiding them. He even imagined that he had seen her shadow at the window, although he could have been mistaken.

He had gone there primarily to invite her along on the journey to Dorset. If she was not amenable to taking up residence for the summer at Salwayash Manor, then there were still many other alternative lodgings available in Bridport or Weymouth that he could offer her, where she would be safe from the privations that the people remaining in London would have to endure in the coming months. He could of course have unlocked the street door to the house in Bow Street with his own key and gone in to investigate if she was at home, but was not so presumptuous. Either Molly was not at home, in which case there would be no point in entering, or else she was there and chose not to answer, in which case the same conclusion applied...

Without Molly, Raven's party bound for Dorset consisted of only four. Martin and Kate Soule sat in the front seats opposite him, and of the two of them, it was Kate who seemed to be enjoying the journey the more. It was taking her back to her home county of course, which made it a welcome enough journey anyway, but especially welcome in this case in giving her the opportunity to sit next to her beloved Martin for several hours. In the seat next to Raven sat a thin and forlorn figure with shorn hair who went by the name of Edward as far as the hired coach drivers were concerned, although Martin and Kate knew otherwise of course by now. Raven turned and glanced at Esther sitting beside him, and regretted again that he had suggested she should travel in male disguise. Dr Croone's maidservant Rose – who had formed some special attachment for Esther, it seemed, since helping to save her – had cut Esther's hair in a masculine style this morning, and made a workmanlike job of it. And the other servants had found her some old breeches and a doublet and shirt to wear, that fitted Esther well enough, who was tall and well-built for a woman. Yet Raven regarded her shorn hair and male costume with unease because her face was still far too beautiful to pass easily for a boy. It had seemed the safest thing for her to travel disguised in this way, but such a strikingly pretty boy was going to stand out on the journey anyway and attract perhaps even more attention than a pretty maid.

He was worried too for Esther's wellbeing and for the health of her mind. He had not mentioned to her that he had seen her accuser Mistress

Worme laid low with the plague, for fear that it might provoke some unwelcome reaction from her. Yet probably the news of her accuser's fate would have had no effect on her at all: Esther seemed to have lost all interest in life, sunk into a severe depression, and taking no interest either in her companions, or even in the views through the coach window of the wild heathland and pine forests of Surrey. Yet Raven could not see what other course there was but to take her to Dorset. He was determined to help her recover her life, and make a new start, although he had no definite plan yet in mind for her future. If the worst came to the worst, and there was no safe opportunity of her beginning a new life with a new name in another part of Dorset, then she still had the option to go abroad to live. Holland remained a possibility because it would be easy enough to obtain passage for her from the port of Weymouth to Amsterdam or Scheveningen. Although the Dutch were presently at war with England, Holland was still a country very like England in its climate and culture, therefore perhaps Esther could find happiness there.

It would be best, though, if she could stay reasonably close to those who loved her, particularly to his sister Catherine. Raven reflected that his sister knew of Esther's arrest, of course, since she had warned him of it in her letter, and was perhaps also aware by now of the dismal news that Esther had been tried, found guilty and hanged for her supposed crime. Therefore he would need to forewarn his sister in some way when they arrived, otherwise this sudden return of Esther from the grave was going to be a great shock to her.

Raven tried to think again of some way to resolve the circumstances of Esther's tragic life. Perhaps he could purchase a new smallholding for her in Dorset? - not in Salwayash, of course, but somewhere far enough away from it – near Sidmouth or Lyme Regis possibly - where she would not be known. For the present, though, he could only hide her at the manor until her spirits revived, where, for her own safety, she would have to continue in her guise as a young manservant for the present. The servants at Salwayash Manor would have to be told the truth eventually about this new "manservant", of course, and that too might lead to new worries of disclosure...

The sweetly shy Kate tried to engage Esther in conversation, and bring her out of her dark mood. 'Mistress, we shall stay tonight at the Greene Dragon in Winchester, which is a most comfortable inn. I think you and I must be bed mates tonight, for the inn is always busy.'

'That will hardly do in Mistress Linney's present guise, Katie,' Martin interrupted harshly. 'And you had better call this lady "Edward", otherwise you might make a slip when we get to the inn this evening,' he added coldly.

Raven spoke up to settle this minor argument. 'I have influence with the landlord at the Greene Dragon so I am sure that I can get three rooms for us tonight,' he said quietly. 'Esther will have her own room, and I shall share with Martin, so that will solve that problem.'

Raven saw that Martin had for some reason taken exception to the presence of Esther in the travelling party, and he had been cold and discourteous to her all day, which was most unlike his normal polite self. Raven reflected that Martin knew Esther slightly of course since, although he himself came from Cambridge, he had often travelled with his master to Salwayash, especially at the times of the harvest feasts which Esther had always attended. Yet that acquaintance should have made him *more* courteous to her, not less, therefore was not easily explained, especially after everything that Esther had suffered. Martin was a young man who could be severe in his judgements of women, though, Raven knew, and perhaps it was the knowledge of Esther's illicit child that made him resentful of her.

Raven too had been upset by that discovery of Esther's intimacy with a man outside the bounds of marriage. In fact it was this degree of hurt that he had felt at discovering Esther with child that had informed him that he still had a considerable personal regard for her. Even today, with her hair shorn and dressed in that poor boy's garb, and with her eyes dulled by all the hardships and misery she had endured of late, her beauty still shone through somehow, and Raven was finding it hard not to lean over during the journey and put a comforting arm around her.

Martin's irritation with her seemed however to bring a spark of life to Esther and she spoke up, more like her usual self. 'Yes, indeed, Kate, call me "Edward." In fact I like my appearance and my new hair so much that I might make the change to the male sex a permanent one.'

Martin blinked in surprise at that but said nothing...

*

At nine o'clock that evening, night had already settled like a soft muslin shroud over the Salwayash Manor estate, as Catherine Raven returned from her usual long evening walk. She liked to wander far on fine summer evenings, and watch the sun set over the green vale of the River Simene, then to walk back through the meadows as the light faded from gold to violet to black. Then, if she was fortunate, and the sky was clear, the stars would erupt one by one from the black velvet vault of the heavens, and make her sprits soar even further. Catherine did not have her brother's knowledge of natural philosophy, yet she had a curiosity and a sense of wonder to match his. As she reached the wooded lane leading to the manor house, she looked up again at the immense swathe cut through the sky by the Milky Way, and wondered again if that milky white stream could really be composed of a myriad of stars. According to her brother, the Italian Galileo had been the first man to see this fabulous sight with a telescope half a century ago, and she longed to be able to look through such a wondrous instrument herself, and get a glimpse of those stars, which were by all accounts as numerous as grains of sand on the seashore. Her brother had a large refracting telescope of his own that he kept at his home in London, and used to make observations of the stars and planets, and Catherine was always begging him to bring it to Dorset on his visits. Yet Henry was reluctant to risk his fine instrument on the rough coach journey, so Catherine had been reduced to listening to his stories of the wondrous things he had seen himself – the rings of Saturn, the phases of Venus, and a great red spot on the face of the planet Jupiter, which Henry's strange friend Mr Hooke had discovered only last year.

Yet tonight, Catherine was in no real mood for pausing to look at the stars. Her mood had in fact been one of considerable dejection all week since she had heard the gossip in the village of the terrible fate of Esther Linney. It had been hard enough to accept the stream of worsening news about her beloved sister that she had heard during the week: that Esther had given birth secretly to a child fathered by some local man; that the child had died and that Esther had been accused of its murder; that she had been tried for this supposed crime and already found guilty. Yet that dire news had turned even worse today...

Only this afternoon Catherine had met her elderly neighbour Lady Onslow, just returned from a visit to Guildford in Surrey, who had heard in that town the dreadful news from London that Esther Linney had been hanged yesterday...

Catherine had not been able to compose herself after this terrible news, and had spent much of the rest of the day weeping and grieving in private for her lost sister.

She could not help but blame Henry a little for this sad turn of events. If he had found Esther quickly as she had asked, and brought her safe back to Dorset, then none of this would have happened. They could have kept the matter entirely private then, and protected Esther's reputation; Esther could have given birth in secret at the manor, and had the baby adopted in time.

Catherine knew that the law must have made a tragic mistake to accuse Esther of murdering her own child. Such a thing was unthinkable for a devoutly religious girl like Esther. Yet even the thought that Esther could have had an illicit love affair was difficult to comprehend, given her sweet and retiring nature...

Catherine jumped in surprise as a figure loomed suddenly before her in the starlight. But her heart settled quickly to its normal rhythm when she recognized Ralph Warboys' distinctive voice.

'Thou art out late, Catherine,' he said.

'Perhaps a little later than usual,' she concurred. 'But the evenings grow ever lighter at this time of the year, and it is difficult to keep track of time.'

Warboys hesitated. 'I suppose you have heard the terrible news of Esther Linney. It is all over the village now, though I know not where the story originates. Yet it seems it must be true – that she has been hanged, and that a terrible injustice has clearly been done. I did not hear of it until today because I have been away making a tour of my tenant farms in Wiltshire this week.'

Catherine stopped in her tracks at the mention of Esther's name, and soon began weeping again at the thought of her sister's sad fate.

Warboys cursed himself under his breath. 'Forgive me for my crass stupidity in bringing up this sad business so abruptly. I had almost forgotten how close you and she were as children. More like sisters, I know. I always wondered why she left the security of your home in favour of keeping house for her reckless brother.'

Catherine dried her tears with a handkerchief. 'I too wonder why she ever left us.'

Standing together under the spreading boughs of an ash tree, Ralph put his hand to her wet cheek, then pulled her gently towards him. 'I hope you know that I would never do anything deliberately to hurt you, Catherine. Your happiness means much to me.'

Catherine's heart was racing again, but now for a different reason. 'Does it?' she whispered, as he bent down his head and kissed her on the lips. At first the kiss was gentle, but then became ever more passionate from both sides.

When his hand reached down to cup her breast, Catherine finally broke away from him.

Ralph was apologetic. 'I beg your pardon, Catherine. That was unforgivable...'

Yet he could not finish his sentence before they were forced to separate completely by the sounds of running feet on the lane and the arrival of several servants from the house carrying lanterns.

Catherine recognized the bulky figure of Dora Bagwell in the lead, together with young Jacob Shawn. 'What is wrong, Dora?' she asked in alarm.

Dora was wheezing and out of breath. 'Ruth Pilcher is missing from the house, Mistress. I have asked everyone. No one has seen her since first light this morning...'

# CHAPTER 16

The King's theatre was a dismal and gloomy place when empty, Molly thought, as she glanced around the circle of her fellow actors, gathered together for one last time on the darkened stage. The only light came from the overhead skylight directly above the stage, and one solitary candle in a tall brass candlestick on the stage, which Sir Thomas Killigrew had lit with a show of reverence, almost as if it were a votive offering in a silent church. Molly was used to rehearsing when the theatre was empty, yet without that activity on stage, the building seemed a haunted and lonely place. Molly's eyes scanned the rows of empty seats in the gallery, the green baize-covered benches in the pit, the silent boxes, while sweet memories of her time in this theatre flooded her mind.

Even her time here as a mere orange girl had been a wondrous experience, because it was the beginning of her love affair with the theatre, and with the art of playacting. Immediately before the performances began, Molly and the other orange sellers would go up on stage and parade before the audience in a last effort to sell their fruit. And it was here, on stage, lit by blazing chandeliers and subjected to the brazen shouts and uncouth wit of the audience, that Molly had first dreamed of becoming an actress. In the end it had taken two years for her to realize that dream (and had required the sacrifice of some pride and dignity in allowing Sir Thomas to make some wanton sport with her.) Yet the price of admission to this world had been worth paying: when the opportunity had come to show her acting talents, she had taken it with both hands and proved herself to be an accomplished actress.

It was here in the theatre, too, that she had seen Henry Raven for the first time, when he had come last winter to see a performance of Mr Etherege's lewd play, *The Comical Revenge, or Love in a Tub*. Molly could not help but glance up at the private box where he had sat that night with his friends, including Mr Mawdsley. Mr Raven had not attracted her attention immediately then because his friends were in truth much handsomer than him.

With his long nose and square jaw and bad complexion, Mr Raven was certainly not gifted with beauty, and, on first inspection, he had also seemed a little gloomy and stern to her, with something of the look of a puritan about him, despite his long curling hair. Yet as Molly got to know him better, she soon began to realize that he was the best of men – brave and resourceful, yet also kind and compassionate. These were rare attributes indeed in such a young and wealthy man, and Molly now felt a warm glow of affection for him stealing through her body at the thought of his fine qualities.

Yet now they seemed to have grown apart for reasons that she could not really comprehend – a mixture of misunderstandings, ill fortune and, perhaps, a dash of excessive pride on both sides. If only M'sieur Desargues had not been with her yesterday morning, then she would have invited Henry in and finally cleared the air between them. She had seen the way that he had looked at during that performance of *The Indian Emperor* last week, and knew well from the lust and hunger in his eyes that he still yearned for her. She did not know why he had not come to her that night, but something important must have detained him. Molly was sure that if she could get Henry into her bed again, then all his suspicions and reserve would soon vanish again. She realized now, though, that *she* would have to make the effort to bring them back together; if Henry did have a fault, then it was his gentlemanly pride, and perhaps also a reluctance to assert himself when it came to his personal feelings...

Molly turned her attention to the rest of the company again. The entire company had chosen to attend, backstage hands and dressers as well as actors, but everyone seemed sunk into the same melancholy mood as she herself. Molly had been summoned personally to the theatre on this Lord's Day by a message left in her doorway last evening, so Sir Thomas had most certainly wanted her to be here today to hear the formal announcement of the closure of the theatre. She knew not how Sir Thomas had managed to get word around the entire company, but from the number here, it seemed that no one of importance was missing. Even some of the company's regular playwrights were here: Roger Boyle, the Earl of Orrery; the young rake George Etherege; and the more gentlemanly John Wilson.

Molly now wished that she had dressed in grander fashion before coming here today, since the rest of the company was decked out mostly in their best apparel. Molly had left her house secretly this morning before first light and had therefore chosen to wear her oldest clothes - a plain dark dress of homespun material with a prim high neck, and a white coif modestly covering her dark hair. She realized dismally that she must look like a servant girl again when surrounded by all this lace and satin finery of the other actresses. All the regular ladies of the company were here, of course - among them the best actresses in all England: Elizabeth Weaver, Margaret Hughes, Anne and Becky Marshall, Charlotte Butler and Elizabeth Davenport. Nell was here too of course, and she seemed to Molly to be the only one in tolerable spirits, though that was perhaps because the handsome Charles Hart sat beside her and patted her hand intimately from time to time. He was at least twenty years older than her, yet Nell was such a mature and knowing girl for her age, that they did not seem mismatched at all. Molly could only envy Nell her reliably promiscuous nature; she would never break her heart over any man, Molly was quite sure, but simply move from one to another like a bee to the next flower. Although, in Nell's case, it was probably more correct to think of her as a flower moving from bee to bee, than the other way round.

Mary Pettican was sitting on a stool directly opposite Molly, so that their eyes frequently encountered each other. For once there was no hostility or jealousy in Mary's eyes, nor even any pointed looks at Molly's plain and unfashionable dress, and she seemed almost amiable and sympathetic today now that she and Molly were enduring the same hurt over the closure of the theatre.

The greatest actors in England were all assembled here too: Michael Mohun, William Wintershall, Robert Shatterell, William Cartwright, Walter Clun, Nicholas Burt and the irrepressible John Lacy. The beautiful Edward Kynaston had chosen to sit a long way from Mary Pettican today, so Molly wondered if that unlikely friendship had been still born. Christopher Malthouse was however sitting next to Mary and paying her close attention, so perhaps imagined that he might step into Edward's shoes eventually. With his plain freckled face and tall gangly figure, though, Molly doubted the success of his venture somehow,

Molly was glad to see that all the company looked healthy, with no sign of any plague symptoms among them. But this thought inevitably rekindled a memory of one person from the company who was missing today from this stellar assembly. Poor Patrick Whelan was already mouldering in his grave in the churchyard of St Katherine Cree in Leadenhall Street, while she, for some unknown reason, had survived the same affliction that had killed him. This sombre reflection gave Molly much pause for thought as she wondered about the vagaries and the vicissitudes of life, and realized how much of human happiness was in the end down to simple blind luck.

Sir Thomas had come today in company with a lady called Mrs Behn, who seemed to have some connection with him, though what it was, no one knew. She had more the look of a society lady than a high class strumpet, so it seemed unlikely to Molly that Sir Thomas was bedding her.

But her presence here was puzzling to say the least, since she had no involvement with the company that Molly knew of.

Sir Thomas finally called the meeting to order. 'Thank you all for coming today, my dear friends and colleagues. I fear that I have only doleful news to impart to you all, but 'tis better that ye know the truth and can make your own plans accordingly. The theatre, as you know, is likely to be closed now for the whole summer, or until the plague is over. I am hopeful that we will be able to reopen in the autumn, provided the plague is on the decline by then.' He glanced around the ring of serious faces. 'You will see that Mr Dryden is not among us today; he has already left the city and gone to the Wiltshire estate of his wife's family. I know that most of you do not have the opportunity to quit the city so easily for the country, though I would suggest that those of you who can should do so…'

'What about you, Thomas?' his old friend William Wintershall asked. 'Will you quit the city?'

Killigrew smiled faintly. 'Nay, I cannot in good conscience leave my beloved city, so I intend to stay. I lived through the plague in Venice many years ago without any ill effects, so I am consoled by the thought that most people here will survive this outbreak, even if they stay. I have even heard of cases of people catching the plague and surviving…' - here he cast a brief if pointed look in Molly's direction which caused some acute discomfort to her, and some extremely puzzled faces elsewhere – 'so whatever else we do, we should not give in to fear.'

Charles Hart took his eyes off Nell for a moment to speak up. 'I have heard that even Cromwell's secretary, Milton, has left his house in Bunhill Fields and retreated to his wife's home in Chalfont St Giles in Buckinghamshire…'

There were a few murmurs of disapproval among this mostly Royalist gathering at the mention of this severe Republican's name, particularly from Sir Thomas's companion, Mrs Behn. But Killigrew put up a protesting hand. 'That disrespect is unworthy of this company,' he said. 'Whatever Mr Milton's politics may be, yet he is a fine poet. They say he presently puts the final revisions to some great work of poetry, even though he is quite blind now…'

Charles Hart would not be silenced, though. 'Yet I doubt that a servant of Cromwell is truly capable of any poetic greatness, Sir Thomas. That gentleman suffers an attack of blindness in more ways than one, if he believes himself to be a great poet.'

Killigrew decided not to argue further, but said instead, 'So let us all make a pledge to come together again in the autumn and begin a fresh and glorious chapter in the history of the theatre in this country. We are not at the end of the journey, my friends, but only at the beginning. We must think ahead to the glories to come on this stage, the wonderful plays not yet written, and to the further applause of the masses. That is our future, my friends, if we choose to grasp it...'

The actors and actresses were tearful as they took their leave. Margaret Hughes was shedding tears like a waterfall, and even bluff and manly Michael Mohun sat with quivering lips while his fellow actor Nicholas Burt did his best to console him...

*

Sir Thomas stole up during the leave taking for a private word with Molly. 'And what will you do, sweet Molly?' he asked. 'Will ye join Mr Raven for the next few weeks in the county of Dorset? I see that you are dressed most plainly today in your old servant's garb, so I wondered if you might be about to travel with him.'

'In Dorset, sir?' Molly said in surprise.

Killigrew seemed puzzled. 'Why, yes. I encountered him by chance in Bridges Street yesterday morning, and he told me of his immediate plans to leave the city for the county of Dorset...' He frowned. 'Did you not know of it, Molly? I thought that you and he were fully reconciled again.'

Molly did not like to disappoint Sir Thomas. 'Mr Raven and I are indeed reconciled, sir, and I knew well of his plans to go to Dorset. He is very attached to his sister,' she said, elaborating her lie with a little of the truth to make it more believable, 'and goes there often to see her.'

Sir Thomas beamed. 'Just so.' Then a shadow fell over his raddled old face. 'Yet while I cannot blame him for his wish to leave the city, yet I think his decision to volunteer to go with the King's navy in their fight with the Dutch is very ill advised. Why should such a wealthy young man risk his life in that way, noble though it be? There is any number of men who can serve this country as cannon fodder, but we can ill afford to lose such a man as him. I suppose you tried to dissuade him from this course, but were unable to, given his innate sense of honour...'

Molly had felt the blood drain from her face at this unexpected news. 'Err...yes, indeed...dissuade...yes, I did try to dissuade him...'

Killigrew put his arms around her and embraced her. 'Yet, God willing, he will come through this ordeal, and come back to you in one piece...'

*

Nell too came to the side of the stage to embrace Molly before leaving. 'I see Sir Tom could not take his leave of you without giving your bum a hard squeeze too. Mine is quite sore from his roving fingers. For all his great age – why he must be over fifty, is he not? - he has the iron fingers of a blacksmith. Yet I shall miss the randy old goat, even if my bum will not,' she laughed.

Molly glanced over to where Charles Hart was saying his farewells to others of the company. 'And what will you do during the summer, Nell?'

Nell turned to look briefly at her lover too. 'I shall take my pleasures

193

where I can find them,' she said coyly. 'Charles and several of the company are planning to tour the country and do outdoor performances at fairs and festivals - perhaps in the West Country where there is no plague to blight our lives.' Nell took Molly's hand and gripped it tightly. 'Why not join us, Molly?' She hesitated. 'Or are you off somewhere with your wealthy lover, Mr Raven?'

Molly was pensive. 'He is gone to the county of Dorset for the present, Nell. I will wait for his return, then decide what to do.'

Nell sighed. 'Then give me a kiss, Molly, and we will say our sad farewells. Nay, not on the cheek like that, but full on the lips like lovers, for I do love thee, Molly, as my best friend in the world.'

Nell gave her the promised smacking kiss on the lips, and then held her in her arms for a full ten seconds. 'Promise me that we shall always be friends, no matter what the future brings, Molly,' she said. 'Even if I were to become the King's mistress...'

Molly laughed at the brazenness of her fifteen-year-old friend, and put her hand to Nell's pretty cheek. 'I promise...we shall always be friends...'

*

After the meeting, Molly walked back alone to her home in Bow Street, congratulating herself that she finally had her house to herself again.

M'sieur Desargues had stayed there for a second night last night, but Molly had finally rid herself of her unwelcome guest before first light this morning. M'sieur Desargues had however refused to simply walk through the front door, since he thought that Bow Street must still be under close observation by the accomplices of his enemy, the Catalan gentleman with the evil reputation, Senor Francisco Nunez de Santiago.

Therefore Molly had been forced to come up with an alternative plan in order to be free of her unwanted guest, hence her choice of her plain old dress today. Under cover of darkness, with the new Lord's day still no more than a few streaks of light in the eastern sky, Molly had led her French gentleman houseguest up to the roof of her own house, from which, by jumping across a small if intimidating gap of four feet, they had been able to get onto the flat roof of the house next door. From there they eventually found a rickety wooden staircase which led down from that roof to the alleyway at the side of the houses. And from there, they had been able to get away from the house in Bow Street undetected, as far as Molly knew.

M'sieur Desargues did not wish to go back in person to his lodgings in Fleet Street either, though, certain that they would be watched too. So Molly had been forced to find other accommodation for him. One benefit of the plague in the city was that there were now many lodgings and rooms newly available for rent. Molly was most familiar with the district of Whetstone Park behind Lincoln's Inn Fields since this was where she had grown up, and where her mother still kept her bawdy house. Molly had soon found a suitable lodging there for M'sieur Desargues - a large garret room in a house just around the corner from her mother's bawdy house, but clean and respectable enough a lodging for all that. It was not the most reputable area of London, of course, being the poor home of whores and vagabonds and criminals, yet Molly reasoned that M'sieur Desargues would be safer in such a place where people minded their own business. She also had many friends in this street who could keep an eye on M'sieur Desargues and who would inform her if any foreigners were seen in the vicinity asking questions about him.

Molly had gone to all this trouble because, although she was anxious to be rid of M'sieur Desargues from her home, she was not so callous as to want to see him placed at risk. After the events of Friday night, the threat to him seemed a real enough one to her, and she did acknowledge some responsibility for him. He had after all probably saved her life when she had come down with the plague, for which generous action she could not be anything else but grateful. And although his pestering attentions since had served to threaten her good relations with Henry Raven, yet she could not be too angry with M'sieur Desargues even about that, given his amusing manners and witty banter...

As Molly walked home from the theatre on this sunny if blustery afternoon, she did glance around briefly from time to time to check that she was not being followed. If that Catalan gentleman, or his agents, really were watching these streets of Covent Garden and Drury Lane as M'sieur Desargues suspected, then they might see her again by accident, and follow her. She was confident, though, that no one could have followed her early this morning when she had taken M'sieur Desargues to Whetstone Park: Molly knew that labyrinth of narrow stinking alleyways like no one else, and could have lost an army of pursuers in there. Yet in these wider thoroughfares of Covent Garden, Molly was less sure of herself, so it was a comfort for her to pat her skirts and feel the reassuring shape of the large bone-handled knife that she had strapped again to her right thigh this morning. She reminded herself that she could not take her own safety too much for granted, now that she was completely on her own at home.

Molly was completely alone now because it seemed her maid Bathsheba had left the city permanently due to the plague and gone back to her family home in Essex to live, while the old woman from downstairs who cooked sometimes for Molly had also chosen to leave for her brother's home in the sanctuary of the Kent countryside. Molly was not concerned about the loss of her servants as such; now that the theatre was closed, she had enough time to look to her own needs and did not require a maidservant to help her with washing and cooking. Yet she was concerned about being trapped in the house, if M'sieur Desargues's enemies should keep it under close observation, thinking that he was still inside. So she was especially wary as she got within twenty paces of her own front door, and glanced around furtively for any signs of being watched.

Yet her watchfulness proved to be wasted against this devil, whose cloaked and hooded figure seemed to rise from the shadows between the houses like something supernatural. Before Molly even realized what was happening, she found herself in a similar predicament to M'sieur Desargues two nights ago - pressed against a wall with the point of a dagger to her neck...

The man had a scarf over the lower half of his face, so all that Molly could see between that and the wide brim of his feathered hat were a pair of black eyes that burned with intensity like hot coals.

'Do not struggle, young Madam,' he said in a hoarse whisper, 'else my hand might slip, and the blade go straight through your carotid artery. Then you would drown in your own fresh young blood, and die most unpleasantly.'

Molly twisted her eyes in panic to see up and down Bow Street but there was not a soul in sight, and certainly no Officers of the Watch, dressed in their distinctive greatcoats, and armed reassuringly with lanterns and wooden staffs. Since the outbreak of the plague, these officers of the law, known popularly as "Charleys", had become conspicuous by their absence from London's streets. Not that an old watchman was likely to be much help against this devil anyway, who would no doubt slit an old man's throat just as readily as her own. Molly's right hand felt through the pocket in her skirts, trying to reach the knife she had secreted there, but the man had her shoulders pinned back in such a cruel and undignified fashion against this wall that her straining fingers could not reach far enough to get a full purchase on the handle.

'What do you want, sir?' she gasped though gritted teeth, as she strained her fingers as far into the pocket of her dress as she could.

The man put his face close to hers so that she could feel his hot breath upon her cheeks. She still could see nothing of this man's features other than the eyes, yet his manner suggested a younger man than she had first thought, if this truly was the man that M'sieur Desargues claimed him to be – the infamous assassin Senor Francisco Nunez de Santiago.

'I want just one thing from you, girl. Tell me…where is the Comte de Mésanger? I know that he is no longer in your home, and that you managed somehow to spirit him away somewhere this morning. I hope this refuge is not too far away, else I will have to take out my displeasure on you, little girl, and slit your pretty white throat anyway.'

Molly felt the blood rushing through her head like an ocean wave. 'The Comte de Mésanger, sir? I know of no such person.'

The man grunted dismissively. "Do not play games with me, girl. You were with him on Friday evening. Philippe Desargues, *Comte de Mésanger*…'

'I did not know that he had a title, sir,' Molly said lamely.

The devil laughed humourlessly. 'No matter. He will not have need of it much longer when I catch him again. Tell me, Madam, where have you hidden this errant gentleman? I shall count to three, and I shall do it in English, in deference to you, so that there will be no error in your comprehension of my meaning. I promise you that you will die horribly when I utter the word "three," if you have not told me by then where M'sieur le Comte skulks…'

The man had stepped back a little, giving Molly a little more freedom of movement. Suddenly she found that her fingers had a firm grasp on the handle of her knife, and she began to withdraw it discreetly from its sheath.

'One…' the man said.

Molly had the knife in her hand now, and even in full view, should the man choose to look down.

But he did not, as his attention was concentrated on uttering the ominous word, 'Two…'

Before he could say "three", though, Molly had taken her knife and plunged it savagely into the man's side below the ribs, with an angled thrust upwards. She would have liked to plunge it into his black heart instead, but that was impossible given the way he still held her pressed so close against the wall, with a knife to her throat.

The knife blade went in a good three inches, before hitting something hard like bone, which Molly guessed must be his lowest rib. His body was jolted back by the blow, and with that immense shock to his system, the man dropped his own knife in a clatter on the cobbles, which reflex action finally released Molly from the cruel pressure of his blade on her throat. Most men would have screamed in agony too at such a severe wound in their side, but Senor de Santiago was apparently made of sterner stuff and merely grunted explosively.

He did however step back further from her to see the full extent of his injury and those fiery eyes opened in astonishment when he saw the bone-handled knife embedded so deep into his abdomen. 'You witch…' he muttered, as the pain began to tell on him, and his knees buckled slightly.

This slight display of weakness gave Molly the only chance she would ever have to escape, and she turned on her heels at once and fled. Despite that waver in the man's step, she was sure that he was not mortally wounded – her knife thrust had not penetrated deep enough for that - and he was therefore still dangerous. In fact he might be even more dangerous in this wounded state, and certainly even more vindictive.

Molly reached her own door within twenty paces, but there seemed to be no possibility of unlocking it and getting through it  safely with that man so close on her heels, so she ran on past this sanctuary, and turned instead into an alleyway that led back towards Bridges Street and the theatre.

From behind her in Bow Street, she heard an animal growl of anger that made the hair stand up on the back of her neck. Then a voice called out a message that she would never forget as long as she lived.

*'When I see you again, witch, ye will die a slow and painful death along with the Comte, I promise you...'*

# CHAPTER 17

The Lord's Day, 14th May 1665

The church clock was striking seven o'clock as the coach-and-four finally brought Henry Raven's party into Bridport High Street on this warm Sunday evening.

It had been a long and dusty journey from Winchester through the New Forest, and all were glad to be back here in Dorset, Esther in particular. After Kate and Martin had stepped out briefly to fetch fresh water from the well by the church, and while the horses too drank their fill from the stone horse trough, Esther glanced through the carriage window at the distinctive green conical shape of Colmer's Hill to the west of the town. 'I never thought to see the sight of Colmer's Hill again. It gives me a timely reminder how much gratitude I owe thee, sir,' she said.

Now that they were alone, Raven took her hand, which she made no objection to, though appearing clearly uncomfortable with such intimacy. 'I have told you to call me Henry,' he chided her gently, 'at least when we are alone. We will be at the manor within an hour, and 'tis best that you go with Martin and Kate on arrival. They will look after you and show you privately to your room. I think you must stay out of sight in the South Wing for the present, away from the rest of the household until I think what to tell them about you. And I fear that you will not able to meet Catherine immediately on arrival. She may think you dead, therefore it would be a great shock for her to see you, unless I can warn her first of these unexpected glad tidings…'

Esther looked down at her boy's breeches and doublet, and almost smiled. 'She will be even more shocked to see me in these ill-fitting breeches, Henry. Despite what I said to Martin yesterday, I do not truly feel comfortable in this guise, and sense that everyone stares at me.'

Raven cautioned her. 'Remember that the woman who gave evidence against you, Mistress Pollock, lives not far from the manor, therefore, if you want to leave the manor and walk outside, I think it best that you stay dressed as you are. I doubt that the law has any further demands on you, yet I do not wish to put this to the test. And that Pollock woman may yet make more trouble for you if she discovers that you live still.' Raven looked at the faded linen shirt she wore, and the worn breeches, with chagrin. 'Although perhaps we can get you some better boy's clothes, at least, as befits your pretty face.'

Esther's face fell. 'I am not pretty, Henry. I look in the mirror now and see only an ugly, ugly woman.'

Raven put his finger under her chin, and lifted her face for his inspection. 'You are partly right, Esther. I look into your eyes and I do not see a pretty face either. I see a *beautiful* one.'

Esther coloured, but did not turn her face away.

Raven finally withdrew his hand as Kate and Martin returned to the coach with their heavy stoneware bottles filled with water.

As they retook their seats for the last leg of the journey, north through Allington to Salwayash, Raven advised Martin of his plan.

Martin still seemed in cold and surly mood, though, and if Esther had not been there to hear it, Raven would have reprimanded him severely for his rudeness towards her. Yet for the moment he held his tongue as the coachman urged the horses into life again and turned the ponderous coach on the road to Salwayash and the familiar Tudor manor house nestling in its green valley...

*

Henry Raven was glad in the end that he had taken the precautions that he had, because the reunion between Esther and his sister Catherine was fraught with enough emotion as it was, even after he had warned her of the truth late that evening after dinner.

Catherine could scarce take in his meaning at first when he told her of Esther's miraculous survival. Overcome with emotion at this unexpected providence, she had gone immediately to sit in her private little sewing room next to the Great Hall, where a cheerful fire burned, and tried to compose herself for the promised reunion. Yet Raven found his sister still wrought with emotion when he returned there secretly with Esther, close to midnight.

Raven knocked quietly at the door of the sewing room, then led Esther over the threshold. Catherine climbed slowly to her feet, then brought a lighted candlestick close to Esther's face to confirm that it truly was her. Then, with a sigh of gratitude towards her brother, she embraced Esther, until both were weeping uncontrollably.

'Shall I leave you to talk in private, sisters?' Raven asked uncomfortably as he watched this outpouring of emotion and mutual affection.

But neither Catherine nor Esther would hear of it, and they made him sit with them while Esther told them both of her terrible experiences during this last week.

Catherine was still shaking and unable to properly control her voice or her expression. Yet gradually happiness and relief took over from the shock and she became reconciled to the miraculous truth. She looked at her brother in wonder. 'You have often been a source of comfort and affection to me, Henry, but tonight you have surpassed yourself, bringing dear Esther back to me alive.'

Raven demurred. 'I did nothing, sister. I was worse than useless in trying to get Esther acquitted. And as for her survival, she did that all herself, though she must have had some considerable help from the Almighty too.'

Catherine smiled. 'Amen to that, brother.' Yet Catherine's emotion returned when she stood up and asked Esther for permission to pull back her man's neck cloth and see the rope marks on her neck with her own eyes. Those eyes filled with tears again when she saw how deep the rope had bitten into Esther's soft white skin. 'I feel like doubting Thomas, who could not believe the Lord's resurrection unless he could feel the wounds in his hands and his side with his own fingers…'

Esther too was weeping quietly. 'Then feel them, Cathy, and your gentle touch may perhaps take away some of the hurt in my soul over what happened.'

Raven preferred that Catherine did not touch Esther's wounds, though, knowing how delicate her present state of mind was. 'Does not the bible say, sister, that "Blessed are they that have not seen, and yet have believed"?'

Catherine took her brother's hint and did not touch Esther's scars further, but merely put her neck cloth back into place again.

Raven cleared his throat – for he too was overcome with emotion, though trying manfully not to show it. 'Do you know if Mistress Pollock has returned to the village yet, Catherine?'

Catherine had retaken her own seat by the fire, and she now frowned at the mention of that invidious person. 'I have not heard it, but she will no doubt soon be back in Salwayash to gloat over her triumph.'

Esther was suddenly afraid. 'Yet even if she were to discover me here, would she be able to do anything against me?' She turned to Raven, seated next to her. 'Did you not say that I was now safe from the law, Henry – that they could not try me again for this crime of killing my own child?'

Raven nodded. 'Before I left London, I consulted with your lawyer Mr Sherbrooke on this matter in law…'

Esther blanched. 'You did not tell him that I had survived the hanging?'

Raven reassured her quickly. 'Nay, I did not, but only couched the question in the most general terms. It seems such a miraculous thing has happened before, though I have never heard of it – a woman called Anne Green survived hanging in Oxford some fifteen years ago, and went on later to marry and have a family. She too was believed to have killed her own baby…'

'I did *not* kill my child,' Esther stated angrily. 'Either he died of natural causes because of his premature birth, or else some evil person smothered him. Yet I cannot conceive why any person would be so evil as to smother an innocent baby, therefore I must assume it was simply a natural death.'

Catherine leaned over and took her hand. 'Of course we know this is the truth, Esther.' She hesitated. 'Will you not tell us who the father was, though? Perhaps you need to see him, and tell him what happened. I assume he knows nothing of these sad events…'

Esther was distraught, as she glanced at Raven for support. 'Please do not ask me for his name, Cathy. This was simply a grievous error of judgement on both our parts, and one we had both better forget.'

Catherine was patient with her in return. 'Then I accept it, and shall never ask you that question again, my sweet...'

*

After Raven had escorted an exhausted Esther back to her bed chamber in the South Wing of the house, he returned to the sewing room and sat with his sister by the dying log fire until the early hours, discussing what needed to be done about Esther.

Raven stifled a great yawn with difficulty but his sister seemed not to notice his great fatigue. 'Considering the terror of what she has been through, it is remarkable that she looks as well as she does,' Catherine said. ''Tis a great pity that you had to disguise her as a boy, though, and that someone had to shear off that beautiful black hair of hers. It must have hurt you to see that further indignity done to her.'

Raven acknowledged that. 'Yet it seemed the safest solution. And it was only a small indignity, when compared to the indignity of being hanged before a jeering mob at Tyburn,' he added sombrely. 'Her height makes her stand out as a woman, yet is not so noteworthy in a man. So I think she must stay in this guise for the present, in order to keep her survival a secret as long as possible.'

Catherine, although still somewhat dubious, agreed finally with her brother's plan that Esther must stay here incognito in her male guise until she was fully recovered in mind and body. 'And we will worry about her future only when she is restored to full health and vigour again,' she declared forcefully.

But Catherine was against her brother's notion of telling the whole household the truth about Esther, given the loose wagging tongues of some of the younger servants. 'None of the present servants know Esther well, therefore they are unlikely to recognize her…'

'Dora will know her at once, even dressed as a boy,' Raven pointed out.

Catherine agreed. 'Yes, she will, not doubt. But she will hold her tongue, as I am sure will Kate and Martin. I will tell the other servants that "Edward" is a distant kinsman of ours, who is recovering his health and needs privacy. Which is almost the truth apart from her sex, of course...'

'They will suspect some deceit, I am sure. Esther is far too beautiful of face to be a boy,' Raven murmured tiredly.

Catherine cast a shrewd look in her brother's direction. 'She is, although her beauty was late in developing. Yet you liked her well enough even she was a skinny and gawky girl, and I often wondered whether your feelings towards her were entirely brotherly.'

Raven stirred uneasily in his chair at such a personal question from his sister. 'No, they were not always brotherly, I freely admit. I missed Esther greatly when I went to Cambridge to study, and not in quite the same way that I missed you and Mary. I had quite a pain in my heart at being away from her then.'

Catherine turned her eyes towards the dying embers of the fire. 'Did she ever suspect your partiality, do you think?'

Raven shook his head woozily. 'Nay, I think not. In any case, she was but thirteen at the time, and too young to be wooed. And my thoughts were soon diverted elsewhere by sad personal circumstances, when our dear mother died. And then Esther left us soon afterwards to take care of her brother, so I reluctantly gave up any thoughts of her in that way.'

Catherine smiled faintly. 'Yet I sense that some of those feelings have been rekindled, brother, in this time of trouble.'

'I certainly feel a great affection for her,' Raven conceded, 'but I have now given my heart elsewhere, as you know.'

Catherine gave a despairing sigh at that, and returned quickly to the subject of Esther. 'I wonder who was the father of her child, though? This seems the most perplexing part of this lamentable business, for I am sure that Esther is not promiscuous by nature.'

'I am sure of that too. I suspect that this unfortunate thing happened during our harvest feast last August, although I do not remember if anyone paid special attention to Esther that evening.'

Catherine too cast her mind back to that warm and pleasant evening, and smiled faintly. 'You drank so much ale that day that I doubt you remember anything of that celebration.' She reflected a little, and her smile faded rapidly. 'It would be strange, though, if all these terrible things that have happened to Esther had their origin at that joyous feast.'

Raven agreed with a wry shake of his head. 'It would indeed.'

Catherine was wistful. 'Does it change your view of her, Henry? The fact that she has been with another man, perhaps a married man? Could you ever love a woman with Esther's personal history?'

'I hardly know what my feelings for Esther are now, so I cannot say how they might have been changed by her recent sad history.' Raven hesitated, before continuing in even more awkward fashion. 'Before I forget, there is something else I need to say to you tonight, Catherine.' He took a deep breath, knowing that she would be upset by this news. 'I have volunteered to go as a ship's surgeon with the Royal fleet, which sails at the end of the month to make war with the Dutch.'

Catherine was exasperated to hear this. 'Why in heaven's name would you do such a preposterous thing? I did not think that you would be a vain chaser after glory, Henry! I suppose your friend Mawdsley put you up to this heroic gesture? Is it not enough that you have risked your life so recklessly during this outbreak of the plague? Now you have to go and risk your neck in even more dangerous circumstances...'

'Mawdsley did ask me to go,' Raven admitted. 'But I do this for my own peace of mind, not because of any loyalty I feel to him.'

Catherine simmered with resentment. 'What of your actress mistress? Even she cannot be happy that you would do such a thing. Could not even her charms, blousy and unnatural though they must be, dissuade you from this foolish bravado?'

'I have not told her yet,' Raven said quietly.

Catherine was surprised. 'Ah, then perhaps your relations with her are in decline, which is the one bit of encouraging news I have heard today.'

'Our relations are not in decline. At least not on my side. I forgot to tell you that Molly caught the plague a month ago, and most severely...'

Catherine was embarrassed and her eyes fell. 'Oh, then I am sorry, brother...Is she...?'

'Nay, she survived it well, and without a mark of it on her skin, which shows both her remarkable will and her bodily strength. If you met her, Catherine, I am sure that you would like her well enough. She has a ready wit and a most appealing manner...'

Catherine bristled. 'Do you truly think that I would like your actress friend? I doubt it sincerely, brother. I would as soon make friends with a black savage as with an actress. They must be the most preening, shallow and silly women in the world, as well as being naturally promiscuous...'

Raven held his temper, since it would do no good to lose it. Yet he resented these insults against Molly greatly. He began to suspect, though, from Catherine's irritated mood that something else must be the matter with her to explain this unusual animosity. 'Something else disturbs your normal tranquillity, sister, I can feel. Has Ralph Warboys come to court you yet? Is it he who has disturbed your natural equanimity?'

Catherine blushed now as the tables were turned on her. 'How know you that, you devil?'

Raven smiled at her endearingly. 'I have known you all your life, sister, so it is not so strange that I should see when your heart is taken with someone.'

Catherine could not help but smile back. 'Then I confess that you are right in your supposition. Ralph wants to marry me, though he is conscious that it is only three months since his dear wife Margaret died in that riding accident, therefore we cannot announce anything yet, and must feign an indifference for each other to stop tongues from wagging.'

'Does not his age worry you, Catherine? You will spend much of your life as a widow, if you marry a man twenty years older than yourself.'

'Nay, his age worries me not at all. He is still a vigorous and handsome man, even though past forty. And all of life is a gamble, is it not – a leap into the dark? I believe that I love Ralph now, and therefore am happy to take that leap of faith with him.'

Raven leaned over and kissed her on the cheek. 'Then I am happy for you, sister, to have found someone who suits you so well.'

Catherine took his hand and squeezed it tightly. 'I only hope that, in time, you will find someone equally suitable for you, brother.'

'You mean someone with no connection to the theatre, I suppose,' Raven said tartly. Yet he noticed a fresh shadow had fallen over his sister's face, and wondered at the cause.

When pressed, Catherine confirmed her worry. 'Yes, something else does concern me, Henry. Two weeks ago, Dora and I walked together in the oak wood, and we came across the body of a young maid hanging by her neck from a tree...'

Raven was shocked. 'What! Here on our estate?'

'Indeed. I did not write and tell you of this because I knew you were occupied in fighting the outbreak of plague, and I did not want to distract you with further troubles. The dead girl was a young milkmaid from a farm on the Warboys' estate, a fair and pretty girl called Lorna Wanless. Ralph was sure that she must have hanged herself over some sad love affair, and the constable who came from Bridport to investigate thought so too. Yet I am not so sure...'

'It does sound the most plausible explanation,' Raven suggested.

Catherine shrugged. 'Perhaps, until yesterday anyway...'

'Why until yesterday?'

Catherine looked down at her feet in distress. 'Because another young maid went missing yesterday, this time from our own household.'

Raven waited expectantly. 'Who was this girl?'

Catherine sighed. 'Her name is Ruth Pilcher.'

Raven frowned, not remembering that name. 'I do not know her, I think.'

'No, you do not. She joined the household but a week after your last visit. She looked very like the dead girl, Lorna. In fact they could have been sisters, the resemblance was so marked. She had not been with us even a month before she disappeared yesterday...'

'Did you find her?' Raven asked quickly.

'Yes, young Jacob Shawn found her in the end – floating face down in the fishpond behind the manor, just upstream of the weir.'

Raven was bewildered. 'Then that is extremely sad. But could it not be a strange coincidence?'

Catherine shook her head vigorously. 'I do not believe that two such similar girls would meet the same fate, unless there was some evil hand at work here. I fear that some devil stalks our lands, Henry...'

# CHAPTER 18

Monday, 15th May 1665

Molly paced the wooden floorboards of M'sieur Desargues's garret. 'It seems that I am as much a fugitive from this devil now as you, M'sieur,' she declared with more composure than she truly felt.

M'sieur Desargues, seated by the leaded window with its view of distant Primrose Hill, was contrite and full of humility. 'Then I humbly beg your pardon, Molly. This was never my intention when I sought your acquaintance - that I should bring this evil down on your head.' He glanced out of the window at the tranquil green fields north of the city, which seemed in their perfection and rich variety of spring colours to resemble more the painted backdrop to an artist's canvas than real life. It was hard to believe from this halcyon summer view that this was a city and a population under grim siege from the plague. 'Tell me again of this encounter yesterday, Molly, and every detail that you can recall with your actress's profound memory.'

Molly told her story again with a little more elaboration than the first time, and M'sieur Desargues was full of renewed admiration for her bravery and resourcefulness. 'I can scarce believe that you got the best of Senor de Santiago. He will not like that story to get out – why, if it did, his reputation would be tarnished, and he would be the laughing stock of Europe...'

Molly regarded him coldly. 'Why, sir? Because it was a mere woman who bested him? And why should that be such a source of amusement to anyone? Do you think a woman can never outdo a man in anything? Are you one of those gentlemen who believe that women are mere drudges provided by the Almighty to do their bidding - to clean up after them, or to cook for them, or to make sport with them, as they wish?'

M'sieur Desargues was taken aback by this broadside. 'Err...indeed no, sweet Molly. I did not mean to suggest such a thing, merely that I doubt that this man has ever lost an encounter of any sort before, even to the greatest swords in Europe. He underestimated you badly, Molly, and will want to make you suffer for it if he ever catches up with you again,' he warned. 'There is no forgive or forget in that man's nature, so I fear that you are right in your supposition, and that you are now as much a fugitive from his vengeance as I am.'

'Your words are less than comforting, sir,' Molly snapped, wondering how she had ever got herself embroiled in this dangerous intrigue, when she hardly knew this gentleman who was the root cause of it.

M'sieur Desargues got to his feet. 'You must not go home to Bow Street for the present, Molly. It would be too dangerous.'

'Indeed?' Molly demanded sarcastically. 'I believe I have already come to that obvious conclusion myself.' Seeing the genuine surprise in his face at her tone, she relented a little in her anger. 'I have already found a new lodging for myself next door, which will do me for the present. Senor de Santiago shall never find me there, though he has a thousand spies looking.'

M'sieur Desargues nodded. 'Then that is well.'

Molly looked down at her clothes and sniffed dismally. 'Perhaps it will keep me safe from harm, sir, yet it mortifies me that I have to make do with only the poor rags I stand up in.'

M'sieur Desargues was alarmed by her words. 'You must *not* be tempted to return to Bow Street, even just to fetch some of your fine gowns, Molly. You would not live long enough to enjoy wearing any of them. That devil will not make the mistake of underestimating you a second time, and will simply slit your throat if he gets within reach of you. He has no normal human feelings to appeal to: no mercy, no compassion. He has no friends, by all accounts; he beds no one, neither women nor boys; he enjoys no pleasures apart from killing and torture.'

Molly said nothing to that, but fear stirred uncomfortably in the pit of her stomach.

M'sieur Desargues looked at her hopefully. 'Perhaps you are wrong, though, Molly, and you wounded the devil mortally? Might not he have bled to death from the wound you gave him? If so, our problems could be all behind us.'

Molly shook her head doubtfully. 'I wish that I could think so. But the wound was not so deep or severe as I would have liked to inflict. And the villain seemed to recover his strength quickly, judging by the foul threats he shouted to me as I fled the scene.' Molly stopped pacing for a moment. 'Given those threats, I will certainly not venture to return soon to Bow Street for more clothes.'

M'sieur Desargues was relieved at her good sense. 'Then you will buy new ones, I presume?'

Molly made a wry face. 'Difficult now, sir, with all the dressmakers and drapers gone from the city because of the plague. But my mother's house is only in the next street, and she keeps some old clothes of mine there still, so I can obtain a change of attire without venturing too far. I will go there shortly, and then return later to discuss what we must do about this. Can we go to the local constable and beadle, or perhaps appeal to the City Marshal, for protection against this man and his agents, do you think? I do not wish to have to hide forever from this man...'

M'sieur Desargues grunted heavily. 'I would not place any reliance on the law to protect you from this man, Molly. For one thing, we have no proof that he even accosted us, or that he is sworn to take my life.'

Molly sighed with frustration. 'Then what can we do, sir?'

M'sieur Desargues took her right hand. 'We can leave this country forever; that is what we can do. I intend to sail to the New World, as I told you, where even Senor Francisco Nunez de Santiago can never find me.' He squeezed her hand between his fingers. 'Why not come with me, Molly, and start a new life there together?'

Molly frowned and shook off his hand irritably. 'What as, sir? You told me already that you have no lustful feelings for me. So what would we travel to the New World as? Brother and sister?'

M'sieur Desargues seemed oddly amused. 'Nay, not as brother and sister. That would be impossible.'

Molly remembered her previous suspicions of this gentleman's motives and was determined to get to the bottom of this mystery. 'Why did you make such efforts to get to know me, sir? You waited outside the theatre for weeks, watching me intently, and then followed me home sometimes. Do not deny it...'

''Tis true enough, so I do not deny it. I desired to know you, but was not sure how to introduce myself. Then one night I followed you and saw that you were ill, and that gave me the perfect opportunity to help and comfort you, which was my hope all along...'

Molly was uneasy. 'And I was most grateful for your attentions that night, sir. Yet why pick on me of all the actresses at the King's theatre? There are many wondrous beauties to tempt a man in that company, so why did your eye fall on me, sir?'

M'sieur Desargues smiled. 'Thou art too modest of thy own attributes, Molly. None of those other ladies of the company can hold a candle to thee, when it comes to grace and beauty.'

Molly was not to be distracted like that and pressed home her advantage. 'You knew of my mother and her business before you ever met me, did you not?'

'I did,' M'sieur Desargues admitted reluctantly.

Molly was triumphant at getting this admission. 'Ah, I knew it! Who told you that my mother ran a profitable bawdy house?

M'sieur Desargues was embarrassed. 'I forget exactly who – perhaps a French acquaintance who had visited her establishment.'

'You have not been there yourself?' Molly demanded.

In exasperation at her angry pressing, M'sieur Desargues ran a hand through his thick dark curls. 'Most assuredly, I have not. It is the last place that I would go in London! Yet I knew of your mother through my acquaintances, and I soon discovered that you, the new young actress from the King's company, were her only daughter.'

'I was adopted, sir. Celia is not my real mother at all, merely my foster mother,' Molly lied without a second thought, maintaining the convenient fiction that all the neighbourhood still believed.

M'sieur Desargues was dubious. 'Are you sure of that, Molly? I have heard there is a great resemblance between you and Madam Hornett.'

'A coincidence only, sir,' Molly assured him. She had a sudden thought as she remembered something the villain Senor de Santiago had said. 'Your enemy called you by a different name yesterday, sir. He used the name "Comte de Mésanger" instead of merely M'sieur Desargues.'

M'sieur Desargues bowed with a flourish. '*À votre service, mademoiselle.* They are both my names, Philippe Desargues, Comte de Mésanger.'

Molly was impressed despite herself. 'Then you are truly a nobleman in your home country?'

M'sieur Desargues smiled faintly. 'I told you that I came from an ancient lineage that was formerly possessed of great wealth and privilege. Did you not believe me?'

Molly avoided his eye. 'I know not what to believe of you any more, sir.'

'Believe at least that I have a great affection for you, Molly, and that I want only the best of life for you.'

Molly weighed him up with a doubtful eye. 'Then tell me what was the cause of this feud that has led to this situation, M'sieur le Comte. It seems the least you can do for me – to explain why this assassin Senor de Santiago wishes to take your life. And now mine too, it seems,' she added worriedly.

M'sieur Desargues agreed, if reluctantly. 'Yes, it seems only just that you should know the cause of this feud, although, to be frank, it does not reflect on me well.'

Molly prompted him to go on. 'I will be tolerant of your failings, sir. We are all human, after all.'

'Yet I am perhaps more human and venal than most, Molly, and was often given to moral turpitude as a young man, especially in my treatment of young women,' M'sieur Desargues admitted. 'My real enemy – the gentleman who has hired Senor de Santiago to exact his revenge - is the Duc de Chavagnes...'

Even Molly had heard that name before – one of the wealthiest noblemen in France, and an important figure at the court of King Louis.

'I see you have heard that illustrious name before, Molly,' M'sieur Desargues guessed astutely.

Molly nodded. 'I have, sir. How did you arouse the ire of this famous duke?'

M'sieur Desargues sighed. 'Alas, I was unfortunate enough to fall in love with his young second wife, the Duchesse Marie, who was a distant cousin of the King himself.'

Molly nodded in understanding. 'Ah, I see. That was most imprudent of you, sir, to choose the wife of such a great man as the subject of your passion.'

M'sieur Desargues grunted. 'Ay, 'tis true what you say. Molly. Yet my family is much older than his. But for the cruel blast of ill fortune, it would be my family who still owned vast estates and exerted great power, not his, and I who could have laid claim to such a wife as Marie.'

'How old is the Duchesse Marie, sir?' Molly inquired.

M'sieur Desargues hesitated. 'She was but one and twenty, when I first met her two years ago.'

Molly hid her cynicism over that, and made only a mild comment instead. 'Then there was a great disparity in your ages, sir,'

M'sieur Desargues shrugged his broad shoulders. 'Not as great a disparity as with her husband, who was forty years her senior, while I was merely twice her age.'

Molly was dismissive even so. 'It seems men can make fine sport into old age, sir, while we women are worn out by the arduous process of love before reaching our fortieth year.'

M'sieur Desargues reflected soberly. 'That is true enough, Molly, and I agree that it is a most unfair part of a woman's life. Yet my affair with Marie was a genuine love match on both sides. I had never been in love before but had left a long trail of broken female hearts behind me. My life had simply been one bedchamber conquest after another, which truly made no more impact on my soul than a raindrop falling on the sea. Yet finally I met a woman who could break my heart in return. I was no callous fortune seeker this time. If I were merely looking for a rich woman to pay my debts, I would have chosen an easier target for my affections than the wife of such an eminent man of the French court...'

Molly was tempted to say, '*You mean an easier target such as myself, sir, a mere actress with a wealthy mother.*' But she thought better of it.

M'sieur Desargues seemed to recognize her unspoken thought simply from her tart expression, and he was thrown off balance for a moment. He tried to recover his composure, though, and explain. '...I wanted Marie to leave her husband forever, and to come with me to...'

This time Molly could not help but say, 'To the New World, sir?'

M'sieur Desargues agreed with a tired smile. 'As it happens, *yes*...'

Molly was quick to respond. 'Then it seems you offered this great love of your life the same arrangement as you do to me. I should be flattered then, I suppose, that I fall into the same group in your affections as this grand lady, the Duchesse Marie.'

'You certainly compare well in beauty, Molly,' M'sieur Desargues assured her, 'yet my feelings for you are not what they were for Marie.'

Molly bit back a more trenchant response, and said only, 'How do they differ, sir?'

M'sieur Desargues did not answer that pointed question, though, and seemed lost for words for a moment.

Molly waited for him to continue, until she saw with distress that his eyes were wet with emotion. 'The Duke discovered that his wife was unfaithful?' she asked him curiously.

'Ay, he did. And I never saw Marie again; the Duke made sure of that. She died only a few months later.'

Molly was shocked. 'How so, sir? She was but a young woman.'

M'sieur Desargues controlled his emotions with difficulty. 'She died supposedly in child birth, along with her son. Yet I believe the Duke poisoned her with salts of arsenic when he discovered that the child was probably mine.'

Molly put a comforting hand on his shoulder. 'Your life has certainly been a sad and tangled affair, sir. And you left for England to escape from the Duke's terrible wrath?'

M'sieur Desargues nodded. 'I did, but 'tis not far enough from France here to be safe, as events have proved. I must now be on my way to the Americas, and as soon as I can. Even such a villain as de Santiago will not follow me to New York and beyond. When I get to the New World, I intend to explore the interior of the Virginia territory. I have heard stories of mountains full of diamonds, and rivers flowing with gold dust.'

Molly blinked. 'Are not the forests of Virginia also full of painted red savages who would take your hair at the first opportunity?'

M'sieur Desargues smiled at that 'Perhaps, but then I have much hair that I can afford to lose. But, in any case, I am not so foolish as to venture there alone: I will hope to link up with some like-minded Frenchmen, and to make some cooperative venture with them into the interior...'

Molly wished to talk some more of these interesting things, but saw from the short shadows outside that it must be near noon, and that she had already been here for far longer than she had planned. She picked up her bag to leave.

M'sieur Desargues was concerned by her obvious intention to go.

'Worry not, sir,' she explained. 'As I said, I go only to my mother's house in the next alley to collect some more clothes, and perhaps to take bread with her.'

'You had better not tell her anything of this sordid business, Molly. You will only frighten her, and there is nothing she can do to help,' M'sieur Desargues said pointedly.

'Celia is not given easily to fright, sir, but I will say nothing to her for the present of my troubles,' Molly promised him, as she turned towards the door. 'I will return later, then we can decide some sensible course of action for us…'

'For *us*, Molly.' M'sieur Desargues reacted with some joy to her use of the plural. 'Does that mean you will seriously consider my proposal?'

Molly shook her head wryly. 'I fear that I have no intention of venturing across the oceans with you, sir. You forget my loyalty to Mr Raven, do you not?'

'Perhaps he has forgotten his loyalty to you, Molly?' M'sieur Desargues suggested acidly.

'If he has, sir, then I will be most sad. But I doubt that even such woeful news as losing Mr Raven's affection would tempt me to change my mind. Yet perhaps I must leave London, therefore we may be able to agree on a plan of action that suits both our needs…'

*

'Why do you want your old dresses, Molly?' Celia asked her suspiciously. 'I would have thought that you would not want to be seen dead in those rags, now that you are a great actress and the mistress of a wealthy man.'

Molly sat in the tiny parlour of her mother's bawdy house, sharing her midday meal of leftover mutton stew. One of Celia's girls, Marion Caster, had joined them at the table for this small repast. Marion was a beautiful blue-eyed, fair-skinned girl from Kent, and a special friend of Molly's since Molly had saved her last winter from the attentions of one nasty customer with a predilection for whipping the soft white flesh of his girl victims until they bled. That "gentleman" had not returned to the bawdy house since the night that Molly had threatened to do the same to his fat white buttocks, which loss of custom was certainly no great personal loss to the girls of this establishment, and particularly to Marion.

'The theatre is closed because of the plague, Mother, and I may have to return to a simpler life for the present,' Molly explained. 'Perhaps I might even have to leave London for a while, therefore it might be politic to wear less grand clothes than I have worn of late. In these troubled times, I think it better not to stand out from the crowd.'

'And where might you go, Molly?' Celia inquired. 'Is your intention to leave London something to do with the plans of your gentleman, Mr Raven?'

Molly hesitated. 'Not directly.'

Celia probed a little. 'How go your relations with Mr Raven, Molly? Are you fully reconciled with him after your misunderstanding with him over

213

that man he found in your bed?'

'*Mr Raven found another man in your bed, Molly*...?' Marion giggled at this unexpected discovery but was soon silenced by Celia's reproving glance.

Molly was tempted to lie, but did not in the end, knowing how easily Celia could see through any of her attempts at deception or evasion. 'I am not sure how Mr Raven and I stand at present, Mother, but I do have hopes that he will return to me soon.'

Celia was disappointed. 'Then I am distressed to hear it. I saw him arrive at your door a few weeks ago, when you were still recovering from the plague, and he seemed most contrite over his earlier neglect of you...'

Marion looked up from her plate of mutton stew in alarm. 'Did you have the plague, Molly,' she asked worriedly.

Molly gave her mother a pointed look. 'Nay, I think not, Marion. I was merely sick with some other lesser affliction, the ague, that was all.'

Celia inspected her daughter closely, and her eyes softened for the first time. 'I must say that you have made a most remarkable recovery from the ...plague...err...*ague*...Molly. I did not believe it when I heard that you were already back performing for Killigrew's company. Yet you look extremely well, my girl, even if your lover has deserted you,' she added tartly.

'He has not deserted me, Mother,' Molly protested. 'His time is merely taken with other more pressing things, that is all.'

Celia snorted in derision. 'That is the very definition of desertion, if a gentleman can no longer find any time for bedding his mistress.'

'He has *not* abandoned me, Mother,' Molly repeated stubbornly. 'I know in my heart that he has not.'

Celia relented a little in her aggressive tone. 'Then, tell me. When did he last spend the night with you, Molly?'

Molly avoided her eye. 'Not since I was taken sick,' she conceded.

Celia shook her head knowingly. 'Then that is more than a month that he has been away from your bed, Molly. Your hold on him must be a tenuous one indeed, for him to stay away from you willingly for so long.'

'Yet he called at my house but two days ago, Mother,' Molly argued. 'He is gone to Dorset now to see his family, and look after his affairs there. I intend to wait patiently for his return.' Molly hesitated. 'But he will not be back in London for long, I fear. He has volunteered to join the King's fleet at Harwich in a few weeks as a surgeon, and to sail against the Dutch.'

Celia bristled with derision. 'Then he is a fool to leave your warm feather bed for such an alternative life. Why should a wealthy young gentleman like Mr Raven risk his neck in such a foolish way? Is the young man mad?'

Molly looked at Marion, appealing with her eyes for her support. 'Henry is an honourable man, Mother. He does not wish to stay wrapped up in comfort and luxury, when his fellow countrymen might be dying for their country. '

'And he would rather die with them, is that it?' Celia muttered. 'Would that ultimate sacrifice make him feel that his honour had been fully tested?'

Molly finished her stew and stood up, desperate to be gone now. 'Perhaps you had better take this up with Mr Raven himself, if his decisions so perplex and distress you, Mother. But for myself, I want only the old clothes I came for, and then I will be gone.'

A worried Celia got to the feet too. 'Have you some other troubles, of which you have not told me, Molly? You seem very distressed.'

'No,' Molly said bitterly. 'I have no other problems other than the theatre where I work is closed, my lover is going to war, and I live in a city overrun with the plague. Is that not enough to distress me?'

Celia took Molly's hand and gripped it tightly. 'Then I am sorry indeed that I could not say a kinder word to you, Molly. I think you should leave the city too as soon as you can, and find a safe refuge to wait for Mr Raven to come back to you. Which I am sure he will, God willing.' She glanced down at Marion. 'As for me, I think I will choose to stay. But I will soon have to close this house, and send the girls away for their own good. With the city so empty, there are few gentlemen customers now, so it is better that Marion and the others go to the country where they will be safe from this pestilence...'

*

An hour later, Molly returned to M'sieur Desargues's garret to inquire whether he had any specific plan in mind for his escape from London. To her surprise, his plans were already far more advanced that she had thought they might be.

M'sieur Desargues sat down facing her at the table by the window and informed her of the arrangements he had made. 'I have booked passage for the Americas in a vessel leaving England this very Saturday, Molly, the twentieth day of May.'

Molly hid her surprise. 'Then you must have already arranged this, I assume, even before Senor de Santiago arrived to haunt your steps.' Molly had a sudden distressing realization that, if she chose to wait for Henry's return, she would be left alone in this plague-ridden city, being hunted by that devil. 'Does the vessel leave from the port of London?'

M'sieur Desargues shook his head. 'Nay, I could not get passage in any vessel from London with so many wealthy people fleeing the city. But I did hear of a vessel that sails for New York this week, from a port called Weymouth on the south coast of England. A friend has gone there already and made the arrangements for me.'

Molly's eyes lit up at this news. 'Weymouth is located in the county of Dorset, I believe. Mr Raven has mentioned it to me several times.' She suddenly saw a convenient solution to her problem. Perhaps she should not simply wait for Henry to come back, but to follow him to Dorset, in which case she could travel with M'sieur Desargues? It seemed such a sensible notion that she suggested it at once. 'Then, since you are determined to make this journey, perhaps I can accompany you as far as Weymouth, sir.'

M'sieur Desargues looked disappointed. 'You go merely to see your Mr Raven again, I take it,' he said with ill humour.

'And what if I do, sir?' Molly asked defiantly. 'What is that to you...?' Molly suddenly stopped in mid-sentence as she heard a heavy footstep on the creaking stairs outside, and her heart leapt into her throat at the thought that de Santiago might have found them here after all. But it was her mother's voice she heard through the closed door, laden heavily with suspicion. 'What games do you play at in there, Molly? Are you all right?'

Molly's heart was still racing because, although this was not as bad as being run to ground by a mad assassin, it was still a nasty surprise. 'My mother must have followed me here from her house in the next alley, sir,' she told M'sieur Desargues in a breathless whisper. 'She will think the obvious when she finds me here colluding with a strange man, no doubt.'

M'sieur Desargues appeared even more concerned about this unwelcome visit than Molly. 'Do not let her in, Molly. I will lock the door, if you will not...'

But it was too late for such measures, for Celia simply barged into the room without knocking at all.

She came to a sudden halt, and eyed M'sieur Desargues with a contemptuous look. 'Ah, I see what goes on here, Molly,' she said with heavy resignation. 'You have deceived me, talking to this "gentleman" behind my back.'

Molly sighed. ''Tis not what you think, Mother.'

Celia ignored her, and chose to address M'sieur Desargues instead. 'You have not changed much, sir. Still handsome, I see, even if a little worn and grizzled at the edges,' she added tartly.

Despite her obvious hostility, M'sieur Desargues bowed gallantly to her. 'And you are still very beautiful, Madam.'

Molly was mystified by this interchange and turned angrily on M'sieur Desargues. 'You know my mother already, sir? You told me that you had not visited my mother's establishment, sir,' she reminded him angrily.

M'sieur Desargues nodded. 'And I told you the truth, Molly. My sin is one of omission, not of falsehood. I have indeed met your mother before, but it was not at her establishment here. We met many years ago in Paris.'

Celia frowned in puzzlement. 'He has not told you who he is, Molly? I thought he must have told you.'

Molly blinked. 'Told me what, Mother?'

Celia took a deep breath. 'This gentleman is your natural father, Molly...'

# CHAPTER 19

Tuesday, 16<sup>th</sup> May 1665

Esther Linney had thought that her mind and soul must have been irreparably damaged by the sad and terrible circumstances of her recent life, yet it seemed that even the most tortured soul was not completely beyond redemption. She realized with some astonishment that, since her return to Dorset, she was capable of feeling almost normal thoughts and emotions again – even if those emotions were mainly dictated by anger, regret and a profound melancholy. Yet she had discovered that she could feel some brighter emotions too. And though happiness was presently an elusive emotion for her troubled mind, she had nevertheless yielded occasionally over the last two days to an odd sort of calm...

*As now...*

She acknowledged to herself with surprise that she was in almost a tranquil mood on this warm May morning. She was not overwhelmed with the joy of life, of course – that degree of happiness and optimism might be lost to her forever - yet she did feel some pleasure that she was back in this special place, and among people she loved and respected. She was even beginning to get used to wearing men's breeches, which she had discovered to her surprise did make strenuous country walking much easier.

Since her arrival at the manor, Cathy and Henry had assigned Martin Gibney as her personal guardian and protector, mainly, she suspected, to keep her away from the curious eyes and questions of the rest of the household servants, who naturally wondered who this pale young visitor to the manor house really was. So far Esther had been mostly confined to her room in the South Wing of the house - which was a more comfortable prison than Newgate, of course, yet which she still found an irksome imposition when she had expected to be free as a bird. It had not been possible to go walking outside at all yesterday, because a towering black thunderstorm had billowed up unexpectedly from the southwest, and had lashed and pummelled the manor house with rain all day, turning the gargoyles on the roof into miniature waterfalls. That frustrating further imprisonment yesterday had made Esther desperate to be allowed out of her room today, especially when she had risen this morning at first light and seen the golden globe of the sun rising above the eastern hills into a clear unblemished sky, heralding a fine spring day to come. She wanted so much to walk through the woods and meadows that she had enjoyed as a girl, and see again the drifts of wildflowers and the familiar sunlit glades that she had known then. Catherine and Henry had been only too happy to oblige her in this wish, of course, provided that she was accompanied, which meant that this escort duty had inevitably fallen on Martin too.

Esther had thought that Martin might resent such a menial task, particularly as he had been so ill-tempered and brusque with her on the coach ride from London. Yet surprisingly he seemed in a better mood today than she had seen him previously, and he had even favoured her with an occasional smile during their long walk, if not much conversation. She wondered if Henry had perhaps spoken to him about his ill manner in her presence, and asked him to improve it.

Esther had been acquainted with Martin for some years, though she hardly knew him well. He came not from Dorset but originally from the university town of Cambridge, yet that was almost all she knew of his personal circumstances. She had first encountered him eight or nine years ago when, as a sixteen-year-old boy, he had been appointed as Henry Raven's personal manservant during his time at the university. Esther had never visited Cambridge herself, of course, but Martin had always accompanied Henry on his visits back to Dorset, and that was where their paths had crossed. Once Esther had left the manor to keep house for her brother, though, she had encountered Martin much less, perhaps only once a year during the summer when Henry and his own servants came back to Dorset for the harvest. Yet, despite the infrequency of their meetings, he had always seemed to make a point of picking her out on those few occasions when they did meet, and favouring her with his attentions. Esther had always found Martin to be a very sober and serious young man not given much to gossip like most of his peers. But she was grateful for that taciturn character today because it meant that he was not constantly trying to gain her attention with idle chatter, which left her mainly in peace to enjoy nature's grand handiwork at every turn...

Now, in mid-morning, they were walking along a footpath at the edge of the oak wood, from where the land fell away steeply to form a natural bowl between the surrounding hills. The distant manor house nestled in the bottom of this hollow, protected by a grove of ancient ash trees, and with its tall red chimneys and brick walls providing a splash of distinctive colour among all this verdure. In contrast to yesterday's storm, there was not a breath of wind today so that not even a leaf stirred, while the trail of white smoke from the kitchen chimney at the manor house climbed straight into the blue sky with nary a waver.

They had already been walking for an hour or more, and Martin now suggested that they should stop for five minutes at this fine vantage point and enjoy the tranquil view. He produced a flask of water, and some bread and cheese from his knapsack, and, since the grass was still damp from yesterday's rain, they found a seat instead on a fallen tree trunk at the top of a grassy bank. In the branches of the oak tree behind them, a robin sang sweetly above their heads. After the terrors that she had been through over the last few weeks, Esther was suddenly overwhelmed by the beauty of this moment, and a tear came to her eye at the thought that her dead child would never grow up to enjoy such a wondrous place as this.

Martin could not fail to see the tear on her cheek, and finally said something to break the silence. 'Mistress Linney...'

Esther wiped away the tear impatiently. 'Please call me Esther, Martin. We have known each other long enough for that.'

Martin nodded. 'Indeed we have. I apologize if I was severe on you during the coach journey to Dorset. I did not mean to be unkind, Esther, but I was much distracted by your suffering, and did not know truly how to speak to you about it. You have been through a great ordeal, which was not deserved, therefore I have found it hard to reconcile your suffering with my belief in a caring and compassionate God.'

Esther took a little of the bread and cheese that he offered her. 'You do not hold with the view that I had a child out of wedlock, and therefore deserved such punishment? I suspect many people would hold that opinion.'

Martin swallowed uncomfortably. 'Indeed I do not. It is not for me to condemn anyone, and especially not you...'

'Then you are very good, Martin, to overlook my shortcomings, and not to blame me for my sins.'

Martin poured some water into a wooden cup and offered it to her. 'Here, drink your fill.' He hesitated. 'I hope that I am not presumptuous in saying this, but do you want to talk of what happened to you? It gives relief sometime to talk of one's troubles, which relief is called catharsis, I believe, after the Greek. Or are the memories of what happened too painful to ever recall with equanimity?'

Esther did not truly want to talk of these things at all, but was forced to say something in response. '*Catharsis*? I have never heard that word. You are well versed in new and impressive words, Martin, I see. Where did you learn such things?'

Martin stiffened perceptibly, seeming to suspect some insincerity in her question, although it was in fact an honest one. 'I learned to read and count in the village school in Trumpington, near Cambridge, where our teacher was most diligent in his duties – and in the administering of floggings if we did not learn our lessons quickly enough,' he answered finally. 'But my late mother was my major influence. She was a genteel woman, though only the widow of a blacksmith, and it was she who instilled in me this love of language. And my master has allowed me to read any of his books that I wish, which has greatly furthered my knowledge.'

Esther paused for a few seconds as the robin above their heads burst into sweet trilling cadence again. Eventually, after the robin had finished his paean to the beautiful day, she spoke again. 'Yet, for a man who loves words, you speak so little, Martin.'

Martin avoided her eye. 'I speak to those I care for.'

Esther realized for the first time that Martin was rather a lonely and solitary man, despite his many years in the Raven household. 'You have no brothers or sisters?' she asked.

Martin shook his head, as he took some more of the bread. 'I had two brothers and one sister. But all are sadly dead.'

Esther understood that feeling of being without a family of one's own. 'Death stalks everyone in the end, but some dear souls are taken before their time, which is always hard to comprehend.'

'Ay, untimely death is hard to comprehend, yet you overcame even such an obstacle as that, and came back from the dead.' Martin shook his head in wonderment. 'You were dead nearly an hour, so people say, although time perhaps means little beyond the grave. Yet, by rights, according to the ancients, the ferryman Charon should have transported your soul far across the river Acheron into the underworld by then.'

Esther could see that Martin was intensely curious about her experiences and clearly wanted to know what she might have seen of the next world. 'Do you not mean across the Styx?' she asked, half in jest. 'Did not Phlegyas ferry Dante and Virgil over the river Styx, and did not Dante make that river the fifth circle of Hell, where the wrathful and sullen are punished by being drowned in the muddy waters for all eternity?' Esther felt a wave of fresh melancholy envelop her at that thought of an infinity of suffering. 'That is surely where my soul should have ended its days.'

Martin tried to calm her. 'In truth it should not, Esther. Thou art a virtuous woman who has been brought low only by evil circumstance, not by wicked inclination.'

Esther would have liked Martin to desist with his questions, but his curiosity on this subject would not be denied despite the clear pain he was causing her. 'Do you remember being taken to Tyburn on the cart?' he asked her. ''Tis but four days ago, after all.'

Esther nodded. 'I do remember that much, and all the vilification and cruel insults I had to suffer on the way.'

'And what of being hanged? Do you remember that too?'

Esther shivered as she thought back to that horror. 'No, thankfully, I can recall nothing of that. I remember arriving at Tyburn and seeing the jeering mob swelling around me, then everything after that has gone from my mind. The Lord God has blessed me and wiped that evil memory away. I remember nothing more until I woke, as if from a dream…'

'You remember nothing at all of what happened in between?' Martin pressed her again. 'You did not see Our Lord or the archangel Gabriel?'

'If I did, then that revelation too has been lost to me, along with memory of the hanging. No, truthfully, I did not see Our Lord.'

Martin was disappointed. 'Yet he must nevertheless have wrought this miracle, or how else could it have come about? Our Lord truly took pity on you and brought you back to life, like Lazarus.'

Esther thought it more likely that she had not been fully dead, but had still clung to life, even though quite insensible, and breathing so little that no one had seen it. 'Perhaps the ferryman refused to take me across the river to the underworld because I had no coin in my mouth to pay the toll?' she suggested bleakly.

'I doubt that was the reason.' Martin let his eyes linger on her face for a moment, until Esther became quite uncomfortable with his close inspection. Finally he spoke again, his voice rising. 'Yet what a wonder it must have been for you when you came back to the world of the living!'

Truly that had been a wonder because Esther had thought at first that she must indeed have arrived in heaven. Lying in a soft feather bed in a sweet bedchamber, with candlesticks burning on side tables, and a fine oak floor underfoot, her eyes had traversed the room looking for clues as to where she might be. Everything was out of focus, yet it seemed to her that the walls were hung with rich tapestries, and opposite the bed was a Flemish triptych, fittingly showing three scenes of the Crucifixion and Resurrection. She saw vaguely that someone was ministering to her, cleansing her body with hot water, and letting her drink a little. If this was not heaven, then she did not know where else she could be. Yet she had soon realized from the sound of earthly voices that someone must have rescued her from her fate somehow, and with that realization that she was still living had come the onset of a terrible ache in her heart…

As her vision began to improve, the first person she had recognized in the room had been Henry Raven. She had tried to ask him how she had come here, but her throat was too painful to speak, and she found she could only make embarrassing animal noises instead of lucid speech.

She remembered that he had come and sat beside her, had held her hand, and spoke comforting words to her. Although she could give him no sensible reply, yet she had understood his words well enough, and was overcome with gratitude for his concern. He had seen her suffer ultimate humiliations and disgrace – conceiving a bastard child, then accused of causing its death; and finally, suffering a trial and a hanging before a jeering and hateful mob. To him she could have been all manner of despicable creatures by now - temptress, whore, murderess. Yet, on recovering her, he had treated her in the same sweet way as ever, as if she was a young and innocent girl again, taken into his home for the first time...

Now, on this fine spring morning back at Salwayash Manor, Esther realized with dismay that these events had re-ignited her love for Henry Raven. Truly she had always loved him somewhere deep in her heart, yet she had been able to leave that unrequited love behind her when they saw so little of each other. Yet now she was smitten with this same longing for him again, and her brief dream of contentment evaporated as quickly as it came. Happiness would always be a fragile thing for her from now on, and would be doubly impossible if she was burdened with a desire that would always be unfulfilled. She told herself that she must escape from Henry Raven's kindness at all costs: staying here at the manor would be sweet torture indeed to her, with him so near and yet far beyond her reach. He had always been unattainable, yet now, because of these terrible events, she knew in her heart that he was separated from her by a gulf so wide and unbridgeable that there was no feasible way across.

Although the sun still shone out of a clear blue sky, it seemed to her as if a black shadow had now fallen across her brow as she faced up to her future. She knew now that she would have to leave this place forever. Not just the manor, not just Salwayash, not even just her beloved Dorset. If she wanted to find peace from this sweet torture, she would have to leave England forever and start a new life somewhere else. In a new land, far away from here, she might just be able to find some salvation for her wounded soul.

That secret decision was made in but a moment, but, once made, was sufficient to calm her again. She would have to stay here for the present, of course, but she would try to keep to herself as much as possible, until she felt strong enough to leave. There were other people she needed to avoid too, and as much as Henry, if for different reasons. She dreaded if she should meet Ralph Warboys while she was here, although perhaps her male disguise would prevent recognition by him, provided it was only from a safe distance. He must, after all, believe her to be dead, which belief would certainly deter him from recognizing her. She hoped indeed that she would not meet him face-to-face, and be recognized, for she had no comprehension of what she would say to him in those trying circumstances.

It had been his child too who had died after all, so Ralph must have suffered some considerable pain of his own at what had happened. *Yet did he even know of his baby son's death, though, and what had happened afterwards?*

Surely that woman, Mistress Worme, must have told him everything? Even if Mistress Worme had said nothing to him, though, he *must* have heard of the death of the baby, and of the trial, because Esther's name had appeared in numerous lurid newssheets and pamphlets (as her hateful gaolers at Newgate had been only too happy to tell her.) *Had he stayed away from the trial then because he believed her guilty of this heinous crime?* That would be the most terrible thing of all, then, for the father of her child to actually believe her guilty of its murder. Yet perhaps he did for, unlike Henry Raven, he had certainly not stepped forward to help her.

Given these uncertainties over what he might believe, Esther could only hope that she would avoid Ralph completely, although she knew him to be a regular visitor to the manor house, which might occasion some risk of an unwanted encounter. In fact it was these regular journeys by horse from Warboys Hall to the manor that had taken him past her own cottage last summer, which chance encounters had been the start of all her troubles. Now, all she could do for him was to give him the benefit of the doubt, and hope that he did not think too badly of her in return. Whatever happened, she was determined to keep his relations with her secret, and to carry that secret to the grave with her...

All these thoughts had flashed through her mind in a few moments, and Martin still seemed anxious to interrogate her further about her experiences. Yet Esther had had enough of being pressed about her experiences of a possible afterlife by now, and she climbed abruptly to her feet. 'Come, Martin!' she ordered. 'Let us walk some more.'

Martin was forced to join her, and they walked on in almost complete silence, taking a familiar path through the oak wood which seemed exactly as Esther remembered it from a child.

Eventually they came to a clearing in the wood, and a stream glinting in the dappled sunlight. The banks to the stream were steep at his point, and thick with stinging nettles and the green stems of young willowherb. The stream was in full spate after yesterday's rain, but the waters still ran as clear as ever, being on chalk soil.

Martin indicated the fast flowing stream. 'This is a sad place, I believe.'

Esther thought he was just making conversation. '*Sad?* Why so?'

'Dora Bagwell told me this is the very spot where my master's neighbour, Mistress Warboys, met her untimely end.'

Esther blinked. 'You mean *Margaret*, the wife of Mr Warboys? *She died here?* When?'

Martin eased himself down the steep bank to the waterside, where he leant down and splashed some cool water on his face. Then he looked back up at her. 'It happened a few months ago, not long after Candlemas, I believe, when she was out riding early one morning, and tried to ford this stream. The water was low then, but it was also icy, and her horse put his foot down a hidden rabbit hole in this steep bank and rolled down on top of her. Her neck was broken instantly, so they say, although the horse, surprisingly, was all right.'

Esther felt a sudden chill in her marrow. Ralph's wife must have died not long after she had left for London to have her baby in secret...

So why had Ralph not told her this notable fact when he had come to see her in London last month? *Why had he not told her that he was a widower?* This could hardly be an oversight on his part therefore he had deliberately chosen to keep this significant fact from her, which suggested some deceit on his part. Not that the deceit had to be due to an entirely selfish motive, she conceded. Perhaps he thought he was being kind to her by not telling her this? Perhaps the truth was that he did not want to raise any false hopes with her that he might one day marry her and make the child his heir.

Of course, such thoughts were no more than academic now anyway, with the child buried in a quiet graveyard in Little Chelsea. Yet Esther could not but feel a little betrayed at the thought that this man would obviously have never married her under any circumstances, despite his suggestions to the contrary.

Because of the heavy flow of water, Esther and Martin found they could not ford the stream at this point today, so made their way upstream a little to a simple wooden trestle bridge. Following the track through the woods on the other side of the stream, they came a quarter hour later to a crossroads, and saw an elderly grey-haired woman approaching the same crossing from the left.

So far today, they had encountered no one at all which had suited Esther perfectly. But this woman was approaching at a rate that meant they would probably meet at the crossroads. They could have slowed their pace down to avoid her, or even stopped or turned back, yet both alternatives seemed an unnecessary overreaction. Esther knew that she would have to meet some local people at close quarters at some point, and see her disguise tested, and now was as good a time as any. Martin too seemed to be of that opinion and chose a rate of walking that seemed almost designed to make the encounter a very close one.

Esther went along with this unspoken plan, keeping up with his pace, but not daring to glance in the direction of the other woman, and instead keeping her eyes firmly fixed on the path ahead. But as they approached nearer the crossroads, Esther heard Martin gasp under his breath and knew that something was amiss. Her gaze turned naturally towards the other woman arriving at the crossroads to see what might have occasioned this gasp of surprise from her companion.

Esther was then barely twenty paces away from the other woman, when she realized with shock that the newcomer was none other than her implacable accuser at the trial, Judith Pollock...

Esther's legs almost failed her at this shocking realization, but prompted by Martin, and with his arm for discreet support, she continued walking towards the crossroads as if nothing was untoward.

As they reached the crossing of the paths, Martin spoke up as if nothing was wrong, and doffed his hat to Mistress Pollock. 'Good day, Mistress,' he said, before squeezing Esther's arm to make her follow suit.

Esther pulled off her cap to reveal her cropped boyish hair, and repeated the greeting in as low and mumbled a tone as she could manage.

Mistress Pollock did not seem to notice anything amiss, and merely nodded in return before continuing on her way.

After they had walked another fifty yards and were far enough away not to be heard, Esther glanced back at Mistress Pollock's retreating figure and complained bitterly. 'Oh, what ill luck was that! What is that woman doing walking here, so far from the village? She must have recognized me!'

Martin silenced her fears. 'She did not, Esther. She thinks you are dead and buried. She cannot possibly suspect that you are still alive.'

Esther sighed. 'Yes, how could she suspect such a thing? I scarce know it myself...'

*

At noon, with the sun beating down fiercely from a cloudless sky, Henry Raven had sought the shade of an apple tree in the walled privy garden behind the manor house. From this comfortable position he could cast his eye over the whole rear west elevation of the house, which was just as grand as the front east elevation that faced the main road to Bridport, though this rear view was much less visible to passers-by. The house had been built a hundred and thirty years ago by a local Tudor architect who had copied many of the Renaissance ornament features from Hampton Court Palace – tall slender chimneys, steep gables and other distinctive roof features - so that Salwayash Manor was in many ways a smaller and humbler version of that great riverside palace built for Cardinal Wolsey. The man who had commissioned the house for himself and his family – Sir Thomas Daplyn – had also been a devout Catholic, though, and in the ensuing decades of anti-Catholic sentiment during the reign of King Henry and his son Edward, had made many modifications to the interior, including installing a secret chapel and a introducing a number of priest holes throughout the house. Now, a century later, the existence of these secret hiding places was known only to Raven and his direct family, on the strict orders of his late mother, who imagined that these priest holes would one day find a useful purpose, if not perhaps to hide Catholic clergy as had been their original intention. One of the priest holes even led to a secret tunnel below the house, which then passed under the privy garden to a hidden exit in the surrounding woods. So far, though, no one in the Raven family had ever been forced to make use of this secret exit from the house, not even during the Civil War when Dorset had been in considerable turmoil from the competing armies of the King and Parliament, and from wandering bands of marauding soldiers with no particular affinity in mind other than their own fortunes.

Raven was still deep in his reflection on the architectural style of the manor house, when he heard a loud cough at his side.

'Ah, here you, Henry,' Catherine said mischievously. 'Skulking in the privy garden, when you should be hard at work checking our accounts.'

Raven smiled at her. 'I was not skulking; I was merely taking time to reflect on the architectural glory of our house, which is a notable example of the harmonious transition in English architecture from domestic Tudor to the Italian Renaissance classical style.'

Catherine turned to face the house too. 'Indeed so. 'Tis not so grand from this aspect, yet delightful enough for all that, and, I suppose, a reasonable reproduction of the style of Hampton Court. I have read that, in building his palace, Cardinal Wolsey was attempting to create a Renaissance cardinal's palace, all rendered with classical detailing...'

Raven laughed. 'I see that you have been spending much time in the library of late, if you know such things...'

Catherine gave a complacent shrug. 'I have, brother. Wolsey was truly an enigma, was he not? On one hand the plain English churchman; on the other, the grand cardinal who made his sovereign the arbiter of Europe and who built and furnished Hampton Court to show foreign embassies that King Henry's chief minister knew how to live as graciously as any cardinal in Rome.'

'Our present rulers are just as much an enigma to me as those Tudor gentlemen of the last century,' Raven observed. 'Sometime I know not what to make of our present Lord Chancellor, or the King he serves. At times, they seem the noblest of men; at others foolish wastrels.'

'Then why do you go to risk your life in their service, Henry?' Catherine asked irately. 'I have not given up hope of dissuading you from this foolish course of action.'

Raven sighed. 'I go to serve England, and my fellow Englishmen, Catherine. I may be able to use my surgeon skills to alleviate the suffering of my fellows; it seems the least that I can do.'

'I hope that you do not need the skills of a surgeon yourself, Henry. The flight of a cannon ball or grape shot is not discerning in its choice of target, and may as well hit a gentleman surgeon as a naval gunner,' Catherine said, biting her lip with worry.

'Then I will have to trust to God to bring me through in one piece, sister.'

Catherine was dismissive. 'You talk of God, brother. Yet God seems to have been most remiss of late in bringing justice to the world, if I judge this from Esther's undeserved sufferings, or the deaths of those two poor girls...' Catherine was halted in mid-sentence by the arrival at the north gate of the walled garden of a gentleman dressed in a fine velvet cloak and riding breeches. Her eyes lit up when she recognized the visitor, but she quickly whispered a warning to her brother. 'Ralph is come to call, Henry. Please do not give away that you know of our engagement. He asked me not to tell you yet until the time was more propitious, and he will be angered that I could not keep my woman's mouth closed for even such a short time as this.'

Raven nodded. 'I will do my best, sister, though it will require some considerable feat of acting on my part to feign ignorance of this affection between you, when your cheeks burn as brightly with passion as the noonday sun.'

Catherine snorted prettily. 'Hush, brother! He comes presently...'

Warboys arrived, breathing hard from his ride, and with his breeches splashed with mud from the wet roads. 'This is well met, Henry. Welcome back to Dorset. I did not know that you would be here. But perhaps the plague has finally forced you to leave London, so that dreadful pestilence may have brought some good at least, in giving us the pleasure of your society for the whole summer.'

Catherine curtsied formally to Warboys. 'Good day, Ralph. Yet I fear your optimism concerning my brother is ill founded. Henry has indeed left London for the present, but now he intends to volunteer to fight with the King's navy against the Dutch...'

'I go not to fight, sister,' Raven protested. 'I go only to serve as a surgeon when the navy is desperately short of such skills.'

Warboys smiled ruefully. 'Yet 'tis a worthy enough thing that you do, for all that, Henry. I wish that I were equally public-spirited, but I feel too old for such strenuous heroics.'

Raven glanced at his handsome face and his fine figure, which were more those of a man of twenty than a man of forty. 'You seem quite as young as me, Ralph,' Raven said.

Warboys stirred uncomfortably. 'Time has been kind to me on the outside, yet inside I feel all the suffering and pain of my forty years on this earth.'

Catherine looked up in surprise at his sudden bleak tone, and Raven too wondered what had prompted this dark introspective thought from their handsome neighbour.

Raven was spared from responding, though, by the arrival of newcomers to the garden, this time at the southwest gate behind them. He saw uneasily that it was Esther with Martin Gibney, just returning from their long morning walk around the estate.

Ralph too had seen the newcomers, even though they were fifty paces away. 'I see that you have brought your excellent young manservant back to Dorset with you this time, Henry.' He squinted into the sun. 'Yet who is the tall young fellow with him? Have you a new servant in your household?'

Catherine interrupted hurriedly. 'His name is Edward, Ralph. He is a distant cousin of ours from the North, and he has been through trying times of late, being struck down with sickness, and now needing rest and recuperation...'

'Not from the plague, I hope, Henry,' Ralph said urgently.

'Nay, not from the plague,' Raven assured him, 'but merely some bodily weakness brought on by his difficult situation in life. We try to leave him to his own company, until such time as he is fully recovered.'

Warboys stared curiously at the two departing figures, who were entering the house hurriedly by the west door. 'I see.' He frowned. 'I wonder, though, if I have met your cousin before, because he seems most familiar to me...'

# CHAPTER 20

Tuesday, 16th May 1665

After her dramatic discovery yesterday, Molly was glad to have an hour alone with her mother to discuss what to do about M'sieur Desargues. Molly had told her mother nothing of this villain who was in pursuit of M'sieur Desargues; that additional information was best kept to herself for the present, given Celia's open hostility towards the gentleman.

They sat together by the fireside in Celia's familiar parlour at the bawdy house. Evening sunlight lit up the room, showing up cobwebs in the ceiling. Molly had spent so much time in this room over the last five years that it was almost the most familiar place to her in the world, and the nearest thing she had to a home. Molly's eyes went around the room, taking in all the comforting ornaments on the mantelpiece that she knew so well, the brass candlesticks, the fire in the hearth that was always burning, summer and winter, the plain wooden lathe ceiling and the worn wainscoting, which was blistered and cracked from the constant heat of the fire. Celia had tried to make this room as homely and welcoming as possible, because it was where the gentlemen guests to the house waited on arrival, and where she could size them up, and decide which of her girls would be most appropriate. Of late, Celia had been turning away the more unsavoury types in her wish to raise the tone of the establishment. Yet with the plague taking hold of the city, gentlemen were now scarce and Celia could presently afford to turn no one away, unless they were clearly poxed. Even so, she was making plans to close the establishment, because the lack of customers meant that it was no longer worth keeping her girls here in the plague-ridden city when there was so little call for their pretty young bodies.

'So, M'sieur Desargues never gave you any inkling that he might be your natural father, Molly,' Celia said, as she sipped a cup of China tea.

Molly had never tried this new drink before because of its expense, but today she had accepted a cup the size of a thimble from her mother. It was not quite the taste she had expected, yet pleasant enough for all that. 'No, he did not say anything directly. Yet now I think back to his behaviour, I see that he came close to telling me, by his words and deeds.'

'*Deed*s? What deeds?' Celia snapped.

'Well, for one thing, he did not try to worm his way into my bed, which is *most* unusual behaviour for a gentleman who is paying me close attention. Therefore I should perhaps have realized who he was, given what you told me of my real father. Yet I did not believe you since you have told me so many contradictory stories over the years.'

Celia snorted angrily. 'I would not put it past that devil to want to sleep with his own daughter! It would mark a fresh triumph over me, to indulge himself in this sordid way. He is a rake and villain of the worst kind, and it gives me no pleasure that he is your father...'

Molly remained calm under this haranguing. 'I think you misjudge him a little, Mother. The night that I was afflicted with the plague, it was M'sieur Desargues who came to my rescue. I believe that I would have died in the street that evening if he had not come to my aid...'

'I thought it was that giant Moor apothecary who saved you, Molly,' Celia said sharply.

'It was Bassam who treated me with his herbs and physic,' Molly conceded, 'yet I would have been dead already by then if M'sieur Desargues had not followed me that night from the theatre and brought me home safe to my own bed.'

Celia sniffed coldly. 'Then 'tis the least that he owes you, though it was probably not his original intention when he followed you home. He no doubt had some baser notion in mind. '

'If you really think him such an evil rogue, then why did you let him into your own bed, Mother?' Molly asked tartly. 'You must have allowed him some liberties once, else I would not be here.'

Celia's tone softened. 'If you had seen him as a young man, in the spring of 'forty seven in Paris, then perhaps you would understand why I afforded him those liberties that I did. He is still a handsome man now, yet his beauty as a young man was something extraordinary. You must understand that I was not working as a whore then, but as a lady's maid. I was a simple and sweet girl from the village of Deptford in Kent, and I knew little of the world then, and of the ways of men. My employer was a Royalist lady who had fled Republican England, and she took me with her, and taught me some French to get by. These English émigrés enjoyed considerable intercourse with French high society, so that I came into contact with many high people in Paris. '

Molly looked up. 'And that was how you encountered M'sieur Desargues? Or rather the Comte de Mésanger?' Molly still could not bring herself to refer to this gentleman as her "father", which still seemed a most bizarre notion, and one hardly to be countenanced.

Celia nodded. 'It was – at a soiree in the salon of my lady's apartments. I was not yet twenty years old, and still a virgin. The Comte seemed to sense this straightaway, and to want to deflower me. Yet despite him being the most beautiful man I had ever seen, I resisted. I was a good and honest girl then.'

Molly smiled faintly. 'Yet you gave in eventually.'

Celia agreed wryly. 'Indeed so. After many months, he wore down my resistance with his charm, and protested his love for me.'

Molly nodded knowingly. 'Did he ever say that he would marry you?'

Celia shook her head. 'Nay, he was not so hypocritical as that. And, though I was a simple maid, I was not so naïve as to believe such a thing anyway. Yet I gave into him one May evening in a French garden in the moonlight...'

'I was conceived outside?' Molly asked in a shocked voice.

Celia shrugged. 'Probably you were. We were never able to enjoy a comfortable bed together, as I remember.'

Molly was intrigued now by her mother's story. 'And what happened when you were with child?'

'My lady caught me with the morning sickness one day and dismissed me, of course, though she liked me well enough, and thought me just a foolish child. She gave me some money to tide me over; she did have a good heart for such a grand lady. I saw the Comte and told him what had happened, and he seemed surprisingly content with the situation. He said that he would provide for the child, but that it was better for now that I should go to the country and have the baby in secret, which I did, to a little village on the River Marne, using the money given to me by my lady. It was a difficult breech birth, and the country physician who attended to the delivery was an incompetent French butcher who made sure with his crude instruments that I could never bear a child again. The Comte came to see me and the child afterwards at the cottage I had rented, and was most affectionate towards us both. But he did suggest that I should return to England for a while, until he could sort out his affairs and send for me to return to Paris.' Celia coughed cynically. 'And that was the last I ever saw or heard of him until yesterday, though I wrote him many pleading letters. After a few months, I gave up writing these foolish epistles of hope, and then I decided to give you to the Titchens, who were my neighbours at the time. At that time, I could not bear to look at you, because you were a visible reminder of that cruel man, and what he had done to me. Now a more worldly woman than before, and deprived forever of the opportunity of having more children, I became a money-seeking whore, which seemed to be a more worthwhile choice than being a spinsterish drudge all my life.

Later I regretted that I had given you away, though, so that when the poor Titchens died in that terrible fire, it seemed fated that you should return to me, for which I was most heartily glad.'

Molly touched her mother's arm consolingly. 'I am sorry that the Comte disappointed you so, Mother.'

Celia's voice broke with emotion. 'He did more than that, Molly. He broke my heart asunder until I thought that I must die from the pain. I never felt as much for a man again, though Captain Tommy did restore some of my faith in humankind later…until he went and died on me while at sea off the Spanish Main,' she added painfully.

'Yes, I remember Captain Tommy,' Molly said with affection. 'He was always kind to me as a little girl.'

Celia's eyes had grown misty at the mention of her old love Captain Tommy, and she wiped them impatiently. 'Tell me how this French rogue came into your life, Molly? And what does he do here in England? Did he come deliberately to seek you out?'

Molly did not truly know the answer to this question. 'I think not, Mother. He came here last winter for other compelling reasons.' She decided to keep these compelling reasons to herself for the moment, or at least to limit herself to half-truths about them, since she doubted that her mother could listen to the tale of the Comte's later philandering exploits with any degree of composure. 'He left France over some money trouble – he is heavily in debt, it seems…'

'It does not surprise me,' Celia interjected tartly, 'for a wastrel such as him. But how did he discover that you are my daughter, and therefore probably his daughter too? '

'He has not told me yet, but then I have hardly spoken to him since I discovered this great surprise. But I believe M'sieur Desargues knows many French émigrés here in London who patronize this establishment of yours, and these gentlemen must have mentioned your name to him. And from there he must have uncovered the fact that I am your daughter, and that I worked as an actress at the King's theatre. His curiosity to see what I was like must have brought him to the theatre. I started to notice him waiting at the stage door in March, and then recently I spotted him following me home.'

Celia's hostility was still simmering. 'Then he has certainly sought this acquaintance with some selfish or evil notion in mind. If not to seduce you, then he must have thought you would help him with money, being the mistress of such a wealthy man as Mr Raven. The Comte knows all about Mr Raven, I take it?'

'Ay, he has even met him by chance once,' Molly admitted.

Celia was anxious. 'I hope you have not promised the Comte any money? You owe this gentleman nothing, Molly, not even loyalty. And certainly not money. If it had been up to him, you would have starved as a child.'

'I have not given him any money, Mother. It is Mr Raven's money that I have in my purse, after all, and I cannot give it away in good conscience, even to my natural father.'

Celia was only moderately reassured by that. 'What mischief is the Comte planning that needs your support, Molly?'

Molly was wary. 'He plans only to leave this country, and Europe, forever, and start a new life elsewhere.'

Celia's suspicions were intensified. 'And where would this new life be?' she demanded abrasively.

'Why, in the New World, in the new colonies of North America. I believe M'sieur Desargues is hopeful to start a French colony there in time, perhaps in the interior of that unknown continent,' Molly explained.

'Then he might lose that wondrous long hair of his, when those red savages catch a glimpse of it,' Celia observed acidly, 'which would serve him right.' She debated aloud. 'But if that is his plan, then we should be grateful for it, for he will trouble us no more. Whatever happens, *you* must have nothing to do with it.'

Molly took a deep breath. 'M'sieur Desargues plans to sail for the Americas from the port of Weymouth in but four days.' She hesitated awkwardly. 'He leaves on the merchant vessel *Lapwing*, bound for the settlement of New York on the Hudson River. I had thought to accompany him by coach on Thursday to the port...'

Celia was aghast. 'Do not do it, Molly! He has some dastardly notion behind this. He will likely knock you on the head and take all your money, or worse, give you some sleeping potion, and you will wake to find yourself at sea on the way to Virginia or some other God-forsaken spot.' She took Molly's hand. 'Please, I beg you, Molly. Do not go with this man.'

Molly patted her hand in return. 'Worry not, Mother. I go to Dorset only to see Mr Raven. It surely cannot cause me any great harm merely travelling in the same coach with M'sieur Desargues as far as Weymouth, can it?'

Celia was angry. 'I see that you have already made up your mind to go, whatever I think.'

Molly was tempted now to tell her mother about the greater threat of this man, de Santiago, and her own pressing reasons for wanting to quit London, apart from the plague, which was a compelling enough reason to go anyway. But she thought better of it; it would only worry her mother to death to know that there was an evil maniac in pursuit of her. She tried a different argument instead, which had the advantage of being also true. 'It is Mr Raven that I truly go to see, Mother. He will soon be off to war, and I must see him and reassure him again of my faithful affection before he goes.'

Celia's face softened. 'Well, if that truly is the reason, then I can understand your need to go, Molly. But do not let the Comte get you anywhere near his ship! And do not listen to his lies either: he will no doubt try and poison your mind and tell a different version of this story if he has half a chance. And that version of how he got me with child will no doubt be much more considerate to himself than I have been...'

# CHAPTER 21

Wednesday, 17th May 1665

Wednesday was a market day in Bridport, and the High Street was a churning mass of local people, engaged in the time-honoured ways of rural commerce. Most of this commerce comprised the most patient and laborious of dealings, as suited Dorset country folk, yet there was some more feverish bartering going on too among the rowdier elements of the town, which occasionally even erupted into resentment and altercation, and sometimes even into fisticuffs.

Henry Raven was enjoying doing business at the market again on this fine May day, in company with his sister Catherine. His business dealings this morning were generally of the quieter and more gentlemanly kind, yet he always drove a hard bargain, having learned a severe lesson from his strong-willed mother that only a fool gives away more for something than he really needs to. Salwayash Manor did have a bailiff of course – the excellent if elderly Mr Solomon Jones - who looked after livestock and crop matters on the estate, and managed all the buying and selling of such on market days. Yet Catherine had worked closely with him for the last three years and, for a genteel young lady, now knew much about the intricacies of farming and commerce, including the right price for every commodity. She showed off that knowledge to her brother now, with casual and unfeigned accomplishment, as they wandered along the long lines of animal pens, and she pointed out cows and bullocks of every breed, sturdy oxen as vast as carriages, sheep of every variety known to man, and cackling geese by the hundred, and pronounced the value of each to a few pence. Raven was amused that she should be so much at home among all these animal sounds and smells of the farmyard, even if those smells were tempered a little by the heady perfume of stocks and meadowsweet, and other cut herbs for sale.

This market scene lacked the intensity and vitality of London's Smithfield Market at its busiest, but the country characters who peopled this market were interesting enough in their way, and varied enough examples of humankind too, despite most of them being born within ten miles of the town. And being mercifully free of the plague, Raven thought that Bridport Market must no doubt be much busier today than the sad and near deserted Smithfield that he had seen before quitting London four days ago, which was but a shadow of its normal self.

Henry Raven had lived most of the last five years in the teeming streets of London (which period of residence in the capital coincided exactly with the restoration in England of the King's rule), and his life had been undeniably content and fulfilled there. Yet he realized that, despite the greater attractions of a vast city like London, he greatly missed the gentler and more convivial atmosphere of this small market town. So much of his life and character had been formed here in this part of Dorset. He could remember walking through this very market as a small boy with his mother, and being consumed with wonder at all the frantic dealings and the wild cacophony of street cries. A country market like this could not compare to the street markets of London for the range of goods that could be bought (at least in normal times) but there was still more than enough on offer here to tempt even the most jaded soul: there were vendors of flatfish and flounders, of crabs and oysters fresh from the English Channel, stallholders selling sheep's trotters and livers, bakers selling pies and tarts, cloth sellers with fine local lace and satin, tinkers selling copper pots and pans, small holders selling poultry and game. Their cries rang out along the straw-covered street, each trying to drown their neighbour's. "*Hot baked wardens!...Crab, crab, any crab!...Buy my crab!...Who will buy my fat rabbits...?*"

The greatest difference that Henry Raven now noticed between a London street market and this country equivalent, though, was the absence of all the throngs of raffish entertainers who would invade a London street on market day: tumblers, jugglers, clowns, beggars, and pickpockets. Such people were rare indeed here, as were professional whores, since the local magistrate Sir Malcolm Batcock and his stern young constables would not tolerate their presence at all, and moved on any loose or lewd women from outside the area very quickly. Yet pickpockets and thieves could still be found even in a town like Bridport, since many people of that persuasion had left London recently to escape the plague, yet still needed to use their thieving skills to keep their bellies filled. In the country these people no doubt found the task of thieving an easier one, when preying on less sophisticated victims than knowing Londoners. Raven had seen many suspicious rogues today as he had wandered through the market stalls - some of them certainly hookers or anglers or rufflers – and he had made sure to keep a tight hold on his own bulging purse, which must be a great temptation for such wastrels.

Not that Bridport market was given over entirely to commerce; there was some entertainment too, if of a low kind. Some travelling players had put up a crude wooden stage at one end of the High Street, and now put on a show for the locals, which Henry Raven and his sister paused to watch for a few minutes. The play was a mixture of bawdy farce and sentimental melodrama, and, although unsophisticated by comparison with the plays that Raven saw regularly at the King's Theatre in Covent Garden, or at the Duke's in Lincoln's Inn Fields, it held this simpler country audience enraptured. The plot was mostly incomprehensible yet featured a romance with a beautiful maid and many contrived swordfights; also a comic housemaid with a vast wobbling bosom and even vaster buttocks who was always dropping plates and bending down to pick them up in a most lewd way. The hero was a fearless if stupid young man with long yellow hair, while the villain was a dastardly individual with dark moustaches and satanic features lined with burnt cork who tried to come between the yellow-haired hero and his virtuous maid. All turned out happily in the end, though, as the villain got his just deserts, and the hero wedded his maid.

Seeing these exuberant players at their work, Raven could not but be reminded of his sweet Molly, and of how much he missed her at this moment. His absence from her life over the last few weeks had mostly been due to ill circumstance, yet he could truly have found more time for her if he had made the effort. He regretted now his foolish petty jealousy, and longed to see her again before he left to join the fleet at Harwich, so that he could tell her again of his true affection.

He was much preoccupied with thoughts of Esther too, and what he could do for her to help her recover her life. Yet it was encouraging how quickly she seemed to be recovering her spirits now that she was back in Dorset and among friends who loved her. Raven had even seen her smile yesterday for the first time, when she came back from her long morning walk with Martin, and looked much more like the happy Esther of old, despite the shorn hair and the men's breeches she wore. Yet he was still glad that he had advised her to maintain her disguise as a boy, because it seemed by some ill chance that yesterday, while walking in the woods, she and Martin had encountered none other than her chief accuser at her trial, Mistress Pollock. If she had been dressed in her normal garb, then the secret of her miraculous resurrection would have been revealed at once, and to the last person in the world they would have wished.

Even Ralph Warboys would most assuredly have recognized Esther yesterday if she had not been dressed as a boy - as it was, he seemed to have come precious close to doing so anyway. Of course Ralph could no doubt be trusted to keep Esther's secret, if he should accidentally discover it, yet Raven preferred that even he did not know of this. The more people that knew, the more chance there was that some loose tongue would betray the information to someone who wished Esther harm, of which there were regrettably a few, even in this neighbourhood...

After watching the short play, Catherine went off to buy some things for herself in the dress shop in the High Street, while Raven went to the King's Head Tavern to drink some ale and converse with some of his gentlemen neighbours. In an hour Catherine returned from her shopping, sporting a new silk bonnet decorated with bold blue ribbons, which her brother duly admired. Yet, as they continued with their business at the market, Catherine was less interested in talking of her new bonnet than of Esther.

'Do you think that Ralph recognized Esther yesterday?' she asked Henry worriedly, when they were out of earshot of anyone else.

Raven shook his head. 'I think not. I believe he recognized something in her face perhaps, but his imagination would not let him take the next step when he knows Esther to be dead. But we should try and keep "our cousin Edward" away from his sight for the present, and not give him a second chance to recognize her.'

Catherine frowned. 'Should we not just tell him of Esther's miraculous deliverance, and ask him to keep the secret? He is our closest neighbour, after all, and an honourable gentleman...' – she blushed a little – '...as well as being completely devoted to me, of course. '

'I do not doubt his honour, sister...' - Raven smiled – '...nor his devotion to you, which is plain for all to see. But 'tis better that as few people know Esther's secret as possible. We will tell him the truth eventually, of course, when we have a better idea of her future.'

'Have you had any fresh thoughts about that future?'

Raven glanced around at the milling crowds in the High Street, and at the line of green hills to the north and west – Frogmore Hill, Symondsbury and Colmer's Hill - which added much beauty to the scene. 'I still hope we can find a place for her in another part of Dorset, perhaps near Lyme Regis. She loves this county so much that it would be a hard thing for her to leave it forever. I will discuss it with her, but there is no need to make a quick decision so long as we keep her secret.'

Catherine hesitated. 'We may not have as much time as you think to come to a decision about Esther's future. I believe that young Jacob Shawn may have overheard some gossip of Dora or Kate concerning "Cousin Edward". Last evening, he asked me some very pointed questions about our new guest, particularly mentioning his great beauty, which perhaps revealed some suspicions on his part.'

'You think he knows that "Cousin Edward" is a maid in disguise?' Raven asked in alarm.

'Perhaps. After all, Esther is far too beautiful to really pass plausibly for a boy, unless that boy be a wondrous beauty with creamy skin and lustrous hair. Yet Jacob has never met Esther before, so cannot possibly know that it is her, unless someone has inadvertently told him. I asked Jacob to stay away from "our cousin" for the good of his health, of course, but if he has seen through Esther's male disguise, then others will too, eventually.'

Raven sighed worriedly. 'I hope he does not share those suspicions elsewhere then.' He had an even more concerning thought. 'Did you not tell me, sister, that Jacob is Mistress Pollock's nephew?'

Catherine looked dismayed. 'Ay, he is. I had quite forgot,' she added dismally.

'Then we must truly hope that he keeps his suspicions to himself,' Raven said grimly. 'And that Martin, Dora and Kate continue to hold their mouths too.'

'Amen to that, brother,' a worried Catherine said, before dropping her voice to an even lower whisper. 'Ah! Here comes Ralph, riding down the High Street on his large bay...'

Raven smiled at her obvious discomfort at this unplanned meeting, thinking that she liked well enough to encounter Ralph Warboys by chance, but would prefer not to do it when in company with her amused brother. 'He seems to be everywhere that you are now, sister. There seems to be some mysterious source of attraction between the two of you, just as there is between the Sun and its planets.'

Catherine coloured. 'Nonsense, Henry. It is market day, and he is always here to oversee the business of Warboys Hall.'

Raven had no time to make an even more jocular reply, before Warboys arrived. Their neighbour did not dismount, thought, but merely doffed his broad-brimmed hat at Catherine. 'I see that you immerse yourself quickly again in the business of the estate, Henry,' he observed. 'I am sorry that I cannot tarry and talk with you both longer, but we are engaged for dinner next week at the manor, are we not?'

Catherine said nothing, but merely smiled innocuously at him. Observing her closely, Raven decided that his sister hid her regard for this gentleman rather well, which gave him cause to reflect wryly on the artful skills of women generally in concealing their true feelings, and most especially, the true directions of their affections, when it suited them to do so.

Raven waved an airy hand. 'Of course we forgive you, Ralph, if you must ride on. You are a busy man, I know, as I am...'

*

As Ralph Warboys rode west out of Bridport at a canter, he reflected on what a picture of beauty Catherine had been today in her new silk bonnet. With her fine complexion and brown curls, blue was a most becoming colour for her. He had always been fond of Catherine as a child, but there had been the very problem. It had taken a long time for him *not* to see her as a child, and to think of her instead as a desirable and beddable woman, yet that profound change in his view of her had eventually come about over the last year, when he had been thrown much into her sociable company.

In truth his affection for Catherine had predated the death of his wife Margaret, and he had been tempted to pursue her for some considerable time. Yet Warboys had always known that Catherine would never enter into an intimate relationship with a married man, so had wisely stayed his hand until the time was more propitious. Once he was a widower, though, he had soon made it clear to her by his attentions that he wanted her for his new wife. She was the obvious choice for his new bride, of course: beautiful, intelligent, strong-willed like her mother, and with a wealthy background similar to his own. She was also young enough and healthy enough to bear him many children in her coming married life, and Ralph Warboys had been filled with optimism of late that he would finally be able to father an heir, and to fill Warboys Hall again with the sound of children's laughter.

For many years Warboys had been resigned to being the husband of a barren wife, and to know that he was therefore destined to be the last of the Warboys' line. Yet Catherine Raven seemed to be the person designed by fate to lift that curse on the Warboys' family forever, and to bring fresh young blood into the family line that would reinvigorate the family's fortunes.

Warboys reached the crossroads at Miles Cross and turned his bay gelding Samson north on the Moorbath Road, as it wound its picturesque way between Colmer's Hill and the hamlet of Symondsbury. This road was one of his favourite local rides - wooded on both sides and laced over with interconnecting branches from the tall oak trees on each side, forming almost a green tunnel, filled with dappled sunshine and the echoing sound of birdsong. Despite the beauty of the scenery, though, Warboys was beset by a sudden attack of melancholy as he thought again of the tragic fate of poor Esther Linney. His guilt over that sweet maid was profound, and something he had not been able to dismiss easily from his mind, despite his new found happiness with Catherine.

In truth he had also been deeply attracted to Esther last summer, and he had made a deliberate point of riding past her cottage to greet her whenever he was close, which innocent enough habit had set in motion this sad chain of events. Yet, unlike his relationship with Catherine, he had never intended at the time that his relations with Esther should go any further than a mere pleasant flirtation to take his mind off his sterile and unhappy marriage. Esther was a most sympathetic listener and he had found that he could unburden himself with her in a way that he could never do with Catherine. Yet an evil circumstance had changed his relations with Esther forever...

Once Margaret was dead, he did briefly consider making amends to Esther for what she had suffered, by choosing her for his new wife rather than Catherine. She did not have Catherine's advantages of family and position in society, of course, yet she was as beautiful and striking as Catherine, and perhaps even more intelligent. For a week or so in April, Ralph seriously entertained this notion. That noble gesture had in fact been the main purpose of his conciliatory visit to her in London in April. Yet, given the unmentionable circumstance that had happened to her, and with that unwanted child on the way, he had soon changed his mind on the coach journey to London, and found that he could not go through with his foolish and naïve plan. If he had married the pregnant Esther and taken her into his home as mistress of Warboys Hall, he could never have lived such a thing down in the neighbourhood, and his reputation would have been blackened forever. And, in any event, by this time his affection for Catherine had become something close to an obsession with him, and had soon eclipsed the modest affection he still felt for Esther.

Yet he had still never wished Esther any harm, and sincerely wanted to help her. What harm he had done her had been entirely accidental, and merely the result of him trying to protect the honourable and ancient name of his family from scandal. He knew that he should have spoken up during the trial and offered her his support, but it was too late now for regret. And Henry Raven had stepped forward anyway and done as much for her as he could. Yet even, with Henry's connections to court, he had not been able to save Esther, so Ralph consoled himself with the thought that it was as well that he had not come forward and risked his reputation for nothing...

The elderly Samson was blowing hard by now as the road climbed higher through the village of Moorbath. Warboys let the old horse recover his breath a little as they reached the boundaries of his own land. He took the side road leading to the hall, but a mile into the beech wood, he turned off the main road again. This part of the estate was not cultivated but had been left as forest for timber, and was therefore a wild and beautiful place, untamed by the hand of man.

Yet this untended wood was the oldest part of the Warboys' land, and Ralph soon saw peering above the trees the serrated outline of crumbling stone battlements that marked his family's original home. Nearly four centuries ago, King Edward I – the famous Hammer of the Scots – had granted this land to his ancestor Sir William Warboys for services rendered during the wars with those dangerous Northern clans, and a grateful Sir William had built his new castle on a hillock looking south towards the Channel. The stonework of the castle - soft marine limestone - had long been crumbling over the centuries since then, and Ralph's father, Oliver, had finally abandoned his cold and damp home completely thirty years ago in favour of a modern Jacobean house built with much sturdier stone, fires in every room, and glass in the windows. With the beech wood grown up about it, the existence of the castle was now almost forgotten to locals, being invisible behind its cloak of trees, and far from the main roads.

Ralph rode into the grassy clearing around the ruins of the castle. The depressed line of the original moat was still visible, although now dry and full of tall fescue grass and wild flowers. The outer walls of the castle were still there too, if laid low to no more than ten feet by generations of locals scavenging stone. The cobbles of the inner bailey too were mostly gone, although Samson's iron hooves did occasionally find a stone slab under the grass and weeds, which did make the gentle old horse uneasy as a result, as if he thought he was stepping on gravestones.

The old keep of the castle was the most intact part of the building, and its battlements were still largely complete, as was the sturdy roof of oak beams. Warboys dismounted and tethered Samson to his usual post by the main door into the keep. Perhaps surprisingly for a castle that had been abandoned so long, the huge timbered door opened easily to his touch, swinging without so much as a creak, on well-greased hinges. Once past the door, Warboys ascended the worn stone stairs that curved up the inside wall of the tower. Sunlight pierced the narrow embrasures in the wall, so he required no candle to see his way up the steps. He passed the doorway to the darkened first floor without pausing for breath and carried on to the next main level, and a second doorway leading into the interior.

Through this doorway could be glimpsed clear evidence of present occupation – in the centre of the straw-covered floor was a table set with a candlestick, and with greasy pewter plates and stale victuals, while up against the far wall was a truckle bed. A burly man hastily stood up to greet Warboys as he entered through the doorway into what was a surprisingly snug and comfortable chamber, if also a distinctly evil-smelling one.

'Good day, sir,' the man said with a bow, hurriedly wiping gravy from his grey whiskers, and trying to pull his thin stringy hair into some sort of order. 'I did not expect you today, Mr Warboys.'

Ralph eyed the man with distaste, regarding his soiled breeches and torn stockings. Mr Lockshear was a most evil-looking rogue as well as being a known refugee from the law, but then a more genteel or honest man would hardly have accepted such a grim assignment and situation as this one, even with the generous rewards that Warboys had offered. Ebenezer Lockshear had been many things apparently – a footpad, a highwayman, and more lately, a pirate on the Spanish Main where he had earned a bloodthirsty reputation as a sadistic torturer of Spanish prisoners. Yet that history made him the perfect man for this miserable task...

'How is he today?' Ralph asked, nodding at a door in the inner wall of the main chamber. The door was a heavy studded iron door that was barred and bolted as if some wild beast dwelled on the other side of it.

'He has been most docile and well-mannered today, sir, almost like a child,' Lockshear answered complacently. 'He has a most comfortable chamber in there, and seems happy to read his books and wile away his time. He does not seem at all disposed to violence, sir.'

Warboys grunted angrily. 'That is what my late wife believed too, Mr Lockshear, and you would be well advised to dismiss such a foolish notion from your mind. I have paid for two men to assist you in your duties, so please make proper use of them. Remember what I told you, and never go into that room with him alone and unarmed!'

'I believe that I could control this man, sir, no matter what the circumstances,' Lockshear boasted.

Warboys came close to him, until he could see the pores in the man's bulbous nose, and feel his sour breath. 'Did I not tell you what he did to his last gaoler, Samuel Cocking?'

'I know he overpowered him and killed him, before escaping, sir,' Lockshear replied uneasily.

'Yes,' Ralph said ominously. 'But do you know how he actually killed Mr Cocking?'

Lockshear hesitated. 'No, sir. You never told me that.'

'Then I will enlighten you. He ripped Mr Cocking's eyeballs out with his bare thumbs. And that, I assure you, is a most unpleasant way to die...'

Ebenezer swallowed hard, his Adam's apple making a huge ripple in the wattles of his white-whiskered neck.

Ralph believed he had made his point satisfactorily, and now made his way across the chamber to the barred door. He opened the viewing panel and looked inside. The chamber beyond was indeed a comfortably furnished room, and did not resemble a cell in any way, though that is what it was, of course. The room had no windows, but did have a skylight in the roof so was well provided with natural light, if not with any view of the outside world. A man sat at the table below the skylight, reading from a heavy leather-bound book. When he saw that he was observed, the man put the book down immediately and stood up. Then he made his way to the door and the viewing panel where he stood looking through the gridiron in return at his visitor.

'It is kind of you to visit me again so soon, Ralph, if a little unsettling when I see what plan is clearly written in your face,' the man said balefully. 'I had almost expected that you would have already ordered Mr Lockshear to murder me in my sleep by now, so I am pleasantly surprised to find myself breathing still.'

Ralph too was unsettled by this accusation. This man must certainly be able to read his mind, because Ralph had indeed been wondering if Mr Lockshear might be amenable, for a price, to rid him forever of this endless burden in his life.

Yet the man's words were not the things that unsettled Ralph Warboys the most; it was more the fact that they came from those familiar lips, and were accompanied by a familiar sardonic smile playing on that handsome face. In truth it was most unsettling for Ralph Warboys to look through this grilled opening and to see his own face reflected there, exactly as if he looked into a polished steel mirror...

# CHAPTER 22

Thursday, 18<sup>th</sup> May 1665

The Dorset-bound coach had broken a wheel in crossing a ford over a stream near Richmond, the repair of which had delayed the coach for a good two hours, and meant that by noon it had only just reached the village of Camberley in the sandy heathlands of Surrey.

Molly was not minded to complain, though, being enthralled with the journey despite its slowness and its many discomforts, since it was only the second time in her seventeen years of life that she had travelled more than twenty miles from London, and the changing scene was therefore a constant source of wonder and delight to her.

As she gazed at the distant vista of pine-covered Surrey hills, she said a silent prayer of thanks to God for delivering her from the plague, and allowing her to see such a wondrous view as this on this glorious late spring day. She glanced across at M'sieur Desargues, who sat opposite her in the coach. She was becoming more used now to the notion that this gentleman truly was her natural father, which did cause her much wonder, and also some undoubted pride to discover that the blood of a French nobleman flowed in her veins.

M'sieur Desargues had studiously ignored the other travellers in the coach for the whole of this journey as they were apparently not much to his taste – a young non-conformist family of four, who also apparently had plans to sail for the New World and make a new life for themselves in the Cape Colony. Now he spoke to Molly again, as intimately as if they were alone. 'Have I told you how pretty and well you look today, Molly?'

'You have, sir, several times. Yet that is one message to a young woman that can never become dull with repetition,' Molly said with a half-smile.

The Puritan father of the travelling family scowled to himself at these improper familiarities, although his pretty young wife seemed less offended, and merely smiled amiably in Molly's direction.

'You do resemble your mother greatly, Molly. She was quite as beautiful as you when she was young, and I saw this week that she has retained much of that beauty into middle age,' M'sieur Desargues said.

'Yet her beauty was not sufficient to tempt you into marriage, was it, sir?' Molly said bluntly. She went on to tell M'sieur Desargues frankly what her mother had told her two days ago of her affair in Paris, despite the increasing frowns of their Puritan fellow traveller, and the increasing interest of his young wife. 'Is all that true, sir? That you broke my mother's heart asunder, and then cruelly abandoned her?'

M'sieur Desargues was philosophical. 'I made no secret of my shortcomings to you, Molly. I am more human and venal than most, I freely admit, and have always treated women with little true regard, perhaps because I had never truly been in love.'

Molly nodded coldly. 'Your frankness does you credit at least, sir, although it hardly lessens the severity of your sins. So you never loved my mother, but merely used her for cruel sport?'

M'sieur Desargues protested mildly. 'I was not so cold-blooded and scheming as that, Molly. I did not say that I had no affection for young Celia at all. I certainly had a great affection for her, yet she did not move my heart the way the Duchesse Marie did later. Perhaps by that time of my life, my character had improved with maturity so that my heart was finally able to be pierced by Cupid's arrows. If it is any consolation to Celia, and to all the other women who have graced my life, I did discover in the end the true pain that comes with separation from the object of one's true love and devotion. I believe, after talking privately to your mother again, that she has now forgiven me for my youthful sins towards her…'

Molly blinked at that. 'You saw my mother again since Tuesday, sir? Then you are a braver man than I thought, because her only wish concerning you, M'sieur, seemed to be to leave a real dagger in your heart to match the imagined one that you left in hers all those years ago.'

M'sieur Desargues smiled. 'Perhaps she is not so severe a woman as you think, Molly.'

Molly blinked even more at that, and wondered if there had been an unlikely rapprochement yesterday between M'sieur Desargues and her mother before they had left London. 'Ay, the human heart is indeed a difficult thing to comprehend, sir,' she said with genuine confusion.

M'sieur Desargues agreed with a nod, then said hesitantly, 'Are you sure that you will not accompany me to the New World, Molly? What joy it would give me to have my daughter at my side in this coming venture!'

'I will not come, sir. You forfeited the right to my loyalty when you abandoned me and my mother all those years ago,' Molly replied sharply. 'As it is, I do more for you now that you have any right to expect.'

M'sieur Desargues was not at all chastened by this stern reply. 'I agree, Molly. But I know that your main purpose in going into Dorset is not to see me on board my vessel, but more to ingratiate yourself again with your lover Mr Raven.'

Molly heard a sharp intake of breath from the Puritan at this mention of her lover, but ignored it. 'I doubt that you can truly censure me for this action. I have told you, sir, that Mr Raven goes to war against the Dutch soon, and it would be most remiss of me not to try and see him before he leaves, and to assure him of my constant affection. And as we both know, 'tis better that I do not wait in London for his return, with the plague getting ever worse in the city, and also a certain gentleman lurking there in vengeful mood…'

M'sieur Desargues was finally chastened by that remark, as he reflected on the evil threat he had brought down on Molly's head by his selfish determination to become acquainted with his daughter. 'I hope it will soon be safe for you to return to London, Molly, at least with regard to the attentions of that villain Senor Francisco Nunez de Santiago.'

'How so, sir?' Molly asked irately. 'I may never feel safe in that city again because of you.'

The coach gave a massive lurch as the driver hit a pothole in the road, yet M'sieur Desargues did not even seem to notice it. 'Once in New York, I will make it known by letter to my true enemy, the Duc de Chavagnes, that I am gone to the American colonies. The Duc is no fool, and will not waste his money after that. He will call off his dogs; even such a vengeful man as the Duc de Chavagnes will know that I am quite beyond his vengeance there.'

Molly sighed. 'Yet he may think that by banishing you alone to the wilderness of North America, he has achieved his aim of revenge anyway, sir.'

M'sieur Desargues laughed humourlessly. 'Ay, indeed he may.' He leaned across the coach and took Molly's hand. 'Yet if you will not accompany me, sweet Molly, then the least I can do is to try and repair your friendship with Mr Raven, even though I think him an unworthy and dull gentleman for the likes of you.'

Molly was suspicious. 'And how will you do that, sir?'

M'sieur Desargues waved a hand airily at the passing countryside. 'Well, we shall spend the night in Winchester, and be in Weymouth by noon tomorrow. That will give me plenty of time to confirm the sailing time of my vessel, the *Lapwing*. After that, I will have a full day to accompany you to the town of Bridport where Mr Raven lives.'

He lives not in Bridport,' Molly explained, 'but in a manor house some five or ten miles distant.'

M'sieur Desargues made a face. 'Five miles is of no matter, Molly. And, if I come along, perhaps I can help you find this place, and also help you gain admittance to see Mr Raven discreetly. You cannot simply knock on his door, and make your claim to his heart. His family will likely feed you to their dogs, if you do.'

This had indeed been Molly's plan, but she saw now that she might embarrass Henry by such a direct and brazen approach, therefore M'sieur Desargues would certainly be useful as a gentleman intermediary. 'Then I accept your kind offer, sir,' she said formally.

*

Mistress Celia Hornett did not much like the look of this new visitor to her establishment, despite his gentlemanly apparel and distinguished look. She had offered him a seat in the parlour while she tried to judge his physical needs, and whether indeed she was prepared to let one of her girls pleasure him as he wished. Yet she was in an amiable and accommodating mood since her second meeting with the Comte de Mésanger yesterday, which had proved to her one thing at least: that she was quite a different person from that naïve girl who had encountered this handsome French nobleman all those years ago. Her heart was a much harder thing to break now, being tempered by age and experience, and she had found that it was possible after all for a mature woman to enjoy some physical intimacy with an old love, without any danger of the experience reopening old wounds. She was only sorry, though, that she had succumbed again to his honeyed tongue (in more ways than one) and given him so much damned money for his journey when she had ordered Molly not to give the worthless devil a penny. With chagrin, she recalled that she had handed it over willingly, and with no fight at all. She hoped sincerely that Molly never learned of this abject capitulation, though, or she would never hear the end of it...

As she brought her new visitor a cup of her expensive China tea, Celia inspected him closely. He was no more than five-and-thirty, and most certainly a foreign gentleman, although she could not say from where. His face was handsome enough, yet seemed also hard and cruel. His hair was thick and luxuriant, yet of a strange dark red colour, like blood mixed with iron. His beard was threaded through with silver, and his piercing eyes were most unsettling, burning with some hidden passion. Yet his manner was polite enough.

Celia knew better than to ask her gentleman visitors their real names, yet she was curious as to this man's origins. Celia was normally able to read her customers like a book, and know their life histories and their professions merely from looking at them, and even hazard a good guess as to how much their purses might contain. Yet with this gentleman she was at a complete loss.

'Where are you from, sir?' she asked. 'I hear a foreign accent. Are you perhaps a Venetian or a Greek?'

The man inspected her in return through hooded eyes like a snake. 'I am neither, Madam. I was born in the city of Barcelona, if that helps you.'

Celia was not entirely sure where the city of Barcelona was, but thought it must be a southerly place given the man's swarthy complexion. She began to run through the names of her girls who had not yet left the city, and came finally to Marion. 'May I recommend Marion in particular to you, sir? She is a most beautiful girl from Kent with the bluest eyes and sweetest dimples…'

''Tis neither blue eyes nor dimples that I come for, Madam,' the man growled suddenly. 'I have come for your daughter Molly.'

Celia was flustered. 'I know not how you have heard of Molly, but I must disappoint you. Molly does not work at this establishment, sir. She is a very accomplished actress with the King's company now, though sadly the playhouse is presently closed because of the plague, as is everything else. Even I will have to close ere long, I fear…If you want one of my girls, sir, then it will have to be Marion.' Celia turned her head as she heard the sound of footsteps on the wooden stair outside. 'Look, here she comes. You will see what a splendid beauty she is, sir, and worth every penny of your two guineas…'

'I do not want this "Marion", Madam.' The man leapt to his feet, and pulled a dagger from beneath his long velvet coat. 'My name is Francisco Nunez de Santiago. You may not have heard of that name before, yet I promise you will remember it long after today, if you do not give me what I want.' He came over to the fire and put the point of the dagger to Celia's throat.

Celia was now naturally terrified of this evil man, yet tried not to show it. 'I have told you, sir. Molly does not work here, nor is she presently in this house,' she protested gamely.

At his point, Marion entered the room behind them, and gasped in shock when she saw Celia threatened with a dagger. Marion tried to leave again rapidly but the ruffian was too quick for her. He abandoned his threat to Celia to pull Marion back into the room by the arm, which he did most painfully. Then he held the terrified girl in front of Celia by the hair, and put the dagger to *her* throat now. Marion squealed in terror at this, but the man merely applied the point of the dagger with further pressure to silence her.

'If she is not here, then where is your daughter, Madam?' the villain demanded. 'Tell me at once, or there will be evil consequences for you and this fair maid here.' He stroked the side of Marion's face with the tip of the dagger. You were right, Madam, in your judgement of this girl. She is a most splendid beauty. I am sure you would not wish to see that beauty marred forever by a twelve inch scar to her cheek.'

Celia could hardly speak as she saw the terrified look on Marion's face.

'Please desist from these cruel threats, sir, and I will do what I can to help you. But first I must know - what do you want with my daughter?'

'That is not truly your right to know, Madam, but I will enlighten you anyway in the hope that it might free your tongue from its foolish defiance. I seek a certain French gentleman, the Comte de Mésanger.' The man's evil eyes burned brighter. 'Ah, I see that name means something to you, Madam. Then you must know that your daughter hides and protects this gentleman, though I know not why she takes such foolish risks.'

Celia tried to control her fluttering heart, which threatened to leap from her chest. 'You are mistaken, sir. I know nothing of this gentleman of whom you speak. And my daughter has nothing to do with any such gentleman either. She has left London because of the plague, that is all.'

'I hope that is not true, Madam, otherwise I shall be heartily displeased with you, and shall have to punish you accordingly,' the man spat out venomously.

Marion rolled her eyes in terror and tried to speak. 'I know where Molly has gone with the gentleman, sir, if you will only release me and my mistress…'

'No, Marion!' Celia screamed. 'Tell him nothing. He will kill us anyway! I see it in the devil's eyes. Yet we have the power to save Molly by telling him nothing.'

The man snarled at her in return, but then calmed himself with an effort. 'I swear, Madam, on my mother's grave, that I will not kill *you,* or even harm you in any way.' He nudged Marion hard in the ribs. 'Now, speak up, girl! Where is Molly gone with the Comte de Mésanger?'

Marion silently begged Celia's forgiveness with her eyes, before continuing in a breathless voice. 'I overheard Molly talk with my mistress just two days ago. Molly is gone to Dorset with this gentleman by coach. He plans to sail from the port of Weymouth in a vessel called the *Lapwing,* bound for York…'

'I think you must mean *New* York, girl, or formerly New Amsterdam before you English thieves purloined it from Holland,' the man said, finally releasing his severe hold on her slightly. He stroked Marion's hair in a conciliatory gesture. 'You are a sensible girl, which is more than I can say for your mistress. Yet I have made a solemn promise not to harm *her,* therefore must keep my word, which is hard indeed on you, my pretty one…'

Celia jumped to her feet in alarm as she understood the full import of the evil man's chilling words.

The man looked at her triumphantly. 'I warned you not to resist me, Madam, yet you foolishly did so. So this blood must be on *your* head.' With that, he grabbed Marion firmly again by the top of her hair, lifted his dagger, and calmly sliced through her throat from ear to ear.

Celia could only watch in horror as the man withdrew from the room, leaving Marion dead on the stone floor in a spreading pool of her own blood....

# CHAPTER 23

## Friday, 19<sup>th</sup> May 1665

At ten o'clock on a rainy Friday morning, Henry Raven and his sister were going through the estate ledgers with their bailiff Mr Jones in the Great Hall at Salwayash Manor when a house servant came to inform them that there was a deputation of three gentlemen just arrived at the door in a dogcart, who desired to see them. When Raven discovered that the three were the Bridport constable Adam Drew, and two of his worthy assistant constables, he asked for them to be shown through to the Great Hall at once.

The aged Mr Jones discreetly withdrew from the room at Raven's request, allowing him and his sister to have a whispered interchange before these officers of the law arrived. Catherine thought that Constable Drew must have come to tell her the result of the inquest into the death of poor Ruth Pilcher a week ago, though Raven wondered, if that were so, why he needed two men as support for such a modest task.

Raven and Catherine stood up to receive their visitors as they were shown into the Great Hall, and looked around in obvious admiration at the proportions of this imposing chamber. The Great Hall was certainly the architectural jewel of Salwayash Manor, having an immense hammer beam roof of ancient and sturdy oak, a vast stone fireplace, and walls covered with wonderful oil paintings by Dutch and Renaissance masters.

Raven had not met this Constable Drew before (since he was relatively new to the post), although he knew the Beadle of Bridport tolerably well, and also the chief magistrate, Sir Malcolm Batcock. Adam Drew turned out to be a very sober and earnest young man, who looked to Raven as if he had never found any cause to laugh in his entire life. Such sternness and sobriety sat oddly with his smooth callow features and beardless chin, though, which seemed to belong more to some truant from the village schoolhouse than to a respected officer of the law.

The two men with him were older and even grimmer representatives of the Watch: one middle-aged and plump, with hair as sharply demarcated into black and white bands as a badger; and the other underweight and scrofulous with thin red hair. Both gentlemen looked probably even worse for wear than normal because they had been thoroughly soaked on the cart journey here by the persistent morning rain. They stood behind Drew like a pair of wet gargoyles, and Drew did not refer to them at all, or even introduce them, as if he was embarrassed to be in the company of such a disreputable-looking pair in such a grand chamber as this.

'Have you news of the inquest on poor Ruth, sir?' Catherine asked Drew, after she had introduced him to her brother.

Drew seemed hesitant for a moment. 'She drowned, Mistress Raven, that is all I can presently say. Yet there were bruises on her neck that showed she might have been held under. '

Raven became alarmed. 'Then she might not have taken her own life? Is that what you say?'

The constable made a grudging response. 'I fear that is a possibility. She had certainly been violated recently, according to our physician, although whether that was done willingly or no is difficult to say.'

Catherine made an angry noise in her throat. 'By all that I have heard of her, Ruth was a sweet and innocent girl. Therefore she must have been violated against her will, Constable. And it was no doubt the same devil who then held her under the water and drowned her...'

Constable Drew seemed unimpressed with this emotional account, and merely stared back at Catherine with his cold fish eyes. 'Alas it is too early to make such a clear cut judgement as that, Mistress. I have need of more facts first. Facts, facts! – these are what matter to the officers of the Bridport Watch – not emotion.' He cleared his throat with deliberate effect, and turned that cold stare on Raven. 'What I and my colleagues have come about, though, is to ask you about another matter, sir. I believe that you have a young man staying with you at present? A youth called Edward....'

Raven felt his blood chill at this unexpected announcement, but tried to keep his face expressionless as he answered. 'Yes, we have. Master Edward Raven.' He glanced at Catherine at his side to see how she coped with this worrying question, but his sister had remained remarkably composed. 'He is a distant kinsman of ours from the North of England, who has suffered great hardships in his life of late and needed somewhere quiet to recuperate,' he explained. 'We have offered him our home as a temporary refuge, in order to help him restore his natural spirit and vitality. What is your interest in Edward, may I ask?'

Constable Drew frowned. 'May I speak with this young gentleman?'

Raven raised his eyebrows in mock surprise. 'Why, may I ask? Of what interest is Edward to you, sir? He is a very shy and retiring youth, and I do not wish to subject him to public attention unless there be a good reason for it.'

Constable Drew looked behind at his grim associates, as if seeking some moral support. 'I have received reports from a certain person that this young man may be no male at all, but in fact the infamous murderess, Esther Linney, who once lived with you here as a child, I believe.'

Raven did not know how he kept his voice calm, or how he managed a disbelieving smile. 'What nonsense is this, Constable? Esther Linney was hanged at Tyburn exactly a week ago. Are you saying that she has been resurrected from the dead? Who gave you this silly and malicious report?'

Constable Drew was defensive. 'I cannot say, sir, for reasons that must be clear. Yet I do not talk of resurrection, sir, but of measures more worldly than that. According to reports, you were at Mistress Linney's trial, sir, and you gave evidence on her behalf, therefore you would certainly do all in your power to save her. This person who made the report accuses *you*, Mr Raven, of rescuing the woman Linney before she was hanged...'

'In God's name, how, sir?' Raven snapped angrily. 'Thousands must have seen Esther hanged.'

The constable would not be deflected from his mission and said stubbornly, 'This person who came to me says that there must have been some devilry at work here.' He gave Raven a sly look. 'Or else another woman must have been substituted and hanged in Mistress Linney's place.'

'Then who was this obliging woman of identical appearance who gave her life so freely in Mistress Linney's stead, I wonder?' Raven was caustic in his response, but inside he was aghast at this turn of events. If Esther was discovered, then this explanation of her survival was far more likely to be believed than the highly improbable truth, in which case she could yet be hanged again for her alleged crime. Of course, in such an event, he and Dr Croone and his servants could give evidence as to what had really happened, yet would they be believed? Would their story not sound like a fanciful invention to help Esther escape justice? That ogre of a judge, Holinshead, would be unlikely to swallow such a wild tale, that much was certain, and would be doubly glad to see Esther hanged a second time, and with greater attention this time.

Drew was hesitant for the first time. 'I do not say that I give this story credence, sir, yet I have been told by my superiors that I must investigate it.'

Raven held up his hands helplessly and adopted a look of puzzlement. 'Sir, I know not what to say further under such a ridiculous accusation as this.'

Constable Drew refused to give way, and said slyly, 'The matter could be easily resolved, sir, if I could but speak briefly to your cousin Edward, and establish that he really is who you say he is. That does not seem too much to ask...'

Catherine interrupted quickly. 'You cannot see Edward presently, sir. In order to recover his strength, he takes long walks around the estate every morning, and will not return until late afternoon.'

There was a convincing tone in her words which seemed to silence even Constable Drew's doubts for a moment. But then he looked at the leaden skies outside and the steady drizzle of rain against the tall window panes, and said, 'Even on such a day as this, Mistress?'

Catherine was unmoved. '*Particularly* on such a day as this, Constable. Edward likes much to walk in the rain.'

Constable Drew snorted. 'Then that is most perverse of him. I will therefore regretfully have to return this afternoon, yet it is a great pity that this matter cannot be resolved more quickly.' He lowered his voice to a warning whisper. 'I regret to say that the Raven family still has many enemies in this neighbourhood because of your father's well-known support for Parliament during the war. As a result, there are certainly mischief makers in Bridport who make great capital of the story I have just told you...'

'How did this absurd accusation reach the ears of these ruffians, sir, I wonder?' Catherine interrupted sharply.

Drew blinked slowly in response. 'I know not, Mistress, yet it is done. I saw a mob of these angry men assembling in the High Street even as I set out here, therefore I need to show them quickly that there is no substance to this rumour. The mob accuses you of harbouring a witch, sir, and they even say that Mistress Linney is responsible for the deaths of these two young maids.'

'Then she would have been in two places at once,' Raven said sarcastically. 'She was hanged at Tyburn only a day before Ruth Pilcher disappeared, was she not?'

Constable Drew's face was impassive. 'That is true, sir. But then witches are not constrained by the normal laws of nature, are they? So that argument will carry little weight with the mob, I fear...'

*

After the constable and his assistants had left, Catherine sat in a chair by the fire and put her head in her hands. 'Who betrayed us, brother?'

Raven paced back and forward in agitation, as he tried to think what to do for the best. 'It can only have been young Jacob Shawn. Did you not say that he had possibly seen through Esther's male disguise? He must have told his aunt of his suspicions after all. The person who made these accusations to Constable Drew can only be Mistress Pollock. Who else here in Dorset would know that I had attended Esther's trial in Newgate?'

Catherine sat up straight. 'Jacob would not betray Esther's secret, even if he discovered it by accident. He is too loyal to this household to do something like that.'

Raven stopped pacing. 'Then who else, sister?'

Catherine reflected silently for a moment, before asking a question of her own. 'What are we to do about Esther now, Henry?'

Raven sat down by the fire next to her. 'We cannot let Constable Drew meet Esther face-to-face - that much is clear. Her disguise will not survive a close interrogation from that suspicious young devil.' Raven tried to think calmly. 'Tell me, is Esther truly abroad this morning, sister, or was that merely a piece of quick thinking on your part?'

Catherine wiped her eyes, which were tearful and red with worry. 'It was a lie, of course. She does indeed like to walk in the rain, yet I forbade it this morning, given her still delicate health. She is safe for the present in her private chamber in the South Wing.'

Raven took his sister's hand and squeezed it in appreciation. 'Then you must go to her now, sister, and move her into a safe hiding place.' His mind raced. 'Luckily there is a secret chamber – much larger than a normal priest hole - behind the fireplace in her bedchamber...'

'This is not purely luck, I think, Henry. I believe that when you picked out that bedchamber for her, you were thinking ahead to some emergency like this.'

Raven acknowledged that. 'Yes, perhaps I did, unconsciously at least. We must hide Esther in that secret chamber for now. Do it yourself, though, and tell none of the servants what goes on, not even Dora or Martin. They do not know the secrets of the priest holes in this house...'

'I am not sure of that, brother,' Catherine said. 'It would surprise me if Dora did not know their locations at least, after all the years she spent cleaning the manor.'

'Perhaps you are right,' Raven conceded. 'Yet even if the servants know what goes on, they will still not tell Constable Drew anything, even if he insists on searching the house for Esther.' His voice dropped to a whisper. 'If necessary, we will have to help Esther escape the law again.'

Catherine was in despair. 'Yes, but how, brother? And where to?'

'I know not, for the present. Yet that secret room next to her bedchamber is even more fortuitous, because it has a vertical shaft in the corner that leads down to a hidden passageway, which connects in turn to the secret tunnel under the house. So we will be able to spirit Esther out of this house that way, if need be.'

Catherine was bitter at the thought of Esther having to flee again. 'Yet once she leaves our protection here, she will be a fugitive from an angry mob.'

Raven said a silent prayer. 'Then we had better make sure that she is not caught, sister...'

On the way out of the Great Hall, Raven encountered Jacob Shawn in the passageway leading to the kitchens. He saw at once from the lad's burning cheeks that he must have had some part in this unpleasant business, despite Catherine's assurances over his character.

Raven put up a hand to stop the lad abruptly in his tracks. 'Have you spoken of late to your aunt, Mistress Pollock, Jacob?' he demanded abrasively.

Jacob took a deep breath. 'I have, sir. I called at her house in the village yesterday while bringing the milk for the kitchen from Kershay Farm. Mistress Pollock is my late mother's sister, and my only surviving kin, so I must see her when I can.'

Raven glowered. 'And did she ask you questions about my cousin Edward?'

Raven saw instantly from Jacob's pink face that the boy knew the truth about "Cousin Edward" now, though whether he had discovered this by himself, or whether he had merely heard some whispers of the truth from Dora or Kate, was hard to say. Servants would always chatter with each other, of course; it was in their nature to do so, therefore it had been foolish of him to hope that Esther's secret could be maintained for long.

Jacob could not hide his deep mortification as he continued. 'My Aunt Pollock said that she had encountered a tall fair-skinned youth in the woods two days ago, and wondered if it might be a new servant from Salwayash Manor. When she described the youth, I knew at once that she meant your cousin Edward, Master.'

Raven sighed at this ill luck. Mistress Pollock must have recognized Esther after all, as she walked in the woods with Martin, yet had been astute enough not to make her recognition known at once. 'What did you tell her, Jacob?'

Jacob stammered. 'I...told her...nothing at all, sir, though I could see my aunt was most curious about this person. I said only that I thought the youth most retiring in nature. Yet I believe my aunt is the person who later spoke to Constable Drew and made certain allegations.' Jacob began to plead. 'You must understand her, sir. She is not an evil woman in herself, only a disappointed and lonely one, and she seeks solace for her empty life by doing what she thinks is morally right.'

Raven grunted dismissively. 'What she has done is *not* right, Jacob – not by any right person's judgement! 'Tis an evil and wicked thing that she has done, and not for the first time. When her time comes to meet her maker, I trust that God will forgive her for the pernicious evil she has done.'

Raven let Jacob go then, his anger now replaced by despair. All his hopes of helping Esther find a new identity and life in Dorset were in ruins now. Her only hope was to flee abroad, and quickly, yet such a move would still require time and planning, if she was to get away free of pursuit.

*Yet time seemed to be the one thing they no longer had...*

*

In mid-afternoon, Molly and M'sieur Desargues stepped out of the battered old stage coach that had brought them on the final stage of their journey, the one from Weymouth to Bridport.

The rather grander (and certainly better sprung) coach that had bought them from Winchester to Weymouth had set off at first light this morning (which at this time of the year was before five o'clock) and had brought them the sixty miles through the New Forest to the port of Weymouth in barely six hours, despite the steady English rain. Molly had not imagined that there could be so many trees in the world before, because her view from the coach window today had scarcely been of anything else but dripping trunks and leaves. She had been glad to finally leave the dark dank forest behind, and to reach the more open country of Dorset where meadow and copse and chalk hills were mingled into a wondrous green landscape that seemed no less picturesque for being set under a leaden grey sky.

Weymouth turned out to be a pretty town of a thousand souls clustered around the quay walls of the harbour. On leaving their coach, M'sieur Desargues quickly made enquiries and soon found a tavern on the waterfront, where ship's captains were known to congregate. In the Anchor Tavern, he and Molly discovered the master of the merchantman *Lapwing*, taking some noon refreshment. This Captain Darby was a drunken one-eyed rogue, who did not seem to Molly to have enough sense of direction to find his way safely through the entrance to the harbour, never mind across the ocean to the New World. Yet M'sieur Desargues seemed to have no qualms about entrusting his life to such a sot, and had soon made payment in gold for his passage to the American settlement of New York.

Molly knew not where M'sieur Desargues had acquired this significant amount of gold that he had on his person, when he had declared himself to be penniless but a week before. Yet it seemed her natural father had not offended everyone in his life, and must still have some other generous friends to call on for financial help. After all her mother's bitterness towards this gentleman, it did not seem possible to Molly that Celia might have contributed anything to his leaving pot. Yet Molly herself knew by now of this gentleman's considerable powers of persuasion…

Regardless of where he had got the gold for his passage, though, the deal was now done. The *Lapwing* would set sail with the next morning's high tide, and M'sieur Desargues had already had his newly purchased sea chest loaded aboard in preparation for the sailing.

Then, with nearly a day more to wait for that departure, he had been as good as his word, and had accompanied Molly on the twenty-mile coach journey to Bridport, which followed the coast road through the coastal villages of Burton Bradstock and Abbotsbury, and, despite the rainy and inclement weather, provided wonderful views through the coach window of the choppy grey Channel and of the endless shingles of Chesil Beach.

The rain had stopped by the time they arrived at their destination, though, and a beam or two of watery sunshine now penetrated the thinning clouds. Bridport proved to be a most picturesque market town, yet set back an inordinately long way from the sea for a place that had the word "port" in its name, Molly thought. Nor was it so tranquil as Molly had expected. A great rowdy mob of forty or fifty had assembled in the High Street near the magistrate's court, and Molly was momentarily curious to know what was the cause of their noisy complaint.

Yet she soon forgot the angry citizens of Bridport in her determination to get to Salwayash Manor. This was her sole purpose in coming here was, after all - to try and see Henry if she could. From the Weymouth coach driver, she had confirmed on the way here that Salwayash Manor was but two hours walk from Bridport for any active person, which turned out to be just as well, for there were no carriages or sedan chairs for hire here at all. Molly determined now to look immediately for the right road, and then to set out at once on foot, in M'sieur Desargues's company. Fortunately she was dressed still in her plain old maidservant garb therefore knew that she would not attract any particular attention by walking there on foot, which a finely dressed lady in silk and lace would most certainly have done.

After consulting a passing shepherd, they were told to look for the road leaving north to the villages of Dottery and Salwayash. Yet, when they found a leafy lane with just such a signpost, Molly was disturbed to see that the great mob of angry residents who had congregated outside the magistrate's court were now on the move, and – even more disconcertingly - seemed to be intending to follow this same road.

Faced with this great swell of people, Molly and M'sieur Desargues took refuge under a spreading willow tree at the side of the road while they passed by. At Molly's urging, M'sieur Desargues went and spoke at length with one of the least angry looking of these angry men – a blacksmith by his clothes and build - and then returned to the willow tree to report his findings back to Molly.

'From your grim expression, sir, it seems that you bring troubling news,' a worried Molly suggested, as she watched this mob of ruffians cross a small arch bridge and disappear around a distant bend in the road.

M'sieur Desargues was unusually serious for once. 'It is indeed troubling news, Molly. You remember that woman we saw hanged but a week ago at Tyburn, Mistress Linney?'

Molly had as yet formed no notion of what troubled this country mob so, yet she had certainly not expected to hear that name again. 'How could I not, sir? It was a most barbarous affair, and one that did this country no credit.'

M'sieur Desargues agreed with that. 'Yet, from what yon blacksmith told me, it seems by some odd chance that this young woman was well known to your Mr Raven. Did you not know that Esther Linney was brought up here in the Raven household as a companion to his sisters?'

Molly was surprised. 'I did not, sir, or I would most assuredly have mentioned it to you before. Henry has never spoke her name to me, I am sure...' – she hesitated slightly – '...although I have not talked to him much of late, as you well know. Yet, if this is true, and with all his influence with the King, I wonder that Henry could not save her from the gibbet.'

M'sieur Desargues made a droll face. 'Ah, but these local ruffians believe for some unknown reason that he did indeed save her! And that he hides her now at his manor house...'

Molly stared. 'How can that possibly be, sir? We saw the lady hanged with our own eyes, as did a thousand others.'

M'sieur Desargues grunted in disbelief. 'Obviously there are no limits to the credulity of the English peasant. Someone has put this poisonous nonsense in their heads and now they go to the manor house of your friend to find Mistress Linney. These yokels believe this lady to be a witch possessed of the devil, and think she has also caused the deaths of two local maidens with her evil.'

Molly shook her head in wonder. 'That defies all common sense, sir. We saw her hanging from the gibbet with our own eyes, and most assuredly dead.'

M'sieur Desargues sighed. 'It seems that the laws of logic matter not at all when it comes to witchery and superstition.'

Molly thought rapidly. 'Then we must outpace these ruffians to the manor house, and warn Mr Raven of the trouble that comes his way.'

'I think that it may already be too late for that, Molly. It seems that this party we saw is merely the rear-guard of a larger mob, and that the majority are already at Mr Raven's door.'

Molly gasped. 'Then we had better hurry anyway, sir, and see what we can do to help this situation.'

M'sieur Desargues touched the handle of his sword. 'Then 'tis well that I brought my blade and my pistols with me. I did not expect to find such trouble here, Molly. It seems you attract danger wherever you go, *ma pauvre fille,*' he added ruefully...

*

'So, Mistress Pollock recognized me in the woods after all,' Esther said resignedly.

'It seems so,' Catherine admitted. It was mid-afternoon now and she was presently making sure that Esther was comfortable in her secret chamber, while doing her best to hide her growing worry over this frightening situation.

Esther was fearful, though, as she glanced around her new prison, and

Catherine felt her heart break that she had to imprison her sister in this place.

'Would it not be better, though, if I simply gave myself up to the magistrate, and explained what had really happened?' Esther suggested wearily. 'I have already been tried and hanged for my alleged crime. Henry said that they cannot hang me for it again. Or can they...?'

Catherine tried not to frighten her even more, but rejected the idea of surrender at once. 'I believe Sir Malcolm Batcock is an honourable man and, if you fell into his hands, would look at the evidence of what really happened dispassionately and honestly. Yet I am not sure that you would be allowed to give yourself up to the magistrate. Someone – I presume this must be Mistress Polock's handiwork too somehow - has stirred up the common folk in Bridport with even wilder stories than the truth...'

'What stories could be even wilder than my own?' Esther demanded.

Catherine was reluctant to tell her, but it could not be helped. 'Two young maids have died on our estate in the last three weeks; one of them – Ruth – was from this very house, and drowned in the fish pond. The other – Lorna Wanless – was from a farm on the Warboys estate. I found her myself – hanging from an oak tree. At first it was thought that they took their own lives. Yet there seems some evidence now that Ruth at least may have been cruelly murdered, which must also throw doubt on Lorna being a suicide too...'

Esther gasped. 'I knew young Lorna Wanless. She is truly dead? Yet how could anyone say that I had anything to do with the deaths of these poor maids. I was far away in London.'

'That means naught to the mob in their black mood, Esther. If they find you alive, they will ascribe your survival to the Devil's work, not to the providence of Our Lord. The fact that your mother was burnt as a witch will tell against you...'

Esther gasped. 'You think they would burn me...?'

'Times have changed since the witch finder trials of twenty years ago, therefore I trust we will never return to that terrible madness,' Catherine said. 'But 'tis better not to rely on the common sense and goodness of people too much, when there is so much wickedness and prejudice in the world.'

Esther sat down on the bed in a daze, and looked again around her hiding place. Catherine too reflected on Esther's new prison. As Henry had said, this chamber was much larger and better provided than any normal cramped priest hole, being the size of a small and narrow room, and one equipped to allow a long stay if necessary, with a chair and table and washing basin, as well as a trestle bed. Although it did not have windows, there were small vents in the external brick wall to allow in air, and a little light. It had no heating, of course, yet in May that was no hardship. In theory it would be possible to hide here for months, provided one was supplied with enough food and water. There was even a privy in one corner with a downpipe that discharged directly into a cesspit in the garden. The entrance to the chamber was also perfectly concealed behind the fireplace in the adjacent bedchamber, and could be accessed only by a hinged panel in the back wall, which was a devil to find even when one knew it was there. Catherine could still remember her wonder as a girl when her mother had first shown her this place privately in the dead of night, with all the servants fast asleep. Yet for all its relative comfort, it was still a small cell-like room without proper windows, and Catherine knew that being confined here for any period would cause Esther untold distress.

Catherine tried to reassure her with a breezy display of confidence. 'No one can possibly find you here, dear Esther. Even our servants do not know this chamber is here, so no one can give you away. And I doubt that you will need to be here long, for any searchers will soon grow weary of their unrewarding task. But in case something untoward happens, and the chamber is discovered by some ill luck, there is secret way out of here too. In the corner there, next to the privy, is a small trapdoor in the floor. Below is a narrow vertical shaft with a ladder, which, if you need to leave hurriedly, will take you down into a secret passageway under the house, and from there to a tunnel that comes out in the woods somewhere, two or three hundred paces from the house.'

Esther tried to smile, but her mood was clearly one of dejection. 'I lived here for twelve years, Cathy, and thought I knew every inch of this house. Yet this is the first I have heard of this secret chamber and tunnel. Someone certainly had considerable foresight.'

'Indeed they did,' Catherine explained, 'but it was not a Raven who took these precautions. The gentleman who built the manor more than a century ago, Sir Thomas Daplyn, was a devout Catholic during the time of King Henry, and expected that he might need to escape unseen from this house at some time.'

Esther looked around her little prison. 'Then it was fortunate indeed for me that he did,' she said without conviction. 'You say that you do not know exactly where the tunnel comes out?'

Catherine was worried at Esther's withdrawn and defeated mood. 'I do not, for I have never bothered to walk through it. But Henry has, a year or so back, and he says it is in good repair and easily passable, although somewhat damp and dirty inside. It certainly passes at some depth under the privy garden, and then out into the oak wood. According to Henry, the exit is well disguised in a dip in the ground, with a dense growth of mayflower, blackthorn and field maple all around it. Even in winter it must be well concealed, for I know those woods as well as anyone, and I have never noticed this place.'

Esther was solemn. 'But if I were to use this tunnel to escape searchers inside the house, where would I go from there?'

Catherine pretended to be sanguine. 'Hopefully it will not be needed, but Henry and I will think of some other refuge in the neighbourhood where you might stay until the search dies down. Perhaps our neighbour, Ralph Warboys, would hide you at his home...'

Esther spoke up in alarm. 'Nay, I could not impose myself on that gentleman, who knows me so little!'

Catherine was surprised at Esther's vehement rejection of this idea, and wondered if there might be some particular sentiment behind it. Perhaps there was some enmity between Esther and Ralph that she did not know of, yet she had never heard of such a thing. And she remembered now that she had seen Esther sitting next to Ralph at last summer's harvest feast and looking most content in his company, therefore her reluctance to seek his help was doubly odd. But Catherine said only, in a soothing voice, 'It was but one idea among many, Esther, so worry not. If you do have to leave here, there are many other places where you could hide in the neighbourhood in comfort and security.'

Esther had a thought. 'What will you tell this Constable Drew when he returns and asks to see "Cousin Edward"?'

Catherine shrugged. 'We will simply say that you are gone: that you returned from your walk, and, when told that the Constable wished to speak to you, decided to leave hurriedly instead. We will say that "Edward's" delicate health and retiring nature made it impossible for him to stay and be interrogated on such a fanciful matter as being accused of being a woman in disguise.'

Esther looked down ruefully at her breeches. 'Will he not suspect that the accusation made by Mistress Pollock is correct?'

'What of it? Of course he will suspect the truth, yet he can do nothing, provided we keep you out of his hands. And these troublesome witch hunting people will lose interest in you eventually, although it may take some weeks...' Catherine saw Esther's face change again and instantly regretted what she had said.

Esther was truly dismayed at the thought. 'I may have to say in this chamber for *weeks*? If my imprisonment is to be that long, then I believe that I would prefer to try and escape through the tunnel at once, and take my chances outside.'

'Nay, that is not a good idea,' Catherine said forcefully. She kissed Esther on the cheek, then left the chamber through the secret doorway in the fireplace, after first checking through a spyhole that the bedchamber beyond was empty of any curious servants. But no sooner had she gone down the main stairs in the South Wing and entered the Great Hall than an agitated Henry found her.

'What is wrong, brother? Is Constable Drew returned?' Catherine could hear a strange rumbling sound outside, like a gathering storm, yet the weather was now perfect, and the afternoon sun shone through the tall windows from a cloudless sky.

Henry's expression was grim. 'Nay, it is worse than that, sister. There is a mob of a hundred ruffians or more gathered in front of the house. Their leader demands that we hand over Esther to them at once, or else they will burn the house to the ground...'

# CHAPTER 24

Friday, 19<sup>th</sup> May 1665

Molly and M'sieur Desargues had made good time on the road to Salwayash Manor, despite the muddy conditions, and the deep ruts left by morning traffic and by the feet of the angry mob who had gone before them. From the churned up condition of the road, it seemed that even more locals had joined on route to add their numbers to the swelling throng. After an hour's hard walking, the hem of Molly's skirt was encrusted with thick brown mud, yet now was not the time to worry over her appearance.

In late afternoon, when Molly caught sight for the first time of the tall brick chimneys of a great house through a gap in the tall oak trees ahead, she realized that they must be getting close to their destination. Soon she glimpsed the front of the house, which would in normal circumstances have taken her breath away with its beauty. Even today, she could not help but be impressed that Henry was master of such a palatial and grand house. She saw that the house was of U-shaped plan, with the main west entrance at the base of the U, and the house then dividing into two near identical wings, north and south. She and M'sieur Desargues had seen no one on the road for the last few minutes therefore Molly had been indulging herself mentally with some sanguine hopes that this angry multitude who had gone before them had been turned back at the door to the manor, and had simply seen sense and melted away before the militia was called. But those hopes were soon dashed, when they left the main road and followed the green lane that led through the woods to the main entrance to the manor. Molly heard them before she saw them - a great angry hum like a swarm of giant bees – then she and M'sieur Desargues turned through a bend in the road and she saw the fierce crowd congregated at the front door. In her fevered imagination there seemed to be a thousand of these angry zealots gathered on the forecourt of the house, yet the truer number was probably nearer a hundred. Yet they seemed to be growing ever more rowdy and angry, and Molly was sure they would soon force their way into the house and begin their pointless search for Mistress Linney. Molly had no comprehension how this mob had come to believe that Henry was hiding a dead woman in there, yet when they failed to find her, no doubt their wrath would be even more frightening and uncontrolled...

M'sieur Desargues stopped suddenly in his tracks. 'I fear that we will find no way through that vengeful mob, Molly. I hope there is some other way out of that house for the Raven family, otherwise I sense that there will be a great tragedy here. Some of the mob carry torches, I see, even though it be broad daylight.'

'You think they might burn the house to the ground with the household still inside?' Molly asked, horrified.

M'sieur Desargues grimaced as he glanced down the lane towards the house, and saw one of the mob pick up a piece of paving slab, and throw it angrily through one of the ground floor windows. 'Ay, indeed they may. As a young man, I fought in Bavaria and Saxony during the Thirty Years' War, so I have little doubt of the evil that is often done by ordinary men in defence of their religion. Do you know anything of the detailed layout of this house? Did Mr Raven ever trade any lover's confidences with you that might help?'

Molly racked her brains. 'He did once mention to me that there is secret way out of the house – a tunnel underneath the ground floor built by some Catholic gentleman a hundred years ago. He said that it was a most ingenious construction, and that he had walked through it a year or so ago, out of curiosity to see where it came out.'

M'sieur Desargues was immediately interested. 'Which was where?'

Molly tried to concentrate her memory, despite the angry roar of the crowd in her ears. 'He said that the tunnel was two or three hundred paces long, and came out in a wood at the back of the house.'

M'sieur Desargues took her hand and squeezed it urgently. 'You are certain that he said the *back* of the house, not the side or the front? *Alors*, then we must go around the back and look in the woods there for the entrance to this secret tunnel. Perhaps the family will choose to escape that way with this bloodthirsty mob at their front gate. Or else perhaps we can find our way *into* the house that way to warn them, and you, sweet Molly, can be finally reunited with your lover...'

\*

Henry Raven had already decided what he must do, as the milling crowd outside broke yet another window in the Great Hall in a shower of glass, while his household servants resolutely manned the door to prevent anyone entering. He saw with pride that his household was bearing up well under this terror, even the young maids among them, and doing their best to hold the door. He noticed sweet little Kate Soule among them and gave her as reassuring a smile as he could muster. He had not expected to put Kate through such an ordeal as this when he brought her back to Dorset from London

'Can we not make some appeal to their better nature, Henry?' his sister gasped, as she heard the sound of a wooden ram of some sort – perhaps a fallen tree trunk - being battered against the front door. The door was of heavy Tudor oak construction, and would not succumb easily to such a battering, yet the mob would no doubt keep trying until they succeeded.

''Tis too late for common sense, sister,' Raven said through gritted teeth, as he pulled her away from the tumult at the front door, and into a quieter corner of the Great Hall. 'I had hoped the militia would hear of this insurrection already and come to our aid quickly. Yet it is already five o'clock in the afternoon, and I cannot wait until these ruffians have burnt our house to the ground. I must break out and go and fetch the militia myself to protect the house, before it gets dark. Even so, it will take at least an hour to summon them since the nearest garrison is five miles away, and I must go on foot since I will have to use that secret tunnel to effect my escape.'

Catherine was breathing hard. 'Should you not better send one of the servants on this mission?'

Raven looked at his servants and shook his head. 'Most are too callow, or too elderly, to do this hard work. I can run five miles in half an hour, especially when my house is at stake.' He hesitated, crestfallen. 'Yet I think not clearly. How can I go and leave you here, with that mob baying for blood?'

Catherine tried to smile. 'Be not feared for me, Henry. I am more than a match for the likes of those ruffians.'

Raven took her hand. 'Then I shall go at once. You had better come with me to the secret room, though, and reassure Esther that I do not desert her. Esther must stay hidden there. It would be too dangerous for her to try and leave the house at present, even by the secret tunnel.'

Catherine went back to the main door and had a quick whispered word with Dora Bagwell to explain where she and her brother were going, then she returned and led Henry to the South Wing, and to the stairs leading up the first floor.

*

Once in Esther's bedchamber, it was but a moment to open the secret door behind the fireplace. Esther sprang up from the bed in alarm at their sudden entry, and Catherine realized that she must have been in torment, being only able to hear what mayhem went on outside, but not to see, therefore imagining the worse – that the house had already been put to the torch.

267

Catherine quickly explained the present situation and what Henry was intending to do about it, and Esther seemed moderately calmed by the news.

Raven kissed his sister on the cheek. 'Protect the house as best you can, until I return, sister,' he said simply.

Then he turned to Esther and kissed her on the cheek too. But Catherine was surprised to see that, for whatever reason, Esther kissed him back, and full on the lips, in a most passionate and abandoned manner. Even more surprising was that Henry responded to her in kind with equal passion.

Catherine was taken aback by the intensity of this kiss, from both sides. She had long suspected that Henry's affection for Esther had not always been merely brotherly, and he had even admitted as much recently. Yet for the first time she saw that Esther had an equal passion for her brother too, which was a revelation to her. How could she not have seen this before, when it was as plain as the nose on her face?

With a quiet shock, it suddenly occurred to Catherine that Henry might have been keeping a dark secret from her.

*Could he have been the father of Esther's baby...?* After all, he had been at the harvest feast when this illicit affair had supposedly happened, and he had also been very drunk that evening. Drinking too much ale was known both to inflame passions and to reduce inhibitions, in women as well as men.

That would explain much if it were true, especially Esther's refusal to name the father of her child, since she would not wish to embarrass Henry in front of his family. And it would also explain Henry's considerable efforts to save her – efforts which had somehow succeeded so far despite all the terrible difficulties he had faced. Yet, if it were true, it did not explain why he had not married her as she should - unless it was the interference of his new actress love, who had seduced him with her many guiles and no doubt turned his mind against following the honourable path.

Yet there were other more important things to worry about at present than Henry and Esther's feelings for each other, Catherine decided, instantly putting this revelation to the back of her mind for the present. If this mob should find Esther, Catherine did not know what terrible evil they might do to her.

Catherine watched as Henry finally released Esther from his arms, then smiled at both of them, before going to the corner trapdoor.

'Will you not take your sword, Henry?' Catherine asked him worriedly, as she saw that he was unarmed.

'Nay, I will not. I left it behind deliberately. It will only get in my way climbing down this shaft, and will also encumber me once I start running,' Raven explained. Even without a sword, the trapdoor proved to be a narrow squeeze for such broad shoulders as his, yet he made it with an inch to spare, and smiled a reassuring farewell to them both, before closing the trapdoor gently behind him.

*

The shaft was narrow all the way down as it was squeezed into the tiny gap between two walls on the ground floor. Yet once below the ground floor, it opened up into a significant passageway, in which it was easy to stand up straight. The passageway was filled with a hundred years of dust and dirt, though, and choked so thick with spiders' webs that they seemed to hang in gossamer curtains. Yet Raven gave no thought to the mess they made of his fine clothes, and forced his way through regardless. He could distinctly feel through the floor above his head the vibrations as the mob continued to pummel the front door with their makeshift battering ram. He could only hope that the stout Tudor door would be able to take this punishment for at least the next hour until he could return with help.

The passageway soon dipped down further below ground into a proper brick tunnel with arched roof. Raven guessed that he must be below the privy garden now, or even the woods beyond already, because the roof of the tunnel was damp with dripping water, while tree roots penetrated through the mortar joints of the brickwork in some places.

Raven had counted his paces from the shaft, and had reached three hundred and forty – more than he had expected – before he came to the entrance that he remembered so well from his first walk through, more than a year ago. He had not expected then that he would ever need to use this tunnel in a real emergency, but he gave a silent prayer of gratitude to the previous owner of this house, Sir Thomas Daplyn, who had provided this useful bolt hole. The tunnel ramped up steeply at the end, and also narrowed to a small vertical shaft again, this one sealed by a stone slab. Raven remembered that last time he had been forced to exert considerable muscular force with his arms to move the heavy limestone slab over the opening, which had obviously not been moved for many years prior to his visit and was overgrown on top with soil and grass and brambles. This time, though, it moved easily, even though still as heavy as he remembered. Raven doubted that a woman could even lift such a dead weight as this, so decided, after climbing through, that he would leave it where it was with the shaft open, in case Esther might need to escape through it before his return. The opening was concealed from casual inspection by a dense growth of mayflower and blackthorn hedgerow on all sides, therefore would not be discovered accidentally, except by a fox or badger.

Raven found the thinnest part of the hedge and forced his way through, ignoring the painful thorns and the damage they did to his exposed skin and his clothes. The oak woods beyond were sunlit and bright in the late afternoon sunshine, despite the close spacing of the trees. Yet with

269

satisfaction he saw the track that he thought would take him safely to Bridport, while avoiding bringing him anywhere near the manor again. Raven would have preferred less light to make sure his escape was unseen, yet there was nothing for it but to hope that none of the mob had chosen to go around the back of the manor house.

Yet he had not run but a hundred paces further down this track, when two men stepped out from behind a tree in front of him, and held up their hands for him to stop. Raven would have liked to simply diverge from his path and run around them, yet there was not sufficient space for that between the dense vegetation encroaching on each side of the track, so he was forced to skid to a halt.

Raven did not like the look of these two men, which was villainous in the extreme. They had more the look of footpads or highwaymen than local religious zealots, therefore Raven suspected that they were not part of the mob who had laid siege to his house.

The older of the two, an ugly individual with evil eyes, bowed mockingly and took off his broad-brimmed hat. 'We will take your purse, sir, if you will be so good. Else we will have to break a few bones in your body, and then take your gold anyway.' His accent was not local, therefore Raven suspected that the pair were thieves from London who had fled the plague, and were now looking for victims wherever they could find them.

Raven saw that they were both armed with thick cudgels of ash, and looked like they knew how to use such weapons in the most vicious way possible. The younger one looked just as villainous as his older companion, and was stronger and more muscular to boot. For a moment Raven was tempted to simply hand over his purse because of the urgency of his mission. Yet he knew in his heart that these men would not then simply let him go, but would beat him insensible anyway, therefore he would have to fight to get past them. Catherine's suggestion that he should take his sword now began to seem like the wisest advice he had ever received, except that a brace of matchlock pistols would have been even more welcome right now.

Raven braced himself for the attack. 'If you want my purse, sir, then you will have to come and take it off me.'

The younger footpad snarled at this defiance and came running at Raven with his cudgel raised to strike. Although a vast man, he was also slow and clumsy, and Raven was able to feint and step aside from his challenge, and then to trip him. Snatching up the fallen man's cudgel, he hit the man over the head with his own weapon, opening a great gash in the back of the man's close cropped head.

Raven now faced the older man, who did not seem deterred by the failure of his friend, yet approached Raven more warily, clearly recognizing a more dangerous adversary than he had thought. The man, for all his greater age, was immeasurably more skilful than his friend, and Raven suspected he was dealing with an ex-soldier of the Civil War here. Yet Raven was faster and stronger even than this man and, armed with a weightier cudgel too than his opponent, soon got the better of him, giving him a blow to the side of his head that might have broken the skull of a weaker man. The footpad did finally collapse on the ground under the force of this savage blow, but he was still conscious and far from beaten yet. Even more oddly, though, he seemed to smile almost triumphantly up at Raven as he lay on the ground, despite the considerable pain he must be in.

Raven was about to batter the man again where he lay, when he heard a whistling sound behind him and realized too late that these two villains must have a third accomplice hiding in readiness just in case. Raven felt a searing pain in the back of his head, then the world went black....

*

Molly and her father had found their way around to the woods at the back of the manor house, but this long and circuitous route took them almost twenty minutes of hard walking. It was then that Molly realized the difficulty of their undertaking, because this wood was not normal open oak woodland, but instead a wilderness as dense with vegetable undergrowth as the wilds of North America. The chance of finding the entrance to a long lost tunnel into the manor in all this wilderness of shrubs and trees seemed as remote a possibility as finding a way into Hades.

Molly sighed. 'What are we to do, sir? There could an army of red savages living in this forest, for all I know. I cannot even see the manor house from here, so cannot hazard a guess where this tunnel might lie, even if it exists at all...' Molly stopped in alarm as she heard the sounds of some fierce altercation nearby in the woods.

M'sieur Desargues held up a warning finger to silence her further, then indicated for her to follow him, which she did.

They carefully forced a way through the thick undergrowth, and came to a narrow track, thick with last year's rotting oak leaves. Molly peered around M'sieur Desargues's shoulder as he looked down the track. She saw three villainous-looking men standing over a body face down on the ground. The man on the ground appeared to be a gentleman judging by his dark hair and his rich velvet coat and breeches. One of the villains was going through his pockets, and Molly realized at once that they must have waylaid the poor man. M'sieur Desargues took out his pistols at once and lit his match cord ready to fire them. Molly could not but be impressed with the speed at which he prepared his pistols, so his boast that he had fought in the Thirty Years War did not seem such an idle boast after all, as she had half suspected.

But he had no need to fire his pistols, for the three highwaymen took to their heels as soon as they saw an armed man approach. Molly noticed that two of the men were in distress themselves, one bleeding profusely, and the older one holding his sore head, so it seemed their victim had not gone down without a fight, which perhaps explained why the rogues fled so easily. They had no doubt got the gentleman's purse, but at least they had paid some price in pain for it.

Yet M'sieur Desargues chased after them a little anyway to make sure that they did not return, while Molly approached the victim of this cowardly attack, who did not move at all, and seemed quite insensible. Molly even feared that he might be dead, so was wary of touching him at first.

When her father came back, Molly asked for his help to turn over the victim, which was no easy task considering his size. The man did groan slightly as they moved him, which reassured Molly that he was alive at least. She gasped, though, when she saw who it was. 'Ah! *It is Henry, sir!* And he seems badly wounded by those ruffians…'

*

Catherine stood at the main door into the Great Hall and saw with trepidation that the stout oak door was finally beginning to yield under the repeated impact of the battering ram on the other side of it. The mob had learned by their mistakes, and found a heavier tree trunk from somewhere to use as a ram, and this weightier one was beginning to cause the door to disintegrate around the lock. The mob had also tried to get into the house through some of the broken windows on the ground floor, yet had been deterred in that object by the thorny blackthorn hedge that Henry had planted there in front of the house for deterring burglars.

Dora came and stood beside Catherine. 'They will be in the house soon, Mistress, and we can do naught to prevent it.'

Jacob Shawn looked most penitent and crestfallen, verging on tears, as he turned to Catherine. 'You think it was truly my aunt, Mistress, who has incited this mob?'

Catherine nodded. 'I fear so, Jacob. But I do not blame you for this disaster, but these gullible ruffians outside who were so easily swayed by the evil gossip of a vengeful old woman. We must hope that my brother returns with the militia before they manage to get in'

Yet Catherine was not hopeful of this. Henry had been gone a full half hour, and Catherine was reassured that he must have got far away by now, and with his powerful running legs must he halfway to Bridport already. Yet he could not be back with the militia for another hour at least, while that front door did not look like it could last five minutes more.

Yet even that proved to be an optimistic estimate. Within a minute, Catherine jumped in alarm as the door finally splintered under the pressure of the ram, and the men outside then took to the damaged door with axes to clear a large enough opening to climb through.

In another three minutes, the first man was through the door, only for the household servants, led by Martin Gibney, to fall on him and beat him with their fists. Soon others of the mob had climbed through, though, and a pitched battle began in the Great Hall with the Raven servants. Catherine saw Jacob Shawn saw fighting like a madman against a much larger opponent, even though his face was bloodied and his fists red raw.

Despite their furious resistance, Catherine could see that her servants would soon be overwhelmed by the mob, as more of them spilled through the opening in the main door.

Dora pulled Catherine away from the fighting and said urgently, 'I know that you have hidden Esther in one of the priest holes, Mistress. Go to her now, and we will hold these villains back as long as we can. I will try and stop them looting and burning the house, until the master returns...'

Catherine did as she was advised, but it seemed some of the mob must have got past the ring of servants at the main door already because she heard heavy footsteps following close behind her, as she ascended the stairs into the South Wing. She only just managed to get up to Esther's bedchamber, and then through the hidden doorway behind the fireplace into the secret chamber, before someone burst into the bedchamber behind her. Catherine embraced Esther who was tense with fright, and then put a warning finger to her lips to silence any enquiries.

On the other side of the fireplace, a muffled man's voice said, puzzled. 'I could have sworn that I saw a lady run in here.'

His lowly companion laughed and swore. 'Be God's sonties! Have you supped too much ale already today, Abraham?'

The first man was resentful. 'I could not have imagined those green velvet skirts she wore, or those white petticoats, or that glimpse I got of silk stocking.'

The second man laughed again. 'Thee and thy cock, Abraham – it is all that ye think of, even though it has brought you nothing but the bone-ache. Forget your dreams of pretty thighs in silk stockings and let us look quickly for things to steal before the rest of our saintly companions find their way here too.'

The first man grunted coarsely. 'They are not so saintly, Jed. Most are like us – taking advantage of the company of this mob of religious zealots to come and take what treasure we can find...'

Catherine was outraged at this blatant larceny, but there was naught she could presently do to prevent it other than remember the names and appearance of these two villains, and hope that she could see some justice administered to them in time. Through the peephole in the wall she saw them looting whatever took their fancy in Esther's bedchamber, and smashing whatever did not. Eventually they tired of the limited pickings in this room and went elsewhere to fill up their sack of loot, and Catherine was finally able to sigh with relief.

Yet the relief was short lived, and Catherine almost jumped out of her skin as she heard another sound - from below this time. Then she realized that it was someone climbing back up the shaft in the corner. She thought with instant relief that it must be Henry returning, yet a warning voice in her head did ask her why he would return this way if he had brought the militia already. Therefore she opened the trapdoor warily to allow the new arrival into the room. When she saw whose head and shoulders appeared through the opening, she gasped again in astonishment, for it was Ralph Warboys...

Esther too was surprised, and gasped even louder than Catherine. But it was Catherine who spoke up first. 'How come you here, Ralph? How did you know of this tunnel?' she asked in wonder.

Ralph pulled himself up into the room, then wiped some of the dust and cobwebs from his coat and breeches. 'I have known for years of its existence. In fact I and my brother Geoffrey once broke into this house through this very tunnel. Geoffrey made me a wager that I would not do it, but then he was always daring me to do foolish things.'

Catherine was still taken aback by his unexpected arrival. 'Yes, but that must be before I was born even, since your brother died more than twenty years ago.'

Ralph smiled ruefully. 'Do not remind me so wilfully of my age, Catherine. The passage of time is difficult enough to bear as it is.'

Esther finally stepped forward from the shadows and asked coldly. 'Why have you come here, Mr Warboys?'

Catherine looked at her sharply and thought her coldness unforgivable in the circumstances, when Ralph had clearly risked personal danger to come to their aid. She was reminded again of her feeling that there must be some enmity between Esther and Ralph, though on this evidence it seemed to be entirely from Esther's side.

Ralph confronted Esther directly. 'Mistress Linney, I was in Bridport this morning and heard these wild stories that you had survived being hanged, and that you were hiding at Salwayash Manor in the guise of a man. I could not believe it, yet I had to come and see for myself. And I am heartily glad to see that these strange rumours are true – 'tis a blessing to behold you alive and well. As for why I have come this way, when I saw the mob at the door, I realized at once that I could not gain entry to the house by conventional means. Yet I remembered the tunnel that my brother and I had used all those years ago, and was lucky to remember where the outside entrance lay. The stone slab over the shaft had even been moved recently so I wondered if someone had left by this way already today...'

'It was Henry, Ralph,' Catherine interrupted. 'He has gone for help from the militia. You did not see him outside, I suppose?' she asked hopefully.

Ralph shook his head. 'I am afraid that I did not. Yet even if he brings help, I think that you ladies must leave immediately.' He turned to Esther again in her boy's garb. 'I still cannot believe that this miracle is true! How did you manage to survive?'

Esther seemed deeply uncomfortable. 'Our Lord must have watched over me, I suppose, although, at risk of being though blasphemous, I wish that he would have watched over my baby with equal attention too. And I had the support of a true friend in Mr Raven…' - she hesitated – '…why have you come to help me now, sir? You have not done so before,' she said accusingly.

Catherine was embarrassed by the ill gratitude of this remark, and wondered again at Esther's open hostility which was most unlike her. Catherine realized that something strange went on between these two people who were both so dear to her, yet now was patently not the time for questions.

Ralph too seemed to understand the urgency. 'I have no time to explain all my actions, Esther. It is already near six o'clock. We must all leave by the tunnel at once; we cannot risk staying here until Henry returns with the militia. In their frustration at not finding you, this mob of zealots may simply burn this house to the ground. I regret that I came here unarmed today, yet even if I were armed to the teeth, I cannot fight off a whole mob.' He offered Catherine his hand to help her down the shaft. 'Come, I will take you both through the woods to Warboys Hall now. You will be safe there until the militia arrives to disperse this mob with their cutlasses and pistols…'

.

# CHAPTER 25

Friday, 19th May 1665

Raven woke up slowly, and gradually the world about him began to resolve itself into some semblance of reality again. He saw that he was lying under an oak tree in an idyllic woodland glade, lit by sunlight casting long evening shadows. He found the length of the shadows deeply troubling, though, yet could not think immediately why that should be so. Then he remembered suddenly the attack on him, and then the details of his thwarted mission to go for help from the militia, which made him jump up in alarm as he wondered how much time he had lost from that encounter with the three footpads. Yet as he moved and tried to stand up, his head erupted again with pain as if it were an anvil on which some demonic blacksmith was practising violent blows with his hammer.

Raven groaned and lay back down on the mossy ground at the base of the tree and wondered who had brought him here, for it was not the place where he had been attacked. Then a figure moved into his line of vision and a sweet, if concerned, face smiled down at him.

'Ah, you are finally awake, Henry,' Molly said, with relief in her voice, putting a damp cloth to his brow.

At first Raven could not believe his eyes, at finding Molly of all people tending to him. 'By God's lid, is it really you, Molly?'

'It is I, sir, and do not blaspheme so, even if you have a sore head,' Molly said primly as she cleansed the blood and dirt from Raven's brow with the damp cloth. ''Tis fortunate that you have such a prodigiously thick head of hair, otherwise those villains who attacked you might have broken your skull in two.'

'It feels as if it *is* broken in two, Molly,' Raven complained weakly.

Molly shook her head with a smile. 'Nay, it is not, Henry. Otherwise the pain would be much worse than it is, and you would not be able to talk so

276

sensibly now.'

Raven grimaced. 'Greater pain is hard to imagine. But what miraculous chance brought you here to this very place, Molly?'

Molly shrugged complacently. 'Why, I came to Dorset to see you, Henry, of course. Sir Thomas Killigrew told me that you intend to fight against the Dutch with the King's Navy, and I could not let you go off to war without seeing you and promising you my continued affection and loyalty. Though I was much upset that you made so little effort to see me before you left London.'

'I did not mean to be so neglectful of you, Molly, but I have been through trying circumstances in these last weeks which have left me little time for my own concerns and comfort.'

Molly nodded. 'Yes, I have seen a little of these trying circumstances today for myself. I saw a great rowdy mob of people assembled in Bridport on my arrival, then heard they intended to march on Salwayash Manor. So I followed on foot to see what I could do to help you.'

Raven was trying to think clearly despite the thundering pain in his head and the continued dizziness. 'You came here alone, Molly, dressed only like that?' He looked at her poor maid's dress and bodice, and thin cloak, all liberally besmirched with mud.

'I am not alone, Henry,' Molly admitted. 'And before my companion returns, I must say something...'

But before she could finish, a man had appeared in the clearing behind her. Raven frowned when he recognized that old French dog, M'sieur Philippe Desargues, whose presence in Molly's life had been the cause of so much irritation to him already. 'What is *that* gentleman doing here, Molly?' Raven demanded peevishly.

Molly chided him in return. 'This gentleman saved your life from those highwaymen, Henry, so please be more obliging to him.' She hesitated. 'And he is also my natural father, sir, so that any small pleasure that you have derived from my company during these last months also owes something to him, for which you should perhaps be duly grateful.'

Raven gawped woodenly at this announcement, and struggled to understand. 'I thought that you were the child of the late Samuel Titchen, a draper of Bartlett's Passage.'

Molly nodded. 'I thought so too until recently, Henry. But it seems Celia misled me, and many others, for reasons that I do not fully understand. Celia is my real mother after all, and this handsome gentleman behind me was the person who aroused the passion in her which resulted in my birth. Though I did not know this either until a few days ago when my mother and M'sieur Desargues were accidentally reunited.' She turned her head to glance behind her. 'Is that not so, sir?'

M'sieur Desargues was in no mood for pleasantries or banter for once, though, and came straight to the point. 'It is after seven o'clock, Mr Raven, and it will be dark within two hours. It is too late to call the militia now for assistance, sir – that is, if your object in calling them was to keep that vengeful mob out of your house. I have been to the front of your handsome manor, sir, where the mob has already succeeded in breaking in. Your servants have all been dragged outside, and the mob is searching and looting inside. But at least they have not set fire to the place, which is one major consolation for you.' The Frenchman hesitated. 'Is it really true that you have Mistress Linney hidden in that house somewhere?'

Raven did not know how this gentleman knew so much of his affairs, but did not choose to dissemble. ''Tis a long story, M'sieur, but ay, she is hiding there, disguised as a boy.'

M'sieur Desargues was astonished that the bizarre rumours that he had heard from the blacksmith with the mob should be true after all. 'How in God's holy name did you save that woman from the gibbet, sir? Such a story defies all rational explanation. Molly and I saw her hanged but a week ago, with our own eyes.'

Raven looked at Molly in surprise to see if this was true. 'By some miracle, the hangman did not kill her. Then, even more providentially, she was taken to the house of a physician colleague of mine for dissection where I found her in time and helped revive her.'

M'sieur Desargues was no less astonished by this explanation. 'Yet the whole affair still seems to require some miracle to explain it...'

Raven interrupted him testily. 'Perhaps so, but now is not the best time for such conjecture. Has the mob got her, sir? Was she with my servants who were dragged outside? Perhaps they caught her but did not recognize her. She is in the disguise of a boy, but a very tall and elegant boy with fair skin. Did you see anyone like that among my captured servants?'

M'sieur Desargues tried to remember. 'I was some distance away from them, yet I did not see anyone so favoured among the servants who were brought out of the house.'

'And what of my sister Catherine?' Raven pressed him. 'Was *she* among the servants? She was wearing a green velvet dress today so should have stood out easily among the plainly dressed maidservants.'

M'sieur Desargues shook his head. 'I saw no beautiful ladies among the captured household, only maidservants in plain dresses and coifs, and manservants in black.'

Raven was relieved. 'Then Catherine and Esther must still be hiding inside. I had hidden Esther in a secret chamber in the house,' he explained, 'and Catherine must have remained there in hiding too.'

M'sieur Desargues sat down on a fallen tree trunk. 'I think not, sir. I overheard the conversation of two of the ringleaders of this mob, and it seemed from their ill-tempered discussion that they had found some secret chamber behind a fireplace in the house, but no one hiding there.'

Raven looked up hopefully. 'Then, if they were not in that secret chamber, Catherine and Esther must have escaped through the same secret tunnel that I did. Perhaps the mob did not find the trapdoor that leads to the tunnel; it is well-concealed after all.' Raven tried to sit up again and see where he was. 'In which case, Catherine and Esther must have passed close by here, since we cannot be far away from the entrance. Molly, have you seen anyone else in these woods while your father was away from you?'

Molly bit her lip. 'I have been fetching water from the stream, and tending to your injuries, Henry, so did not have time to pay attention to anything else. Yet I did not see anyone else that I can remember. Where is the entrance to this tunnel?' she asked curiously. 'Is it near where you were attacked by those rogues? You told me once of this secret tunnel, I remember, but I do not know where the entrance might be.'

Raven scanned the edge of the clearing. 'It is but a hundred paces from where I was attacked, but it is well hidden by vegetation.'

M'sieur Desargues spoke up. 'And I saw no one in these woods either, sir, when returning from the front of the house.'

Raven tried to think. 'Yet Catherine and Esther must have escaped the same way that I did. The question is where would they go from there? To Bridport for the militia? Or perhaps elsewhere?'

Molly took Raven's hand. 'You must know your sister better than anyone, Henry. So you will know better than anyone where she would go for help.'

Raven smiled at her gratefully. 'You are right as usual, Molly. I know exactly where Catherine would go for sanctuary and help. She would almost certainly go to my neighbour's house, Warboys Hall...'

*

It had taken two hour's hard walking through the woods for the party to reach Warboys Hall, and the sun was already beginning to sink rapidly towards the western horizon as they finally approached the imposing house. But when they came within sight of the front of this fine Jacobean mansion, Catherine was dismayed by what she saw. 'The mob is here too,' she said in despair, looking at the milling throng in the courtyard in front.

Ralph pulled the ladies out of sight behind a tree. 'Yes, it seems so. They are far fewer here than at your house, Catherine, yet there are enough of them to concern me. Although it irks me greatly, it seems that I cannot invite you both into my home as I said.' He frowned heavily. 'It also seems that the masses are cleverer than I thought, for they must have discovered you had escaped from Salwayash Manor and guessed you might come here.'

Esther had fallen into a deep and listless melancholy by now, Catherine saw, which lethargy and apathy worried her greatly as it was so contradictory to Esther's normally resilient character. Catherine could scarcely blame her for yielding finally to all this pain and hardship she had suffered, yet part of her was disappointed nevertheless. 'Then where can we go?' Catherine asked Ralph urgently. 'Even though it is mid-May, yet we need to find shelter before nightfall, which is but an hour away. Esther is still not completely well after her physical ordeal of the last weeks.'

Ralph thought aloud. 'There are many cottages on the estate where we could be taken in. But, to be frank, I do not know whom to trust any more among my tenants.'

'What about your old family home, Ralph?' Catherine suggested. 'There is no one living there in that ruined castle now, but I have ridden there often of late, and the old keep still looks habitable enough. It would keep us warm and dry at least, should it come on to rain later. There is also a well with clean water there. We dare not go back to Salwayash Manor tonight.'

For some reason Ralph seemed most reluctant to take them to the ruined castle, but Catherine lost patience with him in the end and said that she and Esther would go there anyway, before dark fell, as it was the only sensible place within walking distance.

Faced with that ultimatum, Ralph gave in reluctantly and led Catherine and Esther for a further half hour through the increasingly wild wood to the ruins of the castle. By this time the sun had set below the tops of the trees and a purple dusk was falling fast.

Esther took in the serrated outline of crumbling stone battlements which seemed in the twilight to have a most sinister aspect. 'I have never been here before, but it looks a most evil place.'

Ralph was in a sullen and resentful mood now after being forced to bring them here against his will. 'You agreed to come here, and 'tis now too late to go anywhere else tonight, Esther,' he snapped, leading them into the grassy clearing around the ruins of the castle. They followed the sunken line of the former moat, and crossed the line of residual stonework that marked the original outer walls of the castle.

Inside the former bailey, now overgrown with tall grass, the old keep of the castle looked much as Catherine remembered it, although at dusk it was indeed a more sinister place than she remembered from her previous visit here on a fresh spring morning.

Esther was unsure about going inside. 'Must we go within the keep? I think I prefer to stay here outside in the courtyard for now. It is a warm evening, and dry enough now.'

Catherine disagreed, though. 'The grass is still sodden from this morning's rain, Esther, and we will all likely contract tissick or the King's evil, if we rest here.'

Ralph spoke up. 'It will be cold if we stay outside. But if we do go in, then I must caution you not to venture above the ground floor. The upper floors are in bad repair, with much broken stonework and missing timbers, and the staircase is very treacherous in some places.'

Catherine was surprised to hear this since the upper battlements of the keep looked in excellent repair from below. But she assented wearily, not wanting a further argument. 'As you say, Ralph. We will stay on the first floor of the keep and not go higher. It will do us as a temporary home for a few hours until the rowdy witch-hunting mob are dispersed and we can finally go home...'

It was just as she was saying this that Catherine's right foot struck against some bulky object hidden in the long grass. She gasped in fright when she looked down in the shadows at her feet and saw that the object she had walked into was the body of a man. At first she assumed naturally that he might be just a drunken labourer or vagrant who was sleeping off his stupor here. But then, as she moved to get a better look in the fast fading light, she saw with horror that the man's throat was slit from ear to ear...

Behind her, Esther screamed even more sharply as she discovered another body in the wet grass, then, while stumbling backwards in a blind panic, a third...

This last one was the most horrible of all, Catherine saw with revulsion as she came immediately to Esther's aid. Not only was the man's throat slit, but his eyeballs had been gouged out by some inhuman fingers, so that two bloody sockets stared up accusingly at the darkening sky.

Catherine was shaking from head to toe at this horrendous sight, but noticed that Ralph seemed remarkably composed at this terrible discovery. 'You know these men, Ralph?' she asked with trembling lips.

Ralph seemed curiously resigned and fatalistic. 'I do. They worked for me here on the estate in a rather peculiar capacity. This one with no eyes is a man called Ebenezer Lockshear.' He shook his head with great weariness. 'I did warn him what might happen if he did not take proper precautions...'

Catherine's heart was racing. 'What does it all mean? Has that wicked mob been here and done this to your poor men?'

Ralph shook his head with bleak finality. 'Nay, not them. What this tells me is that my vicious brother has escaped again, and that my life is now ruined beyond repair...'

# CHAPTER 26

Friday, 19<sup>th</sup> May 1665

With those three horribly murdered corpses lying outside, and the twilight almost gone, Catherine and Esther had needed little further persuasion from Ralph to go inside the keep, and to bar the heavy oak door from the outside. In normal circumstances, Catherine would have preferred to leave this cursed place at once and go in search of help. But she reminded herself that these were not normal circumstances, and Esther was still a fugitive from the mindless retribution of the mob hunting her. And even in the best of times, it would be madness to go walking in these woods in the pitch darkness that was about to fall.

After barring the door behind them, Ralph lit a candlestick that he found by feeling with his hands in a recess in the inner wall, then led them up the curving stone stairs to the first floor. From his familiarity with everything inside the ancient keep, he was clearly a regular visitor here. Catherine saw at once that he had lied earlier about the condition of the staircase and upper floors, since the stonework was fully intact, and even in good condition. Ralph made no attempt to explain or justify his earlier deception, though, and carried on to the next main level, where a second doorway led into the shadowy interior of the keep.

Inside the main chamber at this level, Catherine saw clear evidence of recent occupation – in the centre of the oak beam floor was a table set with a candlestick, and also with dirty plates and half-eaten food – a leg of mutton and some salted beef - while up against the interior wall was an unmade truckle bed. There was also a stash of weapons in the corner: swords, cutlasses and a brace of fine matchlock pistols. She guessed at once that the three murdered men below must have been living here, but as yet had no comprehension of who could have done this wicked and terrible thing to them. Yet, from his strange behaviour and enigmatic words, Ralph clearly believed that he knew who had done it. Ralph had spoken outside of his brother, but Catherine knew that he must be speaking figuratively only, for it was well known that he had no brothers still living.

Through the narrow embrasures in the external west wall, Catherine saw that the last traces of sunlight had almost disappeared from the sky, and that the evening chorus of blackbird, linnet and song thrush in the surrounding woods had now faded to only an occasional distant alarm call. Utter blackness would soon descend on the wild wood outside, yet fortunately such darkness would not last long on such a clear night as this. Catherine remembered that the moon would be in the last quarter tonight, therefore must rise within two hours or so to bathe the world again in silver light. She began to hope that they would not be imprisoned here all night after all, but might be able to walk back to Salwayash Manor after midnight by the light of that old moon. Surely Henry would have summoned the militia by then and dispersed the angry crowd wrecking their beloved home…?

Though whether they would want to walk back to Salwayash Manor in the moonlight, with a lunatic on the prowl in those woods, was questionable at best, Catherine thought. "Lunatic" was the only appropriate word for this devil who had apparently murdered those three men outside in cold blood, while the clear moonlit night to come made the appellation particularly fitting…

The smell of this chamber was most unpleasant, a mixture of stale food and animal odours that suggested that the habits of the three men who had lived here had not been too savoury or refined. Catherine saw that the main chamber did not occupy the whole of the interior of the keep, and that the central area was divided up by a series of internal walls into smaller windowless chambers, like cells. The doors to these chambers were all heavy iron studded oak doors with small viewing panels, and each was barred and bolted as if some dangerous creature dwelled on the other side of it. Ralph's first task on entering the main chamber was to go to one of these particular doors, and to poke his candle through the viewing grille. Then he took the stairs up the roof of the keep where he apparently made a detailed search. Finally he returned to the chamber and made a quick circuit of the whole floor, searching into every dark nook and cranny with his candle, before returning to Catherine and Esther in slightly more reassured fashion. 'He is certainly gone, thank God, so we are safe from his anger here.'

Catherine glanced fearfully at Esther, who clearly shared her deep apprehension. 'Who is gone, Ralph?'

Ralph regarded them both with frustrated bemusement, as if he was trying to explain something simple to a child, but could not make himself understood by any means. 'Why, my brother Geoffrey, of course! Did I not make myself clear before, Catherine?'

Esther merely looked bewildered at this announcement while Catherine in turn struggled to understand what Ralph had said. 'But your brother Geoffrey has been dead more than tw…twenty years,' she stammered, wondering if this savage incident had made Ralph lose his reason.

Ralph sighed like a man carrying the weight of the world on his shoulders. 'Would to God that were true, Catherine! My life would have been much simpler, as would my father's before me. As you know from my family history, my father died on the battlefield at Naseby and left me the master of this estate at the age of one- and-twenty.' Ralph glanced around the chamber in dismay. 'Yet he also left me this family curse to deal with…'

'What curse is this?' Catherine asked, still perplexed.

Ralph swallowed hard. 'I mean the curse on the family of a degenerate son. It was my father who imprisoned my twin brother Geoffrey, for the sake of the family's honour and reputation, and let it be known that he had died of consumption instead. He did not do it lightly, since Geoffrey was only eighteen at the time. It was an awful thing for a father to have to do to his son, yet Geoffrey had given him no choice in the end.'

Catherine finally glimpsed the awful truth. 'Why? Was Geoffrey mad?'

Ralph glanced uneasily at Esther with a look almost of shame, but Esther made no response at all, and seemed in her frozen attitude to have been turned almost to stone. Ralph addressed Catherine again. 'Only if true evil can be considered a form of madness. Geoffrey never foamed at the mouth, or ran completely wild, or fell into strange fits. Yet as he grew past the age of fourteen, my father began to realise that the normal moral restraints that define human behaviour simply did not exist within him, and that he had no regard for human life or feelings at all. At first my father gave him the benefit of the doubt, and did not believe the stories of his wilder excesses. Then, when the sordid truth could no longer be denied, my father became complicit for a while in hiding the evidence of my brother's wickedness from our neighbours and the rest of the world. But as Geoffrey's behaviour became ever more depraved and foul, it no longer became possible to conceal that wickedness. Things came to a head when he raped a young maidservant in our household, then calmly slit her throat afterwards. My father was too concerned with the family's reputation to go to the magistrate and have Geoffrey committed for murder, as he should have. In any case the Civil War raged then and normal law and order no longer prevailed in this neighbourhood. Instead my father had Geoffrey interred here in the ruins of our old home, which was near enough for us to visit him, but far enough away to prevent casual discovery. He had these rooms made especially for him so that his captivity would be as comfortable as possible. To our neighbours, he reported his son as being dead of consumption, and no one at the time had cause to doubt it, the country being in the grip of bloody war and much tumult. My father retained slight hopes at the start that Geoffrey would improve in time and might one day be able to return to the world, should he learn to control these evil impulses that had so blighted our family's honour. The family employed a team of gaolers over the years to supervise Geoffrey, and these men were paid well to look after their charge and to keep their mouths shut. When my father died at Naseby a few years later, this cursed duty of family gaoler fell to me. I have now borne this crown of thorns for twenty years now, and there has not been a day in my life when I have been able to free myself from thoughts of it.'

Catherine did not know what to say after such a sordid tale, and sank down on a bench by the table, still trembling from the shock of what she had seen outside. Esther remained standing, though, and Catherine was worried that she could remain so impassive and calm after hearing Ralph's startling family confession.

Ralph paced back and forward in agitation before speaking again. 'I eventually married ten years ago, as you know. At first I did not tell my wife Margaret anything about Geoffrey, but eventually she began to suspect something from my regular absences from the house, so finally I had to admit to this unfortunate skeleton in the family closet. I tried to represent Geoffrey's imprisonment to her as being a humane and compassionate gesture on the family's part, and not something  derived from fear of scandal...'

Catherine did not much like the direction of this story, which she feared would soon get even worse. 'And...?'

Ralph gave a helpless shrug.  'After I told her the truth, my wife eventually insisted on visiting Geoffrey here. Margaret had a good and kind heart, and wanted to see what she could do to help him and alleviate his suffering in confinement. When I brought her here that first time, she was greatly disturbed by what she saw. For one thing she saw someone who seemed disturbingly similar in appearance to her own husband. Even his behaviour in captivity seemed reminiscent of me. Many were taken in by his sometimes gentle demeanour when confined, even his own gaolers sometimes. Yet I am sure that it was a performance of guile only: Geoffrey is not capable of feeling true human emotions, yet he can simulate them well enough for a suitable audience. His behaviour deceived Margaret completely, who believed that Geoffrey had been imprisoned either in error, or perhaps maliciously by an evil and scheming father. Last summer my wife involved herself more and more in my brother's care, and came here regularly to see him and converse with him though his cell door. I allowed this but made her promise that she would never go into his cell with him.'

285

Esther finally spoke up to disturb her statue-like immobility. 'And what happened, sir?'

Ralph looked desolate. 'Unknown to me, Margaret began disobeying my strict instructions not to enter Geoffrey's cell. In fact she began to do so regularly, with the connivance of the gaoler at that time, a Mr Samuel Cocking. It proved to be a great error of judgement on her part but she desperately wanted to believe that Geoffrey might be able to recover his mind and take his proper place in society again. An even worse lapse of judgment was to come though; she and the gaoler even began to let Geoffrey out of his cell for extended periods at a time, to take walks in the woods, or to go riding again, which he had not done in near twenty years. I did not know of any of these futile attempts at rehabilitation until too late.'

Esther suddenly gasped with pain, as if she had been wounded with a knife. 'It was *your brother* who came to me that night, not you,' she said in horror.

Catherine stood up in alarm as she tried to understand what Esther had meant by that distressed remark.

Ralph could not look Catherine or Esther in the face. 'During the last harvest feast at your home, Margaret took Geoffrey riding to a hill from where he could watch the afternoon celebrations at Salwayash Manor. She told me later that she wanted him to get a glimpse of normal society again, to see whether he would react to it favourably. Yet, if she thought that, then she simply did not understand the true wickedness in his soul. ' Finally Ralph turned to Esther. 'From his vantage point on the hill, he must have seen you and I talking together pleasantly that evening, and planned his revenge against me. Geoffrey then proved his true colours on the ride back, for he tricked Margaret with a simple ruse about his horse being lame, and escaped from her charge.'

Esther was in tears. 'Then I am right. It was not you who came to my cottage that night, but your deranged brother...'

Ralph could only stand in mortified silence.

Catherine finally comprehended too, and took Esther's hand. 'You thought that *Ralph* was the father of your child?' That possibility had never occurred to Catherine before, but now she wondered why she had not considered it. She had even been willing to believe that it might have been her own brother who had lain with Esther, yet not the possibility that it might have been Ralph, which showed her how blind she had been in her devotion to her handsome neighbour. Not that Ralph truly was guilty of this sin, as it happened, yet it seemed he had been guilty of even worse things in covering up the wickedness of his mad brother...

Esther wept bitterly on Catherine's shoulder. 'What else was I to think but that it was Ralph who rode up to my door in the twilight? I had spoken with him earlier at the feast, and it seemed like the same man in every respect. He answered to the same name, and he was even dressed in the same riding clothes that I knew so well.'

Ralph spoke up. 'Of course he would. Margaret would have made sure that he was suitably attired with a pair of my own riding breeches and boots.' His voice broke with emotion. 'I am most grievously sorry that I misled you, Esther. When Geoffrey was recaptured by his gaolers, he boasted to me what he had done - that he had impersonated me in order to make the act of darkness with you. I was horrified to hear of it, and could not bear to hear his evil gloating. When it transpired that you were with child, I could see no other option but to take the responsibility for this on my own head. I still thought mainly of my family's reputation, yet I believe that I thought of you too. It seemed better that I, a married man, confess to something that I did not do, than to tell you that my mad brother was the true father of your child.'

Esther was sunk in despair, and sat down at the table with her head in her hands. 'Did your wife know the lamentable truth?'

Ralph nodded. 'Yes, I told her what misery her ill-judged meddling had led to. Yet Margaret chose wilfully not to believe the truth, and half-suspected that it was indeed I who had lain with you, Esther. I should have forced her to stay away from Geoffrey completely after that, yet foolishly I did not. I did however make sure that Geoffrey was not allowed outside his cell again, and Margaret complied fully with this order during the autumn and winter as far as I knew. Yet eventually, after the cold winter was nearly done, she deceived me again. She was still susceptible to Geoffrey's lies and his pretence of geniality, it seems. One fine day in February, she bullied the gullible gaoler into letting him out again to ride with her...'

Catherine was silent but her mind was in turmoil. She was truly more shocked at Ralph's duplicity than with the fact of his mad brother. She had some sympathy for the situation he had found himself in, yet it seemed he had compounded the evil by his overwhelming need to protect his family's good name. Was this truly the same man she had thought to marry? she wondered. For the first time in many years, Catherine saw her handsome neighbour in a less than favourable light, and was even disturbed by his questionable behaviour.   Catherine had a sudden bleak thought at the mention of the month of February for that was when Margaret Warboys had met her tragic end. 'Was Geoffrey riding with Margaret when she died?'

Ralph looked wretched and was full of remorse. 'Yes, he was. He admitted as much to me later when he was caught again, though this was one time that he made no boast of what he had done, and said it had truly been an accident that had killed Margaret. Yet I did not believe him. Even now I do not know for certain what went on that sad day, but I do not credit that Margaret's horse put her foot down a rabbit hole and fell down that bank into the stream. Margaret knew these woods too well for that and was too good a rider to have such an accident. And the horse was completely unhurt after all, when he was found later, wandering alone. I believe that Geoffrey simply tired of his deceiving games with Margaret and wilfully broke her neck when they were out riding together, then threw her body into that stream...'

Even Esther gasped in disbelief at that, although still in a deep despair of her own.

Ralph continued in this grim vein. 'After all this further misery he had caused, I could at least ensure that my evil brother would not escape again. I hired more gaolers to support Mr Cocking, and demanded more vigilance of him in particular.' He grimaced. 'I should have dismissed the man from my service after all his ineptitude and betrayals, yet the man paid a far heavier price for his incompetence in the end than anything I could have done to him. At the end of April, Geoffrey murdered Mr Cocking most horribly, and escaped again from his confinement. This time he was free for two weeks or more, hiding in these woods until my men recaptured him.'

Catherine went white with shock as she realized the truth. 'You mean that your brother murdered Lorna Wanless and Ruth Pilcher too?'

Ralph hung his head in shame. 'I fear so...'

*

Molly thought that she must have walked for ten miles this evening, from the heaviness in her limbs, and the deadness in her feet. Yet she was more concerned about Henry who was still suffering considerably from the results of that fierce blow to his head, and was truly in no fit state to be wandering so far into the woods as darkness fell.

M'sieur Desargues, however, was in fine fettle, and looked even stronger as the evening wore on. Molly had concerns for him too, though it was not for his physical wellbeing, which was clearly not in doubt, but more to do with whether he would be able to get back to Weymouth in time to sail with the *Lapwing*. She had not told Henry of her father's plans, for fear of distracting him from his more urgent mission to find his sister. That rogue Captain Darby would not wait for his French passenger, though, if he were late, and the vessel would no doubt leave on the morning tide as soon as there was sufficient draught in the harbour to get her over the sand bar at the entrance. Molly did not know exactly when that might be, having no knowledge of tides, but her father himself had mentioned that it might be as early as seven o'clock, which meant he had only ten hours to get back to Weymouth and finalize all his affairs.

On this long evening walk through the woods, Molly had found herself for the first time thinking of this gentleman as her true father, perhaps because of the fact that she knew that she would shortly lose him again forever. She reflected on the sad irony that it had taken her seventeen years to discover the true identity of the man who had fathered her, only to see him leave her again so soon. Yet even such melancholy thoughts as these did not tempt her to the notion of fleeing with him to the Americas. Her future, she hoped, was with a greater man than her father would ever be. She could only hope that Henry would survive his ill-considered decision to sail with the King's navy against the Dutch and come back to her in one piece.

Yet although she was not tempted to go with her father, yet he did now seem a much better man than her mother had led her to believe. He might well be a rogue who had treated women badly his whole life, and frittered his family's fortune away, yet he was also a valiant gentleman, as he had shown in frightening off those three footpads who had assaulted Henry. So on this long walk, Molly's thoughts had been equally divided between concerns for her lover, and a growing respect and admiration for her natural father...

Molly had been relieved for Henry's sake in particular when they had finally drawn close to Warboys Hall. Yet that relief had been short-lived when she saw the remnants of the mob assembled in front of the house, and still in wild and unpredictable mood.

Henry looked at Molly with disappointment. 'It seems that we have walked all this way for nothing. Catherine may have brought Esther this far, but she would not have dared to try and gain entry to the house with that mob of ruffians gathered there.'

Molly was disappointed too. 'Then we will never find your sister and this fugitive lady tonight, unless you can think of some other nearby place they might go from here.'

Henry shook his head, and Molly could see that he suffered still from pain and dizziness, which confused his normally clear thinking. 'I cannot think where she would go from here, Molly,' he said emptily. 'In fact, I now begin to doubt that she would come here to Warboys Hall at all.'

M'sieur Desargues tut-tutted. 'Do not despair, sir. I believe your first instinct about your sister was correct, because I can see the clear signs that she was here. Perhaps I should explain,' he went on airily. 'You see, in preparation for my journey to the wilderness of North America, I consulted an Indian gentleman of the Iroquois tribe called Tadodaho who had been brought back to France by some fur trappers, and who provided an interesting diversion for the ladies at King Louis's court because of his muscular body and semi-naked attire. I became a close confidante of this Iroquois savage, who taught me some of his language, and also some of his interesting skills, in particular how to follow the tracks of game in the woods...'

Henry was presently in no mood for her father's smug explanation, Molly could see, and snapped at him. 'Is this of any relevance, sir, to my present problem of finding my sister?'

M'sieur Desargues smiled in the dusky light, and bent down to examine the muddy ground at his feet in more detail. 'I believe it is, sir. Two men and a woman have passed this way recently. They stopped here for a few moments, then turned onto a different track over there. I deduce from the tracks that the lady was wearing very fine leather-soled shoes, while one of the men was very light of build with a small shoe size, therefore was most probably Mistress Linney in her disguise as a boy. From the size of the man's footprints, he must be someone very tall, and also wealthy, I suspect, from the mark of his substantial boots.'

In truth Molly could see nothing at her feet but a mess of muddied footprints so did not know how her father could be so positive in his judgements.

Yet it seemed Henry did not share her doubts, and he acknowledged his thanks to M'sieur Desargues at once. 'I do not know who the gentleman with them might be, but it could be Ralph Warboys who has found them already by some accident,' he declared with enthusiasm. 'If so, then I believe I can guess where he might take them while the rioters are presently encamped around his own house. '

'Where would he take them?' Molly asked. 'Somewhere close, I hope,' she added worriedly, noticing Henry's still weak condition.

Henry indicated to the northwest. 'Two miles from here is the Warboys' former home, an old Norman castle built by their ancestors four centuries ago. I thought it abandoned completely but I am sure that enough of the stonework stands to provide shelter for a few hours at least.' He looked at Molly's father. 'I think you must be right, sir, so we should make speed to find them before night falls.'

Molly regarded Raven worriedly. 'Henry, you can barely stand.'

He smiled back at her woozily. 'My head is spinning still from the blow those ruffians gave me,' he admitted. 'Yet I can still walk, so we must go on. What else is there to do?'

'What else indeed, sir,' M'sieur Desargues said, indicating the way with his right hand.

*

Inside the keep, they had settled down for the night, lying on the straw-covered floor. Catherine had suggested leaving once the moon was high enough to see by, but Ralph would have none of it, knowing his deranged brother was now prowling the woods outside.

Esther had said little for the last hour, but she now asked, 'Are we truly safe here inside the keep, sir? Your brother might return, after all. Is there no way that he could get back into this keep? '

Ralph was lying at the other side of the room from Catherine and Esther, but sat up at this enquiry and shook his head. 'There is no other way but through that door below, which we barred properly. Not even

Geoffrey could get through such a door without a battering ram. So rest soundly, Esther. In any case, I do not think Geoffrey will linger here in the neighbourhood. He will be long gone after killing those three men. He must know that there will be a hue and cry raised now, and he may even choose to flee the country, with the Channel ports so close to hand.'

Suddenly Catherine screamed as she saw a tall figure appear from nowhere from the shadows behind Ralph and strike him fiercely across the back of his head with the blunt end of an axe

'As ever, you misunderstand me, brother,' Geoffrey Warboys said with grim satisfaction as he stepped forward into the light..

# CHAPTER 27

Friday, 19<sup>th</sup> May 1665

Catherine was shocked at how much Geoffrey resembled his brother. It seemed from this startling resemblance almost as if it was Ralph who threatened her and Esther, and Catherine found it difficult to accept that such evil threats could come from a man with the same face as one she had always held in such deep affection.

Catherine and Esther had both leapt to their feet at his sudden appearance, and now cowered together against a wall while Geoffrey strode backwards and forwards in triumph. Catherine wanted to go and minister to the stricken Ralph who had not made a move or a sound since his brother had struck him down so malevolently. But Geoffrey would not allow it, even after going down to the ground floor and opening the main door to see if anyone else might be out there. 'If he is not already dead, then let him bleed to death slowly,' he said on his return. 'It seems only a fitting punishment after all. He left me here to rot all these years in this filthy place, and now he has compounded the hurt he did me with his sickening speech today. From my secret hiding place on the roof, I was forced to listen to his tiresome cant for the last hour, while he blackened my name and made me out to be some sort of evil monster.'

Surprisingly it was Esther who spoke up boldly in Ralph's defence. 'He was merely telling us the truth, I believe, although I for one wish that he told us it much sooner...'

Geoffrey interrupted her harshly. 'It was not the truth! Do you really think that I killed Ralph's wife Margaret? What reason would I have for that? She was my one ally against Ralph. No, it was not I who killed Margaret, but Ralph himself, for many reasons of his own...'

Catherine wanted to shout her denial of this absurd accusation, but Esther was still in full flow, and clearly gave no more credence to this charge than Catherine did. 'You lie, sir…! As for imprisoning you here,' Esther went on, 'he was simply protecting the rest of us from your evil ways. He could have had you quietly put to death as you deserved. But his ties of blood with you precluded that solution, so he did his best to keep you alive in tolerable comfort. All in all, you should be grateful for such a considerate brother. It is truly much more than you deserve. '

Surprisingly to Catherine, Geoffrey Warboys did not take further offence at this show of defiance. Instead he came towards the two of them, looking so much like his brother at close quarters that Catherine could only blink in amazement at the evil and sordid threats coming from his mouth. 'What have they done to all your beautiful hair, sweet Esther?' he demanded critically. 'I would not have touched you that night if you had looked as drab and mannish as this when I came to your cottage. Yet we made such fine sport together, did we not? Shall we not do it again now, and invite Ralph's betrothed to join us in this wanton pleasure?' He laughed at the expression of disgust on Esther's face, but also at her clear surprise. 'Ah, I see that you do not know that Ralph has pledged himself secretly to your dear "sister" here,' he added shrewdly. 'That is why he killed his wife Margaret, in order to free himself from the burden of a barren wife, and to allow him to marry a fresh young bride. Unfortunately for you, dear Esther, you were no longer quite so fresh any more after our night of sport together, therefore could not compete in Ralph's mind with the intact maidenhead of Mistress Raven here. My father thought that I was the mad one, yet Ralph is madder than I could ever be…'

Catherine looked at him with contempt. 'I believe you not, you foul devil!'

Geoffrey merely laughed. 'Foul devil, is it? Well this foul devil intends to break the glass of your virginity too, as I did with Mistress Linney here, so that Ralph will know that I had the pleasure of both of his women before him and his pathetic little horn.' With that Geoffrey grabbed Esther by the hair and began to rip the boy's jerkin from her. 'Let us rid you of that unflattering boy's costume first, Esther, and reveal the female charms that lie beneath.' Yet Esther fought back like a wildcat, and gave as good as she got, so that Geoffrey soon sported deep scratches on his face.

Geoffrey's mind was so engaged in this fierce struggle with Esther that Catherine was able to slip away from under his threshing arms. She quickly scoured the chamber looking for a suitable weapon from the stack in the corner, but her eyes alighted first on the axe that Geoffrey had used on Ralph, which lay on the floor next to Ralph's still insensible body. Catherine picked up the axe at once and came at Geoffrey with a rush from behind, with the blade raised to strike his shoulder blade. Esther was still putting up a fierce resistance to having her clothes ripped from her body, so that Geoffrey seemed entirely unaware that Catherine was approaching quickly behind him. Yet the axe was such a heavy and cumbersome weapon that Catherine's strength proved inadequate to wield it with any real venom. She did manage to land a blow of sorts with the axe blade on his shoulder, yet the force was insufficient to penetrate his flesh, or even his leather jerkin. Yet the blow took him by sufficient surprise to throw him off balance for a moment, and she was able to follow it up with another sharper cut with the blade to his legs which finally knocked him off his feet. Yet he was not even remotely hurt, Catherine could see, and he would soon be on his feet again to terrorise them.

Catherine instantly dropped the axe, grabbed Esther by the arm and escaped with her through the doorway into the staircase. Breathing heavily, and both in a deep panic, they stumbled up the stone steps in the darkness to the next level, and to a doorway which brought them out onto the roof. They could hear Geoffrey already mounting the steps behind them, so Catherine quickly barred the door behind them - and not a moment too soon, as she heard Geoffrey instantly pounding the other side with his angry fists.

Catherine made a quick circuit of the roof to see if there was any other way down. The forest all around them was a sea of pitch blackness, with not a single light showing. Yet Catherine was relieved to see that the old moon was just rising in the east above the treeline, and providing enough faint light on the roof of the keep to see by. That light was sufficient to show however that there was no way down except by the stairs; the outer walls of the keep were smooth and vertical, with no projections or niches at all that could be used to help them climb down.

Esther and Catherine both jumped in alarm as they heard a more massive blow on the other side of the door.

Catherine cursed to herself in a most unladylike manner. 'That was stupid of me to leave the axe behind! We are done for.'

Esther clung to her. 'Perhaps the door will hold even against an axe. The oak looked very strong despite its immense age.'

Yet even as Esther said these hopeful words, Catherine heard the wood splintering under the fierce blows of the axe, and knew that Geoffrey would soon be through that door. Yet she made light of it, speaking defiantly. 'Even if he gets through, we will still deal with him together, Esther, just as we did below.'

Esther and Catherine retreated to the farthest, and darkest, corner of the roof, just as they heard the sound of the door finally yielding to Geoffrey's axe, before being pushed contemptuously aside by this maniac.

He found their obvious hiding place within a few seconds, as if he had the eyes of a bat after all his years imprisoned here. This time he seemed determined to take out his evil anger on Catherine first rather than Esther, although, from his wild behaviour, it was clearly going to be a swift bloody retribution for her defiance rather than a violation of her body. He pulled Catherine from her hiding place by her hair, and threw her again to the ground. Catherine felt a massive blow to her head as she fell, so that she was badly dazed. Then, pinning her half-conscious body to the ground with his heavy boot, Geoffrey Warboys raised his axe to dismember her limb from limb...

A sudden warning cough behind him stopped Geoffrey from bringing the axe down however, and he turned in astonishment to discover the origin of this unexpected sound.

Catherine, her heart pounding fit to burst, and her mind seized with the terror of the moment, looked up from her trapped position on the ground and saw a tall figure standing on the roof in the dim moonlight. The newcomer was holding a pistol in his right hand and had it trained on Geoffrey Warboys' heart.

Catherine heard the newcomer's voice too, and it was one that gave her some hope since it was a sardonic voice without any trace of fear. 'That is not gentlemanly behaviour, sir, so I must ask you to desist with the axe, and release that poor lady from her demeaning position.'

Geoffrey could not hide his astonishment. 'Who are you, sir?'

The man bowed slightly. 'I am Philippe Desargues, Comte de Mésanger, sir, at your service. Now, please put down the axe or I will be forced to put a lead ball through your wicked heart,' he said with a more baleful note.

Geoffrey now proved his madness beyond doubt to Catherine because he simply ignored the pistol trained on him at ten paces, and charged the Frenchman (for such Catherine took the newcomer to be, from his name.)

Catherine watched in dismay as she saw Geoffrey throw his axe at the Frenchman, just as the newcomer fired his pistol in return. The pistol ball clearly hit Geoffrey somewhere on his person, but certainly not in the heart, for he continued unchecked in his run at his assailant.

As for M'sieur Desargues, the blade of the axe had struck him hard in the side of the ribs, drawing a gasp of pain, before forcing him to his knees. In a second, Geoffrey was on top of him, with the axe recovered and again raised in his hands, and about to dispatch the Frenchman to eternity.

But then Catherine saw someone else arrive on the roof seemingly from nowhere too, this time a servant girl with, bizarrely, a cutlass in her hand who circled quietly around the two fighting men. With a fierce scream, the maid suddenly raised her blade and ran Geoffrey through with it from behind with a force that nearly lifted him off his feet.

Geoffrey Warboys looked down in disbelief at the blade of the cutlass which had penetrated right through his body and now stuck out six inches through his chest, dripping with his own blood. He tried to turn to see his assailant, but, impaled on the blade, could not perform even that simple task, and instead took a few jerky steps towards the battlements. Catherine could not be sure whether what happened next was deliberate intent on the man's part, or simply the result of a lack of bodily coordination caused by his terrible wound. But regardless of the cause, Geoffrey Warboys simply toppled over the battlements in silence to land a second later on the cobbles below with an ugly sound of tearing flesh.

Catherine was too weak with shock even to attempt to get to her feet, yet her wits were sufficiently recovered from her ordeal now to notice that the servant girl went to the aid of the fallen Frenchman first. And Catherine was sure that she heard the Frenchman say gratefully in return, 'Thank you, *ma petite fille*, for your timely arrival...'

# CHAPTER 28

Saturday, 20<sup>th</sup> May 1665

Henry Raven had listened in astonishment to what his sister had told him of her adventures tonight, and of the violent conclusion. After their ordeal, she and Esther had soon returned from the roof of the keep to the floor below, where Raven, just arriving from below, had found them in a state of great distress.

Raven was recovered enough by now from his own blow on the head to examine Ralph Warboys, who was still dead to the world an hour after he had been struck by his evil brother. Yet Raven had discovered from his regular breathing and normal heartbeat that Ralph seemed not to be in mortal danger, and in fact showed signs of imminently recovering consciousness. From what he had understood from his sister's distraught account of this sad business, Raven was now as disenchanted with Ralph Warboys as Catherine, for, although none of this evil was Ralph's doing directly, yet it seemed that he could have prevented his mad brother's wicked deeds if he had shown less concern for the welfare of his family's reputation, and more for the common good. Whatever happened now, the reputation of his family would be forever mired in scandal, even if no criminal charges could be laid at Ralph's door directly.

After Raven had seen Ralph made comfortable on the truckle bed, which was done more from his duty as a physician than from any remaining compassion that he felt for an old friend, he returned to the rest of the party. He saw with admiration that Catherine had recovered quickly from her ordeal and was much more like her normal self again. Esther, on the other hand, had not been so distraught as Catherine, yet neither was she recovered to her former character, being withdrawn in manner and refusing to speak other than in monosyllables. Yet Raven could hardly blame her after everything she had been through; in fact it was a wonder to him that her spirit still survived at all after these terrible trials in her life. Therefore he did not press her to speak, but decided to leave her in peace for the moment, hopefully to recover some of her former spirit and character in time.

Instead he went and sat with his sister again in the hope of getting some greater understanding of events. After a calmer Catherine had explained the whole convoluted story again in more detail, Raven took a few moments to collect his thoughts. 'And Ralph's brother, Geoffrey, has been alive all these years? I can scarce believe it!' he said finally in wonder, although it was hardly a question since the evidence of his battered corpse in the bailey below could not be denied.

Molly, who was sitting on the floor in another corner of the chamber and tending to her injured father, overheard Raven's discussion with his sister, and spoke up. 'Until I finished him, Henry, for throwing that axe so wilfully at my father,' she said without apology. ''Tis fortunate that I picked up that sword in this chamber when I came past, otherwise the outcome would have been far more tragic than it was.'

Raven looked at Molly in bemused wonder that she should be taking things so calmly. 'I should not have allowed you and M'sieur Desargues to go into this keep after we discovered those three murdered bodies below.'

Molly gave him a tart look. 'What else could we do when we heard those sounds of terror and mayhem from above? And you were still in no fit state to rush up those stairs.' She glanced at Catherine. 'It is as well we did go, otherwise your fair sister would be dead now, Henry, as well as Mistress Linney.'

Esther finally aroused herself from her withdrawn mood at this moment and went over to Molly to commend her for her bravery. 'Please accept my deepest gratitude for my own life, which you doubtless saved by your action. I doubt that anyone will blame you for taking that man's life, Mistress. Therefore I trust that you will lose no sleep over what you have done: it was just and merciful to end that worthless man's life that way. Would to God that he had dispatched his own victims so quickly and so mercifully!'

Molly climbed to her feet, and nodded gratefully in return. 'I shall not lose any sleep indeed, Mistress Linney. My conscience is a most pliable thing when it comes to protecting my own, and will certainly not trouble me over a dispatching a devil like that,' she said firmly, before returning to tending M'sieur Desargues's wound.

Listening to this lively interchange, Raven could not but reflect on Esther's particular suffering at the hands of Geoffrey Warboys. Although it seemed that he had murdered many poor souls, yet Geoffrey Warboys' action towards Esther had perhaps been the most reprehensible of all his heinous crimes, in taking his brother's place to make love to her. Raven thought that poor Esther must be in renewed torture after discovering the true identity of her baby's father, which must have been a grim revelation to her indeed.

Catherine leaned over in her seat at this point, and whispered in Raven's ear. 'You know this brave servant girl, Henry?'

Raven smiled faintly and kept his voice low so that Molly would not hear it from the far side of the room. 'I do, sister. That is my lady, Molly Titchen, who, if I remember, was the object of much hurtful derision from you during my last visit to Dorset.'

Catherine glanced at Molly in astonishment but said only begrudgingly, 'Then she is not what I expected, brother…'

*

Later Raven went and sat on the floor with Molly and her father while he checked his injury again. Molly was concerned anew for her father after seeing the nature of his wound, but Raven again calmed her immediate worries. 'The blade of the axe caught him only a glancing blow, Molly. The cut is long but not deep, and has not damaged any vital organs or blood vessels. He will not die from this.'

'Ay, this gentleman is right. 'Tis a flesh wound only, Molly,' M'sieur Desargues said in agreement. 'I have had worse insect bites.'

Molly was not convinced. 'Yet will it not grow gangrenous quickly enough if it is not cleaned properly and stitched, Henry?'

Raven gave M'sieur Desargues a wry look as he got to his feet. 'This is what comes of allowing Molly to read my medical texts. But you are right, Molly, that your father needs the wound stitched and cleaned, and I shall ensure that it is done properly as soon as we can get him back to Salwayash Manor.'

Molly helped M'sieur Desargues slowly to his feet, which caused him to make a grimace of pain. 'I am most grateful to you, sir,' he said. 'But I am not sure that I have time to go with you to Salwayash Manor.'

'Why not, sir? What business do you have elsewhere that is so pressing? I would like you and Molly to be my guests at Salwayash Manor for as long as you wish.'

M'sieur Desargues smiled tiredly. 'I would be most grateful for such hospitality in normal circumstances, sir, but on this occasion I must decline. I must make my way to the port of Weymouth before dawn.'

Raven blinked. 'Why, sir?'

M'sieur Desargues glanced at Molly. 'I leave for America on the morning tide, sir.'

Molly touched Raven's arm. ''Tis true, Henry. My father leaves Europe forever to start a new life in North America. He wanted me to go with him into this wild land of red savages, but I told him that it is impossible since my first loyalty must be to you always.'

Raven was touched by the genuine emotion in her voice, and squeezed her arm affectionately in return, before addressing M'sieur Desargues again. 'Then you must still come back to Salwayash Manor, sir. Hopefully the mob will be long gone by now and we can get one of the carriages from the stables to take you to Weymouth in time to make your vessel. It is only five miles or so back to the manor, while it is twenty or more if you want to walk directly to Weymouth from here, even if you could find your way, which is by no means certain. We will set off for Salwayash Manor as soon as the moon is high enough to light our way home, sir, so we should certainly be able to get you back to Weymouth by dawn.'

M'sieur Desargues bowed deeply. 'Then I am even more grateful, sir.'

Raven shook his head. 'Do not bow your head to me, sir. It is I who should bow to you. You saved my life earlier today. And now you have done me a greater service by rescuing my sister and my dear Esther from an even more terrible fate...'

*

Raven left Molly and her father for a minute as a worried Catherine beckoned him over into a private corner. She glanced at Esther who stood in the centre of the chamber in melancholy silence. 'Henry, that angry mob still looks for Esther, so it is truly safe for us to return to the manor house with her just yet?'

Raven tried to reassure his sister, though he was not completely convinced himself. 'I am sure the mob has long since been dispersed by the militia, sister. And I would hope that some wiser and cooler heads in the neighbourhood will have reflected on the madness of what that mob has done, and will take urgent steps to punish the ringleaders, especially that Pollock woman for inciting them so. Therefore Esther should be safe at the manor for the time being. I will speak to the magistrate tomorrow to tell him the truth about her, but I suspect he will be far more interested in the wicked murders of Geoffrey Warboys than in Esther's sad business.'

Catherine accepted her brother's judgement for the present, but still seemed doubtful. She turned her head slowly and inspected Molly with close attention again as she tended to M'sieur Desargues. 'Is this truly your fine painted actress, brother? How did she come here of all places?' she whispered in bemusement.

'She came to Dorset to see me, of course, before I go off to war.'

Catherine reflected on that. 'I would never have taken that maid for an actress, Henry. She seems more like a simple servant girl in that garb, if a very pretty one. Yet she also seems more intelligent and braver than I had imagined for one of these creatures who parade themselves so wantonly on the stage.' She frowned as she took note of Molly's particular care for M'sieur Desargues. 'And what is that French gentleman to her, Henry? They seem a very close and affectionate couple,' she said suspiciously. 'Is he a rival for her affections?'

'What an absurd imagination you have to think such a thing, sister!' Raven said without a trace of irony. 'That French gentleman is her father, and the man, need I remind you, who saved your life not an hour ago.' Raven could see that his sister was slightly abashed at this rebuttal, and decided to press home his advantage. 'He is a French count, it seems, therefore Molly has as much noble blood in her veins as us, sister...*and possibly more*,' he added tartly...

*

Although the moon has risen well above the horizon by now, Ralph Warboys was still not well enough to walk yet, so Raven decided to delay their departure for a few minutes more to give him time to get some strength back in his limbs. Now that Ralph was fully conscious again, Raven had spoken a few words to him and told him that his brother was dead, which seemed to provoke only a great relief in Ralph's mind. But Raven had also told Ralph of his personal disappointment with him over his deceitful conduct. He had made it clear to Ralph that there was no question now of Catherine ever being allowed to marry him, even if she still wanted to.

Ralph had looked sorely disappointed at this, but made no protest. 'I did not know that you were aware of our plans, Henry, and I apologize for keeping them secret from you. Yet I doubt whether Catherine will ever speak to me again, never mind marry me, Henry. And I can hardly blame her for that rejection; I have made most grievous and wretched errors of judgement in my life so I deserve the opprobrium that will undoubtedly fall on me as a result of this dreadful business.'

Raven made no further comment, but went and talked privately to Molly, away from the rest of the party who were dozing on the floor with fatigue. He took her hand and stroked her fingers. 'Your father is a remarkable and brave man, Molly. It is sad indeed that he now intends to leave you forever. Can you not persuade him to stay and perhaps make his future life here in England?'

Molly smiled sadly. 'I do not think that is possible, Henry. Yet I thank you for suggesting it. I am sad to see my father go, because I still do not truly know him, and would have liked to have more time to get to know his character properly. Yet he does seem to be a most remarkable man in his courage at least, for which virtue in a father I am duly grateful. Yet, if you ask me, I believe that I would rather have had a kindly and unremarkable father who had been with me throughout my life to support me, than a remarkable father who simply abandoned me at birth. So, in my heart I still feel like the child of the simple draper Samuel Titchen, and his good wife Mary, who saved my life as a babe with her last selfless act.'

Raven squeezed her hand tightly and then, making sure that his sister was not looking in their direction, kissed Molly firmly on the lips. 'You have a good and wise head on those young shoulders. I am sure that the Titchens would be most proud, if they were to see the fine woman you have become, Molly…'

*

Esther Linney was not asleep, even though her eyelids were closed, and she could hear clearly the sweet words that Henry spoke with his actress friend, even though they kept their voices low and discreet. Esther owed her life to this girl Molly Titchen, therefore could not be too hard on her because she had won the affections of the man she had always dreamed of. They did make a handsome if unlikely couple, she was forced to admit to herself.

Yet she could not help but wonder why Henry could not have given his heart to her instead. How different her life would be now, if that had happened! Esther had always thought that her own lowly birth was the greatest obstacle between her and Henry, yet it seemed not to be the case, for this girl Molly had no great station in life and seemed to have won Henry's affection merely by her sweet nature and lively wit.

Esther felt a great melancholy descend on her like a shroud, so that for a moment she felt as if she was being suffocated. It had been bad enough to know that the man who had fathered her child had no real affection for her. Yet it was infinitely worse to discover that the man she had lain with had been an evil and violent murderer with the blood of many innocent souls on his withered conscience.

In this dark place, it seemed to Esther that the desolation of her life was complete, and now she wanted only to be gone from this sordid world of death and despair...

*

Raven judged that Ralph Warboys was finally in a fit enough condition to walk, at least as far as his own home Warboys Hall, which was but a mile distant, so he made the party ready to leave the keep.

Catherine, Molly and M'sieur Desargues roused themselves from their half sleep, and got their small possessions together in preparation to leave. Ralph was on his feet too, and there was a moment of supreme awkwardness when he came face to face with Catherine, and seemed about to say something conciliatory. But Catherine cut him dead and would not even look him in the face, so that Henry Raven even felt some small trace of sympathy for Ralph Warboys in his disgrace.

Esther seemed to be fast asleep in the corner now next to the stack of weapons kept by Geoffrey Warboys' gaolers. But when Raven went to rouse her, he found that she was in fact wide awake and merely staring at the blank stone wall with huge sad eyes. Eventually she sat up and tried to smile at Raven, but he could not smile back given the pain and sorrow in her haunted face.

302

As she got slowly to her feet, Ralph came over and gallantly offered her his hand, but Esther refused it with a show of simmering anger. Now standing to her full height, she stared at him accusingly. 'You should have told me at once, sir, that it was your deranged brother who had visited me that day. I am tainted forever now because of your lies and deceit.' Esther narrowed her eyes. 'Tell me, sir, did you truly murder your wife in order that you might marry Catherine, as your brother claimed?'

Ralph coloured under this attack. 'Nay, of course that is not true. I am sure that my mad brother did it himself; if not, then it must have been an accident after all. How can you accuse me of such a thing, Esther?' he asked with deep mortification, conscious perhaps that Catherine stood so close by, listening to every word of this bitter exchange. 'I can only beg your forgiveness again, Esther, for not telling you the truth about what happened to you. And I feel great shame too that I did not come forward to speak at your trial and give the evidence that would have cleared you...' Ralph stopped in mid-sentence as if he realized that he had apparently said too much.

Esther frowned. 'How could you possibly clear me, sir, even if you had come forward? No one knows the truth of what happened that day when my baby died...' She gasped aloud as a shocking realization came to her. 'Yet I see in your eyes that you do know the truth!' Esther turned to Raven to explain. 'You remember, Henry, that I told you that a carriage had just passed my cottage before I found my baby dead.' She turned back angrily to Ralph Warboys. 'That was *your* carriage, sir, was it not? How could I have not seen it before? You were on your way to see me that day, were you not? No one else would have gone to that remote cottage in such a grand carriage...'

Ralph shook with emotion. 'I came only to see how you were in your new home, Esther. I swear that I had no malicious aim in mind.'

Esther was relentless in her blinding anger. 'Yet you did not stop your carriage at the front door of the cottage and get out there, did you? You went past and got out of your carriage around the next bend in the lane - to be out of sight of any curious neighbours, I suppose. I wonder at the need for such a devious approach, though, unless it was I that you hoped to avoid. I was standing at the front of the cottage just after your carriage passed, and I did not see you, sir, so you must have come unseen to the side door of the cottage.'

Ralph lowered his head. 'I did,' he admitted uneasily.

Raven was tempted to intervene to stop this, but did not as he was as curious as everyone else to hear Ralph's explanation of what he had done at Esther's cottage.

Esther confronted him. 'You came in through the side door, and you smothered my child in his cradle, did you not? I had some suspicions of your integrity before when you did not appear to help me at my trial, yet I thought it just the natural reticence of a wealthy and important man. I did not believe that you could have smothered your own child. *But your mad brother's child?* That is a different matter. That you would do gladly...'

Raven and Catherine looked on aghast, almost willing Ralph to deny this terrible accusation. Yet Ralph made no denial, and tried instead to take Esther's hand, but she shrugged it away contemptuously. 'I did not do it gladly, but with great pain. And it was done for *you*, Esther,' he pleaded, 'to save you the years of misery ahead! I swear when I looked at that child in his cradle that I saw my brother's madness in his eyes, Esther. And here God had given me the opportunity to right the terrible wrong that my family had done to you.'

Esther gasped in disbelief. 'You would right a wrong by killing an innocent child? Your brother was right – you are madder than him...!' With that she ran in distress to the darkened corner of the chamber.

Raven thought that she must have gone there to shed private bitter tears, and looked at Ralph more in sorrow than disgust that a man whom he had considered to be so noble in spirit should do such a wicked thing. He and the others stood in shocked silence around Ralph, as the tortured man put his head in his hands.

Raven did not know what to do next, but glanced over to the corner of the room where Esther had gone. Yet she was no longer there, and Raven was suddenly beset with a feeling of impending disaster as he noticed the stockpile of weapons in the corner where she had been...

Suddenly, Esther reappeared from nowhere brandishing a dagger, and leapt into the centre of the room. Raven tried despairingly to make a grab for her arm when he realized what she had in mind, but still suffering from his recent blow to the head, his reactions were unequal to the task and she easily evaded him. As if in a nightmare, Raven then saw Esther plunge the dagger deep into Ralph Warboys' heart, who collapsed to the floor in a welter of blood...

# CHAPTER 29

Saturday, 20ᵗʰ May 1665

In the aftermath, Esther seemed unnaturally calm as she looked around the assembly of shocked faces. 'What else could I do?' she asked them all wearily. 'This monster killed my baby, and then stood by while I was accused of it. I care not what the law does to me now, but natural justice had to be done.'

Raven was distraught at this even sadder turn of events. He had examined Ralph to see what could be done for him, but the man had been dead before he even hit the floor, given the severity of the dagger wound, which had penetrated deep through the ribs, and ripped both ventricle chambers of the heart.

Surprisingly it was Molly who moved first to comfort Esther. Putting her arms around her, she said consolingly, 'No one can blame you, Mistress Linney, for what you did to the man who killed your child.' She looked searchingly at Henry for support. 'If Esther is guilty of wilful murder, then I am too, for I did precisely the same to this man's deranged brother, did I not?'

Raven did not truly think the circumstances were precisely the same, yet he nodded his assent. 'I am sure that neither case can be regarded as wilful murder, but as legitimate cases of self-defence. We will take the bodies in time to the magistrate Sir Malcolm Batcock, and I shall try and explain these sad events to him.'

Catherine seemed also remarkably calm now, Raven thought, considering that she had just seen the man that she had recently loved so well stabbed to death. She gripped her brother's arm. 'We must think carefully on this, brother, and what to tell the magistrate. I believe that the law will hang Esther, if we recount truthfully what we saw here.'

M'sieur Desargues stepped forward. 'I know little of English law, except that it seems to be arbitrary and unfair, and often unjust in its judgements. Therefore I have to regretfully concur with this fair lady here –' he bowed extravagantly to Catherine despite his still obvious discomfort from his wound – ' that the law in this blighted country may well choose to see this as wilful murder rather an act of self-defence. That is, unless we all agree to change the facts a little. I propose that what happened here went as follows: the mad brother killed both his gaolers and then his sane brother.' He bowed to Esther now with an apologetic smile. 'I use the term "sane" only in the comparative sense, of course, Mam'selle. Ralph clearly was near as mad as his brother...'

Raven was grateful for the suggestion, which seemed the most sensible way out of this dilemma. 'And what of Geoffrey Warboys? Who killed him?'

M'sieur Desargues laughed. 'Well, not a mere slip of a girl, that is certain!' He laughed even louder at Molly's pained expression, before giving her cheek an affectionate touch. ''Tis better this way, Molly. I will take the credit from you for killing the mad brother, which I would have done anyway, if I could. I will be gone forever from this benighted country in a few hours, so it will be no hurt to my reputation if you say that I killed this madman. I doubt that anyone will follow me to the New World in pursuit, because of it.'

Esther suddenly spoke up sharply, her face animated again. 'I must be gone from this country too! Can you get passage to the New World for me too, sir?'

M'sieur Desargues bowed to her again, though his expression was wary. 'I am sure that can be arranged with the captain of the vessel, Madam, if you truly wish it. I would be honoured to make the arrangements, and to have your company on the voyage. But are you sure that you know what you do? North America is a wild and untamed land...'

'Yet there are many English colonies there, are there not, where I might start a new life?' Esther asked eagerly.

Before M'sieur Desargues could answer, though, Catherine interrupted with a question of her own. 'Why do you want to leave this country, Esther? With this story we have agreed, there is no need for you to be a fugitive again.' She glanced at Raven for support for her argument. 'We could even obtain a full pardon for you on the charge of murdering your own child, because we here can all swear that we heard Ralph's full confession to that wicked deed.'

Esther shook her head dolefully. 'People like Mistress Pollock will never give me any peace here, I fear. I will always feel like a fugitive in my own land now. Also there are too many enduring sad memories for me here, which will drag down my heart with their weight and cause me endless misery. Therefore, if I am to survive all that has happened and prosper again, then I believe that it must be elsewhere.'

Raven took Esther's hand. 'Perhaps it is the wisest course, dear Esther, if this is truly what you want. Yet I do not like you to go alone to such a fearsome wilderness.'

M'sieur Desargues stepped in. 'Worry not over that point, sir. I will look after her on the voyage, and also ensure that she is taken care of on arrival in the colony of New York.'

Raven looked worriedly at Esther still. 'Yes, but what of later, sir, when you are gone from New York into the interior? Who will take care of Esther then?'

Esther withdrew her hand from Raven's and tried to smile. 'I am not a child, Henry, not after the troubles I have been through. Whatever tribulations I may face in America can scarce be worse than those I have been subject to in my own homeland. And, in truth, 'tis time that I took control of my own life again, Henry.'

Raven was about to make further response to this when he heard the sound of footsteps on the stairs of the keep. He looked around in alarm, yet his relief was palpable when he saw that the newcomer was his manservant Martin.

Martin looked around in wonder at the scene before his eyes, and particularly at the bloodied corpse on the floor. 'What evil goes on here, Master?' he asked breathlessly.

Raven gave him as short an explanation as he could, which only astonished Martin even more. 'How did you find us here, Martin?' Raven wanted to know.

Martin was still heavily distracted. 'Late in the evening, the militia finally arrived at the manor and dispersed that ugly mob in a few minutes. They arrested half-a-dozen of the ringleaders in the skirmish that followed, before releasing me and the rest of your household. The manor is looted inside, but is not beyond repair. As soon as I was free, I discussed matters with Mistress Bagwell, who suggested that you and the Mistress might have gone to Warboys Hall for refuge. I went there by carriage at once and asked for you, but you had not been there, as the house had been besieged by some of the mob too until an hour before. But as I returned home this way, I saw a distant light in these old ruins, so wondered if you might have taken temporary refuge here instead.'

Raven clapped a thankful hand on his shoulder. 'You have a carriage near here?'

Martin nodded. 'I left it tethered to a tree on the nearest road, but it is only a quarter mile walk from here. It is only the small carriage, though, Master, but five should be able to squeeze inside, I am sure.'

Raven looked around the assembled party. 'Then we will all go at once, and get away from this evil place. Our first destination will be the manor, but then some of us need to go on to Weymouth this very night, Martin.'

Martin frowned. 'Who will go to Weymouth, Master?'

Raven gave him a wry look in response. 'That is a good question, Martin. Who indeed...?'

\*

Standing on the quay wall at Weymouth with Molly and M'sieur Desargues, Raven shivered in the half light of dawn. Overhead the stars were fading a little as the black of night turned to purple, and a thin sliver of yellow sky blossomed into a rosette above the eastern horizon. The coming dawn had also brought a fresh wind blowing in off the dark green sea, so there seemed little doubt that M'sieur Desargues's vessel, the *Lapwing*, would be able to leave with the high tide in an hour or so.

Martin had driven them here in the carriage from Salwayash Manor, and, with enough moonlight to light the way, had made good time and got them here a full hour before dawn. Catherine had stayed behind to take charge at the manor, and there she had said a tearful farewell to Esther, which had been a hard thing for Raven to witness with equanimity. Esther had dressed again as a maid for her journey, and her cropped hair was now concealed beneath a dark and lustrous wig that had been worn regularly by Raven's mother in her later years, when her own hair had become prematurely white with grief over the loss of her husband. Catherine had also packed a chest for Esther with as many of her own suitable clothes and other useful possessions as she could manage to fit in.

Once at the port, M'sieur Desargues had gone immediately on board the *Lapwing* to talk with Captain Darby (though it was still an hour before dawn), and an arrangement had been made with him for Esther to travel to New York too. Esther would have to share a small cabin with two other intrepid young ladies who were making their way to the New World, yet Raven was disappointed to see that this likely discomfort did not cause any waver in her determination to leave these shores forever.

Now, at first light, Martin had taken Esther into the town to buy whatever other provisions he could find for her journey, even though it would mean waking up shopkeepers from their beds. Yet Raven had given Martin a large bag of gold sovereigns to ease these shopkeepers' ire at being roused so early from their slumbers, so he was sure that Esther would be able to obtain most things that she needed for the journey and for her coming life, despite the limited time available. Raven had pressed a considerable sum in gold into her own hands too, and, despite her protests, had forced her to take it as a condition of bringing her here to Weymouth.

Raven had not accompanied Esther and Martin on their shop expedition though, and had chosen to stay instead with Molly and M'sieur Desargues on a quiet corner of the quayside while they said their sad farewells too. Raven was still worried that, in a fit of daughterly sentiment, she might change her mind and leave on the *Lapwing* too, which was in truth his main reason for not leaving her alone with M'sieur Desargues for too long. Although M'sieur Desargues had proved himself a most gallant gentleman in the last twenty four hours, Raven was still not sure that he trusted him entirely.

Molly finally embraced M'sieur Desargues as they said their last whispered words to each other. Yet just as M'sieur Desargues made to leave, they were all surprised to see a most unexpected visitor walking along the quay wall from the direction of town.

Raven recognized Madam Celia Hornett at once, despite the fact that the sun was not properly up yet, and the pre-dawn light insufficient to penetrate the deep shadows on the quayside. Molly was the most astonished of all, though, at seeing her mother here, of all places. 'What business brings you here, Mother?' she asked worriedly, as Celia came closer.

Celia stepped forward into the pool of light from a nearby lantern, so that finally they could see her face properly. Raven was bemused to see that she addressed M'sieur Desargues first rather than her daughter, though. 'I came to warn you, sir, that an evil individual called Senor de Santiago is in pursuit of you, and knows you will be boarding that vessel yonder soon.' Now that the light of the lantern shone full on Celia's face, Raven saw with astonishment that her eyes were red with weeping, which distressing aspect of her countenance was not something he had seen before in the worldly Mistress Hornett. She finally turned to Molly and embraced her daughter tightly. 'This foreign villain murdered poor dear Marion before my very eyes, not two days ago.' She cast an accusing look back at M'sieur Desargues. 'As usual, you have brought only misery and evil into my life, sir.'

M'sieur Desargues was contrite. 'I am most dreadfully sorry, Celia…and I thank you most heartily for coming here to warn me…'

Celia wiped her streaming eyes with a handkerchief. 'I did not come here for your sake, sir! If it had only been your life at risk, I would have gladly let this villain catch you and slit your throat from ear to ear too. Yet I love my daughter too much, and knew she would be here to see you off, and therefore in harm's way from this foul murderer…' Celia gasped in alarm as she saw a tall imposing figure step out suddenly from behind a stack of barrels and fishing nets twenty paces away. The man regarded them in ominous silence, and from his belligerent stance clearly intended to block their way to the *Lapwing*, which was berthed at the seaward end of this same quay wall.

The newcomer finally unsheathed his sword, which he then pointed at M'sieur Desargues. 'Your warning is too late, Madam,' the man said starkly. 'But provided you and your daughter stand aside with this other gentleman here, and do not interfere, then I may let you all live. And since you, Madam, seem to have no great regard for the Comte de Mésanger, you may even enjoy the spectacle of seeing me cut this gentleman's tongue out as a bloody souvenir of our encounter...'

# CHAPTER 30

Saturday, 20<sup>th</sup> May 1665

Raven quickly moved Molly and her mother a safe distance away from M'sieur Desargues and his frightening opponent and ordered them both sternly to wait there. Yet he himself immediately ignored the stark warning given him by this villain de Santiago and returned to M'sieur Desargues's side. Raven had been tempted to go and look quickly for some officer of the local Watch on his rounds of the port, but this quiet area of the quayside seemed entirely deserted of life at this hour, so Raven suspected that this unequal contest would be finished long before he could ever return with help.

M'sieur Desargues eyed de Santiago warily, who was still standing patiently a bare twenty paces away and blocking his way to the distant end of the quay wall where the *Lapwing* was berthed. Raven saw that the vessel was presently taking on the last of its cargo and provisions in readiness to set sail, yet he dared not call out for help from the crew either for fear of arousing this dangerous villain into immediate hostilities. 'Perhaps this gentleman can be persuaded with a generous bribe to let us all pass?' he suggested hopefully under his breath to M'sieur Desargues, seeing that de Santiago seemed to be in no great hurry to begin the fight.

M'sieur Desargues grunted cynically. 'Not he, sir,' he whispered. 'He waits merely for the light to get better, so that he can see properly to do his bloody work of butchery. He wishes to exact revenge for all the irritation and trouble that I have caused him in his search, and no doubt wants to cause Molly great distress too for her defiance towards him. Therefore, with her to witness this, he will make this revenge as bloody and painful for me as he can, no doubt. The enemy who sent this devil after me, the Duc de Chavagnes, has apparently asked de Santiago to cut out my tongue while I am yet alive, and that barbaric request may perhaps give me some small advantage, since he will not want to kill me outright, but only wound me sufficiently badly at first to allow him to do this piece of savagery.' He grimaced wryly. 'Needless to say, I will place no similar restrictions on myself, and will kill him the first chance I get. '

'Then we will at least fight this villain together, sir,' Raven suggested. ''Tis the least that I can do in return for all your services to me. And two blades must be better than one. Together we might prevail against this man, despite his great repute with the sword,' he added.

M'sieur Desargues shook his head bleakly. 'Two blades will not help in this case, sir, and you may be more of a distraction to me than a help. You are simply no match with a sword for a mercenary villain like this. I am a far better swordsman than you, I suspect, but even I am no real match for him. I will just have to trust to God to see me through this trial.' He sighed. 'Yet I wish that I had not already put my pistols aboard the *Lapwing*, for I could have made good use of them now...'

Raven still remonstrated with him. 'You are also wounded, sir,' he reminded M'sieur Desargues. 'I have stitched and cleaned the axe wound you received earlier tonight, yet you must be sore and stiff still. You will certainly be no match for this devil in this condition.'

M'sieur Desargues forced Raven away. 'You have had a knock on the head too, sir, so are in no fit state to help me either. Let me do this work alone, as I wish. De Santiago has recently received a severe knife wound in the side too, which may slow him a little, and perhaps help to redress the imbalance in our skills a little in my favour...' The Frenchman took Raven's hand in a tight grip. 'Promise me on your honour that you will not interfere and fight this man, sir. I have done Molly much hurt in her young life, yet it would be the most evil of all my sins towards her if I was to deprive her now of the man who loves her. You do love my daughter, do you not?

Raven glanced back at Molly, who stood watching their whispered conversation with deep trepidation written on her sweet face. 'I do love Molly, sir, most heartily.'

M'sieur Desargues smiled. 'Then stand back from this fight, sir, and look after Molly and her mother. Should the contest go against me, I believe de Santiago will be appeased in his anger, and will leave you and Molly be, provided you take no hand against him. But in case he does not keep his word, please ready yourself to flee with Molly and her mother at a moment's notice...'

*

Raven reluctantly did as he was told, and stood back to watch the swordfight with Celia and Molly.

Molly seemed curiously resigned to the likely outcome of this fight. 'He is sacrificing himself, Henry, in order to avoid further hurt to me and my mother. He told me himself that he is simply no match for this devil with a sword.'

The sun had now finally risen over the green headland to the east of the port, flooding the quayside with a wash of golden light, as M'sieur Desargues and Francisco Nunez de Santiago approached each other warily and began their fight to the death.

Strangely enough, the duel began at a very cautious and sedate pace on both sides. De Santiago seemed content at first to fight defensively and let M'sieur Desargues come to him, which tactic surprised Raven given the man's reputed superiority with the sword. Yet Raven was sure that it was no more than a deliberate cunning ploy to let M'sieur Desargues expend all his strength as he made many futile attempts to break through the other man's defences.

The pace of the duel began to increase inexorably as the minutes went on, each cut and thrust and parry coming faster than those before. Raven found it a most unsettling experience to have to watch this titanic struggle, yet not interfere. Time and time again he gripped the hilt of his own sword in preparation to draw it and come to M'sieur Desargues's aid. Yet he had given the man his solemn promise not to interfere, so on his honour could do nothing directly with his own blade.

Molly and her mother watched M'sieur Desargues's determined struggle with grim faces, and frequent gasps of horror every time that he came under threat from de Santiago's flashing blade. For all her supposed indifference, and even hatred, towards the Frenchman, Celia was the more vociferous of the two in her support, and even cried aloud in alarm on some occasions as M'sieur Desargues came close to being run through.

M'sieur Desargues might be carrying that debilitating wound, yet Raven saw with admiration that he was not weakening as fast as he had feared, and indeed continued to fight like a man possessed the longer the fight went on. Yet despite this show of bravura and skill, Raven could still see only one final outcome to this contest, for despite everything he did, M'sieur Desargues was nevertheless being steadily outmanoeuvred and outfought by his more skilful opponent. Raven had never seen such dazzling swordsmanship as this villain displayed – such speed, such virtuosity, such skill. This Spaniard, or whatever he was, seemed to have acquired his skills with the sword from the Devil himself, and nothing M'sieur Desargues could do seemed able to break through the man's implacable and inhuman defences.

Engrossed in the intricacies of this fierce struggle, Raven had entirely lost track of time, although the fight could not have gone on for more than a quarter hour at most. M'sieur Desargues was finally showing clear signs of weakening as the effects of his long night awake on the road, and of the wound in his side, began to take their toll on him. Noting M'sieur

Desargues's slowing responses and his wheezing laboured breath, Raven could see now that the end of this fight must surely be imminent. De Santiago seemed to be simply toying with the Frenchman now, and it was only a matter of time before he delivered the *coup de grace*.

Would this devil really simply wound the Frenchman mortally, then cut his tongue out while he still lived? If de Santiago made any such barbarous move, then Raven knew that, despite his promise, he would have to finally interfere to prevent such a thing, no matter what the risk to himself and Molly. Raven glanced down at Molly's tortured face now and wondered what she would think of him if he merely stood aside and watched this villain cut her father's tongue out while he was still alive...

Yet, just as he was thinking these dark thoughts, Raven finally noticed something about the Spaniard that he had not observed before. He noted one slight chink in the Spaniard's armour when the man parried a weak thrust from M'sieur Desargues and gave an audible gasp of pain. For the first time, Raven also noticed the man's waxy white face and bloodless features, and some evidence of a growing heaviness in his own limbs. Raven remembered that the Spaniard was apparently carrying an old knife wound of his own, and wondered hopefully if his exertions might not have opened up that wound again. Yet it soon seemed that Raven had simply misread the signs, for the Spaniard quickly seemed to shrug off this apparent weakness, and with a dazzling fresh series of thrusts and parries, finally had M'sieur Desargues at his complete mercy.

Raven could see that M'sieur Desargues barely had the strength left to lift his sword and defend himself now, and de Santiago was finally able to turn his opponent's blade contemptuously aside, then disarm him completely with a casual flick of his own blade. Molly grabbed Raven's arm in alarm as she saw her father's blade skitter along the ground and end up six feet away from him. Then the Spaniard forced M'sieur Desargues to kneel before him on the cobbles as he made ready to run him through the heart.

Yet the villain did seem fully intent on fulfilling his grizzly promise to the Duc de Chavagnes, Raven saw, because he held back from impaling his disarmed opponent through the heart at once. Instead de Santiago merely raised his blade again and pointed it at M'sieur Desargues's exposed throat. Then the Spaniard did an even more ominous thing, as he pulled out a knife from under his coat with his left hand. Raven realized with dismay that this was no false threat that the Spaniard had issued, and that he really intended to take M'sieur Desargues's tongue as a bloody souvenir, before finally dispatching him...

In desperation to stop the Spaniard from finishing M'sieur Desargues in this barbarous fashion, Raven called out the first thing that came into his head. 'Stop this evil deed now, Senor! You will suffer hellfire and damnation for all eternity if you do such a terrible thing! Be merciful, for God's sake…!' When the Spaniard ignored this inane appeal for mercy and still made ready with his knife to slice the tongue from his opponent's mouth, Raven called out again even more desperately. 'You have the plague, Senor! Have you not felt the signs of the weeping black sores on your face? Can you not feel the growing weakness in your limbs? You must stop this exertion at once and go to a physician for help! There is no time to lose!'

The villain gasped in bemusement at this bizarre interruption, but did step back from M'sieur Desargues for a moment and feel his face gingerly with his sword hand. Though he still seemed unsettled by Raven's bizarre pronouncement, he glared balefully at Raven in return. 'I warned you not to interfere, sir. Now, for your impertinence in trying to frighten a man who is beyond fear, you shall die a bloody death too when I have finished with this *gentleman…'*

Events moved swiftly after this. M'sieur Desargues, kneeling apparently helpless before de Santiago, saw this brief moment of hesitation in his opponent, and took the only opportunity he would ever have to escape his awful fate. Even Raven could not quite believe his eyes, but somehow M'sieur Desargues managed in an instant to open his own coat and pull out a concealed dagger from within its folds. Raven saw the Frenchman's right hand move with an incredible speed for one in his supposedly weakened condition. The eight inch blade flashed in the sunlight, and with a movement too quick to follow with the human eye, M'sieur Desargues thrust it deep into the Spaniard's heart with a vicious rising blow that almost lifted his opponent off his feet. De Santiago gasped in pain as the blade sliced through his flesh and his organs. The Spaniard looked down in disbelief at the blade buried deep inside him, then he tottered forward a few paces in silent agony, blood frothing from his mouth. He stood swaying on the edge of the quay wall for a full ten seconds, before pitching head first into the dark green water below, where he disappeared without a splash beneath a thick bed of waving kelp…

*

Despite all the noise they had made, no one on board the vessels in the harbour had apparently seen or heard any of this momentous swordfight, so Molly quickly came to her father's aid and lifted him to his feet. Giving her mother a look of hurt at her refusal to step forward and help too, Molly took M'sieur Desargues's arm and supported his considerable weight, then helped him along the quayside to the *Lapwing,* with Henry following behind carrying the Frenchman's bloody sword and his remaining possessions that were not already on board.

M'sieur Desargues was still breathing hard as Molly helped him up the gang plank and onto the mid-deck of the vessel. M'sieur Desargues glanced at Henry Raven, who had remained on the quayside after returning his sword to him, and who now raised his hand in farewell before returning along the quay wall to where Celia still stood alone. 'I should be angry at that gentleman for coming to my aid when he promised not to,' M'sieur Desargues said moodily. 'It was not an honourable thing that he did.'

Molly snapped at him. 'Then, if you thought so, sir, you should not have taken advantage of Henry's help! He did not do it lightly, I assure you, being a most honourable man. Yet, for my sake, he could not simply stand by and watch you skewered, sir. And he did not exactly fight the gentleman, did he? Which was all the promise he made to you, as I recall. Therefore he did keep his word.'

M'sieur Desargues smiled at her fierce defence of Henry Raven. 'I am glad truthfully that you take his side. 'Tis only right that a woman should protect her lover and stand by him in all things.'

Molly gave her father a shrewd look as a sudden thought occurred to her. 'Perhaps you were not so weak at the end of that fight as you made yourself appear, sir. Perhaps you always intended that the fight might end in that fashion, and that you actually expected Henry or myself to intervene and cause a suitable distraction. So Henry's plea for mercy on your behalf merely provided you with the most opportune moment...'

M'sieur Desargues said nothing to that in reply, yet Molly sensed that she had determined the truth of the matter, and that her father was therefore a most determined if devious character.

He glanced at the frenetic activity all around him as sails were raised in preparation to leave, and deck hands swarmed all over the ship doing the myriad things needed to get the vessel in motion. ''Tis time that you went ashore, Molly,' he said regretfully. 'They will soon take away the gangway.'

Now that the time was finally come for a last farewell, Molly found it hard to leave her father. But as she looked ashore and saw Henry and her mother standing together in the distance, she finally broke away from her father's embrace and stepped towards the wooden gang plank.

M'sieur Desargues called after her as she stepped over the gunwale and onto the gangway. 'Do one more thing for me, Molly, before you go.'

She turned on the gangway and looked back at him. 'What thing, sir?'

M'sieur Desargues smiled again. 'Say to me "*Au revoir, mon père*".'

'Why, sir?'

He smiled again, but sadly this time. 'Because it would mean so much to me if you did use those words.'

Molly raised a hand in final farewell, inexpressibly sad too that she would never see this gentleman again in her life. 'Then I will say it, sir, but most regretfully. *Au revoir, mon père...*'

\*

Mistress Celia Hornett was clearly as relieved as Raven when Molly finally stepped ashore again. She nodded in vague acknowledgement at the distant figure of M'sieur Desargues, who now stood on the forecastle of the ship with his hand raised in farewell to her, which gesture she did finally and begrudgingly return in kind. 'That gentleman always had the luck of the Devil,' she observed tartly to Raven. 'Yet Molly did not go with him in the end, as I feared she might, so he has lost the one true gem in his life.'

Molly finally re-joined Raven and her mother. She was in a melancholy state, Raven could see, yet made no mention of her sad mood. She glanced down instead in the water at the spot where the body of Senor Francisco Nunez de Santiago had fallen. 'What do we do about that evil gentleman's body in the water, Henry?' she asked.

Celia spoke up. 'We should leave that foul devil in the water to have his body devoured by snails and fishes as he deserves. For what he did to poor Marion, I hope that his soul will burn in hellfire for all eternity.'

'I hope so too, indeed,' Molly said, 'yet we can hardly leave his body there, even if his soul burns in hellfire.'

Raven shrugged. 'I am afraid that is exactly what I intend to do, Molly. He will be discovered soon enough in a few hours when the tide is low again. But I already have five corpses to explain to the magistrate in Bridport, and even a man as tolerant and understanding as Sir Malcolm Batcock may draw the line when I tell him of a sixth body, lying impaled with a French dagger in the mud in Weymouth Harbour. Therefore I think it best that we leave here as discreetly as we can, once we have seen Esther on board the vessel too. Yet where can she be?' he wondered aloud, though without any true concern that she might be too late to board, because he still preferred that Esther did not leave on the *Lapwing* at all.

Molly interrupted his thoughts. 'Did that man de Santiago truly have the plague, Henry, as you said? I know that he could have been afflicted so, since I myself saw him touched on the face by a woman with the plague. Yet I suspect you said that merely to distract his attention for a moment.'

Raven was not sure that he should confess his sins to her, but finally admitted the truth. 'I do not truly think that he had the plague, yet what I said was not entirely a ruse. De Santiago did most assuredly have an ailment of some sort that slowed his reactions considerably, at least towards the end of that fight...'

'The French Pox, most likely,' Celia said malevolently.

Raven laughed. 'Nay, more likely it was an attack of Lethargy or Impostume, brought on from the recent knife wound that M'sieur Desargues said he had suffered.' He turned to Molly. 'I think that is the only reason that your father managed to resist him so long. Also, I think de Santiago might have been able to avoid that last dagger thrust from your father if his reactions had not been slowed by his own wound. So I would say that whoever gave de Santiago that earlier wound was the real person who saved your father's life, not I.'

317

Molly's face gave nothing away of what she might be thinking. 'Then 'tis a pity we shall never know who this kind benefactor was.'

Raven was not listening to her with his full attention now, though, as he wondered again what had become of Esther and Martin. But his frequent backward glances towards the town were finally rewarded when he saw them hurrying down the quayside steps towards the *Lapwing*'s berth. It seemed they had been successful in their mission for they were accompanied by several shopkeepers and servants encumbered with baggage and goods.

Raven ran along the quayside to meet them. 'You must go quickly, Esther, if you truly wish to leave.'

Esther nodded, and asked the shopkeepers and their servants to carry her provisions on board the *Lapwing* at once. She hesitated, not sure what to say next, so Raven took her hand and looked searchingly into her eyes. 'Are you sure that you wish to go, dear Esther?' he asked her. 'Truly I do not want you to go, and would prefer it if you stayed here with us in Dorset for all time.'

Esther seemed unmoved, yet Raven saw tears welling in her eyes therefore suspected that her calm mood was but an act. But she wiped her eyes quickly and looked at him defiantly in response. 'I am sure that I must go, Henry,' she declared finally.

'But how will you fare in that wild land alone?' Raven asked her helplessly.

Martin stepped forward abruptly. 'She will not be alone, Master. I have spoken with this lady today and offered to go with her as her husband. I have already seen the captain of the *Lapwing* and given him money for my own passage...'

Raven was completely taken aback. '*You* would go to the New World, Martin! A month ago, you would not even consider a move to Newcastle as my mine manager, never mind to a new and unknown life in the New World.'

Martin glanced uneasily at Esther for support. 'Nevertheless, Mistress Linney has accepted me as her husband, and that is a much greater inducement even than your kind offer was, Master. So I will gladly go with her to the ends of the earth.'

Esther looked at Raven, and gave him a rueful half-smile. 'I cannot turn down such a man, who will stand beside me, even after all the evil things that I have suffered, and done, in my life.'

Raven was still astonished, yet if Esther had to leave, then he could not think of a better man than Martin to go with her. He took both their hands, then placed them together. 'Then I am equally glad for you both...'

*

The sun was rising fast as Henry Raven stood with Molly and Celia and

318

watched the *Lapwing* as it cleared the harbour walls, and its white canvas sails fluttered fitfully into life.

Raven could still make out the distinct figures on board the vessel. As the ship hit the Channel swells, he saw M'sieur Desargues brace himself against some rigging and raise a hand again in farewell to Molly on the shore. Martin and Esther stood close by amidships, taking in the vanishing coastline of England, yet neither raised their hand in a final farewell, which left Henry Raven a little disappointed.

Raven turned to Celia as the vessel finally vanished from sight behind the harbour wall. 'I hope you will not need to return to London at once, Madam, now that the plague has taken rampant hold there. Instead I hope that you will stay as my guest at the manor this summer, together with Molly. You will both be safe from the plague here, I am sure. And perhaps my sister will also appreciate your company once I am gone.' He smiled at Molly. 'You and my sister may even become tolerable friends in time.'

Molly was still sad at the departure of her father, which Raven could see had affected her much more deeply than she cared to reveal. 'Do you truly have to go to fight the Dutch, Henry? Can you not change your mind and stay at the manor too?'

Raven shook his head firmly. 'Nay, I cannot. I have made my decision and must go to do my duty.'

Molly bit her lip and fought back a fresh tear. 'Then I hope your duty does not include giving your life, because that life is very important to me, sir.'

Raven was touched by her clear concern for him. 'Then I will make sure in the coming weeks always to duck my head promptly at the first sign of danger, and to avoid the flight of any troublesome cannon balls, should they come anywhere near me.'

Molly stood up on tiptoes and, ignoring her mother's presence, kissed Raven hard on the mouth. 'Ay, make sure that you do, sir...'

# EPILOGUE

Saturday, 3rd June 1665

A fortnight later, Henry Raven stood on the aft deck of the Duke of York's flagship, the *Royal Charles,* in company with his friend Anthony Mawdsley. His head was still ringing with the heat of battle, as he wondered wearily whether it would not have been much more sensible of him to have taken Molly's advice and avoided this unnecessary call to arms in the service of his king and country. It would not have been difficult for him to have contrived to arrive in Harwich too late, that much was certain...

In fact he had only made the departure of the fleet with a few hours to spare, after a mad dash to the eastern port of Harwich by coach from Dorset. Even then he would have missed the sailing, but for the delay caused by the protracted business of victualing. Raven had arrived at the Essex port to discover that it was not only the victualing that had delayed the departure, though, but also the crew's taste for whoring and merrymaking which were difficult habits for men to forego without a struggle, especially when about to go to war. The whoring had not been confined to the lower ranks, though, and seemed to be the prerogative of everyone, from cabin boy to Admiral. Raven had been astonished, once on board the *Royal Charles,* to find the vessel filled from the bilges to the deck with women of all classes, from sailors' wives and sweethearts, to countesses, courtesans and boisterous country wenches, who jostled one another shamelessly in cabin and forecastle.

Mawdsley had been much amused by all this riotous wenching, and his only surprise, once he discovered that Raven and Molly were fully reconciled again, was why he had not brought her here to Harwich with him. One of the King's favourite libertine courtiers, Lord Buckhurst, had brought *three* women in total to see him off on his adventures, and had even composed a playful song of farewell that every woman on board the ships was now singing with gusto:

*"The King with wonder, and surprise*
*Will swear the seas grow bold;*
*Because the tides will higher rise,*
*Than e're they us'd of old:*
*But let him know it is our tears*
*Bring floods of grief to Whitehall stairs*
*With a fa, la, la, la, la..."*

Yet eventually all the women had been evicted from the vessels, and the three squadrons that made up the English fleet had sailed in search of Admiral de Ruyter's Dutch fleet; the white squadron, commanded by the Duke of York, the blue with Prince Rupert in command, and the red squadron led by the Earl of Sandwich.

For many days, the Dutch fleet lay low, and the boredom of life on board the ships of the English fleet became intolerable without any women to stave off such feelings, leading to much temperamental feuding and bickering among the crews. The bickering was quickly curtailed, though, on this third day of June, when the mighty Dutch fleet of eighty one warships and eleven large Indiamen was finally sighted off the Suffolk shore. The Duke of York in his flagship, the *Royal Charles,* had immediately led the fleet to engage the enemy.

The battle had raged all day, and Raven had been on the aft deck at the start of it, watching with admiration how the Duke of York had marshalled his three squadrons in the favoured "line-ahead" formation. This great fleet truly was an inspiring sight for an Englishman – more than a hundred ships with billowing white sails strung out over seven miles of windy blue ocean, and divided into three distinct lines; white squadron leading as usual with the Duke of York in command; red in the centre; blue bringing up the rear. A mass of smaller vessels - fifth- and sixth rate vessels – also sailed alongside the main squadrons, ready at a moment's notice to tow away damaged ships and to relay signals.

Yet no single vessel in the fleet could compare in magnificence to the one on which Raven stood: the Duke of York's flagship, the *Royal Charles.* As the English fleet bore down on the Dutch, Raven took the opportunity to stretch his neck and admire the perfection of this great fighting ship, whose tall oak masts and vast sails towered above him. Following her refit last winter, she now had a hundred cannons on her three decks instead of the previous eighty, enough to blow any ship on earth out of the water. And at 1,229 tons, she was also far larger than any of the older three-deck ships of the line.

The two fleets had passed each other on different tacks, and at five hundred yards, the white squadron opened fire on the Dutch with a great cannon broadside. Soon events descended into mayhem as vessels came within grappling distance, and soldiers with muskets rushed on deck to prepare for hand-to-hand fighting. By this time Raven was fully occupied tending to the wounded below so saw little of the action that followed. Yet from what babbled accounts he heard below, it seemed that the Duke of York was using his fire ships - small boats filled to bursting with pitch and tar, and anything else inflammable - to terrible effect against the Dutch warships.

Raven heard from the frantic gossip below that the Dutch ship *Oranje* had been grappled and then burned with fire ships, and that its sails and rigging had gone up like an inferno. Then, as he was taking off the mangled right leg of a gallant young midshipman above the knee, he learned from a wounded officer the even more encouraging news that the Dutch admiral Opdam had been killed and his flagship blown up.

It seemed as if the English triumph was complete and, during a break in the battle, Raven went back on deck to discover from Mawdsley whether these reports were all true, which excuse also allowed him to escape briefly from the gore and horror below

The Duke of York was still commanding the fleet from the aft deck, and on seeing Raven appear with Mawdsley on the deck below, beckoned him to come up. The King's brother looked at Raven in alarm when he saw his surgeon's apron so liberally covered in blood and dirt. 'It must be grim work indeed below decks, Mr Raven,' he said without irony.

'It is indeed, my Lord,' Raven answered honestly, struck as always by the Duke's fair and handsome countenance and his long yellow hair, so unlike his brother's darker features. Three courtiers were standing next to the Duke of York, and Raven recognized in turn Lord Muskerry, Richard Boyle, and the King's particular favourite, Charles Berkeley. The King had recently made his most favoured friend Berkeley the Keeper of the Privy Purse, as well as granting him the titles of Baron Berkeley of Rathdowne and Viscount Fitzhardinge of Berehaven, which, being Irish titles, could be conferred without the King having to ask the Privy Seal and the Commons for approval. Berkeley was hardly worth such generosity from his monarch in Raven's opinion, though, and was by all accounts a most vicious character: Mawdsley had told Raven that Berkeley had recently brazenly offered three hundred pounds a year to the wife of the King's surgeon, Mr Pierce, to become his mistress, and there seemed to be no limits to his debauchery, or to the depths to which he was prepared to sink in order to pursue his personal and political ambitions. He gave Raven and Mawdsley friendly greetings however, and Mawdsley responded generously in kind, though in truth he too had a great distrust and dislike of Berkeley.

The mood of all the Duke's party was buoyant after what seemed to be a great victory, yet Raven could see from the confusion of vessels around them that the battle was far from over yet. Mawdsley too was worried as he looked through the smoke and haze and espied a Dutch warship bearing down at them unexpectedly from starboard and about to fire a fresh broadside. 'The Dutch fleet comes at us again, my Lord,' he pointed out unnecessarily

The Duke smiled. 'Then, if you are nervous, you had better keep your beautiful head as low as possible for the next few minutes, Mr Mawdsley.'

Even as the Duke said this, Raven heard the screaming flight of a stray approaching cannon ball and dived instantly for cover. Then he felt a prodigious explosion that seemed to lift the entire vessel out of the water, and deafened him with its power and immense noise. When Raven raised his ringing head off the deck again to look about him, he saw the Duke of York still standing by the rail of the aft deck, but now in a bewildered daze, his beautiful uniform spattered with blood and brains. Of the three courtiers and his beautiful friend Mawdsley, Raven saw with a cry of despair that there was nothing left of them but a mass of torn limbs and bloodied headless torsos, one of which still threshed about in sinister fashion on the wooden deck...

*

Sitting in the privy garden at Salwayash Manor on this fine summer's day, and practising her sewing, Molly felt a sudden chill malaise inside her, and wondered what it was that ailed her so.

Catherine had not noticed her discomfort, though, and smiled engagingly at her companion. 'Your sewing skills come on in leaps and bounds, Molly, I see – you make capital work of repairing that old gown of yours.' She glanced at Molly's plain dress with chagrin. 'Yet while we talk of gowns, I think that we must get you some more presentable clothes in time for Henry's return from sea.'

Molly quickly dismissed her feeling of unease, and smiled back. 'I have many fine dresses in London waiting for me when I return, Catherine. For now it is better that I wear the poor garb that I was born to.' This thought rekindled some memories in Molly of her childhood, and then, inevitably, some fresh concern over her mother's recent departure from Dorset. Molly was sorry that her mother had decided not to stay longer at Salwayash Manor, even though she had frankly found it difficult to be comfortable here with Celia always in close attendance. Molly could not help but be concerned for her mother's welfare given the risks she was taking in returning to a city in the grip of the plague. Before leaving, Celia had expressed to her worried daughter her determination to keep her many businesses open as long as she could, a course of action which seemed admirable to Molly in some respects, and downright foolhardy in others. Yet despite the worsening reports from the city, Celia had stuck resolutely to her plan to return to London, and in the end could not be dissuaded from it, even after an unfamiliar show of tears from her daughter...

Molly thought again with renewed concern about all her many other friends and acquaintances still in London; fresh reports from people fleeing the city said that the plague was now killing thousands every week, and might even get worse in the coming months. Henry had predicted bleakly before he left for Harwich that half of the city might die eventually from the plague, which made Molly wonder if London could ever be the same vibrant and populous city again that she had known since childhood.

With regard to her own situation, though, Molly could only be grateful that she had managed to escape the city before the plague took such savage hold, and to find a temporary home here at Salwayash Manor with Henry's sweet sister. Molly and Catherine were not great friends yet, but there was a tolerable affection growing between the two of them, Molly decided, which gave her much pleasure. To entertain Catherine in the evenings, Molly had even begun giving recitals of some of her more stirring speeches from recent plays, and Catherine had been duly impressed, both by her prodigious memory and by her powerful delivery of such fine words and sentiments.

Molly knew Catherine well enough by now to know that she also was not fully recovered from the events of last month. Catherine still clearly endured much sadness over the permanent departure of Esther Linney, as Molly had over the departure of her father. Yet Catherine had a greater cross to bear too in that, unlike Molly, she had lost the man she had been betrothed to, her neighbour Ralph Warboys. Even worse than losing him, she had discovered that her lover had feet of clay, and was not the noble man she had thought him to be, which realization should perhaps have helped to cure her remorse more quickly than it had. Yet Catherine had clearly loved Ralph Warboys with her whole being, and so her heart could not be so quickly or easily mended as that, Molly could tell.

The Bridport magistrate and his constables had investigated the strange happenings on the Warboys' estate, and Sir Malcolm Batcock and Mr Drew had apparently accepted the version of the story that Henry had reported to them, although with some suspicions that this was not quite the whole truth.

Only today, a distant cousin of Ralph's had called at Salwayash Manor to make himself known to his new neighbours. It seemed that this callow (and regretfully plain looking) individual, a Northern gentleman called William Godber, had arrived to claim ownership of the Warboys estate. As Catherine had said farewell to him at the main door, she had turned to Molly and smiled with relief. 'At least Mr Godber is so plain that I will not be easily tempted a second time to become mistress of Warboys Hall,' she quipped uneasily.

Sir Malcolm Batcock and Mr Drew had given up all interest in the Ravens' "Cousin Edward" when Henry had told them that their cousin had simply returned north to find some peace and solitude after all the trouble with the rioters. These officers of the law also seemed to have lost all interest in pandering to Mistress Judith Pollock and to her wild stories that Esther Linney had somehow survived being hanged. Mistress Pollock was now ostracized by most of the local community for her malevolent interference, and for her provoking of the rioters, and had as a result become an even lonelier old woman than previously.

Magistrate Batcock had been most diligent, though, in pursuing the ringleaders of the rioters and bringing them to summary justice. Several had been condemned to hang already, and many more were to be transported shortly to penal colonies in Virginia.

Molly wondered again about her father and how he would fare in the New World, yet had few doubts that he would prosper in the end. She had more doubts about the fate of Esther Linney, though, and whether that poor young woman would be able to survive the rigours of her new life. Yet from what Molly knew of Martin Gibney, she was sure that he would make her a kind and considerate husband, and one who would do his best to help her recover from the sadness and disappointments of her life. Molly could not imagine the full depth of pain and distress that Esther had gone through. She had taken her revenge in the end on the man who had caused her hurt, but Molly thought that it would have been better for the good of her soul perhaps if she had not.

Catherine had noticed Molly's preoccupied mood now. 'You seem a little melancholy and out of sorts today, Molly. Are you sickening for something? Or do you miss your father? Is that what causes your eyes to mist over a little?'

Molly nodded. 'Of course I do miss him, Catherine. Yet I only discovered his existence so recently that I had no time to form any great attachment to him. Therefore the pain of losing him is commensurately small,' she lied.

Catherine regarded her shrewdly. 'Then something else troubles you. I suppose it is Henry and his reckless heroics which cause you worry.'

Molly sighed. 'It is indeed Henry who troubles me more. I worry about him endlessly, and I am always imagining the worst things that might befall him at sea.'

Catherine took her hand and consoled her with a firm pat. 'Worry not, Molly. I know my brother too well. Henry will return in one piece. He has promised me so, and he always keeps his word.'

Molly smiled, despite the dark murmurings of doubt in her head. 'Then I will trust his promise too...

THE END

# ABOUT THE AUTHOR

Gordon Thomson is a civil engineer by profession, a Geordie by birth, and Sunderland supporter (and therefore masochist) by inclination. His professional engineering career took him all over the world - Africa, the Far East, South America, as well as Holland and the UK - and this experience of exotic places and different cultures is what gave him the urge to try writing.

He has a Japanese wife and two grown up sons, one of whom was born in Holland, so he does claim to be a citizen of the world, if a very English one.

*Summer of the Plague*, which is set in Restoration London, is a 17th century mystery thriller, and a sequel to *Winter of the Comet*. He has previously published the Victorian thriller *Leviathan*.

Printed in Great Britain
by Amazon